ONE MONDAY MORNING

One Monday Morning

Jennifer Burke

POOLBEG

Published 2016
by Poolbeg Press Ltd
123 Grange Hill, Baldoyle
Dublin 13, Ireland
www.poolbeg.com

© Jennifer Burke 2016

Copyright for editing, typesetting, layout, design, ebook
© Poolbeg Press Ltd

The moral right of the author has been asserted.

1

A catalogue record for this book is available from the British Library.

ISBN 978-1-78199-906-6

 www.facebook.com/poolbeg
 @PoolbegBooks

Printed and bound by CPI Group (UK) Ltd, Croydon, CR0 4YY

Typeset in Bembo 12/16

www.poolbeg.com

About the Author

Jennifer Burke's first novel, *The Secret Son*, won Poolbeg Press and TV3's *Write a Bestseller* competition 2013 and was published to critical acclaim. Her second novel, *Levi's Gift*, was published in September 2014. Jennifer also writes short stories – she was published in the 2012 *From the Well* anthology and, in 2013, contributed a short story to the book *If I Was a Child Again*. Since 2012, Jennifer has been longlisted once and shortlisted three times in the *Fish Publishing Flash Fiction* competition. *One Monday Morning* is her third novel.

Acknowledgements

I would like to start by thanking Paula Campbell of Poolbeg Press for being an honest, constructive and encouraging champion of my work. Also thanks to my editor Gaye Shortland for helping to make my book the best it can be. To all at Poolbeg Press who played a part in bringing *One Monday Morning* to the shelves, I will be forever grateful.

My writing has benefited hugely from the critique and encouragement of the "Second Mondays" writing group. Thank you all for your continuing support.

Particular thanks to my good friend Amy Holmes, of Fitness Aims. Your help with my research into the life of a professional runner has been invaluable. A huge thank-you also to Sarah Jane Searle, for sharing your experiences working as international cabin crew. Any inaccuracies in this book are entirely of my own making.

Thank you to my extended family, especially all my cousins, for your interest and support. Special thanks to my brother Richard – even miles away across the sea, you never fail to be my cheerleader! To my parents, Michael and Denise – without you I would not be the person I am today (the good bits, anyway!). Your never-wavering support, considered advice and love has kept me going. I love you dearly.

At its core, this book is about the importance of friendship. *One Monday Morning* is written for all my friends, who have made my life so rich, meaningful and above all, fun. I am especially dedicating this book to my good friends Ann and John Keegan, as a small token of thanks.

To Ann and John

Prologue

TRISH

Gazing outward from the top of the world is calming. There are mountains all around, some with dizzying vertical drops, others rippling down, sliding to flatness below. I stand at the edge of the highest cliff, with a dazzling view beyond. The city sparkles up at me, mirroring the dots shimmering in the sky. Up here, in the dense darkness, the stars shine brighter than can be seen from below.

Still, they are mere specks, probably burned out already in a distant galaxy. Not enough to light the abyss, only steps away. How easy it would be now to end it all. No more mother, no more sister. Not even my friends. But they will disappear from my life anyway. Tomorrow, once they find out the truth, they will be gone as quickly as gravity would pull me over the cliff.

I cannot make out the drop with only those useless, dead stars to guide me. I could close my eyes and run until the ground disappears and I fly, landing with a crack I will not hear on the rocky ground below.

1

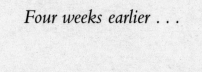

Four weeks earlier . . .

Chapter one

TRISH

I scramble along the grassy rocks until I can climb no further. Standing alone, I hold out my arms to the air.

The jagged mountaintops smash the wind into pieces, casting them howling into the curves of the cliffs. Squinting into the force, I breathe in its purity. Alone up here, I am free. I could fly. I like to come to this spot early, to suck in the sights, the whistling sounds, the sense of release that I hope Gerry felt before he dived off the edge, all those years ago.

"There she is."

"Trish! Over here."

Having finished my own personal tribute to Gerry on the mountains, I have retreated along the walking trail to my friends. They are waiting, huddling around the warm bonnets of their cars like two neglected cats. The sun has been up for hours but it is still curdling in a buttery ball of whiteness, barely dispelling the shadows of dawn.

"Morning," I say, unzipping my jacket. The trudge down has

rosied my cheeks and I can feel a thin layer of perspiration oozing into my clothes.

Stephen, the biggest and hardiest of men, shoves his hands into his pockets, eyeing my movements with distrustful disdain. "How can you possibly be hot, Trish?"

Ciara hops from foot to foot. "It's September. Why is it like the inside of an Eskimo's fridge out here?"

"You should be well used to it, Ciara," I say. "You come running up the mountains every week."

She grins. "Running in this godforsaken weather is one thing. Waiting for you to show up is another."

"All right, sorry I took so long," I concede. "I'll get the flasks."

Once a year, on the anniversary of the day Gerry left us, we meet by The Kite pub. It's not far from where he jumped – and was found spread-eagled on the rocks below.

For the first few years, other friends and sometimes his family showed up too. We wept inconsolably and stayed mere minutes. Inevitably, the numbers dwindled over time but Ciara, Stephen and I never missed it. We began to be able to talk about what happened. It took five years to think of bringing coffee and pastries. Now it is a tradition. Instead of crying, we toast to him with smiles, and joke about the good times.

"Gimme!" Ciara grabs the flask gratefully.

"Climate change, my friends," Stephen grins, cupping his hands around a mug as Ciara tips coffee into it. "It wasn't this wintery when we first started coming up here. Seven years." He shakes his head. "Can you believe it?"

"I still can't get over that he did it," Ciara says with a bitterness that snaps my head up.

"Ciara!"

She shrugs. "The four of us were friends so long. We were all so miserable when we met in that summer camp. That's why we became friends – to see each other through the hard times. He should have come to us. We would have helped him."

We go through this every year.

"He did what he thought he had to do, Ciara," I say gently. "It's no reflection on our friendship."

She tries not to react, but I can see her biting the inside of her lip. "I know. I wish he'd talked to us, that's all."

I say nothing, stroking the side of my mug. We talk about Gerry often, but the pain flashes acutely on this day.

For me, the worst part is that we didn't know the truth until after he jumped. I often wish he had come to me, for consolation at least.

But I have no right to wish that. I have a secret of my own. I would never tell Ciara or Stephen, though they are the closest friends I have in the world. I ought to confide in them – it's what we all wish Gerry had done. But I'm not about to throw myself off a cliff. I don't have to tell anyone.

"Remember the first night we sneaked out of our dorms in summer camp?" Ciara's tone has thawed, a hint of humour in her face.

Of course we remember. We often refer to it.

"Gerry was so nervous he ran through the woods and smacked face first into that tree."

Stephen blurts out a laugh at the memory. "It's a pity he's not around now, Trish," he says. "He'd be all over you about your TV appearance this week."

Ciara snorts through a gulp of coffee and nudges my arm. "Can't you imagine Gerry? Director-extraordinaire – he'd want to be on hand to give you step-by-step instructions."

I try to grin along with them but my chest tightens painfully. I stand against the sensation. The last thing in the world I want to do is take part in a nationally televised interview. I'm doing it for Conall, I repeat over and over in my mind.

"I wish Gerry was here." I keep my voice light. "I could do with a few tips."

"He'd probably have made it to Hollywood at this stage." Stephen waves away my remark.

I wonder if he is right – if Gerry's dream of being a world-famous film director would be flourishing if he was alive. The thought distracts me for only a moment until Ciara resumes the conversation.

"Will it be a live interview?"

I curse myself for not changing the topic when I had the chance. I stare ahead of me as the clouds thin, the sun bullying through.

"No," I answer. "It won't be shown until Thursday but we're filming tomorrow. Hopefully that will give them time to edit out anything stupid I say."

Stephen punches me lightly, but with his big fist it stings. "Come on, Trish, I bet they'll hardly talk to you."

"Yeah, this is about your sister and Conall at the end of the day, not you. How is the baby?"

My spirits lift. Conall may be the reason for this whole ordeal, but he is all that keeps us going. "He was six months old last week."

Ciara's eyes bulge. "Six months? That's amazing."

I nod. It is truly incredible. Conall was never meant to survive outside my sister's womb. Every day since then has been a torturous wait for death.

"It's odd," I say, still gazing outward instead of at my friends, "the difference a year makes. This time last year, Conall wasn't born." I glance at Stephen. "You and Lisa hadn't moved in together."

"And you were engaged to Brian," Ciara adds.

I jerk my head toward her. Her eyes are glowing with compassion. I sigh. Neither Ciara nor Stephen understand why I ended my engagement. Even Brian doesn't know the whole reason.

"Do you want to come around to mine on Thursday to watch the interview?" Ciara asks, her face brightening. "That way you can at least avoid your mother analysing every second of it. Stephen, you and Lisa should come too."

"Thanks, Ciara," I say, "but I'm working. I managed to swap shifts with another crew member so I'm flying on Thursday." Anything to avoid being here when the interview airs.

"The life of a jet-setter." Stephen says it in an off-hand way, but I hear the envy. His grand plans to travel the world got cut along with his job.

I open my mouth to argue that working as cabin crew for an international airline is far from a constant holiday. It's tough work with little sleep. But I hold it in. Ultimately, my job gives me freedoms I never had before. Stephen can no longer say the same.

Suddenly, Ciara stands away from the bonnet and faces us. "I have news," she says, her voice vibrating with excitement.

I wait, watching a slow smile transform her face.

"I was going to tell you if you came to my house on Thursday – it would have been a distraction for you, Trish. But since you'll be away . . ." She takes a deep breath. "You know I've been training hard all summer –"

"Nothing new about that," Stephen cuts across her.

He's right – Ciara's obsession with winning every race in which she participates is well-known. I shush him and motion for her to carry on.

"I know, but this training is more focussed. There's a race in November. A trial. If I get the time I'm aiming for, I'll qualify."

"Qualify for what?" I ask, thinking of the European Indoor Championships. Or the Outdoor Championships. Ciara is not one to limit herself.

Her mouth slopes upwards cheekily. "Rio."

Stephen slaps his hand on the bonnet of the car in elation. I gasp. The 2016 Games are less than a year away in Rio de Janeiro but I hadn't expected to be cheering Ciara on. We all thought her Olympic dreams were over.

"Do you think you'll qualify, Ciara?"

"I do," she says with a steady confidence that convinces me completely. "It's not guaranteed – and even if I make it I'll have a lot of work to do before the Games next summer. The time I need to get isn't easy. But I'm putting everything into my training. I can do it."

"Damn right you can do it!" Stephen grabs her up in a hug, shaking her from side to side.

"Careful, Stephen," I laugh. "Don't break her before the big race."

As soon as he releases her, I skip around him to congratulate her warmly.

"When did you decide to go for it, Ciara?" I ask, conscious that her previous two attempts to enter the Olympics ended in tears.

"They released the qualification times in late spring. Adrian and I have been preparing since then. November is only two months away so it's crunch time now." She rubs her hands together. "I have a race in three weeks in Morton Stadium. It'll be an indication of how my training is progressing. If I do well in it, I'll have a real chance."

"We'll be there to cheer you on," I say immediately.

Stephen nods with absurd rapidity. "Wouldn't miss it."

"I know it'll be tough," she says, suddenly quiet. "I'm thirty now. I'll be competing against young things in their prime."

Stephen's frantic nodding changes direction with a sickeningly audible crick. He carries on shaking his head as Ciara screws up her face at the noise. "No negativity, Ciara. Isn't that what you always say? Running at your level is more about mental than physical strength."

"And if we've learned anything from Gerry's death," I say, feeling like a fraud, "it's that we need to rely on each other. You've got us behind you, and you have the experience those younger ones won't have. You're so much stronger, and you're ready for this."

She smiles widely. "I am. I am ready."

As one, we look across the road and up the curving trail, out to the cliff beyond. There is something particularly poignant about this anniversary. Ciara, Stephen and I are all in our thirties now. We have moved on from the decade of youthful expectation that defined Gerry's personality. We are not merely leaving him behind in time. We are developing into people he did not know.

"Let's toast once more to Gerry before all the coffee is gone," I say.

Stephen and Ciara raise their mugs. The wind, though not as blustery as on the edge, cuts into us. As one, we cast our eyes toward the spot from where Gerry jumped seven years ago.

"To Gerry," Stephen says softly.

I regard my friends, and think of all the changes that have occurred in our lives over the past year. Ciara on the cusp of

Olympic glory. Stephen living with his girlfriend. The birth of my darling nephew Conall.

Of course, it hasn't all been rosy. My split with Brian. Conall's constant illnesses. Stephen losing his job just as the worst of the recession seemed over.

Gerry is missing it all. The good and the bad. Sometimes I envy him, when my own past and fears threaten to crush me. But right now, as I click mugs with my best friends to dispel the bitter cold with memories, I feel sorry for Gerry. However many cracks form in our lives, he is missing the love that pours from our friends to fill them.

Chapter two

TRISH

My stomach is bubbling fizzily. I can taste it in my throat.

"What's the matter with her, Mum?" I hear Beth whisper.

"She's just nervous."

Sitting in front of the mirror, they stare into it at my reflection. To avoid their gaze, I glance down at the deep-green dress Beth picked out for me to match the colour of my eyes. The make-up artist did an acceptable job, even finding an identical shade of eye shadow, although it is a bit over the top. She pre-empted any complaint by explaining that the camera does not appreciate subtlety.

"We shouldn't have brought her, Mum. She'll ruin the whole interview."

I force a smile. "Sorry, Beth," I say, and I mean it.

I had promised my sister I would do this to help her. Help Conall. So I arch tall – one of my survival techniques – and step forward to where she and Mum are sitting side by side, waiting for their make-up artists to reappear with more supplies.

I place a hand on each of their shoulders.

"Careful," Mum snaps, adjusting the overall that has been slung across her body to protect her dress.

"Sorry," I say again. I look at Beth in the mirror as she fixes her own white cover. "It's the idea of being on TV. Scary!" I try to keep my voice bright but it comes out squeaky.

Beth starts to frown but at that moment the door bursts open and a large woman with a vacant air bustles in. A shorter, skinnier girl scuttles behind her. Mum's eyes lock hard onto the older woman. I slide out of the way, glad I arrived early and so my make-up is already done.

My phone rings. I snatch it up gratefully.

"Trish?" It comes through as a shout, but I can barely hear her through what sounds like swooshing wind around her.

"Hi, Ciara. Hang on a second." I indicate to my mother and sister that I'm stepping out. They ignore me. I shut the door of the make-up room behind me and make my way to the exit, my head down to avoid eye contact with the myriad of minions scurrying around the studio.

"Trish, are you there?"

"Yes, I'm here," I say as I reach the door.

"I wanted to wish you luck today!" Ciara shouts. "What time are you filming?"

"In the next half an hour. Where are you, the centre of a cyclone?"

"I'm up at The Kite. All that indoor training with Adrian has me antsy. Mind you, I thought the wind would have died down by now. I could get blown off the cliff." She gasps at her own words. "I'm sorry." Though scarcely a whisper this time I can hear her perfectly.

"Don't worry," I say quickly.

She says something else but the wind has picked up again and I have to ask her to repeat herself.

"I said, are you all set for the interview?" she yells down the phone.

"I suppose."

14

"You'll be fine, Trish," she says. "Let your mam and Beth do the talking."

After a few more attempts at conversation, we give up, unable to hear properly. "Bye, Ciara!" I shout into the phone. "Thanks for ringing. Good luck with the run."

I end the call and tip back against the wall, breathing deeply. I stay there for some time, listening to the cars speed by on the distant road. The wind whips my hair across my face. I pick it away, barely caring that it is undoing the newly blow-dried look, so different from the frizzy mess that usually hangs around my shoulders.

By the time I return to the make-up room, it is empty. The flush of panic is almost welcome – anything to dispel the nerves. I stride as purposefully as I can in my heels along the corridor. They will kill me if I'm late.

At first I had refused outright to do the interview. I had conquered some of the crippling shyness of my youth since I started working with Aer Clara seven years ago, but not to the point that I could happily make an appearance on television.

"Why do you need me there, Beth?" I had asked when she and Mum arrived at my house to invite me on air. Mum's home-baked carrot cake and a box of biscuits from the corner supermarket were not nearly enough to bribe me.

"Listen, Trish," Beth said, "you know finances are hard with Conall's medical expenses."

I said nothing. At six months old, Conall has lived most of his life in hospitals, and any time at home is mostly spent in the arms of a nurse. Medication is his breast milk and, only for the donations, the family would be financially crippled. But I didn't see how my quivering on television could possibly help.

"I've been interviewed loads of times, as has Mum." Beth inched forward.

I nodded. Mum enjoys her status as the most vigorous and uncompromising pro-life advocate in the country. Whenever there is a whisper of a debate about ending Ireland's ban on abortion she turns up, waving posters of mangled foetuses dumped in rubbish bins.

15

"There are a lot of wealthy pro-lifers, Trish," Beth said desperately. "Their contributions have been saving us, keeping Conall alive. Now *Current Times* wants to interview us. That's huge. You have no idea of the difference it would make."

"Exactly, Beth. This is a big deal for you. You know I'll only blow it."

Mum, who had been watching me with her steely gaze, sat back. "I told you she wouldn't be up for it, Beth." She directed herself at me sharply. "You're too timid for your own good, Trish. I've always said it."

She was right, of course, but I had to justify myself.

"You're the one with the influence, Mum. Beth and Larry, they are the parents of the miracle baby. Why do you need me?"

"Mum is old news." Beth waved her away cruelly. "They've told the story of me and Larry struggling to get pregnant a million times. They want a new angle. The Olden family. The strong woman who raised her girls without a husband – and the result." She grabs Mum's hand, her best friend once more. "We were taught to never give up and that's the reason Conall is still alive. I never stopped believing in him. You're part of the story too – and you're the one person in our family they haven't talked to about Conall, about our decision to fight for his life."

I squirmed in my seat. "I love Conall," I said quietly.

"Then do this," Mum said loudly. "The interview won't take long. Beth and I will be there beside you – we'll answer most of the questions. Just talk about how much you love Conall and how we support each other as a family."

I pinched my lips together. We support each other when it suits us, I wanted to snipe. If Mum didn't agree with a decision Beth or I made, that scaffold would vanish from beneath us. Beth rebelled against Mum's strictness as a teenager, but it didn't last long. They had that same personality which had the potential to stir sparks into flames, and the common cause united them in a fiery duo. I was left on the edge, half-lonely, half-relieved.

My sister was asking me to help her. I don't do enough for

16

Conall – there is only so much anyone can do for the boy – so I reluctantly agreed.

Some help I am, I think, rushing lost around a television studio.

"*Trish!*" Beth's loud whisper, so similar to our mother's, hisses at me from down the corridor.

Relieved, I clunk along at speed. Her face is orange with make-up, her eyes popping alarmingly with exaggerated eyeliner and annoyance. "Where were you? They're prepping us now, come on."

She shoves me into the room ahead of her. It's a small studio with two couches surrounded by large box cameras on swivel-boards, and piercing lights. Men dressed in black adjust them as Beth ushers me over to Mum on the larger couch. My mother seems oddly diminished as she stares in awe at the interviewer sitting opposite us.

Margaret Elderfield is a tall, imposing woman with jet-black hair and engaging eyes. She has that rare talent of being able to overpower those she needs to break – evasive politicians, for example – and yet radiate a motherly tenderness toward her more vulnerable interviewees. She does not look up as we lower ourselves quietly onto the couch on either side of my mother.

I cast a glance at Mum whose make-up is more understated than Beth's, but nevertheless unnecessarily gaudy, like mine. I had not complained when I was doused in concealer, powder, blusher. The more I could hide behind, the better.

Margaret Elderfield looks up eventually and smiles. Not a genuine smile, but not an unpleasant one either. The broad beam of a professional – I'm sure she shoots that welcome across to this couch every week.

"Beth," she says warmly, as she rises to shake our hands. "And Deirdre. Lovely to see you again. Excuse my rudeness, I needed to check my notes before we start. And you must be Trish Olden. Or, I'm sorry, do you have a married name?"

I squeeze my left hand into a fist, missing the cool touch of my engagement ring. I sense my mother holding her breath. Beth fidgets beside her. If Margaret Elderfield notices, she does not say anything, but stares down at me expectantly.

"No," I say, through a sticky swallow. "I'm not married."

Margaret Elderfield nods vaguely and glides back to her seat. I have barely recovered when a row of bright lights are flicked into my eyes. I squint as Margaret Elderfield stands and motions at us to get ready. I look around frantically. A man is counting down from five.

It begins.

Margaret starts with Beth, asking her about her now-famous decision to bear Conall despite devastating odds against his survival.

A flush of hypocrisy shames me as she speaks. I am not an avid pro-lifer like Mum and Beth. I shouldn't be here. But it is too late. I hardly hear Mum and Beth as they answer her questions. My ears pulsate harshly. It is a familiar sensation from my childhood, when bullies teased me in the schoolyard, or the teachers tried to make me partake in public speaking to help my confidence. Same as then, I want to rush from the room and hide under my pillow.

It doesn't help that when Margaret Elderfield addresses me for the first time, it is with yet another question about my marital status. I look at her sharply. I want to snap that she already knows the answer. Her lack of tact infuses me with an unexpected conviction.

I answer her comments bravely, and manage to spout some admiring lines about Beth. Thankfully this prompts her to redirect her questions at my sister. I arrange my expression to appear engrossed as Beth gives her usual speech about her difficulties conceiving and the quiet promises by the doctors that Conall would not survive.

Margaret Elderfield cuts off that discussion promptly, seeming more interested in Mum's story. "Deirdre Olden, your husband died young, leaving you with two small children. Do you think he would have been proud of Beth's decision?" Her question drips with dreaminess, hopeful of capturing the hearts of her audience.

I close my eyes. *Just say yes,* I think desperately, *just say yes, Mum.*

Dad was always a sore topic in our house. I don't remember him and Mum was quick to plug any attempt to talk about him. I was a baby when he passed away from cancer. I look at my sister. I have often thought it must have been such a confusing time for a six-year-old. Her father gone, a new baby taking up her mother's time. It's no wonder she never showed any natural sisterly affection toward me growing up.

"My husband was a complicated man," Mum says, somewhat cautiously.

I glance at Margaret but she wasn't about to let that go.

"What do you mean by that, Deirdre?"

Mum does not falter. "He did not hold the same beliefs I did. He felt women should have access to abortions in this country if that was their choice."

I stare at Mum. She never, once, in all the time I asked about my father, mentioned this to me.

She continues. "So you can understand why, if he were alive today, he might not appreciate Beth's need to birth Conall. But I do. I am so proud of her."

Margaret's voice has lost its caramel quality. "Did you and your husband debate this regularly?"

"It was not until after he died that I got involved in the pro-life movement. We did not discuss it often. Only once, actually."

Mum glances at me. I know my mouth is hanging open but for once I don't care what anyone thinks of me. My mother is revealing a part of my father I hadn't known existed, not to ease our grief but for entertainment. To grab Margaret Elderfield's attention. To boost ratings.

Margaret asks her to elaborate but Mum does not answer immediately. She keeps her eyes on mine. My lungs constrict. She is about to say something else, something she knows will upset me. My breathing becomes shallow and I blink rapidly. What can she possibly say about my dead father? I try to ask her with my eyes. The urge to jump up and stop this charade is paralysed by her stare.

Then she turns away from me, back to Margaret Elderfield, to answer the question.

Chapter three

CIARA

Running is more than a sport. I am not religious or even spiritual. But when I run, I feel the life in the earth – that same life that grows plants and feeds animals – rush up through my feet and spin through my body. Running brings me truly alive.

I smile smugly when I hear strangers describe how they ran for the bus or raced around with their children in the playground. Casually using your legs to carry your body is not marginally equivalent to serious running. In that there is technique and strategy and overall bodily fitness.

Most importantly, the mind must be sharp. Running fast is not enough to win. The key is running smart.

I'm scheduled to do a short run today – eight or nine miles. It suits me, because Trish's interview is being aired tonight. I messaged her after it was recorded on Tuesday but she never replied.

I slow to a walk at the end of our cul-de-sac and warm down in the front garden, stretching tall. Thankfully the wind is not as vicious as it was earlier in the week. I don't mind running in the cold – it is easier to breathe than in the clammy hotness of summer. But battling elements that won't be present in Rio de Janeiro next summer is not helpful. I am glad of the relatively neutral mildness of the evening.

I turn the key in the lock and am surprised when the alarm beeps, seeking to be deactivated. I punch the code into the pad.

"Nikki?" I call out. Silence greets me. In the kitchen I find a note on the table. I scowl as I read it. She has gone out to meet a friend but hopes she won't be late. I crumple the note in my fist.

I had planned on driving to the mountains where Trish, Stephen and I met for Gerry's anniversary three days ago. When I returned there on Tuesday the hilly terrain was perfect for the quad-strengthening runs my coach Adrian has advised. Although it means I'll get to watch Trish's interview, my reason for staying nearer to home today is mainly so I will not be gone from Nikki for the whole evening.

There has been a strained distance between us lately. Nikki and I have lived together for the past three years and were civilly partnered last year. We celebrated the legalisation of same-sex marriage with the rest of our friends and intend to convert our civil partnership to marriage next year. We are totally committed to one another. But there has been another conversation about our future that is clouding the atmosphere of our home.

Nikki has always championed my running career. "Your ambition is infectious," she told me a few months after our civil-partnership ceremony as we lay in bed, enjoying one last lazy Sunday before I left for a two-week training camp in Germany. As Nikki stroked my arm, I flexed my bicep playfully.

"You know you have the perfect body, don't you?" she whispered, with a sad lilt I was not quite able to read.

I dipped my head to look into her eyes.

"I'll never have that physique," she said. "You could have anyone you wanted, you know."

I laughed. Someone else might have chosen a sensitive response, massaging her ego. But to me, it was ridiculous that she should be self-conscious. I was the lucky one. Yes, I had a defined figure, a toned stomach while she was soft. But Nikki – she's classically beautiful. A doll. Porcelain-smooth skin, and a full womanly figure. "My darling," I said, "you are the most beautiful woman I have ever met."

Her face glowed. "And you are the most wonderful. I love everything about you, including your obsession with winning. It makes you who are you. Don't fight it. Don't feel guilty about going to Germany. Go. It's who you are and I don't want anybody else."

I have relived that conversation many times in the past few months, as Nikki has drifted further from me. Since they announced the times required for Olympic qualification, she has been less forgiving of my training schedule.

I know the problem. She wants a baby.

As I stand under the pumping showerhead, I picture myself on the podium, cameras flashing as they announce my victory – "Winner of the 2016 Olympic Games 5000 metres race . . . from Ireland . . . Ciara Kavanagh!" I grin into the water. It can happen. I will make it happen.

I have two hours until Trish's interview airs so, once I am dried and dressed, I spend half an hour poring over my training plan for the weekend. It's pretty hectic – even my rest periods are crammed with life chores to free up as much time as possible during the week.

If we didn't have a mortgage to pay, I would be able to train full time. Nikki's primary-school teacher's salary will only get us so far. Adrian secured me a position as a personal trainer with a chain of gyms around Dublin and I take on corporate clients when Nikki and I need an income boost. The flexibility it gives me to work around my training is invaluable. Most of my clients want lunchtime or evening sessions, which leaves me the mornings and afternoons to run. I have reduced my hours as a trainer since Adrian and I decided to go for Rio so I have tonight off work. Still, I passed on a mountain run to be at home. I had thought Nikki would be pleased.

Though some residual annoyance at her absence tightens my shoulders, I cannot deny that I enjoy the quiet of the house. I stand with my hands on my hips, scrutinising the meal plan on the fridge.

The sole aspect of serious running that I do not enjoy is the dietary strictness. It had not been necessary in the beginning – I simply ate healthily. But I have now twice missed out on Olympic qualification – eight years ago because I failed to meet the required time and four years ago due to an injury. This time around, as I get older and my chances dwindle, I am doing everything I can to give myself an edge. Including planning my meals like a dictator.

Until six months ago, I took at least one evening off a week so Nikki and I could binge together on the couch, or go out for a Chinese guilt-free. With my qualification race only two months away, there can be no such concessions, no cheating. I have to give it my all.

Having prepared a protein-laden dinner, I drop onto the couch with a sigh of contentment and switch on the television. I curl my legs under me as a cheery tune announces the end of the news and Margaret Elderfield appears on screen.

"*Stay tuned for Current Times, next. Tonight we talk to Beth, who gave birth to a son six months ago despite being told he was unlikely to survive outside the womb.*"

I squirm uncomfortably, as Trish must have as she sat in the hot seat. The underlying judgement of any woman who chooses not to carry such a baby to birth is scarcely concealed. I spear a piece of chicken with my fork, waiting impatiently. I message Stephen as the final adverts lead into the programme.

Are you watching?

He replies almost instantly. **Not at the moment. It's recording.**

Finally, the screen illuminates dramatically with the *Current Times* studio. Margaret Elderfield twirls on the spot to face the camera and spouts her standard introduction. I munch my lettuce impatiently as she takes her seat. A zoomed-in shot of the three women on the couch reveals my best friend on the left, sitting tall and tense. Her

24

make-up has clearly been professionally done – there is more rouge on her cheeks than she would normally wear, even when working, and her eye shadow is a bold green she would never have chosen herself. It is applied well, however, and complements her dress. She looks classy.

I laugh out loud. "Trish, you're famous!" I lower my plate onto the coffee table with a clatter, directing all my attention at the screen.

Margaret Elderfield goes right for the main attraction. "*Beth Barkley – a woman we have all come to know since you spoke openly about your decision to give birth despite the medical diagnosis you received.*"

Beth nods serenely. "*My husband and I have never regretted the decision. Conall is the light of our lives and every second with him is a blessing.*"

"*Your husband Larry Barkley has been at your side during every interview, but tonight we are meeting others who are equally important in your life.*"

Beth allows herself to smile, though it does not compete with the lipsticked beamer of Margaret Elderfield. "*Yes, my mother and sister have been magnificent. They dote on Conall. I don't know what I would do without them.*"

"*Well, another woman who needs no introduction is your mother, Deirdre Olden. Deirdre, you are a prominent pro-life activist who will no doubt be familiar to many of our audience. Tell me, are you proud of your daughter?*"

My forehead furrows as Trish's mother begins to speak. Perhaps not surprisingly, given the difficulties I have faced in being accepted for who I am, I have naturally liberal tendencies. Deirdre Olden is entitled to hold her opinion, and hold it passionately.

Yet her righteous refusal in newspaper and radio interviews to display sympathy for women who have felt forced into terminating their pregnancies has grated on me more than other commentators. Perhaps it is because I can see the constant battle Trish wages for her mother's approval. For someone who claims to care so deeply about the lives of babies, Deirdre Olden is not a warm mother. I listen crossly as she lists the attributes her eldest daughter possesses – courage, strength, solid morals.

Finally, the camera zooms in on Trish. Her eyes widen alarmingly as Margaret Elderfield addresses her, and her hands twitch rapidly in her lap.

"*Your younger sister has also been a source of strength for you, Beth,*" Margaret says, as though she would scare Trish by speaking to her directly. After a brief pause, she takes the chance. "*Trish Olden . . . it is Olden, isn't it? You're not married?*"

"*Shut up!*" I yell at the screen. Whether or not Margaret Elderfield knows Trish's engagement has just ended, it is an insensitive question, and blatantly unnecessary given the lack of a ring on her finger.

Thankfully, Trish manages to speak.

"*No, I am not married.*"

"*So, Trish Olden. You have grown up with a mother and sister who are not afraid to stand up for what they believe in. What do you think of your sister's decision to have her child in the circumstances she faced?*"

I lean forward. Trish and I have never discussed our personal thoughts on the issue of abortion. This would not be surprising – it is far from typical dinner conversation – except that Trish is my best friend. She sustained me in the hardest moments of my coming out, and I made an extra effort to be there for her during the many years she lived with her overbearing mother.

There is only one time Trish and I drifted apart that I can remember. She had a serious boyfriend, Alan, who she met a couple of years after she left school. They broke up around the time Gerry died. I tried to be there for her, but Trish refused to see me or talk to me. Stephen and I offered each other mutual comfort, but Trish stayed away. Stephen was keen to force her to interact with us, but I knew she just needed time. Finally, after nearly six months, she managed to turn her life around. That was when she first took up her job as cabin crew for Aer Clara, and moved into her own place. Soon we were back to normal, and we never mentioned that period of distance.

I always assumed Trish held the same pro-life beliefs as her family. It would not be easy to express a contrary opinion in her household. But seeing her shift self-consciously on the couch, I tilt my head to the side and wonder if I have been wrong. Her answer is evasive.

"*I have always been proud of my sister. My nephew Conall is a beautiful child. I am honoured to be his aunt.*"

This seems to satisfy Margaret Elderfield who twists around again to Trish's sister.

I message Stephen for the second time. **Trish looks like she wants to vanish. She's doing great though.**

I half-listen to Beth rehash her story as I tap around on my phone, waiting for him to reply. He does not. I look up when Margaret Elderfield asks about Deirdre's husband. Trish was a baby when he died. She rarely speaks of him.

"*My husband was a complicated man,*" Deirdre says.

Margaret inches forward on her seat. "*What do you mean by that, Deirdre?*"

I can only gape as Deirdre reveals that her husband believed women should have access to abortion, and might not have approved of Beth's choice.

Margaret presses on, asking if Deirdre and her husband used to debate the matter.

When Deirdre answers "*Only once*", I feel a chill run through me. Trish's Mum is the most militant pro-lifer I have ever met. I am not surprised that she has never revealed her late husband's belief before – but why is she bringing it up now? She could easily have sidestepped the question.

Margaret, practically salivating, asks her to elaborate.

Deirdre is staring strangely at Trish. I hold my breath.

"*The truth is, Margaret,*" Deirdre says, "*my husband was very ill at the time I became pregnant with Trish and thought it wasn't the right time to have another baby. He worried it would be too much for us. He wanted me to have an abortion.*"

"*No!*" I say it loud into the empty house. My stomach lurches as

27

the camera zooms in on Trish. The make-up seems to have dissolved from her face, now pure white. I wriggle forward until I am practically off the seat.

"Tell me this isn't the first time she's heard this, you selfish wagon!" I shout at the screen, though Trish's expression confirms otherwise.

Deirdre Olden might be a snarky know-it-all, but I never imagined her doing anything as cruel as announcing such a profound personal detail to a watching nation.

"So you see, Margaret, my daughter Beth and I are very alike. We were each given a supposedly valid reason to abort our children, but we value life too much." She puts her hand on Trish's knee. I don't know how my friend doesn't jerk away. *"If I had done as my husband asked, I never would have had Trish. If Beth had acted as everyone expected – travelled abroad to terminate her child's life – I wouldn't be going home after this interview to hold my only grandchild. Even when everyone is against you, abortion is never the answer."*

I want to scream. I message Stephen. **Are you watching this? We need to talk to Trish.**

Knowing that she is in the air, I call Trish's voicemail and leave a garbled sympathy message, insisting she ring me as soon as her flight lands. She must have spent the past two days trying to convince the station not to air the programme.

The interview ends soon after, with the usual begging advertisement for donations for Conall, the little boy whose mother would not give up on him.

I switch off the television with a firm push of the button and stamp into the kitchen. From what Trish tells me, the child is in constant pain and won't live much longer.

Suddenly exhausted, I drop my plate in the sink. As I stare at my phone, willing Stephen to call and wishing Nikki was here beside me, a heaviness settles on me. The interview is over. Yet somehow, though I cannot explain why, it feels more like a beginning.

Chapter four

STEPHEN

I switched my phone to silent after Ciara's first message, knowing she would continue to bombard me until I replied.

I won't get a chance to watch Trish's interview until later tonight, when we're having dinner. I scrub the potatoes until the skin is almost shaved off, the way Lisa prefers it. I have some making-up to do. At least I know she loves my cooking, and I'm always off to a good start in winning her over if I serve up something with a strong sweet-and-sour flavour.

"How's it coming in there?" she calls from the living room.

"Another hour or so." I pause. "Why don't you go for a walk – I'll have it ready by the time you get back."

At first she says nothing. Then, "Good idea."

I jump.

She is suddenly behind me, her voice silky in my ear. "All right. I'll go for a walk. It'll work up my appetite."

Once she's gone, I splash oil in the pan and set about dicing the chicken. Since I've been living with Lisa, we've taken to eating much later in the evening. It is almost half nine at night and I am only preparing the dinner.

Lisa enjoys eating late. She considers it continental. I know she fantasises about us dining by the French Riviera or on a Spanish mountaintop, instead of in our increasingly dated semi-detached house in west Dublin. As little as six months ago, it wasn't an idle dream. I was earning significantly as a senior accountant in Likeman Tiles, the largest home-furnishing business in the country. I had been saving my holidays for an extended trip with Lisa next year.

I can picture her lounging on a wicker chair in an intimate restaurant by the Italian coast, her blonde hair flowing out behind her in the breeze, her eyes glowing with a tender love. It is a picture that has never been drawn, yet it is so vivid in my mind sometimes it is all I see. We weren't intending to limit ourselves to Europe. We were going to ski in New Zealand, shop in Dubai and sunbathe in San Francisco. Now, without my salary and caught in the mortgage trap with a starter house barely out of negative equity, we'll be lucky to get a weekend in Galway this year.

I realise with a jolt that I've been standing rigid for nearly five full minutes, staring down at the half-prepped chicken. Blinking back to consciousness, my hands slip expertly around the meat, and I force myself to think about anything except Lisa and our ever-evaporating plans. I think, as I often do in moments like these, of Gerry.

Ciara and Trish are my best friends and I wouldn't swap them for anything. But it's not the same without another man in the group. Gerry was always the life of the party – whenever I came home from a night out with a funny story, it was thanks to Gerry's antics. Feeling my stomach sink lower, I reach across the chopping board and switch on the radio. It blares so loudly I cannot hear the memories.

Only when Lisa's key turns in the lock do I spin down the volume.

"I'm going to have a shower," she says, popping her head in the kitchen door.

I open the oven at exactly the right moment and a puff of hotness spurts out. She sniffs appreciatively before disappearing.

By the time she comes down, I have the food spread out buffet-style on the coffee table in our living room.

Lisa stops at the door. "Why are we eating in here?" she asks.

"I recorded Trish's interview while I was cooking dinner." I gesture to her favourite chair — a brown leather one-seater that reclines with the pull of a lever on the side. She eases into it. Her silk pyjamas hang loosely from her body. She is so slight, even her tight-fitting clothes have some flow to them. Her hair is wet from the shower but tied up into a loose bun. Without thinking, I bend down and kiss her.

When I pull back, she smiles at me. A warmth ripples through my chest. I wish our home could be this way all the time. Without the screaming and the blaming and the anger that storms around us.

"All right, Stephen, let's watch it," she says, and I feel a rush of appreciation toward her.

I know it's the last thing she wants to do, but she's doing it for me anyway. She loves me. We love each other. I have to remind myself of that sometimes.

She doesn't make the viewing easy though. She sighs when Beth is introduced and protests under her breath at Deirdre's every comment. Lisa and Beth were best friends in school — it is through Trish's sister that I first met Lisa. They have drifted apart in recent years. Beth's marriage and obsession with conception is far from Lisa's idea of interesting conversation.

My musings are blasted aside when Deirdre Olden makes her unnecessary revelation. I cast a look at Lisa. Despite her apparent disinterest in the interview, she is sitting forward with a dropped jaw. As Margaret Elderfield struggles to contain her glee at the scoop, Lisa turns to me, her face contorted.

"Why is she saying this?"

I try to answer but my own voice has locked. There is no reason for Deirdre Olden to bring Beth and Trish's father into the discussion. Certainly no need for this particular disclosure. I scan through Ciara's messages and immediately think of Trish, serving drinks on a long-distance flight, urging the plane to take her as far away from her home as possible.

The audience clap Margaret Elderfield when the interview ends, but it is my friend who deserves the applause for remaining so dignified in the debris of Deirdre's bombshell. Her lips are tighter than usual, and her fingers are gripped so tight in her lap they could easily snap. But she sits tall.

Both Trish and I come from difficult families but, whatever my father did to me, no matter how many physical bruises he inflicted or mental put-downs I suffered, it was all behind closed doors. I never had the country watch as my greatest insecurities were brutally revealed.

"I need wine," Lisa sighs.

I don't argue, and tell her to pour me a glass too. "Choose any bottle – I'm just stepping out for a minute. I need some fresh air."

She surveys me with a frown but does not complain. Once outside, I dial Ciara's number. She answers after one ring.

"I saw it," is all I can manage.

For once, Ciara is lost for words. At her despair, my own head clears.

"We'll see her when she gets home at the weekend," I say. "She'll be fine."

"They filmed on Tuesday. She's had this hanging over her for days. Why didn't she tell us?" Ciara sounds hurt, like earlier this week when she asked aloud why Gerry had failed to confide in us before he died.

"Maybe she didn't want to talk about it. Or she has spent the past couple of days with her family, trying to get to the bottom of why her mother brought it up in the first place."

Ciara snorts disparagingly. "I'll tell you why, Stephen. To create a story where there was none. To keep Beth in the papers and the money rolling in. And don't think for a second this is about the baby's wellbeing. Deirdre has her own agenda. The anti-abortion cause is more important to her than her own family, and this is some publicity, isn't it? Two generations of Oldens standing up to the liberal apologists. Trish and Conall – two human beings alive because of the pro-lifers."

Ciara takes a deep breath as if to continue on her rant, but in the same moment deflates. I can visualise her lying back onto her couch, absorbing Trish's pain as her own. I squint in the kitchen window and see Lisa pouring expertly, her hand cupping the end of the bottle.

"What did Nikki think?" I ask, not taking my eyes from Lisa.

"She's not here this evening."

At her tone, I refocus on the phone. "Everything all right, Ciara?"

"Yes, fine."

I cannot help a small smirk playing on my lips. Ciara is a fixer – her big heart wants all her friends to entrust their woes to her so she can help. But she is less inclined to do the same. I don't pry. Ciara and Nikki might be fighting, or going through a rough patch, but if any couple can come out the other side, it's them.

I dial off, promising Ciara that we'll find time to meet Trish at the weekend. I walk into the living room and pick up the dirty plates. I watch Lisa as I make my way to the kitchen and place the dishes carefully in the sink. She is scrutinising the bottle of vintage red from which she just poured.

I wrap my arms around her waist. "It's late," I say, nuzzling into her. "You take your glass upstairs. I'll do the dishes and follow you shortly."

She leans back into me. "Okay."

I load the dishwasher and take my time scrubbing the pots. All the while, Deirdre Olden's confession repeats loudly in my head.

I climb the stairs slowly. It is the first night this week that has not ended in Lisa and me having a blazing row over something minor. I'd like to keep it that way.

Lisa is sitting on the bed, sipping her wine and flicking through an old magazine. "I still can't believe Deirdre Olden said Trish's father didn't want her," she says without raising her head.

"I know," I answer placidly, stopping by the bedroom door.

She glances up, considering me. "Did you know that was going to happen? Did Trish tell you?"

"No. She didn't say a word. Some things are too painful to talk about, I suppose."

We lock eyes and I hold my breath. Everyone has their secrets, even me and Lisa. In that moment, we acknowledge ours with a shared look. I bow my head.

"Let's get to bed," I mutter.

Not wanting the truth verbalised any more than I do, she tosses the magazine aside and walks into the bathroom, slamming the door behind her.

I undress and crawl into bed, exhausted. In six hours my alarm will ring, and another day will start.

Chapter five

TRISH

I am impatient to get home so I can begin the important task of working my way through the fresh batch of giant Toblerones I bought at the airport. My flight lands in Dublin airport early on Sunday morning. The trip was a godsend. Not only did I miss the airing of the interview, but the rest of the cabin crew did too. Since no one had subscribed to the Irish channel outside of the jurisdiction, they couldn't stream it once we arrived in Shanghai.

I told them it was pretty boring, that my sister had done most of the talking. They believed me and were soon distracted with the usual sightseeing and shopping expeditions. I did not join them, but chose to pamper myself in the spa. I rarely indulge in self-pity but I thought I could be forgiven on this one occasion for acknowledging the stress-knots in my shoulders. The massage eased my muscles significantly.

Afterwards, I didn't bother changing out of my hotel robe. I sat in my room munching on Toblerone and watching trashy pay-per-view films. Still my mother's voice rang in my ears. *My husband worried it would be too much for us. He wanted me to have an abortion.*

It tolls shrilly even now, as I drag my suitcase from the bus through the estate, shivering against the unusual bitterness of the September breeze. As I often do, I had chosen not to drive to the airport on Thursday to avoid rush-hour traffic. It always makes sense at the time but the long journey home from the airport by public transport makes me regret it every time. Home might be a pokey, dilapidated terraced house with nosy and noisy neighbours, but it is mine. All mine, and I long for its solace.

I falter as the headlights of a parked car flash at me. I raise my arm to cover my eyes, then lower it instantly as Stephen and Ciara emerge.

I stop, waiting for Ciara to charge at me with a fierce hug and Stephen to mutter condolences. Instead, Ciara punches her hand into the air like a rally rouser, a large packet of Maltesers dangling from her fingers.

"Chocolate!" she declares with a grin. I look at Stephen, who makes the same gesture on the other side of the car with a six-pack gripped in his fist.

"And booze, baby," he winks.

I roll my eyes and, with a laugh, gesture them to come to me. I should have known better than to assume they would treat me as a victim. They probably want to sympathise, but the best part about our friendship is the relief we offer from the ills of the world. From the moment we met in that summer camp, homesick and sad, we provided a distraction and entertainment. Those are our survival techniques and, as I hug my friends, I realise how much I need them right now.

Soon we are inside, huddled around the electric fire while the central heating clicks into gear. Although it is barely ten in the morning, Stephen pours us all a beer along with the mugs of tea we cradle fiercely. I think of Brian, and how he used to have the house toasty warm on my winter landing days, with a pot of tea warm in its cosy and a fry sizzling on the hob. I shake him from my mind before melancholy at our broken engagement takes over. I already have plenty to bring me down this week.

Ciara is the first to bring it up as we huddle in the living room. "Trish, we wanted to say we're sorry about what you had to go through during that interview. It must have been awful."

I eye them, doubting whether they truly understand. Despite what everyone will think, it is not my father's sentiment that is stinging my chest. It is my mother's insensitivity.

My father had cancer for a year before he died. He was riddled with it even as I was conceived. He must have been so worried about how his wife and six-year-old daughter would cope without him, never mind with a new baby on the scene. He wasn't cold-heartedly disposing of me. He was trying to do the right thing, knowing he had limited time in which to do that. I think of Gerry, struggling like my father, hiding how little time he had left.

My mother, for all her grand declarations to Margaret Elderfield that she wanted me, deliberately chose to hurt me on national television. She knew how nervous I was, yet she convinced me to do it, all so she could use me as bait to reel in more funding. She chose Beth over me, so how dare she deride my father for contemplating the same?

I realise I have been silent for several minutes. "I'm not going to pretend it was easy," I say carefully. "But it was worth it. The money has been rolling in for Beth."

Stephen interrupts this time. "This is us, Trish." He doesn't say any more, but studies me with sincerity shining in his eyes.

Stephen has been honest with us about his own father, whose abuses were far worse than my own mother's strictness and unrealistic expectations. But I cannot do the same.

"You know what my mother is like," I say by way of concession. "There's no talking to her."

I had tried, though. After the interview, once we arrived at Beth's house in a taxi courtesy of the television station, I opened my mouth to challenge my mother. To my surprise, Beth got there first.

She rounded on Mum as soon as we entered the house, not bothering to keep quiet for the baby. "What the hell was that?"

Mum said nothing. She took off her coat and handed it to my

brother-in-law as he raced into the hallway, enquiring about the interview. Beth and I followed her into the kitchen.

"You'll see, Beth," Mum said finally, refusing to look at me. "This is the new angle they need to keep the interest. To keep the donations coming."

Beth stamped her foot. "Is it even true? Dad wanted you to abort Trish?"

I winced at her bluntness, but Beth didn't seem to notice.

Mum insisted my father had made his wishes clear, and that she never told anyone because it would have caused us pain.

I finally spoke then. "And you didn't think it would hurt me now, Mum?"

"I know," she said faintly.

It was the nearest I would get to an apology.

"But we have to think of the baby. You can deal with a few hard family truths if it pays for Conall's medication, can't you?"

I relay the exchange to Ciara and Stephen who do not find the argument to be as strong as Mum made out. Ciara actually growls.

"I don't see why Beth needs money anyway," she says through gritted teeth. "They must have health insurance, and the hospital isn't going to turf a little baby out on the street."

I sigh. "There's more to it than that, Ciara. The insurance doesn't cover everything, and Conall's condition is so serious he needs round-the-clock care. Some of the medication is experimental, from England and America – it costs serious money. Plus, we don't know how long he's going to live, and what treatments might be needed in future. Larry doesn't earn hugely, and all their savings went on IVF before Conall was conceived."

"All the same, Trish," says Stephen, "it's not fair that you should have to bear the brunt of it."

"I'd do anything for the baby."

Ciara reaches for the pot to top up her tea. "I know what you mean. I feel the same about my nephews and niece. It's funny, really. They're not my children but I can't imagine loving anyone more than I do them."

Stephen shrugs. "But, Trish, it's not as though you and Beth are especially close."

I know what he is asking – how I can feel such strong protectiveness toward Conall when our connection is the girl who ignored me for the better part of my childhood. It's tough to verbalise. She is still my sister. She has been a constant my whole life. In some ways, how well we get on is irrelevant. Our bond cannot be severed.

"She's mellowed since Conall was born," I offer Stephen by way of explanation. It's too difficult to describe the complexities of siblinghood to a man who has no brothers, sisters, cousins – no family at all to use as a reference.

What I say is true. Beth's attitude has altered since her pregnancy. Before, she would cast me aside, ignore me if I asked her questions and scoff at any attempts to engage her. It was brattish behaviour that carried on long after we finished school. She left home when she turned eighteen, and never bothered to keep in touch. I used to see her when she'd come home to visit Mum, but she never showed any inclination to have a relationship with me.

I had given up on any hope of a sisterly connection long ago, and settled for hearing about her achievements through Mum. Beth's jobs, loves and general life accomplishments were relayed daily with more pride than I could ever hope to extract from her. I was invited to their pro-life meetings, but I always found an excuse. It wasn't that I was avidly pro-choice, rather I had no time for the die-hard passions of either side. Mum knew I didn't have the fiery debating skills or demonstrating temperament, so she didn't push the issue. Beth was enough for her.

Beth begrudgingly named me bridesmaid, along with Lisa, at her wedding to Larry. Once they started trying for children, it claimed her entire focus. I could contribute nothing and generally stayed away, for fear that I would do or say something unhelpful.

Finally, when she became pregnant with Conall, and received the devastating news early in her pregnancy that he had Edward's Syndrome, the fight seemed to seep from her. We did not become bosom buddies, but she noticed me more. Perhaps the realisation that I would be her baby's aunt softened her. I didn't question her newfound friendliness, and enjoyed the talks she initiated.

When Brian and I broke up three months ago, Mum was devastated. She had taken to calling me 'Mrs O'Connor' since our engagement, and her reversion to 'Trish' was made pointedly. Every use of my name was a rock dropped on my self-esteem. Mum had considered Brian a vast improvement on my first proper boyfriend Alan, and reacted with more annoyance than concern when I broke the news to her. Beth happened to be visiting when I arrived to tell Mum and, as I left, she followed me out to the car.

"Trish, wait!" she called.

I turned, not knowing what to expect. Certainly not the arms she flung around me, hugging me awkwardly. I patted her back, unsure what to say. She pulled away, and looked at her feet, embarrassed.

"Sorry about you and Brian," she said. "It can't have been an easy decision."

I glanced at her but she gave no indication that she knew the real reason behind the break-up. All I had told her and Mum was that we had fallen out of love – a shameful untruth.

I promised Beth I was fine, and left feeling uplifted. Our relationship has improved even more since then.

"Brian rang me," Stephen announces out of nowhere. Ciara slaps his arm. "What?" he whispers, as if I cannot hear him. "Maybe it would help if he came over."

"I don't need Brian," I say loudly. "Thanks, Stephen, I know you mean well, but the last thing I want is more drama. I'm dying for a long soak in the tub and to forget about the whole interview. There's nothing anyone can do about it now. I'm fine."

"Oh, really?" Ciara asks. "Then why are there three Toberlones poking out of your bag?"

For a second, we all stare at my bulging handbag, then catch eyes and burst into laughter.

With the mood lightened, they ask me what I got up to in Shanghai. I don't know why I'm too embarrassed to admit that I holed up like a babe in the womb, so I describe some tours I did months ago. I've done plenty of trips there, and know what I'm talking about.

Even after six years with Aer Clara, I try to do at least one excursion per trip. It is the reason I decided to become an air stewardess in the first place – a chance to see the world. Taking the job was terrifying – until then I had only ever been out of the country once. It was the shake-up I needed after my break-up with Alan and a fresh start after Gerry's death. Aer Clara saved me.

I had let myself grieve on this trip but from now on, once the chocolate is eaten, I will be back to my normal self.

Chapter six

CIARA

My stomach muscles blister as I tremble to hold the position in place. Our overly enthusiastic Pilates instructor yells at us to hold it. In my peripheral line of sight I see Nikki wobble until he finally releases us. I lower myself easily to my knees. Beside me, Nikki collapses onto her mat.

"All right, pet?" I ask half-mockingly.

She sticks out her tongue at me and scrambles upright as we begin our final warm-down.

"Slowly. *Slowly!*" our instructor shouts as Nikki rushes to finish.

The night before our classes, she is always eager. She waffles on about Pilates being such a healthy way to start the week. A proper dose of exercise to invigorate her for work. But when I shake her awake at half five on a Monday morning, the torture of core-strengthening somehow loses its charm.

"Good work, ladies!" The instructor claps as we pile our mats in the corner. "You feel better for it, don't you?"

I agree with a stretch while Nikki grunts and slouches from the room. But I can see that Pilates works for her. It takes her some time to recover but, half an hour later, once the memory of the pain has faded and she has a strong cup of coffee in her hands, she will be full of energy and chat about the week ahead. We saunter to our regular café around the corner and I order while Nikki slips into a booth by the window.

We are a fifteen-minute walk from the primary school at which Nikki teaches, so she has no excuse for avoiding our weekly Pilates class, except for apathy. She's not lazy. Actually, she is one of the most active people I know – constantly coming up with projects for her kids, volunteering at a homework club in the inner city, and her plans for improvements to our house seem never-ending. We are active in different ways and I like to think we spur each other on with our own interests. She'd never bother about keeping her fitness up if I didn't literally drag her out of bed, and I would let the house fall apart without her keen eye.

She watches me unload the tray, her face unusually sombre. She has been quiet recently – when she's around, that is.

"One extra-strong coffee," I sing-song as I hand her the steaming mug, "and a muffin."

"A muffin?" she asks quizzically. "Are you trying to undo all the effort I put into class this morning?"

I snigger as she sinks her teeth unrepentantly into its spongy sweetness.

"It's all right for you," she mumbles accusingly. "You're going to be running and training all day. Pilates is all I have."

"Then don't eat the muffin." I incline my head to the side.

She stares at me, her grinning mouth already crammed full. "It's a bit late now," she says, bits of chocolate-chip spewing from her lips. "Would you like some?"

She holds out the smallest scrap.

"Your generosity is astounding," I say sarcastically, and she flicks her eyebrows playfully.

Instinctively, I reach out and touch her arm. This is what has been missing lately – the easy, everyday banter that makes us who

44

we are as a couple. I don't want things to change, and I don't know why they have. I'm working longer and harder hours, but I'm making a real effort not to take Nikki for granted. She is the one who is never around. I remove my hand.

"Are you coming home straight after work?" I ask, taking a falsely casual sip of my lemon water. "I'll do my famous veggie stir-fry."

It is a few seconds before she answers. "I need to pop into town after work."

I take another lengthy sip. "Isn't your homework club on Wednesdays now?"

"Yes, it's not that. I have to pick up a few things in the shops, that's all. I might stop off and get a new wallpaper sample for the bedroom while I'm there."

There is already a line of wallpaper squares lining our dressing table. I don't know how many more she needs to make up her mind but I don't argue. At least she's not talking about decorating the spare room with stork patterns again. That sparked one of our worst arguments.

While Nikki has always backed my career, she has dreams of her own. At first, it was easy to put off her request to start a family. We were still young, only just living together. When we got civilly partnered last year, she brought it up again. I panicked. I had assumed my attitude towards having children would have aligned with Nikki's at that stage, but becoming a mother seemed too much. I wasn't ready yet. So I suggested we postpone for a year, to give ourselves time to settle into life as a civilly partnered couple. She was reluctant – this was the second time I had put off starting the process. So, to appease her, I promised we would do it this year.

In my mid-twenties, shortly before I met Nikki, I got injured. A bad fall on the track left me with not only a broken ankle but ligament damage. It took months to heal properly. I kept training, and was racing as soon as I could but the injury came during what Adrian called my 'peak period' of fitness, and it set me back. I had previously missed the qualification times for the Beijing Olympics in 2008. Adrian had not been worried – he assumed I would be ready for London in 2012. But, with the injury, I missed out again. I could still race, but the Olympics are the Holy Grail of sport, and I had resigned myself to the fact that I had missed my chances. Both of them.

Turns out Adrian had never taken his eye off the prize. He had pushed me in the years after my injury without admitting the greater plan. Until last year. Until a few months after I had promised Nikki we would settle down and start a family. I am now finally on course, and given my age I don't have much time left to be striking for Olympic Gold. I need to focus. Parenthood will have to wait.

I don't know what Nikki thinks avoiding me is going to achieve, and I have half a mind to insist she leave wallpaper sampling for another night, and spend some time with me.

"I can keep a plate for you," I suggest.

"No, don't bother. Some of the teachers want to meet for dinner and since I'll be in town anyway . . ." She trails off.

I watch her pick at the crumbs of her muffin. I open my mouth to make a comment about the oddness of teachers choosing a Monday night for a get-together but I bottle it at the last second. It would inevitably lead to another fight.

Instead, I shrug. "Maybe I'll pop over to Orla tonight, then."

Nikki's face breaks into a smile and she nods spiritedly at my suggestion. "You should, Ciara. I bet she would love that. Definitely go visit her."

I frown at the extent of her enthusiasm for my impromptu visit to my sister. The cynical part of me worries that she wants me to spend more time with Orla's kids in the hope that they'll ignite a broodiness in me. If that's the case, she'll be disappointed. I am crazy about my nephews and niece, but I'm perfectly content being 'Aunty Ciara'.

Thinking about it now, I realise it's been weeks since I've seen my sister and the little ones.

As I start to message her, Nikki looks down at her own phone. She reads something on the screen, then flicks her eyes to mine.

"Someone looking for you?" I ask.

She gawks around the café. I copy her. A few other customers are dotted about. A man in jogging gear scoffs a doughnut messily. A woman with a pram, also dressed for an active day, sips an expresso while reading a magazine.

"It's the deputy head. She wants to know if I'm on my way."

I glance at my watch – we usually have another twenty minutes before she is due in. But Nikki is already scraping back her chair.

"You know what they're like – there's always something more I could be doing."

"They'll run you into the ground," I complain as we gather our belongings and head for the door, almost bumping into a frazzled businessman as he bundles his way in from the cold.

"If anyone's doing the running, into the ground or otherwise, it's you, Ciara."

I punch her arm playfully and for a moment everything is normal. We stroll in silence toward the school. After a few minutes she asks about Trish. There is nothing more I can add to what I told her last night.

"The interview must have been horrible for her."

"She's putting on a brave front," I answer. "That mother of hers is a right weapon."

"I know." Nikki seems agitated. "She does her cause no good with her inflammatory comments."

We reach the corner by the school and she leans in to peck my cheek. Without thinking, I grab her shoulders and kiss her. She stumbles in surprise, but returns it with feeling.

"I love you, Nikki," I say with as much passion as I can squeeze into the words.

She doesn't hesitate. "I love you too, sweetheart."

We kiss again, an act that would have been unthinkable in public when we started dating four years ago.

We met in my running club. It was my first night back there after ditching the crutches and everyone was buying me drinks to celebrate my ongoing recovery. As the club's best chance for glory and sponsorship, I was surrounded for hours by well-wishers. Through the throng, I spotted her.

I was attracted to her immediately. Round blue eyes in a flawless face, with blonde hair curling naturally around her shoulders. I was sitting on a high stool by the bar when she came to order a drink, but even in her heels I could tell I was taller than her. She bent over the bar, seeking out the busy barman, her ample chest crushed against her arms.

"Hello," I said, a simple word I would not have had the confidence to utter had I not been emboldened by the admiration and praise I'd been receiving all night. "You're new here."

"Just a hanger-on, actually," she grinned, her face lighting up. She nodded to a woman sitting in the corner, watching us converse. "My friend has started training for her first ever marathon. She tells me you're the club's hero."

I gestured for her to sit on the stool beside me. "That's a fierce exaggeration. I was doing well but I'm recovering from an injury." I pointed to my foot. "So, what about you? Are you a runner?"

She laughed, and told me in no uncertain terms that the last time she ran anywhere was to chase the ice-cream van as it drove down the road. Her eyes watered when she laughed, I remember. Soft, intriguing eyes. After five more minutes of easy chat, I made a joke and she touched my hand. I flinched away instinctively, darting glances around the room.

Nikki leaned in. "Still in the closet?"

I took a shuddering breath.

"It's okay," she said. "We've all been there."

It was true. Even for her with a lesbian aunt. There were no ingrained prejudices for her family to overcome. Yet it was not easy.

We talked for so long that night we closed the bar. She walked me to my bus stop, holding my arm as I hobbled a little on the dark, uneven surface. In the concealed darkness of a side alley, with no one else around, she kissed me.

We have been together ever since.

"I'll see you later," I say as I shift my bag on my shoulder.

"I'm going into town, remember, so there's no need to wait up!" she calls after me.

I frown. "You won't be too late, will you?"

She smiles at me, already crossing the road. "No, of course not. See you later." She blows me a kiss and walks into the school grounds.

I stand watching her for some time before turning and beginning my run home.

Chapter seven

STEPHEN

It is late when I leave the pub. I am not drunk — with my six-foot three-inch frame it would take more than a few pints to floor me. But I am tipsy, my feet tripping clumsily over each other.

"You'll be in trouble with the missus when you get home!" one of the regulars calls to me.

I beat away his warning with a flap of my arm.

The fresh air outside steadies me. I picture Lisa pacing the living room, wringing her hands and peeking out the window every few minutes. I don't want to go home. It used to be a place of excitement, when Lisa would leap into my arms the moment I crossed the threshold.

Things have changed since my redundancy, and it is hard to visualise any kind of future. History is repeating itself in a way I never thought it would. As a child, my home life was always tense. My mother spent all her energy keeping my father's temper at bay. I used to hate her for being too weak to walk out on him, and take me with her. Only when she died did I see her for what she really was: a shield of iron I could never hope to emulate.

I promised myself I would never become my father. If I ever found love, and a family, I would treat them tenderly. I worked hard not to let the years of bitterness toward my father pollute me. I have tried to be a good man.

Yet, somehow, my home has become one of hostility. I cannot stop it. It comes from nowhere, although it doesn't take a huge amount of self-awareness to see the triggers. Lisa and I have not coped well with our reduced income. The strain curdles around us without let-up. It is in recent months that I have truly come to realise how many friends Lisa and I have let go since we started dating. Absorbed in each other, we refused invitations to birthday parties, group trips away, even weddings. The invitations became less frequent and now we are left alone, with money and prospects replaced by a buzzing anger and resentment that has progressed, despite my best efforts, to violence.

Trish and Ciara are the only friends who refused to accept my slide into romantic isolation. They have been my family since we met in that summer camp at the age of fourteen. We hung out at the weekends, took holidays together, talked to each other about the important events in our lives. Or most of them, anyway.

There were lulls – like around the time Gerry died and Trish broke up with Alan. Ciara suggested we give Trish time. Eventually, she came back to us. When Ciara went abroad to train, we didn't keep in touch as much as we'd promised at her farewell drinks. Then there were the few months after Lisa and I first got together, when I hardly saw my best friends. But we never completely lost touch, and our friendship remained intact.

Lisa and I met through Trish. On the night I accepted the job with Likeman Tiles – the single greatest achievement of my life – I took my colleagues out for drinks to Café en Seine, a trendy bar on Dublin's well-to-do Dawson Street. Of course, I invited Ciara and Trish along. Their respective others, Nikki and Brian, came too, full of handshakes and congratulations.

At about eleven o'clock, Trish, Ciara and I were grouped in a huddle, knocking back tequila, when Trish grabbed my arm.

"Hey, look! There's my sister."

Ciara and I swung around. I managed to elbow the nose of one of my junior colleagues. I gave a rushed apology as I scanned the room for Trish's infamous sister. We had never met her, as she and Trish were barely in each other's lives. Ciara and I eyed her over our champagne glasses, ignoring Trish's pleas that she did not want to approach her. We insisted, threatening to introduce ourselves if she did not.

So the three of us stumbled across to her sister, who was drinking with an attractive blonde at one of the high tables by the wall. Beth reacted without much interest and her friend did not seem particularly pleased with the intrusion – until she noticed me.

Trish begrudgingly introduced us to Beth.

Ciara grabbed her hand and shook it dramatically. I laughed into my drink but my attention was soon fixed on the friend, who was appraising me with more pleasure than Beth had her sister.

"This is Lisa," Trish said as an afterthought.

I sidled up to her. Perched on her high stool, she was a slip of a thing. I knew she would not even reach my shoulder. She introduced herself properly and soon the two of us were locked in conversation.

She was impressed with me, and I did not restrain myself. My new job and the drink combined to infuse me with confidence. I'd never normally have expected anything but pitying rejection from such a beautiful woman.

Months later, when we reminisced about our first meeting, Lisa snickered at the idea of my nerves. The truth is, since I managed to escape from the suffocating strictness of my father's control, I made it my mission never to be treated that way again. I joined a rugby club. I beefed up. I scrutinised the other accountants and corporate types I worked with – the senior ones who spoke eloquently about wine and knew how to invest their money. I learned how to come off as cocky and handsome, but it was a façade. My father's disapproving voice would not be silenced in my head. My assumption that pretty girls like Lisa would see right through me was absolute.

But Lisa stroked my rugby bicep and commented on my height, my sparkling eyes, my high-achieving career. She lapped up the compliments I doled out in return and happily slipped me her number when Beth managed to drag her away.

As Lisa and I got to know each other over the next few months, I discovered we had more in common than I could have known. Her home had also been one of anger, with a father whose method of education was fear. Her mother wasn't able to handle it. She left when Lisa was small. Lisa says she 'left' – really she died. But it was a death she did not fight. Gone within weeks of the diagnosis and happier for it. Her older brothers and sisters had their own lives to lead – they were willing for Lisa, the youngest, to be sacrificed as their father's distraction.

While her father was not as physically abusive as mine, there were incidents where he hit her – and his emotional put-downs were at least as brutal as my father's had been. She accepted it for years, knowing she had no choice while she was under his roof. But she had not let it ruin her life. Her determination to better herself, to get everything she didn't have as a girl, resonated with me. Her job was not as highly paid as mine – she was an office administrator and PA to the CEO of a small finance company. But she had made herself indispensable, and was on a far more decent wage than I would have guessed.

I did notice her obsession with materialism, but I could identify with it. That was merely her marker, her measure of success. My own work acted as an elevator for my ego and, as we separately thrived, so did our relationship.

My redundancy six months ago hit us hard. No more foreign holidays or expensive handbags for Lisa. We were not married, or even engaged, but we acted as one. We had long ago set up a joint bank account and my financial losses were hers too. Threads of inadequacy and fear were woven into our relationship, bringing out the worst in us.

The arguments were putrid, and often I heard my father's voice coming from my mouth.

For the first few months, I treated finding employment as a sprint. I worked from morning until long after Lisa had gone to bed – researching work, approaching employers, networking with my contacts. I apologised every evening when I came home unsuccessful.

I managed to get a temporary position three months ago. It is a job for which I am absurdly overqualified in a small accountancy practice, Zedmans. I am paid a pittance yet it is enough to dampen my enthusiasm for job-hunting. I know I need to find a permanent position but my will is fading rapidly. Lisa tries to encourage me but I don't want to hear it. I don't want to be around her – her criticisms and snipes and useless suggestions. So I have been going for drinks, staying out later. Anything to avoid her and the inevitable aggression that is unleashed when I arrive home, drunk and harassed from the inside out.

Lisa wants a ring. I'm not stupid, I know that. But I cannot afford one right now, never mind the lavish wedding she would inevitably plan.

I simply want some quiet.

I feel the tension building apace as I walk up the gravel driveway and jab my key into the lock.

"Lisa?" I call out, hearing her name slur on my lips.

She hurries into the hallway. "Where have you been?" She sounds whiny, an irritant.

In that moment, as in so many others recently, I loathe her.

For a moment, we stare at each other, the fear and uncertainty and weaknesses festering. It comes without warning, just like it did from my father.

Slap.

Chapter eight

TRISH

I am surprised when Beth arrives at my door with a basket of cupcakes. I cock my head to the side.

"Hi, Trish," she says breathlessly. "Do you mind if I come in?"

I stand aside to let her through. "I'm not doing any more interviews." I nod at her offering with a hesitant smile and she laughs, relieved I've broken the ice.

"How's Conall?" I ask as I switch on the kettle.

"He's good, actually. He's having a good week."

I probe no more. I have learnt the hard way that discussing details is more upsetting for Beth than people accepting her word. We make small talk for about half an hour. We're good at that. There's something about siblings – they are the easiest people in the world to talk to, even sisters like us who rarely speak except when necessary. You fall back into your childhood when the other person was an extension of yourself. Beth was mostly annoying and domineering, but she was always present, a sort of extra parent.

After half an hour, she glances at her watch but says nothing.

"Beth, why are you here? Do you need something?" I am recovered from the jetlag of my last flight but a general tiredness pervades me. I don't have the energy to be second-guessing my sister.

"No," she says defensively, then sighs. "I'm sorry about the interview. You know, what Mum said about Dad. If it makes you feel any better, I remember Dad talking about the new baby and how exciting it was going to be having a little sister or brother. Whatever Mum says, he wanted you."

"I'm sure he wanted lots of things, Beth." I rise abruptly, my chair scraping on the floor. "Not least to have lived a longer life than he got. But we take what we can get, right?"

"Like Conall." My sister's face brightens. "I don't know how long I'll have with him, but every second is a miracle." She dwells on this for a moment, flexing her fingers nervously. "The interview was a success, you know. More cheques arrived during the week, and two more standing orders were set up for us. People are so generous."

"I'm glad," I say, and I mean it. I study my sister, her face lined and drooping, with too much experience for her age weighing her down. "Beth, when was the last time you and Larry had any time to yourselves, without the baby?"

She laughs disparagingly before realising I am serious. "Well, not since before Conall was born anyway."

"I'm free on Thursday evening. Why don't you let me baby-sit? If he's having a good week he should be fine for a few hours."

She fidgets. "I don't know . . ."

"Come on, Beth," I plead. "He's my nephew, you know. Let me mind him for a few hours. I've met the nurses – I'll have their numbers on speed dial. Go to dinner with Larry – talk about something other than baby stuff."

Beth refuses to commit but she is not gone from my house an hour when Larry calls me, asking if I'm still prepared to baby-sit on Thursday.

I agree readily and, as I make my way to their house later in the week, I find I am strangely excited. I rarely get quality time with my nephew.

According to the limited statistics available, Edward's Syndrome is often cited as one of the reasons Irishwomen travel abroad for terminations. Often they are women who desperately want a child, but the slim survival rate and knowledge of the suffering the child will endure for the short time they are alive prompts an early ending to spare everyone involved. I comprehend, where my mother and Beth do not, the logic and well-meaning motivation of such a decision.

Conall is an anomaly. Only twenty per cent of those with Edward's Syndrome are boys. Most die before they are born or shortly afterwards, and the average lifespan for a baby with Edward's is two months. A mere ten per cent will survive their first year. Those that do will need constant medical care, and not just physically – Conall has brain abnormalities too.

The statistics are stark and depressing. Yet I saw the need shining in Beth's eyes when the diagnosis was first revealed. She had wanted a baby for so long. She might never have another. And even if she did, it wouldn't be this one, this little darling in her womb. She was determined to find a way to manage Conall's pain, and let him live as long as he could.

"He'll be the most loved baby in Ireland," she said, in one of the first televised interviews. "Of course he'll thrive."

It takes Beth and Larry fifteen minutes to leave – Beth keeps rushing back in with further instructions. Finally, I suspect Larry locks the car door and they drive away, Beth straining out the window as I wave from the house until they are out of view. I retreat into the living room and sit next to Conall's crib. He is sleeping peacefully, although he is snuffling.

He has some of the classic outward symptoms of Edward's – a scrawny little body with an unusually shaped head. I have seen strangers recoil when they peek into his pram with delighted expectation, unable to stop the reflex. The back of his head bulges. Larry says he has extra intelligent brains in there. His face and jaw are small. His lungs, even in rest, seem to pound inside his chest. Beth's ears are constantly attuned to his laboured breathing. Then there are the problems not obvious to a casual observer. Impaired kidney function and muscle deterioration, which makes feeding an impossibility, at least at the moment. I've stopped noticing the plastic tube providing sustenance through his nose, the tape securing it covering almost all of his little cheek.

I'm scared for Beth that he won't make it to his first birthday. But I'm also scared for myself. I love the kid in a way I have never loved anyone. Not my mother, not Alan, not Brian. It is a visceral love that touches my very core. When he passes away, I think he'll take a little part of me with him.

For now, we keep going, pretending everything is normal.

I pour a glass of wine from Beth's fridge and nestle into the couch. I flick around the television channels until I hear a little whine from the crib beside me. I freeze, waiting. After a few seconds his breathing levels.

Looking down at him, I whisper quietly, "Let's see if Mammy and Daddy have any good films stored for Aunty Trish."

I click into their planner and see it immediately. They have recorded the interview. It is a full week since it aired and I have manged to avoid watching it. Why would I, I think to myself. I know how it goes. Yet in the quiet of Beth's house, I suddenly feel the urge.

I hit play. Margaret Elderfield's smug face looms large in front of me. I am surprised at how mellow the make-up appears on screen. On the day, we had practically glowed.

I cringe as the camera zooms in on me for Margaret Elderfield's first question. A zap of anger pulses through me when she asks about my marital status. She damn well knew the answer, but was hoping I would elaborate. Provide some gossip. Had Mum given her a head's-up that my engagement had recently ended? It wouldn't surprise me.

Brian had sent me a message after the interview, asking how I was and offering to come over if I needed someone. I had never been so glad that I was travelling that day. If I had been in the country, I don't know if I could have resisted his comfort. That wouldn't have been fair. I broke up with him for a reason.

Brian and I met each other at exactly the right time for both of us. I had been through a difficult time, but was finally in a good place, enjoying my new job with Aer Clara. His company had been on the brink of dissolution for months, but had received a fresh investment and was out of the red for the first time in two years.

When he boarded my flight one early morning, flashing me that winning smile, I was flattered – but I never thought it would lead to anything. I was pleasantly surprised when he gave me his business card as he disembarked, though mortified as the other cabin crew would tease me incessantly. I was shocked when he actually asked me on a date.

Our love flourished intensely during the next few years but, in hindsight, I should have anticipated the end. We lived in the present while our futures were diverging. We wanted different things, had incompatible views of how our lives would evolve.

I shiver and return to the programme. Thank God Margaret Elderfield had not pried further.

Mum's revelation comes soon. Watching her mouth form the words fills my throat with a sickly sweet taste. *"My husband worried it would be too much for us. He wanted me to have an abortion."*

I recall Ciara and Stephen's protective reaction. I'm sure it took all of Ciara's self-control not to scream out a rant against my mother. Even the usually calm Stephen had grimaced as I tried to defend her. Mum was never the cuddly, affectionate mother that many of my friends seemed to have. She was forever deriding me for not living up to Beth's standards, for being too timid, or clumsy, or slow.

I understood she was just being honest. I was an excessively shy girl and gawky teenager. I took her criticisms and jibes for what they were – attempts to improve me so I could have a better life. She was strict by nature but not abusive. We were a poor family and Mum worked hard to provide for us. Beth and I never felt wanting. It wasn't easy for her without Dad, and I must have been a burden. Another mouth to feed. A poor replacement for an earning father and husband.

My life was restricted at the best of times. Mum's reputation scared off many of the girls who might otherwise have been my friends in school. When she got one of Beth's friends expelled for having an abortion, even the considerate ones who used to toss me the odd friendly greeting kept their distance. If it hadn't been for monthly catch-ups with Ciara, Stephen and Gerry, I could have become a total recluse.

The real saviour, of course, was Alan. My first real boyfriend. When I finished school, I had no idea what to do. Few students from my school went on to college; most went into family trades or emigrated. I did a one-year business-administration course that Mum paid for on the agreement that I would reimburse her as soon as I was earning.

It was pure luck that, as I finished, Orwell Travel were hiring. A neighbour recommended me to the owner and manager, Josh. He had built the business up from nothing and was the most relentless worker you ever could meet. Eccentric, with receding yet unruly hair, Josh had a loose smile that revealed stained, crooked teeth. I had worried I was being too reserved in the interview, but he told me some months later that he had intuited my eagerness for work. Apparently my quiet demeanour appealed to him – the others he met had been brash and mouthy. He hired me on the spot, and I remained his office administrator for five years.

Nine months after I started at Orwell Travel, Josh took some of the staff out for my birthday. When everyone else had left, he insisted I stay on so he could find me a man. I told him he was transforming into an old-fashioned matchmaker – he had recently snagged a wife for himself, and so felt it necessary to marry off everyone else. He admitted that I was probably right. Undeterred, he resumed his task of pointing out any eligible men who passed by us. Unbeknownst to him, I had already spotted one.

Almost as soon as we arrived at the bar a man with sparkling blue eyes had winked at me through the crowd. When Josh left me alone to go to the bathroom, Alan made his move.

"That fellow your boyfriend?" he asked.

I shook my head and patted the seat beside me in offering. I felt a red flush creep up my neck at my own boldness. Alan grinned and slid in beside me.

When Josh came back a few minutes later, he stopped short, his eyes wide in disbelief that I had managed to nab a man in his short absence. I think he was disappointed he hadn't played a role in my success. He strutted over and grabbed his jacket from the seat beside me. He narrowed his eyes at Alan.

"You take care of this one, do you hear?" he said, channelling the father I never had.

Thankfully Alan found it amusing, and we sat in the corner of the bar talking for hours. I missed the last bus home and had to get a taxi. He insisted on paying. I felt guilty about that until a few dates later when I learned he could afford it. He worked construction, and it was boom time. His job didn't pay much but he worked the hours to make it profitable and supplemented it with nixers.

My mother never warmed to him, even when he saved her a plumber's fee by calling over after the pipes ruptured one cold winter night.

I fell quickly into the giddy affections of youth. Alan made a tidy amount during the first summer we met. We wasted his money gladly on amusements – cinema tickets, ice creams in the park, trips down the country in his banged-up old racer.

Alan was not afraid of hard work. He was not afraid of anything. He took care of me, and was ready for our future. The following year he bought a small flat not far from where I lived but, though I was now twenty-one years old with a permanent job in Orwell Travel, my mother would not hear of me living with Alan.

So I rebelled, for the first time. I told her in no uncertain terms that I was an adult, earning my own money and entitled to live out of home like a real grown-up.

"The sin!" she exclaimed, but knew there was little she could do about it. It fell apart two years after we started living together. She was gleefully smug when I had to move home.

Alan and I drifted apart. His hours of work only increased with the passing years, until the recession hit. He couldn't handle being unemployed. He took to the drink. I was unable to deal with his moods or soothe away his idleness. In the end, he got work in Australia. He asked me to go with him, but I knew it was a half-hearted offer. We both cried when he left. He had paid the full month's rent and so I had a week in the place on my own before moving back in with my mother. Watching a new, young couple cheerily haul their boxes into his flat was devastating.

Just over two months later, having learned that he had pancreatic cancer and mere months to live, Gerry threw himself off a cliff near The Kite. It was almost a relief when we learned the truth about his illness – it at least explained his actions. It did not ease my stomach-churning grief. Gerry had been so kind to me on my break-up with Alan, and I had wallowed selfishly, taking his soothing comfort but never asking whether he needed any in return.

I shake my head, dragging my thoughts from the past and centring my mind once more on the interview. It is nearly over and Margaret Elderfield is finally asking me a question I am content to answer – about my job as cabin crew for Aer Clara. It is the first time I am pleased with my response.

I look down into Conall's crib. "See, darling," I whisper, "Aunty Trish isn't a complete waste of space after all."

"*Before we go,*" Margaret Elderfield is saying, "*I want to say how lucky you are, Beth, to have such a supportive family. Can I ask about your friends? Are they equally helpful?*"

I had squirmed in my seat at that question, hoping Beth would not mention Lisa, if only because I didn't want Stephen to inadvertently get dragged into our family drama. In school, Beth and Lisa were two parts of an inseparable trio, until the third girl made a mistake and my mother destroyed their friendship.

"*My friends are great,*" Beth answers in a measured tone, "*but it is obviously difficult for those who don't have children to appreciate our daily struggles.*"

No one else would have noticed, because they would all have been concentrating on Beth, but I can see myself holding my breath, begging Margaret Elderfield not to bring it up. I should have known better.

"*Deirdre, you became head of Pro-Life Ireland many years ago after a highly publicised – and I might add successful – campaign to have one of Beth's best friends expelled from school.*"

Please don't! I hear the voice in my head shouting, though I know what's coming.

Mum does not hesitate. "*Yes, Beth's friend became pregnant at the age of sixteen. Obviously, you can imagine my distress at the type of girl befriending and influencing my daughter. The school tried to help her, you know. I was on the parents' association at the time – we offered financial help, talked to her about adoption opportunities, but the girl wasn't interested. She just bought a flight to England, brazen as you like, and had an abortion. I couldn't let Beth, and my younger impressionable daughter, be exposed to that. We were successful in securing her expulsion.*"

Margaret Elderfield shifts in her seat, as do a number of audience members. I remember speculating in that moment that Mum had gone too far.

"*Now, Deirdre, a lot of people think that, regardless of our own beliefs, you did not treat that girl very compassionately. Beth, what is your view on this?*"

"*Margaret, my mother did not march into the school and demand an expulsion. She tried, as we all did, to convince my friend not to go through with an abortion. It was as a last resort that the school decided the other children should not be exposed to that sort of morality. I agree with my mother's stance. I have not seen that girl since she was expelled all those years ago.*" My sister faces the camera. "*And if anyone doubts my mother's sincerity, I urge you to look at this.*"

She holds up a photograph and the camera zooms to a tender picture of my mother holding Conall in the hospital, tears of joy streaming down her cheeks.

Finally, Margaret Elderfield ends the interview, with me almost hyperventilating on the couch opposite her. I could not believe I had somehow survived it.

The usual angry letters and leaflets and demonstrations by the pro-choice side followed, but I was soon out of the country and it has died down now. Despite the harshness with which my mother portrayed herself on the programme, donations are continuing for Conall.

I am glad of it as I stare down at my beautiful nephew. He is just an innocent child, with no conception of the bigger-picture arguments his birth has fuelled. All he wants is warm arms to rock him to sleep. I reach down and graze his cheek with my forefinger. His skin is so soft, it might flake off in my hand.

I sit back and let out a long sigh. For some reason, a feeling of doom settled on me during the filming of the interview and it hasn't left. As Conall stirs, whimpering, I think how this moment is mirroring my life – waiting anxiously for an eruption of tears that is inevitable – it is purely a matter of when.

Chapter nine

STEPHEN

I know it is wrong on all levels.

Yet I realise why it is happening. It is a cliché that the product of a violent home will in turn inflict that aggression on a loved one. But it's true. As is the reverse – someone so used to being downtrodden will put up with it, thinking it is normal on some level.

I could be a real man and face up to it. But it's easier to stay out of the house because, once it starts, I am not able to stop it.

I didn't think anyone would question my taking Brian O'Connor out for a round of golf. Our standing monthly arrangement fell apart after he and Trish broke up. I have been anxious to re-establish it for some time. But when I mentioned it to Ciara in passing, she insisted I check with Trish first.

"I like Brian," Ciara said, "but Trish has broken up with him, and she is our friend."

Trish, the angel, smiled when I told her. "You don't need to ask my permission, Stephen," she said, patting my arm. "Brian was part of our little group for years. I don't expect you to sever all ties with him."

"I don't want you to think that I'm – picking his side or anything," I stammered awkwardly.

I felt my shoulders unclench as she once again reassured me. The truth was I didn't want to cancel my game.

Trish used to thank me for making an effort to be welcoming with Brian when they first started dating, but I enjoyed his company. My colleagues were Wall Street caricatures – either boring to the point of having no life, or so manic they could go for a week without sleep and still close a deal. My buddies from the rugby club were a great bunch of lads but everything transformed into a competition with them.

Ciara and Trish are my best friends. But Brian is someone I need – a normal, decent man. No ego, not out to prove his masculinity at every opportunity. Easy to be around.

He is having the game of his life.

"Nice drive, mate." My voice cracks in awe as he holds his position, club swung over his shoulder.

With his body curved into a professional stance, he watches the ball land dead centre on the green.

I tried to encourage him to join the club a few years ago, when he was first dating Trish. But while green fees once a month was doable, membership was too much for frugal Brian.

"Stephen, even if I went to the pin of my collar to make it happen, the time commitment won't be on the cards until I retire. Keeping a business profitable is not easy these days, as you well know."

The recession may be on the way out, but the practicalities of recovery have not yet solidified. I don't envy him, running his own company. He isn't at the mercy of management like I was, but he can just as abruptly lose everything he worked for, and take his employees down with him.

Brian whoops as he taps another perfect ten-foot putt.

My own game is falling apart. Drives knocked off the tee, 'gimme' putts smacked over the hole into the thicket off the green, fresh air swipes in the bunkers. When I finally sink my ball so many shots above par I don't know what bird to call it, Brian laughs.

I grin, but it's forced. "I'm not letting you win, mate, if that's what you're thinking."

"Well, you're not making it very challenging, Stephen." He thumps my arm as I pass him, sliding his putter into his bag. "You're the seasoned player, not me."

At the start of the next hole, after he has hit another straight shot, I swipe off, sending the ball far into the rough. At least I hit it. I reef my tee from the ground.

"I may have to cancel my membership this year," I say.

Brian exhales deeply. He doesn't seem surprised. I suppose it must be obvious that money is tight since the redundancy. Just when the country was supposed to have crossed the line into recovery mode, our office collapsed. I wasn't prepared. I have not cut back on the luxuries Brian would have severed immediately – golf-club membership, my year-old convertible Audi. Perhaps if steered in that direction, I might have caved. But Brian knows I am not the only one with a penchant for the finer things in life.

"What does Lisa think?" he asks predictably.

I shrug as we set off down the fairway. "She thinks I should stay a member."

Something to hold over me, I think wretchedly. Though I know it's unfair, anger bubbles up once more. I am unable to find the love in our actions anymore.

I turn to Brian suddenly. "Why don't you come to ours after the game? I stacked the freezer with steaks yesterday – we could throw on dinner, have a few beers?"

He seems gratified by my eagerness but shakes his head. "I can't tonight, Stephen."

I say nothing as I step up to the ball, my head down to hide my disappointment. Having another person in the house would act as a buffer, if only for a few hours.

"I have a date," he blurts out.

My club swings wildly, missing the ball.

"Did you just say that to ruin my shot?" I puff, not certain either answer would please me.

"No, buddy," he laughs. "I'll let you retake it. I do have a date. Trish made it clear we're finished. I offered to be there for her after the interview was aired last week. She didn't want to talk to me. It made me realise I have to move on."

I nod reluctantly and bend to re-align my shot. What he's saying makes sense, but I had always pictured Trish and Brian going the distance. He was much better for her than Alan, who was forever working. Brian doted on Trish, and I still cannot fathom why she decided to end it.

"How are Ciara and Nikki?" he asks, in an apparent attempt to change the subject. "I gather they're going through something similar to myself and Trish?"

"What?" I straighten, staring at him.

He holds up his hands. "I'm not saying they're about to break up. No, I just meant they're having the same kind of trouble Trish and I did."

"What sort of trouble? What are you talking about?"

Brian eyes me suspiciously. "I thought Trish would have told you? I wanted to try for a baby soon after the wedding. But Trish wouldn't have it."

"She probably needed some time."

"No, Stephen. She doesn't ever want kids. It was a deal-breaker for her. Nikki is like me in that way — she wants to be a parent. I don't think Ciara is as enamoured with the idea. But they'll work it out. Lots of couples disagree about that sort of stuff, and compromise. But Trish wouldn't even consider it. She said if I couldn't agree from the outset to a childless marriage, then we should call off the wedding. I didn't think she'd go through with it."

I take a swift swipe at the ball and we move on. Trish has never told me the reason for her break-up with Brian, but neither had I known of her aversion to motherhood. Deirdre Olden won't be happy, I think spitefully. She is bound to expect grandchildren from her daughters as a right.

Ciara had mentioned in passing that Nikki was pressing for them to start a family, but had shrugged off any follow-up questions. Kids were a long way off – she had been firm about that. Apparently Nikki didn't feel the same way.

The thought of them breaking up is devastating to me. Our epic group of four was diminished to three after Gerry's death, and now the rest of us are in relationships that are falling apart. Or in Trish's case, already over. At least Lisa and I are still together. We have not given up, despite our problems.

Children are not something we have ever discussed. It wouldn't surprise me if Lisa wasn't certain about the idea. Messy, screaming children would not slot easily into Lisa's version of a sophisticated life. I never really thought about it, but I suppose I'd like to be a father someday. I shake myself. That's for down the line. We have more serious issues right now.

"Trish doesn't mind us playing golf together, does she?" Brian inspects his club as he asks.

"No," I say truthfully. "You know Trish – she wouldn't want me or anyone else to be affected by your break-up."

Brian gives a tight smile. He might have a date tonight, but it is not hard to see that he is pining for Trish. If I was a woman, with their unselfconscious words, I would tell him that I will always be his friend, no matter what. But I can't bring myself to speak that openly.

I scuff the ground with my foot. "Brian, why don't we play another round in two weeks? No point leaving it a whole month."

He smiles widely, and I think he appreciates the sentiment behind my offer. He agrees, and we resume the business of golf gladly.

Having reached his ball, Brian raises his hand to shield his eyes from the low afternoon sun and surveys the course. "I should have listened to Trish more, you know? She's a tough one to crack, she holds everything in. I ought to have handled it differently. Taken better care of her."

"You did take care of her, Brian." I sift through my bag of clubs noisily.

He doesn't seem to notice my discomfort, and shakes his head. "No, I thought I did. But I was thinking of my own priorities. Don't make the same mistake I did, Stephen. When Lisa talks, really listen. Whatever she needs, give it to her. Or you could lose her." With a sudden swipe of his arm, he waves away his own remark. "Sorry, buddy. Ignore me. I don't know what I'm talking about. You'll take care of Lisa without my advice, am I right?"

He bows his head over his club to line up the shot, concentrating hard enough not to notice my failure to answer.

Chapter ten

CIARA

My mind is clear of every thought but my own body and the ground in front of me. People often ask if I am anxious before a race but I am not. The nerves build in the weeks leading up to it. In the days prior, I am often so jittery I will vomit. But in the moments when I am waiting to start, even with cheering from the sidelines, I am calm. Ready.

Such single-mindedness is a relief. Nikki's lengthy disappearances from home have been frustrating but, now Saturday has arrived, I put all that far from my mind. It doesn't matter if I come first or last in this race, but my own personal time will be a strong indicator of whether I can achieve what is required for the Olympic qualifier in less than two months. So I used Nikki's absences as opportunities to study my form, to squeeze in small bouts of extra exercise and to maximise my relaxation periods.

"Rest is as important as training," Adrian had lectured me again during the week.

It is all part of his *'Train smart, Run smart, Win"* philosophy. That is not to say he hasn't been pushing me outside of my rest hours.

I had been preparing for a final session with Adrian in the local gym two nights ago when Nikki arrived home to announce we had to talk.

"What's up?" I murmured, distracted, as I scanned the room for my keys.

"No, I mean a proper discussion. I need your full attention, Ciara."

I sighed. "Nikki, of course we can talk but I'm meeting Adrian in half an hour so it will have to be quick."

"Can't you put him off?" she said sharply. "You're supposed to be unwinding for the race anyway."

I stopped rummaging in my gym bag. Nikki rarely snapped at me in that way. She was standing in the centre of the room, my keys dangling from her fingers. I walked over and snatched them from her.

"What's wrong?" I stood, waiting.

"Do you have time to listen or not?"

I grazed her cheek with my fingers. She jerked away at the gesture.

"The race is in two days. We can talk after."

Without giving her a chance to argue back, I marched out the door and slammed it behind me. I hovered on the doorstep. Nikki and I have the usual tiffs all couples do about whose turn it is to clean the bathroom or how often we have to visit the in-laws. Our new type of fighting is based on avoidance. Her sudden need to converse unnerved me. I contemplated going back in, but I resisted. I needed to concentrate on the race.

My mind is empty of it all now. My body is ready – I did some extra stretches this morning on account of the cold day. The rain is not due until later. Right now, the early afternoon sky is clear. The looped track is before me. The stands, mostly empty, are filled near the starting line with family and friends. I know Nikki is there with my sister Orla. Stephen messaged to say he wouldn't be able to make it but Trish promised to be the loudest voice in the crowd.

I breathe out as we bend into position.

74

The gun cracks and I rush into the wind, as if it is a portal to another world. I leave everyone behind – immersed in the movement, the jostle, the grinding of every muscle in my body. It is a freeing sort of control, feeling each joint and fibre work together to propel me onward, leaving the others in my wake.

Nikki cannot fathom why I enjoy running. All she experiences during intense exercise is the painful heat stinging her. For me, the sensation is not external. I am one with the motion, knowing exactly when to steady off and the right moment to surge ahead.

When I round the final corner, I cannot help but hear an eruption from the stands. Or it could be the thread of the wind in my ears.

I push toward the finish line but do not truly become aware of it until I cross. It is my reawakening from the self-contained land of running, a step back to reality. I throw my body across the line, alone, with my nearest contender a full four seconds behind.

I squint up at the crowd, visualising Nikki's beaming face. But I can't see her. I can only make out blurry outlines of my supporters jumping up and down, screaming at my victory. Club photographers shout at me and cameras flash as I bend over, the exhilaration bubbling with the blood rushing through my veins, pinching me at every joint.

Smiling and waving for the photos, I scan around for Adrian. None of the faces calling to me are recognisable. The other women are finishing, some making their way to me to pat me on the shoulder. I acknowledge them briefly as I cast around, frantically searching. Finally, I see him, barging his way through the photographers.

I find I am wiping tears from my cheeks as he rushes to me. He holds up a hand and I hoot loudly as I high-five it.

"Fifteen minutes, twenty-five seconds! You only need another five seconds off that to qualify, girl!"

I feel a flutter of disappointment. "I didn't make the time?"

He grips my shoulders, staring into my eyes. "No, but that's a good thing. You don't want to peak too early. We have six weeks to go until the trial – we'll use those weeks to boost you that extra bit. This is perfect."

"Really?" I've studied the stats, I know the theory behind working to reach full potential at exactly the right moment but my lip still trembles. I wanted to hit the time today. I wanted that buffer.

Adrian reads my agonised expression. "You know I wouldn't lie to you, Ciara. If you'd beaten the time, the immediate pressure would be off. Not consciously, maybe, but you would relax. That's no good. We need to keep your body and mind working. If you'd been further behind, I might have been worried about getting you there by the trial race. Five seconds off is optimal. We're exactly where we need to be."

I nod, his technical assurances setting the excitement bubbling once more in my stomach. Adrian is always honest with me – he can be brutal at times. If he thinks I'm in a good position, I believe him. I simply have to keep centred. I let him drape a towel around me and lead me inside.

He leaves me outside the changing room, promising to meet me in the running club within the hour. I take a leisurely shower and trade polite congratulations with the other runners. I gather my belongings, hoping Nikki will be outside to greet me.

As soon as I leave the changing room door, a mob is upon me. It is the women from the running club, all delighted for me. I beam at their admiration and allow myself to swell with their praise. They all recognise the importance of this race in my Olympic journey.

Two of them link my arms, demanding to take me to the club where there is a celebration waiting for me. I start to object, looking around for Nikki and Orla.

"It's all organised," one of them says forcefully, dragging me through the corridors of the stadium out into the chilly September air. "Nikki and your sister have gone on ahead. We're to drive you."

I allow myself be shoved into the back seat of a car and, although the journey takes nearly an hour due to unexpected road works, I barely have to speak the entire way. The girls quote statistics at me, predicting my victory and glory.

"I mean, you *have* to make it with that PB."

I sit up. Had I hit a new personal best? In my disappointment at not making the qualifying time, I had not realised.

The driver jabs at the radio and I try to bounce energetically with the others. But my mind is pounding. Why isn't Nikki the one driving me to the club, as she always does after a race? She is making me feel like I'm losing her. The fear inside me climaxes, morphing into anger, an emotion much easier to handle. This race is a milestone in my career, and apparently I achieved a personal best. Nikki should be at my side.

"For God's sake, Ciara, give us a smile," one of the older women teased. "You're on your way to the top now, what's the matter?"

"Nothing," I lie, arranging my face into one of glee. "I'm in shock, that's all."

The running club explodes when the girls pull open the door and propel me inside. I let them grab me in turn – the president of the club, the captain, the women who joined the club with me so many years ago. The kitchen has put on an impressive spread of sandwiches and salads, and I am passed at least three plates with congratulations and insistence I keep my strength up. After all, I am told endlessly, I am the only club member who has ever had a shot at the Olympics.

Finally, Orla is before me. "Congratulations, little sister."

She is hugging me tightly when suddenly we are leapt upon by her husband Thomas. I laugh as the three of us are crushed together. Within seconds, little arms are encircling my leg.

"Liam! Kate!" I bend down, though my quads tighten. I did not have time to do a proper cool down after the race. Adrian would kill me – I'd better not mention it to him. At five and three, my nephew and niece are too young to appreciate the significance of my victory, but they understand the giddy atmosphere, and that I am the cause. They cling to me, squealing as I spin them around.

"What a race, kiddo!" Thomas squeezes my shoulder. "It's going to be some year for you."

"Where's the baby?"

Orla attempts to tug her hyperactive children off me. "Nikki is holding him." She nods to the corner where Nikki is rocking the nine-month-old in a motherly way, oblivious to the rest of the room. I watch her with the baby. A baby. The source of so many of our arguments in the past year.

Adrian yanks my arm, hauling me from my family circle. "I'm sorry I had to rush off. I had an important call to make."

He grabs me up in a bear hug and I laugh as he lowers me to the ground.

"*Everyone!*" he announces suddenly. "Gather around, please."

I try to object but he ignores me as he grips my wrist and pulls me to the top of the room.

"We are all very proud of the terrific race Ciara ran today, beating not only her own PB but a club and county record."

There is a loud cheer.

I try to catch Nikki's eye but the crowd have pushed up in front of her.

The local, and even two national, sports journalists are upon me, wanting quotes and offering congratulations. Adrian stays by my side, making sure they have all the facts and teasing hints about Rio. Trish passes behind them more than once, grinning and waving at me. I manage to wink back as they look down at their notes.

It must be at least another half hour before I escape, wanting Nikki, but Orla is upon me first. She hands me my phone.

"It's Mam. She's been trying to ring you for the past hour. But keep it short, your battery is almost flat and you know what she's like – she'll think you've hung up on her if it goes dead."

I manage to duck out of the main bar into the small training room next door. I sit up on one of the exercise bikes and hold the phone to my ear. "Mam?"

"Oh love! Finally! I've been trying to ring for ages. Congratulations, Ciara. We're so, so proud of you."

My whole body swells. I try to respond but she keeps babbling, her excitement raising the volume and decibel of her praise until mercifully my father takes the phone from her.

"New personal best?" is his opening line. "Atta girl, Ciara!"

My eyes well up. My parents, who knew nothing about the world of professional running until I was discovered, have taken it on as a project. When I was young, they considered my speed nothing but an asset on the camogie pitch. When it became clear that I wanted to make a career out of running alone, they were worried. It's not exactly permanent or pensionable like Orla's nursing job. But I kept winning races as a teenager, and once I secured a sports scholarship to college, they never looked back.

They study the stats and follow the international trends. I will often get calls from them at random times informing me that a rival has picked up an ankle injury, or that there is a new type of shoe I should consider.

Their pride in my running has never dwindled and I grasp at their joy.

I manage to sign off before the battery dies. As it bleeps loudly, warning me of its imminent expiration, I click on a message from Stephen. **Congrats, you absolute legend!**

Before I can react, the screen blanks out and the door squeaks open. I look up to see Nikki creeping in.

"There's my winner," she smiles, shutting the door quietly behind her. "Well done, sweetheart. You were brilliant."

I search her face for an answer to the doubts that almost distracted me from the win. Her face glows with happiness for me, and suddenly I wonder if it was all in my head.

"Where were you?" I grab her arms, kissing her. "I couldn't find you afterwards."

"I was with your sister. She needed help with the kids." She hesitates, her face tight. "I'm sorry if I pressured you the past few days. I know how important it is for you to focus coming up to a race. This one was especially important. I should have been more sensitive."

"It's okay." I lean into her, relieved. "I know you want to talk. How about tomorrow?"

She nods, but she is clenched. The veins in her neck spike

outwards like straw. I hear a cheer go up in the next room.

"Go," she says, giving an encouraging nudge. "You deserve this. Go."

"Are you sure?" I say, hesitantly.

She nods, ushering me to the door.

I sweep around. "Oh, can I borrow your phone? My battery died and I need to message Stephen."

Her head snaps up. Slowly she removes her phone from her pocket and stares at it gripped in her fist. "Ciara," she shakes her head, placing it on a bench beside her instead of handing it to me, "I don't think you should contact Stephen."

"What? Why not?"

Another round of raucous cackling erupts from the bar.

Nikki shifts her weight. "I don't want to ruin your day . . ."

"Is he all right?"

She assures me he is, but I will not let it go. We sit together.

"Two days ago, I ran into Lisa near the school. She seemed distracted so I suggested we go for coffee. We had just sat down, when a man at the next table asked her the time. She pulled back her sleeve to check her watch and I saw it."

I stare at her, watching the words sticking in her throat until I can wait no longer. "Saw what, Nikki?"

"A bruise. On her wrist." She swallows thickly.

Suddenly, the door is flung open and two of the girls who drove me to the club fall across the threshold, giggling. "Ciara!" they cry. "We've been looking for you everywhere. Adrian is telling us the funniest stories about you."

"Can you give me a minute, girls?"

They stop laughing on seeing my pained expression. I force a smile.

"I'll be out in a minute. Tell Adrian to pour me a cup of tea, will you?"

They back out, closing the door so the noise of my party is muffled once more.

I twist slowly around to Nikki.

Her chest rises and falls rapidly. "Ciara, you know I love Stephen . . ."

"What are you saying? That someone hurt her? Did she say it was Stephen?" I ask harshly.

Nikki stares at me. "Well, no. I asked her what happened and she got all flustered. Said she didn't want to talk about it and that I was to mind my own business. When I tried to press it, she stormed out. She messaged me later to apologise. Claimed she was having an off-day but not to worry, she was fine. She said a box of old plates fell on her when she was tidying out the kitchen."

"Well, maybe it did," I say indignantly.

"No, it didn't." Nikki sounds stronger. "Since when would Lisa ever tidy out the kitchen? Remember when Stephen was away for a week for work last year, and she got in cleaners rather than do it herself? Anyway, Ciara, it wasn't that type of injury. I could all but make out finger-marks."

I take a deep breath, putting my hands on my hips. "What is it you're saying, Nikki? That Stephen is beating Lisa up?" I scoff at the image.

"I don't know, Ciara. I'm just telling you what I saw."

"No, you're not. You're telling me not to talk to one of my best friends because you saw a mark on his girlfriend's wrist."

Now that she has started, Nikki seems determined to make her full point.

"Ciara, you know I'm very fond of Stephen. But, if you remember, his father was abusive. And I know what I saw."

"You saw a bruise. That's all. Nothing to do with him. Stephen suffered at the hands of his father. He'd never do that to anyone else."

A red flush creeps up her neck. "It's hard to break the cycle of violence, sometimes."

"*Enough!*"

I know Stephen. I know what he went through as his father's victim. I won't sully him by even contemplating him inflicting the same misery on another person.

I round on Nikki. "Why are you trying to ruin this day for me?" She starts to object but I cut her off. "I mean it, Nikki. You announce we need to talk when I'm rushing out the door to training. After I win one of the most important races of my career, you accuse my friend of – what, domestic abuse? Why are you trying to hurt me like this?"

"That's not fair, Ciara. I'm not trying to hurt you."

"Then what's been wrong with you these past few weeks?" I throw my hands into the air. "This isn't just about Stephen and Lisa! What's going on?"

She presses her lips tightly shut and I can see her face closing with them. She shakes her head, her eyes watering, and she rushes from the room. My legs begin to lurch forward automatically but I stop.

I spot her phone where she left it lying on the bench. I don't care what she says, I'm contacting my friend. I pick it up and type in the code. Nikki and I share passwords – we have no secrets from each other. The screen opens straight to her messages, and the thread that she had last been reading lights up in front of my eyes.

The words imprint on my mind before I can look away. My head pounds.

I barge from the room, shoving past well-wishers, searching. I spot her in the corner with Orla and weave my way over to her, not caring about the scene I am about to make. But when our eyes meet all the fight melts from my body and my eyes prickle with tears.

My voice catches with emotion but I know she hears me as I lean in, holding up the phone for her to see.

"Who the hell is Ann?"

Chapter eleven

TRISH

I am tempted to call Ciara but instinct holds me back. I message Stephen instead. **Have you heard from Ciara today? She left the club early.**

He does not reply. I potter around my kitchen, preparing a light snack to have with my cup of tea. We picked at sandwiches and fruit at the running club, but I am planning on painting the living room this evening so I need something else to sustain me.

It has been a long time since I've had any work done on the house. When Brian and I bought it, he did all of the necessary DIY work, and I have realised recently how incompetent I am at home maintenance. Brian had been threatening to paint the living room for the past year. Now he is gone and the house is mine. I will just have to do it myself. In a strange way, I am looking forward to it. Hardly the most exciting Saturday night for a thirty-year-old but I am feeling unusually impatient to be productive.

As I sit in my denim overalls, sipping my tea, I can't wrench my mind away from Ciara rushing out of the club. I watched Nikki's strained face as she tried to explain to the gathering crowd why Ciara had left, citing a combination of illness and tiredness and stress that garnered sympathetic noises from others but didn't fool me. I asked Nikki if she wanted me to go after Ciara but she didn't seem to hear me. I had stood back then, knowing I was in the way while Nikki bent low and whispered urgently to Ciara's sister.

Nikki stayed for another hour, then slunk out the door with false smiles to the few she passed. She gave me an apologetic wave and I mirrored the gesture merrily, pretending along with her that everything was normal.

I check my phone once more. I was surprised when Stephen did not show up to the race. He had been so enthusiastic about it during the week. His message to me was short to the point of rude. **Can't make Ciara's race. Talk soon**.

I wonder if he is fighting with Lisa. Their lives have not been easy since he lost his job. I have known Lisa for years. She and Beth brought out the worst in each other – they competed to be the smartest, the prettiest and, as they grew older, the most successful. Beth's definition of success was a classic family of two-point-four children, while Lisa dreamt of riches and travel. Conall's problems appear to have united Beth and Larry more fiercely, but it would not surprise me if Lisa's reaction to Stephen's redundancy was less than bolstering.

I give in and ring Ciara. It goes straight to voicemail.

I stare at my phone. Ciara won't answer my call. Stephen is barely communicating with me. Gerry is dead. I think of our final group hug on leaving summer camp, when we promised to keep in touch no matter what. A bout of loneliness engulfs me. I know I shouldn't indulge but my legs are already carrying me upstairs. I rummage in the drawer by my bed, through old bank letters and shopping lists, tubs of hand cream and half-read books, until I find it. An old photo of the four of us – my favourite one.

I sit on the bed and run my finger over our faces, all beaming into the camera.

From the moment I arrived at the camp that hot summer of

1999, I was homesick. My mother had shipped me off to Kerry with strict instructions as to my behaviour. I cried more than if she had tenderly embraced me. I was sharing a room with five other girls, four of whom were best friends from another school. They ignored me and the sixth girl – Ciara, an athletic camogie player from Donegal.

Ciara and I stuck together for the first few days. She missed her family too, but the warmth she described was alien to me – the smell of her mother's scones, the touch of her father's rugged hand as he stroked the back of her head after a long day. She had been sent to the summer camp for the sporting elements. Apparently there was a coach from Dublin who had convinced her parents to let him train her. The summer camp was not a holiday for her. It was an opportunity to improve her fitness.

Although it originally started as a sporting camp, it had expanded in recent years. I could have taken part in musical activities, art classes or dance troupes. Driven by the usual teenage desire to be with my friends, I joined the gymnastics and athletics classes with Ciara. That's where we met Stephen. Even then he was taller than the rest of us, but in a gangly way that exposed his growth spurt as relatively recent. That, and the fact that his trouser legs hung an inch too short.

Both Stephen and I injured ourselves on the third morning. Stephen landed awkwardly out of a handstand onto his shoulder. I wobbled precariously on the balance beam until my ankle buckled and I landed with a crunch on my arm. Neither of us were hurt enough to need to go to the hospital, but we were advised by the blunt nurse to choose activities that did not require a high degree of physical grace.

Over lunch, we scrutinised the list of alternatives.

"Any chance going home is an option?" I had sighed.

Stephen smiled but didn't expressly agree. It was only in later years that I realised he was miserable at the summer camp not because he wanted to go home, but because he wanted to go back in time. His mother was not even dead a year. He missed her, and there was nothing that could be done about that.

With most of the popular activities full, Stephen and I ended up joining '*Film Making and Appreciation*'. Gerry was the entertainer of the group and, with floppy blonde hair and sparkling eyes, he stole my heart immediately. He was not as tall or strong as Stephen, but he exuded a presence that captivated me. He had a girlfriend at home, much to the dismay of the camp's giggly teenage girls. He had been relieved to discover he was not confined to sporting activities.

"I'm going to be a director when I'm older," he announced when introducing himself. "I've got my sights set on an Oscar someday."

He often talked through our lunchtimes about camera angles and storylines. Stephen and I listened politely, with nothing more than a vague interest, until he confided in us that he was planning a night shoot.

"None of the leaders know about it," he said, bending his head toward us as class was ending. "They'd never allow it. I'll be at the river at midnight. Come if you dare."

I had no intention of sneaking out at night until I mentioned it to Ciara. Gerry intrigued her, and she was fascinated by the idea of a night shoot. Stephen seemed torn between the rush of breaking the rules and the potential consequences. Ultimately, Ciara convinced us both. That was the first night the four of us spent together.

Gerry had a modern handheld camera with a strong flashbulb that allowed him capture the scenery around us. He made Stephen and Ciara act out scenes of terror, *amour* and debate by the river as he danced around, searching for the best perspectives. I refused to be involved on-camera, so was designated as look-out.

After an amusing half an hour on the sidelines watching the drama play out, I heard a crack behind me. I swung around, scanning the trees. Nothing. The moon had provided a helpful glow by the riverbed but, further in by the trees, darkness pervaded. I rushed to the others.

"I heard someone!" I cried, unable to control my anxiety.

Stephen and Ciara exchanged a look of panic, obviously contemplating our next move.

Gerry did not stop to consider anything. "Run!" he yelled and sprinted into the woodland.

For a second, we stared after him, our mouths open. We rushed to follow him, goaded by fear of being caught by the leaders, or worse, stumbling across a real-life psycho out here in the woods. We had not made it more than a few metres when we heard a thud and a cry.

"Gerry!"

We raced after him, to find him lying on the flat of his back, his camera on the ground beside him.

"Ran into a tree," he groaned, clutching his face.

A fox scurried past us at the same moment, and I realised that must have been what I heard through the trees. Stephen, Ciara and I burst into peals of laughter.

From then on, the four of us were inseparable. We spent lunchtimes conspiring and took many night-time jaunts together, though none as eventful as the first. We promised to keep in touch when summer camp ended. A part of me suspected it was just talk. After all, Stephen and I lived on opposite sides of the city. Gerry was an hour's drive away by the outskirts of Meath while Ciara was up the other end of the country in Donegal.

We did write letters and, as we acquired mobile phones, made sure to text every week. The contact dwindled after a few months, until Ciara announced she was coming to Dublin one weekend for a session with her coach. We begged our parents to let us meet in town and, some more reluctantly than others, they agreed. The reunion was so much fun I didn't want the afternoon to end. We fell back into our old conversations easily, and spent hours lounging in the park.

After that, we knew we had something more than a passing summer friendship. Ciara made an effort to visit every few months and we were a solid group until Gerry leapt from that cliff. Ciara,

Stephen and I have remained each other's most intimate allies.

On a day like today, decorating my house for no one but myself, I miss them. All of them.

I pick up the roller and survey the room. The furniture I was unable to shift is covered in old sheets. Masking tape is stuck up on the wall edges. I roll in a can, pop the lid with a kitchen knife and tilt it over the paint-tray. The suffocating smell makes me cough as the paint pours out thickly. I step back, inadvertently streaking my forehead with paint while wiping my brow.

The phone rings.

I look down at the fresh paint. It will wait, I think, almost tripping on the roller on my way to the phone.

"Hello?" I answer breathlessly.

"Trish, it's Lisa."

I frown. When I saw her number I assumed it was Stephen using her phone to call me. Lisa has never phoned me directly in her life. We have spent a lot of time in each other's company since she began dating my friend, but never alone. I immediately ask if something is wrong with Stephen. This seems to annoy her, but I cannot imagine why else she would be ringing me.

"How was Ciara's race?" she asks, clearly stalling.

"She did really well," I play along. "She beat her personal best."

Lisa barely acknowledges this and coughs distractedly down the line.

I say nothing, waiting for her to speak.

"Trish, I need to tell you something." She stops, taking a shallow breath. "I don't know how to say this."

I walk into the kitchen to avoid the paint fumes already wafting into the hallway. "What is it, Lisa?"

The words spill from her with the sudden rush of a waterfall. "In the *Current Times* interview, your mother talked about a friend Beth and I had when we were younger. The one they managed to get kicked out of school when she went to England for . . . well, you know."

My body tenses. I try to answer but my mouth is suddenly gluey.

"I didn't particularly subscribe to your mother and Beth's pro-life fanaticism at the time. But everyone was agreeing with them and once our friend was expelled there was no point siding with her. You remember her, don't you, Trish? You know her name?"

It is out of my mouth before I can think about it. "Abby."

"Yes, Abby Walsh."

There is a silence. The question forms on my lips but I can't ask. I can't possibly comprehend why she is bringing Abby up, now, to me.

"Abby rang me," she says, just as I am on the verge of hanging up in a panic.

"I didn't know you were still friends."

"We're not," she says quickly. "But we have had dealings recently."

I hear a little gasp escape my lips. "Dealings?"

"Yes. You know what I mean, don't you, Trish?"

My body bends. Lisa knows.

"Trish, Abby rang because she wanted to warn me about something."

"Warn you?"

"Yes."

The paint fumes have drifted into the kitchen but it is not them that are making my head swim.

"What are you saying, Lisa?"

She gives a bitter laugh. "I'm trying very hard not to say anything, Trish. But I honestly don't have any more details. All she said was that news is about to break, and I should be prepared."

"Why are you ringing me?"

"Abby asked me to call you. You are Beth's sister and I'm her friend. Abby obviously thinks we confide in each other."

"Then she's deluded." My voice sounds unfamiliar.

I hear Lisa's breathing down the line, as laboured as mine.

"I'm simply relaying the message, Trish. I didn't know you had a connection with Abby."

"Well, I didn't know you did, either."

Lisa's voice is determined. "So we'll both keep silent. I honestly don't know what news is about to break, Trish. We'll have to wait."

I say nothing. I can sense her holding something back. Before I can ask her what it is, she stammers out her fear.

"Don't – don't tell Stephen I rang, will you?"

I have held in my secret so long that the thought of Lisa knowing, of it somehow being revealed, is nauseating. "No," I say unnecessarily. "I won't tell Stephen, or anyone."

She hangs up. The deadened tone hums in my ear as I lower the phone. I grip the sides of the table and pull myself upright. I never thought I'd have to hear the name Abby Walsh again. My stomach lurches. I make my way slowly back to the living room. I pick up the tray and roller.

Suddenly I hear myself scream. The tray is heavy in my arms, with white paint sloshing over the sides. Years of fear escape as I roar, throwing the full tray of paint hard at the wall.

Chapter twelve

CIARA

It is the worst row we have ever had.

Nikki arrives home over an hour later than me – nearly half past five. She finds me out back, slouched over our garden table, halfway through a bottle of wine. It's not a large garden, but there is room by the wall for the wooden table and chairs, allowing grass to grow over the rest of the space. The swing is the one personal touch we added. I was thinking of Orla's kids when we bought it. I suspect Nikki foresaw other children playing on it.

I don't move as she comes outside, wrapping her arms around her body for warmth.

"What took you so long?" I slur slightly, from fake apathy more than the effects of the wine.

Her voice is measured. "I had to stay to make your excuses. I told people you were dizzy after the morning and had to leave. You can expect some concerned messages. Adrian was raging – he had invited a potential sponsor from a clothing company."

I shrug. Adrian will sort it out. He's my agent as well as my coach

– it's his job.

Nikki snatches the glass from my hand and tosses the remainder of the wine onto the grass. "You're not supposed to be drinking while you're training," she says blankly.

I look up, squinting into the late afternoon sun. Her face is pinched. For a second, I feel confused. I am the one who should be angry.

"Who is Ann?" I ask simply.

She turns away, blinking back tears. Then she glares down at me. "Who do you think she is?"

"How should I know?" I say irritably. "You never mentioned an Ann. Those messages . . ." My accusation fades away in hurt. I sit up straighter, pulling her phone from my pocket to scroll through the messages. "'*Dinner last Monday was lovely.*' You told me you were meeting the teachers for dinner that Monday – after shopping in town."

"What are you accusing me of, Ciara?"

I stand, mimicking soppy speech as I read out another. "'*Sorry I missed your call, Ann. I couldn't answer with Ciara here. I'll ring when she's gone for her run.*'"

Nikki's eyes pool further but she is not defeated. "So you think I'm having an affair."

The wine shapes my words, hurling them from my mouth. "What else am I supposed to think, Nikki?"

She steps toward me. Our noses are almost touching. Every neighbour on the road must be hearing our fight and I really couldn't care less.

Nikki and I have all our major conversations, arguments, discussions – call them what you will – in the garden. It is less oppressive, feeling the wind swirl around with our emotions.

"*Anything* else! You're supposed to think *anything* else, Ciara." She grabs my arms. "How can you not know how much I love you? I want to marry you. I want a family with you. Don't you know that?"

I can't stop the righteousness spilling from me. "You've been lying to me, Nikki. Sneaking around behind my back, messaging another woman. And all the time making me feel bad for not being ready to have children."

Nikki releases me. "I wasn't trying to make you feel bad."

She walks away and sits on the swing, her fingers grasping the chains. The sky overhead is darkening, not just from the early autumn nightfall but from the cluster of storm clouds gathering in the west. She looks up at me.

"Ciara, I want us to have a baby. We had a deal. We have been civilly partnered for a year, and we're going to be married next year. You promised me we would start the process. Now, suddenly, you're not ready? Haven't we been discussing this for ages?"

"Constantly. It's all you ever talk about. You and Brian, whispering in each other's ears. Making me and Trish feel like crap."

I used to blame Brian for Nikki's persistent insistence on having a baby. He divulged to Nikki that he was trying to convince Trish to try for a family and that she was reluctant. I resented it, what I saw as Brian and Nikki's conspiracy to guilt us into parenthood. Trish refused to talk about it the few times I brought it up, except to admit that it would never happen, no matter how much Brian pushed. She never said, but I assume it was at least part of the reason they split.

A family is something Nikki has always wanted but, for me, it was a future plan, and still is. My races are more pressing. The years are slipping away from me — I won't have the physique or the energy in another few years to win that Gold. But Nikki and I, we are only thirty. We have years to find a sperm donor, or if needs be go down the adoption route.

I was less hard-line than Trish. I would have a child if Nikki really wanted one, but we both had to be ready. Right now I'm not, and I'm too caught up in the Olympics to give it the attention it needs.

Nikki isn't giving in to my accusation.

"What Brian and I crave is perfectly natural. We want to grow our families with the women we love."

"By hounding us into it." I can hear the unfairness of my words

93

but I don't care. I am not the one meeting other women. For so long I had felt nothing but guilt at my inability to get excited at the prospect of becoming a parent. Now, I am the victim instead of the one supressing Nikki. It is equally as devastating.

"All that baby talk, was it a distraction? Something to throw me off so you could carry on your clandestine meetings with Ann?"

Nikki laughs, a harsh sniff without amusement. "Listen to yourself, Ciara."

She kicks at the ground, propelling the swing back and forward. I watch her glide through the cold air, needing the motion to keep from disintegrating before me.

"Tell me!" I call to her. "Who is Ann? Are you having an affair?"

"You are unbelievable!" she shouts. "You're the one who lets her job take over her life!"

She grips the chains of the swing tightly, and scuffs her feet into the ground as the swing descends. She releases the chains and stands up, facing me squarely.

"I know you love running, and I get why the Olympics are such a big deal. Truly, I do, and I'm one hundred per cent behind you. But you're not simply asking for support. You're asking me to put our lives, our future on hold."

"The Olympics will be over next summer. I'm only asking you to postpone for another year." I sound so reasonable, I almost believe it.

Nikki tilts her head shrewdly. She knows me better than I know myself.

"But that's not what you're asking me. I wanted a baby before we were ever civilly partnered. You insisted on waiting. You've already postponed it twice. Now the Olympics is your excuse. Next year, there will be another one."

I say nothing. It would be so easy to argue back, but there's no point. I'm not ready, and I'm not prepared to dissect the reason because I need to focus all my attention on Rio.

"We're a family now," Nikki says, inching forward in what I know is intended to be a comforting closeness, but which feels like

94

a threat. "You need to grow up and put us first."

My speech is shaky as I cut across her, unwilling to deal with my own insecurities when she has yet to answer my questions. "You're trying to put this on me. Don't think I haven't noticed that you're talking about everything under the sun but Ann."

Nikki folds her arms. "What do you want me to say?"

I breathe out a harsh, unforgiving sigh. "I want you to deny all this. To tell me you're not having an affair." I am in control once more, my argument rational and ready.

Nikki's usually mild timbre is as cold as the dusk air whipping around us. "I shouldn't have to tell you that, Ciara. You should know it already. You should know what's really important in life."

I step back from her. "My goals and dreams are as important as yours, Nikki. Just because I want a medal in my hands, not a baby in my arms, doesn't mean my life is meaningless."

"I never said that." Nikki recoils. "Haven't I stood by you all these years? Gone to every race, put up with the crazy training schedules, given up my holidays to follow you abroad for your competitions? Don't put those awful words in my mouth."

I stamp my foot. "I'm sick of arguing with you, Nikki. That's all we've done for months. You're asking me to trust you but you won't tell me the truth."

"No, Ciara." Nikki shakes her head sadly. "I'm saying that of course I'll tell you the truth, if you can say that you trust me. Do you?"

My heart's response is absolute but my solid head wavers. Perhaps my trust is purely habit. She still has not told me about Ann.

At my silence, Nikki lowers her head. "If that's what you think of me, then you should go."

I gape at her.

"I mean it." She shivers.

We are both freezing and a drop of rain lands on my head, but we don't go inside. Too much emotion, too many horrible things to say to confine ourselves indoors.

I want to fight, but I don't have the energy. I'm tired after the day

– after the race, and the wine, and the emotions of finally speaking the simmering tension aloud. Time apart might be the best thing. I think about the past few months and my taut conversations with Nikki about our future. It has been coming for longer than I realised.

"I'll stay with Orla for a few nights."

I hear her sniff as I walk slowly into the house. Upstairs, I throw some essentials into a bag – running gear, pyjamas, toothbrush. My movements are sluggish, almost as if I am in a dream. But the tension stinging my eyes is no delusion. This is happening.

I trudge down the stairs. Nikki does not come to me. I open the front door and am almost over the threshold when she says my name. I look back to see her leaning against the kitchen doorframe.

"Congratulations on your win," she says.

Her compliment is genuine, but laced with a sadness that twists my heart. I can think of nothing to say to ease her, or me. I place her phone on the hall table. I draw out my departure, waiting for her to call out again. To stop me.

The only sound is the click of the door as it shuts behind me.

Chapter thirteen

STEPHEN

"We need to talk."

I am in the door less than a minute after spending all day in that wretched firm Zedmans, when Lisa starts on me. I shut my eyes and will patience.

I have taken to stopping at the pub on the way home. Usually I can persuade one of the guys from my previous job to come along, or there are older regulars who camp at the bar and are always willing to engage in meaningless chat. I don't get wasted, but one or two pints take the edge off. It helps to shake off the day and prepare me for home. Today though, being Saturday, it was full of young groups, rowdily drinking before hitting the clubs in town. Frustrated, I had kept walking past the pub, with nowhere else to go but home.

I try to act unconcerned, dumping my bag by the stairs and heading straight for the kitchen. I launch into preparing dinner, clicking on the kettle, gathering the vegetables from the fridge, reaching for the chopping knife.

"So what's up?"

She does not immediately respond so I say nothing, waiting for her to speak.

"I think we need to get away, Stephen. Just the two of us."

I halt my preparations abruptly. Resting my hands on the counter, I shut my eyes once more. I spend too much time these days with my eyes closed, withdrawing into myself. I know what Lisa wants, she doesn't need to say it. Time together to reconnect. Some sun to boost our vitamin D for what is forecast to be a harsh winter after this unseasonably chilly September. I bet she will even throw my redundancy in my face – we deserve a holiday after the tough months.

"Lisa –" I turn to see her binding her fingers together in apprehension. Clearly, she has anticipated my response. "No one would love a holiday more than me, but you know we can't afford it."

I despise that sentence, and Lisa for making me say it. I used to talk about my financial situation and my work with pride. After all, I studied damn hard for those accountancy exams. I passed them the first time around, which is not as common as my father liked to believe. Being offered the traineeship, and ultimately the job with TJ Simons, one of the largest accountancy firms in the country, made my heart glow with hope and possibility.

The day I got my first pay cheque, I left my father's house. I was no longer a dependent boy. I was the Mr Roche of the family now, and I allowed myself be free for the first time.

Lisa blames me for accepting the job with Likeman Tiles. She didn't complain when she first met me and Likeman had just headhunted me, throwing bonuses and perks upon my already inflated offer. They dazzled me into overlooking the job security I was leaving behind at TJ Simons.

About two months after the redundancy, Brian asked to bring a friend to our golf game. I couldn't refuse, although I dreaded the inevitable questions about work. When his friend asked what I did for a living, two holes into the game, I tried, as always, to sound indifferent to my situation.

"Nothing right now. I was an accountant with Likeman Tiles

but, you know, cutbacks."

Brian's friend had nodded sympathetically. His cousin owned a small accounting practice, he told me a few holes later. One of their staff had been taken ill. "Cancer," he said quietly, as though the beast might hear. "Going through treatment. Hopefully she'll be fine, but in the meantime they're considering hiring someone to fill the gap. It'd only be temporary but I can give them your name."

I agreed immediately, and proactively chased the contact the next day. I accepted Zedmans' measly salary, without benefits, graciously. I feigned interest in the mundane, small-client work my new boss dumped on my desk. Living week to week, I ignored the guilt swimming in my stomach at wishing only a gradual recovery from cancer on a mother of two. They anticipate they will need me until at least the summer.

"It's not as though I'm sitting on my laurels in that place," I try to explain to Lisa. "I am searching for real work. I'm keeping up with my contacts from TJ Simons and sending my CV out. I've even talked to a recruiter in England."

"England?"

I curse myself inwardly. I hadn't intended telling her that unless something came of it. Lisa, for all her nasty childhood memories here, has no interest in living abroad. Luxurious travel is a different story – she'd tour the world ten times over if you gave her business class and five-star hotels.

I shuffle nearer to her, though it scares me what might happen. Our home is volatile these days. "I'm sorry," I say, folding my arms around her waist. She lets me draw her near. I breathe in her scent, remembering the early days of our relationship, filled with holds like these. "I want us to have that holiday. The longer I'm out of a large firm, the more difficult it is to crack in. I have to try everything."

I could go on explaining but she pulls away. She stares up at me, her expression unreadable.

"Why don't you go watch some TV?" I pat her cheek gently, wanting her and her judgement out of the room. "I'll call you when dinner's ready."

She smiles suddenly. "You like cooking, even after a full day at work."

"It's relaxing," I lie. "Now go on, I have to prepare the vegetables. It won't take long."

I watch her walk into the living room. I resume my chopping, the blade slicing hard on the board.

Cooking was just one of the many skills my father used against me. After my mother died, he sent me on a week-long cookery course during my Easter holidays. The fact that I was a grieving thirteen-year-old was irrelevant to him. He needed someone in the house to prepare his meals. As always, I put my heart and soul into anything that might earn my father's acceptance and found I enjoyed it. Cooking is a busy activity that demands concentration both physically and mentally. Surprisingly, it was the perfect distraction for an antsy teenager.

When I came home, I slaved for hours over a roast lamb with crispy potatoes and steamed greens. My father enjoyed it. "Figures a pansy like you would cook as well as a woman."

His comment smashed into my heart but I didn't stop cooking his meals. I never complained. I kept on going, trying in every way possible to please him. I did not fail at anything, except for that one goal: I never won his approval.

He did not beat me much as a young boy. A clip around the ear if I was cheeky, the old-fashioned 'six of the best' if I deliberately disobeyed him. My mother – my loving, soothing mother – was there to protect me. She provided a buffer for me, but was not powerful enough to stand up for herself. When she died, it got worse. He was not an especially stout man, and as my growing spurt finally kicked in the year my mother died, the physical pain was not severe. It was sore, but I coped. The howling loneliness every slap imprinted on my mind was devastating.

A teacher in school once challenged my glowing red cheek. She kept me behind after class and promised me I could confide in her if I had any problems. I lied. I assured her everything was fine. My mistake was telling my father later. I thought he would be happy that I had maintained our privacy. His fist caught my stomach, winding me.

"She should never have guessed in the first place!" he yelled, as I doubled over, gasping. "Be more careful, boy, or I won't go so easy on you next time."

There was no next time. My body was bulking out. My father's figure, which had never been impressive to begin with, was becoming stooped with the years. His job as a civil servant had been a source of much pride in his early adulthood. But with a weak mind and nervous disposition, he did not advance, enduring the humiliation of watching many junior colleagues pass him out over the years.

I like to think he might have been a different father had his work life provided the validation he craved. Instead, a knot of resentment warped his character. He took power from the one place he could captain – home.

Little changed when I finished secondary school. No matter how much I excelled in college, he derided the tuition as a waste of money. When I finally moved out of home, I felt a niggling guilt about leaving him alone, especially when he retired, bitter and friendless from a forty-year career of misery. He used my weekly visits to cook him a Sunday roast as little more than opportunities to vent. On my qualification as an accountant, he claimed to be too ill to attend the graduation ceremony, but I knew he was shrivelled with jealousy that my career prospects were so much greater than his had ever been.

My career became my own internal point of pride. My father might not have been able to verbalise praise but I knew I was achieving what he could not – financial success and status. People trusted me with their money. I was respected, trusted, and work made me the man my father had tried so hard to convince me I was too stupid to be. When I was headhunted by Likeman Tiles to be their in-house senior accountant, my father said they must have had sand between their ears to think I was worthy of the position. It was then I stopped visiting my father. I told myself I didn't need him any more. He had made it clear from the day I was born that I was a burden. My final gesture toward the man was to pay for the nursing home into which he was forcibly placed two years ago. Lisa never met him. She had no interest, no more than I had any desire to meet her father.

When my father died last year, just a few months before my redundancy, I was surprised at the depth of my sadness. My heart clenched tightly for weeks afterwards; my mouth lost its sense of taste for days. My head pounded during the day and swam when I lay down in bed.

Lisa's assurances that I was better off without him did nothing to ease the sleepless nights. It was Trish and Ciara who soothed me by repeating that I was a good son, and that deep down he was proud of me. I found it hard to believe what they were saying, but hearing it from the mouths of my friends made it seem possible, at least without him there to contradict them.

I think the combination of my father's death and my redundancy changed me. Until then, Lisa and I were a power couple. We complemented each other. Our goals were aligned. Now, I don't know who I am or what I want. As a couple, we are turning toxic. The disappointment at the direction our lives are taking has spilled into physical violence in recent months. But the emotional abuse began long ago. I am not a stupid man. I am not oblivious to our problem. But I am powerless to stop it. It takes over.

Shaking these thoughts from my head, I call Lisa in from the living room, placing a plate in front of her. We eat silently. When I have finished I recline back in my chair, sleepy and prepared to crash in front of the television for the night in peace.

"Stephen?" Lisa is staring at me. "I meant what I said when you came in. We need to talk."

Knowing it is easier to let her waffle on, I sit up straight, feigning attention. She pulls at her sleeve to reveal a pale bruise on her wrist. Finger-marks – my finger-marks – are still visible days later. Dread lightens my head.

"I ran into Nikki last Thursday evening. I was passing her school on the way home from work." Lisa pauses, swallowing. "She insisted we have a coffee, and she saw my wrist. It was much worse then."

I say nothing.

"I told her a box of plates fell on it," she continues quickly. "But she was suspicious. She knew it was you, I could tell."

I press my fingers into my eyelids. I always liked Nikki. I thought we got on well. That she would immediately jump to the conclusion that I am hurting my girlfriend angers me. But before righteousness can overpower me, Lisa hurtles me into reality.

"There's nothing we can do about it. I mean," she holds up her wrist, "you did grab me pretty hard."

My mouth falls open at her brazenness.

"Listen," she says, "I know things have been difficult lately, but that's why I want us to take a holiday. We need to get away. *I* need to get away."

"Wait." I stand up, glaring down at her. "Is that why you convinced me to go to work today instead of to Ciara's race? Because you didn't want Nikki to question me about your wrist?"

I had been looking forward to watching my friend compete. I knew this was a particularly important race for her. Besides, it had been a while since Lisa and I had been out as a couple. A part of me hoped if we were able to capture some of life's normality, we could bring it home with us.

This morning, as I got out of bed, Lisa had put a hand on my arm.

"I hope they don't work you too hard today."

For a second I was confused, until I remembered that Zedmans had called last night asking me to work, even though it was a Saturday, as there was a pressing deadline. I had politely refused, but Lisa had obviously assumed I was going in.

When I explained that I wanted to go to Ciara's race she had become inexplicably distressed. She almost cried as she insisted I had to do everything in my power to make myself indispensable to Zedmans. They could let me go at any minute. I needed to put myself – and her – ahead of jumping up and down on the sidelines of a sporting track. To appease her, I agreed.

Now, as the real reason for her interference becomes clear, a boiling hotness rushes through my body.

To my annoyance, tears spill down her cheeks. "Nikki rang me yesterday afternoon. She said she was ringing for a chat, but when has she ever done that? She was asking me all these nosy questions, about you, about us."

"What did you say?" I ask, with a hint of panic.

Her tears dry immediately. "Nothing. I just don't think it's a good idea for us to be around her right now." She stands and rests her head on my chest. "I'm sorry. I should have told you the truth. I want things to be good between us again, and I think they can be. That's why I want us to go away together. It doesn't have to be anywhere exotic as long as it's out of the country. We can get a ferry to France at a reasonable price this time of year. Let's go."

I tilt my head. "What's the matter?"

As long as I've known her, Lisa has had an obsession with keeping her holidays for sun-drenched summer destinations. A choppy boat ride to the chilly north of France doesn't fit.

"It's all coming apart," she blubs, lowering herself on the couch.

I stare down at her, frozen.

Her phone rings and vibrates on the table. She ignores it, wiping her eyes. Unable to take any more of this, I grab it.

"Yes?" I say harshly.

"Can I speak to Lisa, please?"

I cast a glance at my girlfriend. "Who is this?"

"Abby."

I have not heard the name before but that means nothing. Lisa's boss sends her on regular networking lunches. She is forever meeting new people. I hand her the phone.

"It's Abby," I say.

Lisa is on her feet at once. She shakes her head, and scurries into the living room.

Perplexed, I raise the phone to my ear and ask to take a message. Without a word, the mysterious Abby hangs up.

In the living room, I find Lisa sitting on the couch, her head buried in her hands. This time last year, I would have gone to her immediately, gathered her up in my arms and encouraged confidences from her. Not now. I doubt if any holiday, any apology can fix us. It is pure curiosity, rather than compassion, that prompts me to kneel in front of her.

"Who is Abby?"

Lisa shakes her head, wrapping her own arms around her body in the absence of mine. After a moment, she jerks her head up, as though suddenly realising I am there. "Abby," she begins, "is an old friend. She rang me earlier today. I don't know why she's calling again."

I stare at her. She isn't lying. I can see it in her shimmering eyes. "What did she want?"

Lisa shakes her head, more brusquely this time. Then, to my surprise, she buries her head in my chest. "We used to be so happy, you and me." She pulls back, looking up into my face with round bug eyes. "We were a team. A partnership. It's been tough for you losing your job and I should be making things better for you. I know why you grabbed my wrist last week. I need to be a better girlfriend. I know it's all my fault. I'm sorry. Forgive me." She strokes my arm. Her watering eyes and cracking voice unleashes from me a surge of protectiveness.

Roughly, I sweep her from the seat and start up the stairs. There has to be hope for us, I think, as I drop her on the bed and kneel over her. We let the past months sour our relationship to the point of reverting to our childhood defaults. No more.

If violence can start that suddenly, it must be capable of ending too. For a moment, as she reaches up and kisses me with a tenderness I had forgotten could exist between us, I actually believe it.

Chapter fourteen

TRISH

It has been three days since Lisa's call and I think I am going crazy. I wake in the night, sheets damp with perspiration, screaming for help into the empty room. According to Lisa, news is about to break and if Abby is involved it can only be about one thing. My one solace is that I broke up with Brian before Abby barged once more into my life and re-opened the wound I have been papering over for so many years. It would not be fair to put him through these terrifying nights, and equally fearful days.

Stephen arrives at my house out of the blue on Tuesday evening. "Oh great, you're home," he says, smiling, when I open the door. "I couldn't remember if you were flying."

"Tomorrow," I say grumpily. He raises an eyebrow. I take a deep breath and stand back to let him in. "I have a three-nighter to LA tomorrow. Then I have Sunday and Monday off."

"The flight attendant's weekend – take it when you can get it." He sounds slightly mollified after my initial dour greeting. "Sorry I didn't make it to Ciara's race last weekend."

I nod vaguely. It seems a distant memory now.

Stephen asks if he can hang out for the evening. Lisa, apparently, is out with work colleagues. At her name I tense but readily agree. Not alone will company distract me, I'm having trouble undoing the mess I made when I flung the full tray of paint at the wall on Saturday.

"What did you do?" Half-grinning, half-appalled, Stephen stares at the bumpy white clumps stuck to the green wall.

"I tripped," I lie easily. "The paint went everywhere."

"Come on then," he sighs. "Pass me a scraper and let's get to work."

The next hour passes relatively pleasantly. The squirming anticipation of doom in my stomach calms to a flutter as we scrape and wash the worst side of the wall.

"Have you talked to Ciara?" Stephen asks.

"No, she's not answering her phone," I say, although I have only tried to ring her once since the race. Lisa's call about Abby threw everything else to the side.

"I wasn't able to get through to her earlier so I rang Nikki. Did you know Ciara is staying with her sister this week?"

I stop mid-brush. "No. I didn't know that. Are she and Nikki fighting? She rushed out of the running club pretty quickly last weekend."

Stephen shrugs. "Nikki said her sister needed some help with the kids, so Ciara's gone to the rescue."

I continue painting. Ciara would certainly be the first to volunteer to help out someone in need, especially her sister. But she's so fixated on Rio, it surely wouldn't be wise for her to interrupt her routine right now, and leave Nikki behind in the house. Before I can dwell on it any further, Stephen announces he has done as much as he can without a caffeine injection.

I clatter around the kitchen, enjoying having someone else in the house to fuss over. When I return to the living room, Stephen has thrown the sheets off my couch and is sprawled out, remote control in his hand. I snigger and nod at his outstretched legs as I lower the tray onto the coffee table.

"Making yourself at home, Stephen?"

He grins and sits upright, rubbing his hands together as I pour us the coffee.

I sit and cup my hands gratefully around the mug he passes to me.

When the news headlines are read out I realise that, with Stephen for calming company, this is the first time since last Saturday I have sat down to watch the news without quivering. As the first, explosive news item is read out, I feel the irony for a fleeting moment, before it is crushed under the weight of my terror.

"*Irishwoman dies following abortion attempt in the little-known Charrings Clinic in south-east London.*"

My entire body clenches. I retch.

"Trish, are you all right?" Stephen's hand pats my back.

"I'm fine." I force myself to sit upright. "I swallowed the coffee down the wrong way."

Satisfied, he refocuses on the television. The rest of the headlines are over and the newsreader is seconds away from launching into the main stories. I take a deep breath.

"*Good evening, and welcome to the Nine O'Clock News.*"

I bite my lip to stop it trembling as a photograph of the house to which Abby brought me seven years ago fills the screen.

"*An Irishwoman has died following a botched abortion attempt in London,*" the presenter reads calmly from her notes. "*Twenty-two-year-old Mary O'Sullivan, originally from Cork but living in Dublin during her college terms, is believed to have travelled to London late last week. On Saturday morning, she stumbled into St Ignatius' Hospital with acute abdominal bleeding and, following unsuccessful surgery, died as night fell. Our UK correspondent, Susan Young, reports.*"

A middle-aged woman appears on screen, her hair blowing across her face in the wind. She tucks a clump behind her ear and begins filling in the details.

"*It was in this house behind me that Mary O'Sullivan is believed to have been brought on the promise of a safe, clean abortion. One man has been arrested on suspicion of breaching the English Abortion Act 1967,*" *including performing an abortion in an unlicensed clinic and without the consent of a second doctor, as are required by the Act. Police have indicated that further charges may follow."*

As she speaks, the images on screen alternate between close-ups of the house, the hospital where the girl died and, finally, a shot of the man being arrested. I stare at his arrogant face, his lips curled into a leer as he is led away in handcuffs. It has been seven years since he stuck a belt between my teeth and thrust his hand inside me so roughly I cried. I would know him anywhere. The doctor with no name.

Stephen tuts in dismay. "Poor girl, only twenty-two."

A wail escapes my lips. Stephen's response is urgent, trying to calm me by rubbing my back but my shoulders shake violently. He manages to pull the quivering mug from my hand. After a few seconds, I hear his frantic questioning offer me a lifeline.

"What's wrong, Trish? Did you know that girl?"

With a gulp, I steady myself. Charrings Clinic has been exposed, but I have not been. Yet. I will not reveal myself unless absolutely necessary. I can still lie.

"Yes," I breathe. "I knew her. A little. Sorry, I just got a shock."

Stephen carries on caressing my back. "Of course you did, Trish."

Together, we stare once more at the television.

They are talking about Mary O'Sullivan, the girl I never met but to whom I am now connected forever. She was a social studies student who had been repeating her final year. A fellow student with popping eyes materialises to testify that her friend Mary was dedicated and driven, and that she had been working really hard to pass this year.

"Hey look," Stephen says, "it's your mum."

My stomach lurches. Of course my mother, as the face of Pro-Life Ireland, would be first on the scene.

"Poor Mary O'Sullivan's death is a tragedy," she says. *"It goes to show that abortion is never a good option. Had she chosen to have her baby, these wasteful deaths would not have occurred. Instead, a young mother and her unborn child are dead."*

110

A new face, a serious woman in her forties, now dominates the screen, interviewed from another venue. I recognise her vaguely as a rival of my mother's from a prominent pro-choice organisation. She speaks passionately about how Mary spent all her money on her repeat year, and would not have had the luxury of travelling to a safe, private clinic. "*Mary's death,*" she says with feeling, "*is a direct result of the lack of termination options in this country. Her only choice was a run-down dive in London, where she was treated so poorly she died.*"

"*Mary O'Sullivan's death is heart-breaking,*" says yet another new face.

A dizziness weakens me at the number of people weighing in.

She goes on: "*But let us not pretend she was forced to have an abortion. She chose to do this. We should not let the crimes of a clinic in another country bamboozle us into legalising what is clearly a dangerous and terrible practice here.*"

It is already happening. The Charrings Clinic story will lead to nationwide protests from both pro-life and pro-choice groups, each claiming Mary O'Sullivan's death as an irrefutable argument for their own agenda. She will be relegated from human to a rag doll, pulled from side to side in a larger game.

It will be the sole topic of conversation everywhere I go.

The news item ends with a description of Charrings Clinic. A seemingly innocent suburban redbrick that was, for over a decade, a house of horrors.

Then, to my dismay, the Minister for Justice, Elaine Masterson, weighs in from outside government buildings. "*I have already been in contact with my counterpart in Westminster. The other ministers and I will be reviewing the details of this case over the next few days.*"

My mouth goes dry.

"*Be assured I will be taking a personal interest in this case. That's all I have to say for now,*" she declares loudly, pushing past the swarm of journalists surrounding her at the gates.

I watch her stride away, staying resolutely silent as they follow her, flashing their cameras and calling more questions.

I blink at the screen. The newsreader is now talking about a car crash in the city centre, as if she has already forgotten about Charrings Clinic.

"I'm sorry," Stephen says softly, picking up the remote control to lower the volume. "It must be hard to hear about it on the news."

I nod, every movement painful.

"How did you know her?" he asks.

"Oh, from school." I am surprised at how easily the lies tumble from me. Desperation makes strangers of us all.

Stephen frowns questioningly. "But you wouldn't have been in school with her, would you? She's twenty-two years old. And she's from Cork."

I take a sip of my drink as I hastily concoct an explanation. "Her sister was in my class. Beth and I both knew her before her family left for Cork." This is a dangerous game. The story will be in the papers tomorrow, and could easily expose Mary O'Sullivan as an only child, or having not travelled to Dublin until college. I place my head gingerly in my hands.

"I think you need something stronger than coffee," Stephen says.

I let him race into the kitchen, eager to be useful. I sit back, relieved that at least it is not Brian here beside me.

It does not surprise me that Minister Masterson is taking an active interest in Mary O'Sullivan's death. She has been an outspoken advocate of women's rights for years, and is one of the few politicians who has not shied away from the debate about legalising abortion. It scares me. The more people get involved, the less likely all this is to just go away.

Stephen returns with two wineglasses clicking in one hand and a bottle tucked under his arm. A packet of mini Toblerones is clutched in his other hand. "Check out what I found."

"Ah, my buried stash!" I give a half-smile, knowing how important it is to appear normal.

He unscrews the top and pours. "You hide your sweets in the same place Lisa does – behind the health food. Nice try."

"It rarely works," I admit, as casually as I can, but his comment about Lisa triggered something in me. She rang me last Saturday evening with the warning. Abby must have known, even as Mary O'Sullivan staggered into hospital on the Saturday morning, how it would end.

"So, if your sister knew that girl who died, then Lisa probably did too," Stephen muses.

In that second, I miss Brian. Having someone who, even when they are comforting a friend, will think of me first.

Sarcasm spurts from my mouth. "Lisa knew her all right." I am barely aware that I am speaking. Hysteria bubbles up from my stomach at the insaneness of it all but I push it back down.

"That poor girl is not the only friend from the past popping up out of blue," Stephen says, eyeing me cautiously as he takes a sip of his drink.

"What do you mean?" I sniff.

He sits forward. "Well, last Saturday Lisa got a call from an old friend. She seemed . . . I don't know, almost afraid of her. She wouldn't take her call. I wondered if you or Beth knew her? Her name is Abby."

I lean over, fat tears leaking from my eyes. I wipe them away hastily, but Stephen is no idiot.

"Trish!" He sets down his glass and pries my hands from my face. "What's going on? You do know her, then?"

I shake my head.

He sits back, folding his arms with an eyebrow raised.

"Who is she, Trish? Who is Abby?"

My ringtone vibrates shrilly throughout the room. I stare down at it, but the screen is facing the table and I am too afraid to turn it over. It is as if Abby knows we are talking about her.

When I remain fixed to the spot, trembling, Stephen leans across to pick up my phone.

I know I should say nothing, but my head is pounding. "If that's Abby, I don't want to talk to her!" I burst out shrilly.

He holds it up so I can see the name flashing across the screen. "It's Lisa," he says.

I try to snatch it from him, but he answers.

Chapter fifteen

STEPHEN

"Lisa? It's Stephen."

"Stephen? What . . . ?" Her voice trails off. I can visualise her staring at her phone, trying to figure out if she accidently called me. "Are you with Trish?" she asks, her accusation thick with indignation.

"Yeah." I almost laugh at her tone except I can feel my hatred of her insecurities rise like bile within me. "What's wrong, Lisa?"

She stammers a bit, then asks to speak to Trish. I pass my friend the phone. Her hands shake as she takes it.

"Hello? Yes, yes."

I watch her eyes dart to mine before she scurries past me into the kitchen.

I sit down, unable to hear anything except strained mutterings coming from the other room. I knead my forehead with my knuckles. Lisa phoning Trish when she is supposed to be out with her work colleagues stretches beyond unusual.

There was a marginal cooling of my friendship with Trish when I started dated Lisa. At first I thought it was Lisa's connection with

Beth that made the situation awkward for her. I soon realised that Trish simply did not like my new girlfriend.

Trish didn't actually object. She didn't have to – I wasn't completely naïve. I could see the distaste in her eyes. But I recognised the real person beneath Lisa's prickly façade. While Trish saw a girl greedy for designer shoes, I knew she had a genuine interest in the fashion world. Trish might have scoffed internally at Lisa's preference for fine dining, but for me she brightened up an ordinary dinner with her passion for perfection.

In a way, my refusal to let my friend's obvious dislike colour my view of Lisa reminded me of how I championed Trish, Ciara and Gerry at the summer camp when we first met. I saw Trish's shyness for what it was – inner tenderness. I knew Ciara's brash personality was masking insecurities. As for Gerry, his never-ending soliloquys and reflections were the mark of an artistic genius. I didn't judge my three friends then, and I wasn't about to cast Lisa aside because of Trish's concerns.

Things reverted to normal once Trish – and even Ciara, who seemed to share Trish's wariness of my new girlfriend – realised this wasn't a meaningless fling. I fell hard for Lisa, and my friends accepted her as part of our group, though they never warmed to her as I did to Nikki and Brian.

Aside from Lisa's call to Trish, something else is baffling me. Abby. A name I never heard until three nights ago when Lisa quaked in our living room, refusing to answer her phone. Tonight, an already-upset Trish seemed as fearful as Lisa at the prospect of speaking with this old friend. I cannot figure out the connection, but something isn't right here.

Trish slinks into the living room. "Sorry about that," she says with false cheeriness.

"What did Lisa want?" I ask.

"Oh, nothing. She was asking how Beth is getting on. With the baby."

"Beth," I say, as if in agreement. "Trish, can I ask you something?"

She sits so dejectedly I almost hold my tongue. But questioning Trish will be easier than confronting Lisa later, so I make myself speak. "Who is Abby?"

She shakes her head.

"Lisa nearly jumped out of her skin when she realised it was Abby ringing the other night," I say, "just like you did when you thought Lisa's call was from her."

"Don't worry, Stephen." Trish stands. "Abby was a friend of Lisa's when they were younger. I knew her from around school. She wasn't a nice person and I think she's trying to make contact with us all again. But we're not interested. That's it. End of story."

"But . . ."

"Leave it, Stephen!" she snaps.

I stare at her. It is not the first time Trish has blocked me out, but for her to bark at anyone suggests something deeper is at work.

"Maybe it would be best if you head off." She folds her arms tightly across her chest. "I'm flying to Los Angeles tomorrow. I have to be up early."

I do not argue. As I pick up my jacket, I remember what happened before Lisa called.

I lean in and give Trish a hug. She returns it feebly.

"I'm sorry about your friend – the one who died in England. Mary O'Sullivan, wasn't it?"

She nods without meeting my eye.

"Trish," I duck my head to see her face properly, "are you sure you're all right?"

She lifts her chin and gives me a weak smile. "I'm fine, Stephen. I'll talk to you when I land in a few days, okay?"

Accepting the dismissal, I rub her arm and bundle out into the late-September darkness. I sit in my car for a few minutes without starting it up.

I have so many questions for Lisa, not least about the reason she was phoning Trish. Perhaps Trish was telling the truth, and it has something to do with Beth. But I can't imagine what it could be – Lisa and Beth's friendship has fizzled out completely. Their only other common connection is me. A bolt of insecurity physically rattles me. I shudder. What could they possibly want to discuss about me?

Regardless of that, it is clear that both of them are in fear of a person called Abby, and I have to get to the bottom of this. I'll talk to her tonight, though I know how such a confrontation is likely to end.

I take a deep breath and chug the car to life, driving out of Trish's sheltered cul-de-sac and into the night mist.

Lisa is standing at the kitchen counter with her back to me, pouring one of her low-fat slimming drinks that looks like sludge into a tall glass.

"Where have you been?" she asks as she scrapes the bottom of the blender with a spoon.

"You know where I've been. I went to Trish's house."

"Why?"

A familiar burning tickles my ribcage. I take a deep breath. "Just to say hi," I try to answer calmly, but a hint of annoyance slips into the cadence of my words. "I helped her clean up the living room," I continue quickly. "She spilled a whole tray of paint last weekend."

Lisa chugs down the last of her drink. She turns around. "I thought you'd be here when I got home."

I take a deep breath. I don't want us to fight, but it seems inevitable. If we're going to argue, I may as well try to get some answers. "Lisa, why were you ringing Trish this evening?"

The slap comes sharp and fast. I hold a hand to my stinging cheek. She raises her hand again and I reach out instinctively to stop her. We freeze mid-motion. She smiles crookedly, and nods at my hand, inches from grabbing her wrist.

"Go on then," she says silkily. "Try and stop me. Big man like you, you barely have to touch me and it'll show." She reaches out to stroke my cheek. "What would Nikki think if I showed up at her door with more bruises?"

She pushes past me and stalks upstairs. I want to run from the house but my legs belong to Lisa. I bow my head and follow her up. She looks up at me loitering by the bedroom door.

"Come in and sit," she orders.

I obey.

She lowers herself onto the bed beside me, and takes my hand. Sometimes I think the worst part isn't the slaps, the punches, the name-calling. It's the hot and cold. I can never tell whether she is about to kiss me or hit me.

"What do you want to know, Stephen?"

Her voice is lenient so I take my chance.

"What were you and Trish talking about this evening? Did it have anything to do with that woman Abby?"

"What?" she says, clearly startled.

"When the phone rang, Trish thought someone else might be ringing her. Someone who scared her. Abby."

Lisa's hand twitches in mine but her expression does not alter so I barrel on.

"You said Abby was a childhood friend. But you seemed afraid of her, and so did Trish. What's going on?"

She says nothing.

"I don't want you to be frightened, Lisa. You or Trish."

Her mouth narrows to a thin line. "Real hero, aren't you?" She stands. "What you need to do, Stephen, is mind your own business. Abby is exactly who I said – an unwanted friend trying to claw her way back into my life. Probably doing the same with Trish, and her sister Beth, and the rest of our school friends and neighbours. Forget about her. I have already."

I remain silent but unconvinced.

"You shouldn't have gone to Trish's tonight," she says accusingly.

I glower up at her, determined to challenge her for once. "Why not? You weren't here."

"No, I was with my boss, greeting clients. Working, for us." Her voice is rising. "It's not like you're bringing home anything decent in that excuse for a job. You're hopeless, Stephen, you know that? I used to feel sorry for you, when I heard the names your father called you, but I'm beginning to have some sympathy for him. What would he think of you, if he could see you?"

I want to cover my ears with my hands. I stand and make for the door.

She follows me, yelling. "He'd see you for what you really are – pathetic! You can't even stand up for yourself!" She swipes at my back. It does not hurt – I think of the broken bones and stinging tackles from my years of rugby. But, on the pitch, I can muscle against my attacker and I have my team around to defend me. Here, alone in the house with Lisa, I cannot return her blows.

Last week, I defended myself for the first time. She tried to slap me in her usual way – a crack across the cheek. Her aim was off and instead she clocked my temple. It stung. She lifted her hand to hit me again and I grabbed her wrist. I held it in place, my lips pressed tightly together, my whole body shaking. For a few seconds, she eyeballed me, ordering me silently to let her go. When I didn't she started to struggle, then a whimper escaped her lips. I released her as though burned.

"Lisa, I'm sorry."

I followed her into the kitchen, watching uselessly as she rummaged in the freezer and gingerly placed a towelled icepack on her wrist. Still, the bruise swelled up within minutes. She did not speak to me for the rest of the night. I was making to climb into bed after her when her leg shot out, striking me squarely between my legs. I moaned pitifully and toppled sideways onto the floor. She stood over me as I lay there.

Then she flung a pillow down on me. "I don't want you in bed with me tonight. Go sleep on the couch."

I pattered downstairs without complaint, though I am too tall for the couch. Aside from that, it is hard-backed and, while it looks stylish, it is far from comfortable. Yet it was preferable to lying next to Lisa when she is in one of her rages.

When she came downstairs the next morning, I tried to talk to her but she ignored me as she left the house, slamming the front door behind her.

Now as she yells at me, the old nagging self-doubt – that my father was right about me being a gormless idiot – resurfaces with renewed punch. Lisa used to love me, but I have failed her. I lost my job, I cannot provide for us. She is refusing to confide in me and why should she? I can't defend myself from a little woman, so how can I be any use to her? I don't know who I am anymore, except a total failure. The hitting, the slapping – I know it's wrong. She shouldn't be doing that. But it's not as if she is able to cause me any serious damage. If I wanted to, I could pick her up one-handed. I could stop her any time. Except I can't.

I stride out of the bedroom.

"You're spineless, Stephen. I don't know why I'm with you sometimes."

I spin around at the top of the stairs. "Then leave," I say, out of nowhere. It is the first time I have ever said that. I hold my breath, unsure if the words have truly left my mouth.

Lisa's face changes. Her eyebrows fly up and her cheeks flush red. She opens her mouth as if to answer but nothing comes out. For a moment, I think she's about to apologise. She does that sometimes – says she is sorry at exactly the right second, just as I am on the cusp of losing my patience. I always forgive her.

But she is unpredictable. As soon as I start to feel in control with Lisa – that maybe I can handle myself around her – that is the very time she explodes.

I stand before her now, a strange superiority calming me as she looks up at me.

Her two fists punch at my chest, hard. I step back to steady myself. My foot finds nothing but air. I land with a clatter and tumble down the stairs.

I gasp, a piercing pain shooting from the back of my head. I sit up, my back twinging painfully, and place a hand on my head. I flinch as my fingers touch it.

I hear Lisa walking slowly down the stairs. She is always sorry for her bouts of violence. After the worst occasions, she apologises. Mostly she tends to whatever wound she had given me with round, regretful eyes.

I wait for her apology, writhing against the sharp pains spiking my spine.

"Get up, you fat lump!" She kicks my leg.

"Lisa, for God's sake," I shout, the spasms spurring a newfound defiance. It does not phase her. It only enrages her further.

"I said, get up. Get up, *get up!*"

I scramble to my feet and hobble into the living room. I hear her rustling in the kitchen, and a moment later she appears at my side, holding a pack of ice. She presses it roughly to my head. I don't complain. She kneels in front of me on the ground, like a child.

"You're angry with me?" she says. "Why?"

I grimace. She shoved me down the stairs. On purpose.

Her push stirred something in me. I know I deserve the insults she shouts at me. Although it is not right that she lashes out at me in that way, I understand why she is driven to that. But shoving me at the top of the stairs? She could have killed me.

For the first time, I feel a trickle of something more than inadequacy. I feel wronged.

"You – you pushed me down the stairs, Lisa." My voice vibrates but I hold my stare. "I just wanted to know who this Abby is, and what she has to do with Trish."

To my surprise, Lisa just sits back and bites her lip.

"Listen, Stephen," she says, running a hand through her hair, "Trish and I are not best friends, but we go way back. I spent a lot of time in her house when her sister and I were teenagers. It's not uncommon that we know the same people."

I say nothing.

"I told you, Abby is an old friend. I haven't seen her in years. She contacted me and Trish. We don't want to see her. That's all."

I chew down on my tongue until it stings hotly. What she is saying is logical, but I just don't buy it. There was too much fear in their reactions to Abby.

A thought occurs to me at the reminder that Lisa and Trish's connection goes back to their childhood.

"I'm sorry about Mary O'Sullivan."

I know it is a mistake the moment it leaves my mouth. Lisa's face visibly greys. She had calmed enough to try to alleviate my concerns about Abby. I should have left it at that.

I try to repair the damage. "I was watching the news with Trish, and she got all upset because this girl she knew from school had died . . . she said you knew her too."

Lisa seems to tremble as she stands up, but once she is towering over me all sense of unbalance disappears.

I force myself to rise too. Now I am the tall one, the one with every physical advantage. But I cave, as I always do. I keel back from her screams, her punches, and crouch on the floor. I cannot fight her – she's a little slip of a thing. I would hurt her. Even if I wanted to, I know from experience my body won't react except to defend. I shield my head with my arms until it finally stops.

It takes me a few minutes to recover. I stay crouched on the floor, with Lisa leaning on the doorframe, her arms folded.

"I don't know what your game is, Stephen," she says evenly. "You need to learn your place."

I want to shout that she sounds insane. I just squat there.

"Except for work, you're not leaving this house. It's time you grew up and took some responsibility."

"Lisa . . ." I begin, but her eyes narrow and I press my lips together.

She gestures to the icepack, now starting to thaw in my hand. "Don't let that spill. I'm going to bed. You sleep on the couch."

I look at it, then back to her, but she has already started toward the stairs. She stops at the living-room door.

"I expect you home straight after work tomorrow. No later than six."

She waits until I nod, then turns her back and walks up the stairs.

123

Chapter sixteen

CIARA

"That poor young girl." Orla sounds almost on the verge of tears as Margaret Elderfield recaps on the main story – a twenty-two-year-old college student dead due to a botched abortion in England.

Orla, Thomas and I have been watching the news, and afterwards the *Current Times* special on abortion they've managed to pull together. My legs are curled under me, my hands clutching a now cold cup of tea.

Thomas stands with purpose. "I hope they lock that man up and throw away the key."

I incline my head toward him, recalling a conversation we had some years ago, when the abortion debate last took off in Ireland. "I thought you once said you wouldn't be comfortable performing terminations yourself, as a doctor, if it ever became legal?"

Thomas swipes his arm, beating away my remark as irrelevant. "I'm not talking about whether abortion is right or wrong. I'm talking about a young, vulnerable girl trusting a doctor who treated her so brutishly she died from infection. We have a duty of care to our patients. Look at her, she's practically a kid."

We all turn toward the television, where a picture of Mary O'Sullivan fills the screen. She wears a plain blue dress, her curly hair bouncing around her shoulders and a cute fringe covering her forehead. With a naturally round face, she comes across as younger than her twenty-two years. Margaret Elderfield must agree, as she confirms the photo is recent, taken last month at her grandmother's eightieth birthday. I cringe at the thought of that elderly lady being told the news, and then watching her family's loss unfold so publically.

Orla looks up at her husband. "I'd question whether he's even a doctor, love," she says quietly. "With these back-alley places, it's often medical-school dropouts or struck-off physicians who run them."

Thomas is as incensed as I have ever seen him. It makes me feel strangely protected. I was right to come to this house after my fight with Nikki last weekend. It's a safe place, and Orla's home-baked scones smell of my childhood. Our farmhouse in Donegal is a long way from Dublin, but Orla and Thomas's warmth reminds me of my parents in a visceral way that makes me mourn the passing of time.

When I arrived at their door last Saturday night, having braved the thunderstorm that eventually cracked overhead, it was Orla who answered it.

"Ciara!"

Her exclamation somehow calmed me. It is easy to pass worry to a mother, any mother – they take it on naturally and expertly. Exhausted, I let her grab me and drag me inside.

My clothes were dripping with rain. My hair was matted to my head, with my face just as wet from crying. The rain had begun pouring as I stepped off the bus less than a ten-minute walk from Orla's house. I could have called her to collect me. In fact, she or Thomas would probably have driven all the way to my house if I'd asked. The truth was I needed the space of the journey to reflect, and regret.

The woman who sat beside me on the bus had cast worried glances in my direction as I wiped the tears from my eyes as discreetly as possible. She stopped short of saying anything and I was glad. I wasn't looking for attention. I'm hardly a celebrity but I do get spotted the odd time by other runners or athletes in training. I managed to get to Orla's house without incident, unless you count the turmoil in my head.

Orla peeled me out of my soaking jacket as I kicked off my shoes and dropped my bag by the wall. Out of nowhere, little Liam was on top of me.

"Not now, Liam," Orla said.

I squeezed him fondly. He squealed and threw me off, rushing out of the hall screeching my arrival to his little sister.

"What did you give him for dinner, a bowl of sugar?" I laughed, rubbing my hip where he had leapt on me.

Thomas emerged from the kitchen. "Ciara, what are you doing here? You're drenched!"

"Get a towel for Ciara, will you, love?" Orla said before I could answer.

Thomas headed up the stairs as she steered me into the living room. He returned a minute later with a hand towel.

Orla flicked her eyes upwards. "I meant a decent-sized one, Thomas – look at her! No, no, don't worry about it now – just get the kids into bed, will you?"

He blew her a shy kiss as he backed out the door.

"Men," she tutted. "Completely useless."

"Women aren't much better," I replied dourly.

"It'll be okay, Ciara," she said with a certainty I didn't understand. She hadn't even asked why I was there, but I supposed it wouldn't take a genius to figure it out. She stripped off her dressing gown, revealing cartoon-printed pyjamas.

"Wow, Orla," I grinned, momentarily distracted. "How does Thomas keep his hands off you?"

She shoved me playfully. "The kids gave it to me for Christmas. These are the indignities you have to suffer when you're a parent. Now, dry off and put on this dressing gown. I'll get another one from upstairs."

She slipped out of the room quietly, no doubt hoping to avoid getting caught up in the bedtime ritual. I couldn't help smiling at the carrying cries of "Mammy, Mammy!" from the bedrooms and Thomas's vain attempts at distraction.

As I undressed and patted my body dry, I scanned my sister's living room.

It is the definition of homely – blankets on the plump couches, a large television in the corner and photographs papering the walls.

I noticed a few of me and Nikki on the mantelpiece and in a collage beside the door. Boxes of toys were piled in the corners and fluffy teddy bears lay abandoned in various corners.

This is what Nikki wants. A family home. Maybe she is sick of waiting for me, and that is why she turned to Ann.

Orla crept into the room after a while, clicking the door quietly behind her so as not to disturb the kids. She was carrying an enormous slab of chocolate.

"Now, don't you dare talk to me about race diets. After your fantastic win today you can have a few squares of chocolate."

I didn't argue and broke off a large chunk. Orla settled into the corner seat, almost as far away from me as the room allowed. I felt my body loosen. She knew I needed space or I would clam up.

"So, you had a fight with Nikki I take it?"

I curled into a ball on the large couch. "A big one. Can I stay here for a few days?"

"That bad? Of course, for as long as you need."

"It won't be too long. I know it's not fair to land in on you with the three kids. Where's the baby?"

Orla pointed upstairs, her words muffled through a large mouthful of chocolate. "We got him a play-mobile that keeps him occupied for hours. Don't worry, Thomas can take care of them for the evening." She swallows thickly. "So, you ran out of the club in a hurry earlier. Nikki did a stellar job of convincing everyone you were sick, not rude."

I shook my head. What was happening to me? I claim not to want children right now because I need to concentrate on my running, but when the opportunity comes to secure support and even sponsorship, I run from the place like a first-class drama queen.

I glanced at my sister. "I want that Gold so bad, Orla."

She nodded.

I don't know what I'd do without her. It wasn't always that way. As children, we weren't close. With barely three years between us, there was an unspoken rivalry, and probably natural jealousy on her part when I came along.

I was the baby, the one who popped suddenly into the world to usurp our parents' affection. I was also the pretty one. Not that Orla isn't attractive, but I got the dark eyes and hair, the tanned skin and naturally athletic physique.

"There's a Spanish sailor in our ancestry, for sure," my father used to chuckle when commenting on my continental beauty.

In our village in Donegal, right on the western coastline, hurling and football are the ultimate sources of county pride. With no sons to cheer on, my father threw me and Orla into camogie – what was commonly known as the girls' version of the sports. Orla wasn't bad at it but I excelled. More than excelled. I was on the school's intermediate team by the time I was ten, and the senior first team before I was fourteen. My father was beside himself.

Running was only ever a part of training, a means to fitness. But I enjoyed it so much I would go for early morning jogs alone, and while the others wanted skills training and matches, I advocated laps of the pitch. Our PE teacher encouraged athletics outside of the camogie season which helped improve my distance performances as a young teenager. It was not until a scout for the Donegal camogie leagues came to watch our games that my talent was spotted.

I owe everything to that woman. She identified my real talent not as a camogie forward, but as a runner. She all but barged into the school to insist I be mentored and coached at the highest level. She demanded to see my running stats from our athletics season, and when our bamboozled PE teacher handed over my times with shaking hands, the scout's determination was sealed.

After a reactionary refusal from my parents, who wanted my

efforts primarily focussed on camogie, a coach was sent up from Dublin to speak to them. At first they were sceptical of the young, long-haired Adrian's interest in their teenage daughter. He sat with them for an hour detailing his résumé. He was at the time working with the Irish women's team who were training for the Sydney Olympics. That got their attention. Adrian impressed them with a pre-prepared plan and training schedule that would see me work with my own PE teacher weekly, an assigned coach on weekends, and him bi-weekly or monthly depending on his own schedule.

"There is a career to be made from this," he said after watching me run laps of our local park. "Her technique needs honing, and it will take a lot of work. But she's hitting records now, without proper coaching. Imagine what a few years of committed training will do. A scholarship to university at the very least."

That secured it for my parents. I was diligent. I pushed myself. I knew what I wanted – not to be good, or in the top ten. I wanted to win. That drive, Adrian promised, was what would get me there.

I looked at Orla sitting across from me, whose own accomplishments and ambitions were so often side-lined in favour of mine. "It's what I've always wanted, Orla."

"Maybe that's the problem," she said, breaking off another row of chocolate.

I frowned at her in confusion.

"We change as we grow up, Ciara," she said, knowingly. "Just because Gold was your dream when you were fourteen, doesn't mean it will always be your priority. If there's something else you want more, it's okay to chase that instead."

I raised a single eyebrow. She was only three years my senior yet she seemed to know so much. I scrutinised her living room again. In a way, she lives in a completely different world from me.

"Nikki and me, it's not just today. We've been fighting for months."

Orla sat up straighter. "For months? What about?"

I paused with a silence borne from loyalty. Then I blurted it out. "She wants kids."

"Oh, Ciara. That's wonderful." Orla's face lit up.

"I promised her we'd do it now, this year. But . . ." I paused, embarrassed to admit it, "I don't know if I want that, Orla."

"What's the problem?" she asked bluntly.

"You were there today, you know how close I am to finally getting that Gold. I need to keep my focus."

To my surprise, Orla shrugged. "You think Thomas didn't need to focus on his consultancy interviews when Kate was born prematurely?"

I gaped at her.

"All I'm saying is there's never a right time to have a baby. If you're waiting for everything to fit into place, it doesn't happen that way. Life is short."

A hotness rose, flushing my cheeks. "Running has always been my goal and I want the win. I want it so badly. I'm not giving up on what I really want out of life."

Orla bent forward. "What is the real reason, Ciara? I mean, I can understand you putting it off so you can give your attention to the Olympics for the next six months, but what about after that?"

I said nothing, inspecting my fingers twisting in my lap.

"It's okay not to be ready, you know."

I glanced up. "I'm not sure Nikki agrees."

"Well, sometimes you just need to go for it, don't you? Whether you're ready or not. If you had waited until you were ready, you never would have got Nikki in the first place, would you?"

I opened my mouth to argue, then shut it again. She was right, of course. In the midst of my acquisition by the running elite of Ireland, I was going through my own discovery. I didn't put the label on myself for a long time. I fought my urges hard. But when I officially left the camogie team to specialise in running at the age of sixteen, my team threw a party for me in the club. A group of us were huddled around a makeshift bonfire when, one by one, they all dawdled inside and I was left alone with Sandra. The kiss was quick and unexpected, and neither of us mentioned it again. But it crystallised for me what I really wanted, though it took me a long time to accept myself, and a decade more to tell my parents.

Orla was right. I wasn't ready when Nikki came along. I was nervous and scared and only partly out. But I took that leap of faith and never regretted it. Perhaps that was what I needed to do now.

"I don't know, Orla." I shook my head. "I look around here. You are a parent. You know what to do when Liam, Kate and Donal cry. I haven't a clue."

"I hadn't a notion either," Orla laughed. "No one does. It's the biggest shock to the system ever. Listen, Ciara, I'm not telling you to go have babies if that's not what you want. I'm just saying that when it comes to kids, you'll never be ready. No one is."

"You were," I said, almost indignantly. "You and Thomas planned to have Liam. You tried for months until he came along."

"Yeah, and when I finally got pregnant I nearly had a meltdown more than once."

I blinked. "I didn't know that."

Orla eased out of her seat and sat beside me on the long couch. "You're my little sister. I'm the one who should be taking care of you. I don't necessarily tell you when I'm having a hard time."

"Well, you should," I said crossly. "We're both adults, Orla. A three-year age gap is nothing now. If there's something wrong, I want you to tell me."

"Why?"

I spluttered the obvious reply. "Because you're my sister. I want to help you."

"And that, Ciara, is why you will make an excellent parent someday."

I narrowed my eyes as she grinned knowingly.

"You care about the people in your life. You're a good person, full of love to give. That's all a baby needs."

The truth seeped out of me. "I never thought it would be possible. Nikki and I, we can't make a baby together. I assumed it was an avenue that was closed off to me."

Orla stroked the damp hair from my face. "You never thought you could truly be happy."

A memory flashed before me. Orla and I grew up separately. We each had our own group of friends and, while I basked in the admiration of our parents, she played shyly in the corner. Strangely, our parents became more involved in her life after she left home for college, suddenly missing her constant, steadying presence.

She helped me move into my new college dorm in Dublin but, even though she lived a mere ten minutes away, we rarely saw each other during the first few months. Then, one night, she came to visit me unexpectedly. I was beginning to test the waters, very gingerly, and she found me kissing a girl from my biology lecture outside the dorms.

"Ciara!" she had exclaimed, just as she did when I arrived on her doorstep dripping with rain.

I hissed at the girl to leave, which she did, though with a hurt look on her face. My worst nightmare was coming true and I felt my stomach muscles contract severely. My breath came short and shallow.

"Please, Orla," I gasped, stumbling over and clutching her arm. "Please don't tell Mam and Dad."

I expected a smug pout, a recognition that finally she would be the golden child, and I the outcast. It just shows how little I really knew her. She gathered me into a hug so resembling our mother's I almost cried.

"I won't tell Mam and Dad."

I struggled out of her arms to stare into her face. "Really?"

"Of course not," she said meaningfully. "You'll tell them yourself someday, when you're ready."

My throat tasted sickly. "They'll never look at me the same again."

"Oh, come on. We're not living in the eighteen hundreds anymore. There's nothing wrong with being a lesbian, Ciara."

I said nothing. It was difficult to vocalise the fears that had kept me up nights for so many years. But Orla refused to accept they could become a reality.

"Ciara, I had no idea you liked girls but I've seen friends go through this," she said. "Parents grow to understand. Not always at first, but they come to realise it's completely normal. Mam and Dad love you."

"Because I'm perfect!" I spat. "I'm pretty, and I'm a champion runner and I got good results in school. Once they find out that I'm . . ."

"You're still perfect," she smiled, generously offering me the validation I needed.

I felt I was meeting her for the first time — a sister I never took the time to know.

Orla linked my arm and steered me away from the dorm. "Come on, let's go for a few beers. I haven't seen you properly since you arrived."

We have been as devoted as it is possible for two sisters to be since then. I was the first in the family to meet Thomas. I held Liam in my arms before our parents made it to the hospital. Her daughter's middle name is Ciara. Orla was friendly to Nikki at first, but not overly so. I called her on it after a few months, asking her why she had not embraced Nikki as I had Thomas. Her answer sums up the strength of our sisterly bond — "I like Nikki a lot, but you are my priority. Even if you end up married someday, she will only ever be my sister-in-law. You are my sister."

She always believed in me and, as we held hands on her couch, she didn't doubt my ability to be a mother someday. I pressed my teeth tightly together with worry. Maybe I'd messed everything up.

"I think Nikki is sick of waiting for me," I whispered.

For the first time, Orla's expression crinkled with worry. "What do you mean?"

"I think — I think she's having an affair."

Orla's eyes popped. The door opened behind her.

"Liam, get up to bed this instant," she snapped without moving. Hearing the edge in her voice, he pattered out without argument, closing the door again. Orla didn't take her eyes from me. "Why do you say that?"

I looked down at my fingers, intertwined with hers. "I found messages on her phone to another woman. They were talking about waiting until I left the house so they could talk. They met for dinner on nights Nikki told me she was doing other things. She lied to me."

Orla bit her lip. "That doesn't sound like the Nikki I know. What did she say when you confronted her?"

I shifted uneasily. "She didn't deny it. She didn't admit to it either."

We sat in silence for some time, until I couldn't bear to think about it any more. I gave a watery smile. "Aren't you going to offer your little sister some wine?"

Orla eyed me shrewdly. "Not a chance. You're the one talking about Gold. A bit of chocolate won't hurt you but Adrian would murder me if I let you get sloshed. We're all so proud of you, you know. You got a new personal best today – it's incredible, Ciara."

My phone bleeped and I whipped it out, the thought of seeing Nikki's name on the screen enough to fill me with hope. My pounding heart tightened with disappointment. I glanced up at Orla's expectant eyes.

"It's Stephen congratulating me on the PB," I said.

Suddenly I remembered Nikki's vicious accusation about my friend.

"Go to bed and rest," Orla said. "Tomorrow, you can ring Nikki and talk."

I nodded, but continued gazing at my phone. Nikki was trying to poison me against one of my best friends while carrying on covert meetings with a woman I'd never heard about.

Earlier that day, while I was sitting in the garden waiting for Nikki to come home and my own phone was charging, I had read the messages over and over. When I heard her key in the door, I knew I could not return her phone without taking action. So I copied the number into my phone.

Tomorrow, I knew, I would be calling Ann.

But, the next morning, I woke up with a pounding headache. I staggered out of bed, assuming it was a reaction to my fight with

Nikki, though I had slept long and dreamlessly. I met Kate on the stairs. She took one look at me and dashed ahead into the kitchen.

"Mammy, Aunty Ciara's a ghost!"

Orla's laugh shuddered to a halt. She was upon me before I could catch my reflection in the mirror, pressing a cooling hand to my forehead and ushering me up the stairs to bed.

"Kate, go get Daddy for Aunty Ciara, now."

My motherly sister bemoaned my pale skin and clammy hands as Thomas pressed his cold stethoscope onto my chest. I moaned pathetically and shoved him off. After more poking and prodding he told me I had contracted a throat infection and needed to starve and sleep for the next twenty-four hours.

"Lucky this didn't happen to you before the race, Ciara," was his parting reassurance as he left his worried wife to fawn over me.

I knew that it was very much because of yesterday that I was suffering. The race, the wine, the emotional upheaval. One tiny whiff of an infection and my body collapsed.

"Do you want me to ring Nikki, love?" Orla asked as she peeled the sticky sheets off me.

I shook my head gently so as not to dislodge the cold cloth she had placed there. "It's just a temperature," I croaked, though my shredded throat felt like fire. "I'll be fine."

I wanted Nikki, of course. But I was sick, weakened – who knew what I might say? Orla rang her anyway, and she messaged me promising to visit if I wanted her. I sent her a short reply: **Come over if you're willing to tell me the truth about Ann.**

She didn't respond and never appeared. My sister did not mention her again. I spent the next twenty-four hours writhing until finally the fever broke and my appetite returned. Orla insisted I stay until I fully recovered, and it was not until earlier this evening that I felt well enough to join the family downstairs for the evening news.

Just in time to see the Charrings Clinic story break.

Chapter seventeen

TRISH

When I discovered I was pregnant, three months after Alan boarded his plane to Australia, I vomited.

My body vibrated so viciously I threw up a second time. This was more than morning sickness. From the moment my pregnancy was confirmed, my life became one constant panic attack. I clutched at my head, wanting to be out, out, out of my body.

On some level, I must have suspected for weeks but I couldn't bring myself to contemplate it seriously. The changes in my body – I explained them away as physical reactions to the pain of losing Alan, and then my good friend Gerry. I eventually took the pregnancy test on a Friday evening, after work. I holed up in my bedroom for the weekend, screaming into my pillow.

Mum did not disturb me, thinking I was pining for Alan and of course Gerry, who only two months after Alan and I split threw himself off that cliff. Even my friends stayed away. We were taking some space, grieving separately. It left me alone with my dilemma. There was no way I would be able to look after a kid alone – I barely made enough in Orwell Travel to pay my mother rent. Emotionally, I was a wreck – an immature twenty-three-year-old, living in her old childhood room. How could I be anybody's mother?

These arguments, though they spun in my head all weekend, were not the real reason I decided to go to England. Objectivity, rationality, pros and cons. All irrelevant. The truth – and I think I knew it from the moment I watched the little lines surface on the pregnancy test – was that I just couldn't do it. It was nothing more complex than a base reaction that conquered me. I just couldn't do it.

Abortion was illegal in Ireland, and people like my mother would use all their strength to ensure it stayed that way. I didn't know anyone who had travelled abroad for a termination – or at least no one who admitted it.

So I began my internet search. At first, the easiest option seemed to be buying pills online. The sheer volume of choice made me doubt. For every offer of abortive medication, there were articles describing sickening side effects and failed terminations. Ultimately, I was too scared to ingest an unknown substance in my bedroom with my mother downstairs. Naively, I thought I would be safest with a doctor. The official statistics quoted thousands of women travelling from Ireland to England and beyond every year for abortions. I guess I assumed that, because it was legal abroad, dangerous back-alley clinics were a thing of the past.

Given the numbers travelling annually, I thought a termination would be accessible. In a way, it was, but the expense was beyond my means. The price of the procedure itself was far out of my range. Factor in last-minute flights, hotel rooms in England and other costs – buses, taxis and medications – it simply was not feasible. Perhaps if I saved up for a few months – but by then it would be too late.

Asking my mother for money was out of the question for obvious reasons. I contemplated borrowing from Ciara or Stephen, but they were still starting out in their careers. They wouldn't have much to give me. Besides, now that I was living with my mother, they were bound to ask why I possibly needed more money. I couldn't take the chance they would guess. I had just lost Gerry. I couldn't lose them too.

I wanted to get rid of the problem and continue as if it had never happened.

Ironically, it was my mother who gave me the idea. I was hiding in my room on the Sunday evening of that awful weekend, when she shouted up to me.

"Trish, I'm going to a pro-life meeting in the community hall. I'll be late. Don't wait up for me – you have work in the morning."

At first, her destination prompted a fresh bout of tears onto my already damp pillow. Suddenly, I sat upright, remembering. My mother's leadership of the largest pro-life organisation in Ireland was secured when she successfully got Beth and Lisa's friend expelled for having an abortion at the tender age of sixteen. They had cut off all contact with the girl, but I had heard rumours every so often that she helped other young girls in similar positions. A frantic Google search revealed nothing.

I sneaked into Beth's old bedroom and rummaged through the boxes of her old school stuff. It took about twenty minutes but eventually I found it. An old, dog-eared address book, decorated with pink stickers and graffitied with loopy scrawls of *Mrs Beth DiCaprio*. I flicked through to the end and found the name I was searching for. No address, but a landline telephone number.

With shaking hands, I dialled it.

"Hello, is that Mrs Walsh?" I asked.

"Yeah. Who wants to know?"

"I'm an old school friend of your daughter's," I said breathlessly. "I am in the area and was thinking of dropping by, if she is around."

"No, Abby doesn't live here anymore. She has a house with her husband on Sycamore Lane."

It didn't take much persuasion for her mother to give me the exact address. I didn't even have to identify myself. I scribbled it down before hanging up, then sat staring at the address for hours. The enormity of going through with it petrified me. I had to do it as soon as possible before I lost my nerve. So the next day, straight after work, I told Mum I was meeting Ciara for dinner. I got the bus out to Sycamore Lane.

The neighbourhood was more well-to-do than I had imagined. The row of semi-detached houses was tidy, with Mercedes and BMWs parked outside most of the flower-studded driveways. I walked hurriedly down the road toward Abby's house, passing a man with a panting dog and a woman pushing a buggy. I looked away from them.

Abby recognised me when she opened the door.

"I know you." Those were her first words to me.

I would not have recognised her as the lanky girl who hung around with Beth and Lisa years ago. She had put on weight since then, but not in an unattractive way. Her figure-hugging dress complemented her curvaceous figure. Her looped earrings and thick bangles were gaudy. The mere possibility that she could betray me to my family sliced through my abdomen. I bent over and threw up on her feet.

She was kind to me. She ushered me inside and sat me into a chair in the kitchen, pressing a glass of water into my hand. There is something comforting about conversations at a kitchen table. Maybe it's an Irish thing. As for me, I was headed to England.

I surveyed her kitchen. It was an odd combination of modern and cheap. With a marble island in the centre and minimalist fittings, it gleamed. But the tacky ornaments on the windowsill undid any impression of style.

I had finished the water by the time she cleaned up my mess on the front porch. She made us tea without speaking and sat opposite me, eying me shrewdly.

"Where do I know you from?" she asked eventually.

No point hiding it. "I'm Trish Olden. Beth's younger sister."

She threw her head back and laughed. She laughed so hard it was unnerving. Finally, she recovered and stood, putting her hands on her hips triumphantly.

"Well, isn't this some karmic redemption?" she said loudly.

"What do you mean?" I clutched my mug nervously as she

leaned against the kitchen counter.

"Love, there is only one reason why young women show up at my door to throw up on my shoes. You're pregnant, aren't you? Deirdre Olden's daughter coming to me for help."

"Please, Abby." I realised I was shaking. "Don't tell her about this."

"Oh, I wouldn't dream of it," she said, her teeth gleaming in a way that made me feel like a vulnerable Little Red Riding Hood. "So tell me," she folded her arms, "why don't you go to England?"

"I can't afford it."

"Have you thought about getting a loan? Although I hardly think you can ask your mother for money."

That set her off again, and I was on the verge of leaving when she collected herself and took her seat.

"Listen, Trish —" she smiled and pushed a plate of biscuits across the table to me, "there's a reason you have come to me. You must have heard that I can help you. And it's true. I can. Think of me as a charity. I know what a huge responsibility it is to have a child. Not everyone who gets pregnant can cope — whether for financial or emotional reasons. I'm not telling you to have an abortion . . ."

Instinctively, I flinched at the word, my mother's image sparking in front of my eyes.

". . . but if you do decide that's what you need to do, there is a clinic in the outskirts of London. It's small and little known. They won't keep records so no one will find out. There's accommodation around the corner that's affordable for a night or two if you don't want to come home immediately."

I shook my head. "Even at that . . ."

"Trish," Abby said solemnly, "I'll lend you the money."

I stared at her. "Why?"

Abby stood and busied herself at the sink. The sunlight streamed through the window with the noise of a distant lawnmower. "I know what it's like to do this without help."

I took my chance. "Abby, what happened after you left school? How did you end up in this lovely house?"

She rotated on the spot, smiling. It is a different, harder smile than before. Her cheeks tautened and her eyes remained large. I was wary. But her reply was a gel to my burning heart so I let myself believe.

"I found my vocation from my own suffering. I've built a life for myself. I have a beautiful home, a devoted husband. It didn't come easy. I was lost for a long time. It happens to everyone at some point. For you, that's now. Having someone to help will make all the difference. Don't get me wrong, you'll repay the money."

I nodded furiously. It seemed such a reasonable request at the time.

"We can work out a payment plan so you won't be under any pressure. Take a couple of sick days from work, or go at the weekend. You won't be alone. I'll be with you. This time next week, this nightmare can be behind you."

I arrived in London a complete mess.

I had never been abroad. We could not afford anything beyond a trip to Galway when I was a kid. The airplane terrified me. I gripped the seat, breathing deeply while the man beside me turned his head away, embarrassed by my display of fear. I took his wordless criticism on board. Stay silent. Show no emotions. Feel nothing.

In Gatwick Airport, I found the pace intimidating. Men swung laptop bags onto their shoulders as they strutted ahead. Women pulled wheelie-cases with frightening intensity. I felt old.

This was not an adventure. Aside from my boss, no one knew I was out of the country. The plan was for Abby, who flew over a few days before to help some other unfortunates, to meet me at the airport. All I had to do was make it to the arrivals area. I followed the crowd like a nameless drone.

I meshed in with the myriad of other travellers, yet felt completely alone. They were coming here on business, or as tourists. Perhaps to visit family and friends. My eyes darted around at the women. Were any of them there for the same reason I was? Could they tell from my jagged gait, my shivering body, that I was just like them? I shook my head, thinking of the man beside me on the plane. Don't feel.

Abby was waiting in Arrivals. She signalled me over but did not greet me with a hug or even a handshake. She beckoned me to follow her, which I did, gratefully. I watched her as we weaved our way to the exit. She was wearing a chic dress with a leather jacket zipped tightly up the front. I envied her dark leather boots and handbag. I pushed down the thought that the money I owed her might end up lining the pockets of next year's designers.

She stopped abruptly on the pavement. I nearly crashed into her. The air was a different cold to home. Rather than a damp closeness, the wind cut into me. My skin froze.

"Are we getting a taxi?" I asked, anxious to get inside from the frost.

Abby ignored my shivering. "No," she answered curtly. "A friend is collecting us."

"A friend?" I repeated, a pitch higher than I had intended.

As if suddenly remembering why I was there with her, Abby faced me, her expression softening. "Don't worry," she said quietly. "This is all part of the service."

"We agreed a price," I said, more bravely than I felt. The whole journey had ended up more expensive than I had anticipated, even before she tacked on the extortionate interest. I had to make sure she wasn't going to add on a list of extra expenses at the end of the trip.

"All included." Her mouth flinched oddly, as if she was trying to smile. She put her hand on my arm. It did nothing to placate me. "Here she is now."

A car pulled up, screeching to a halt beside us. It was dark blue, an almost navy colour, but otherwise nondescript. Roomy inside, it was devoid of any personal touches. There were no CDs or air fresheners. It was clean of even the odd bit of paper or drink bottle. It was not a taxi, but Abby treated it as such. She ushered me hurriedly into the back seat and slid in beside me. The driver, an older woman with a short bob, sped off without greeting us.

As she drove through the streets, Abby began to explain the process of the day. I jerked my head pointedly toward the driver.

"Chill out, Trish. You're not the first girl Polly has driven around, is she, Polly?" Abby slapped the driver's shoulder with unnecessary force.

I flinched. Polly grunted and kept driving. I relaxed slightly. I was obviously nobody to her, and that was the way I wanted it to stay.

"Once you check into your hotel you'll have a few hours before you have to be at the clinic. I'll come for you at about one o'clock. When you're done, I'll take you to the hotel to sleep it off. Most women are fine by the next day. Polly will collect you about eight tomorrow morning so you'll be in plenty of time for your flight. Back for an afternoon of work."

I thought about Josh, and how interested he had been in my time off. I rarely took holidays, and as a travel agent he found it incredulous that I had never been out of the country.

Abby insisted the clinic could only take me Thursday afternoon, so I asked for Thursday and Friday morning off work. I had considered avoiding any mention of London, frightened he might suspect. But Ireland is too small a place – I could easily bump into a client or someone Josh knew at the airport. If he found out I lied, it would cause greater suspicion.

So I chose an excuse he was unlikely to crack. I made up a friend. Catherine. She was an old neighbour, I told him, who had invited me to visit her in London for her graduation from veterinary college. It was a random story, but it fell from my mouth when Josh asked why I wasn't staying on for the weekend to see the sights.

"Oh, she'll be spending time with family. I'm better off getting home, Josh."

He had shrugged and insisted that, if I decided to stay, he wouldn't begrudge me the Friday afternoon off work. "You should treat yourself, especially after your break-up with Alan and your friend passing away. Take a few more days off. It would do you good, Trish. You've been pale recently."

I thanked him for his concern and busied myself with papers, my head down. Josh treated me as a daughter, one who needed protecting. He worked like a Trojan and trusted me with his workload but in the quieter moments was great for gossipy chats, and was forever offering me life advice. Taking more holidays was one of them. He was thrilled I was visiting London and pressed a worn *Lonely Planet* guidebook into my hands as I left, excitement stretched across his face, as if I was off on a Columbus-style adventure.

I flicked through the guidebook on the plane to keep me occupied, but knew this was not a trip on which I would see any sights. Abby made the same suggestion, incredibly.

"You have three hours," she said, sliding across the seat as I got out. She stuck her head out of the car window. "Why don't you get a bus into the centre of London, see Buckingham Palace or the Tower of London?"

It was beyond me to fake enthusiasm.

"Suit yourself," she shrugged. "Remember, you're booked under my name."

I opened my mouth to reply, but Polly sped away. Alone on the street, I blinked at the hotel in front of me. It looked respectable expect for the neon sign which was missing letters. I was apprehensive about going inside, but too scared to stay outdoors. I wished Abby had stayed with me.

The man behind reception was foreign – I had no idea what nationality. He scratched my name off a list and looked at me with dead eyes as he dropped an old-fashioned key into my hand.

I climbed two flights of stairs and unlocked the door at the end of the corridor. The room was clean but basic. It lacked any sort of comfort. I walked over to the small window. The view was the brick wall of the building next door. I sat on the bed. It sank beneath me with a creak.

I don't know how long I sat there, but soon had to rush into the en-suite bathroom to throw up. While I knew I was doing the right thing – I couldn't have a baby – morning sickness acted as the great doubter for me. It confirmed that my body was changing, that there was something inside of me. It made me question my certainties. But it also weakened me physically, and I never had the strength in those moments of misgivings to act on them.

I staggered into the main room and fell onto the bed. I lay still, staring at the off-white ceiling.

When Abby at last called me I proceeded downstairs with such trepidation that I tripped twice. The second time I slammed down, cracking my wrist off the ground. No one was around. No one saw. I picked myself up and cradled my arm, continuing down to the ground floor. Abby stood back from the counter where she was talking in a low voice to the dead-eyed receptionist. She smiled almost fondly, reverting to the friendly Abby I first met in her house.

We travelled in silence. I had no idea where I was being taken or what to expect. My stomach sloshed. This was actually happening. I was alone, but for Abby, who was inspecting her fingernails, and the seemingly mute Polly. They probably shepherded at least three girls a day to their appointments. I felt the loneliness with a guttural intensity. I breathed deeply. All I had to do was seal my mind to the present and get through the next few hours.

During my initial research, I had read the website of one of the more prominent abortion clinics in London. The one I could never afford. I had asked Abby about using the money she was lending me to have the procedure there. Its website was reassuring, and I would have felt looked after and safe. But she had shook her head with an amused grin.

"Trish, where do you think I get the money to lend you? Charrings Clinic knows not every woman can afford an abortion. They put up the capital."

I said nothing. I had considered applying for a credit card and just doing the whole thing myself, without Abby. But aside from the clinics and last-minute flights being prohibitively dear, I would be alone. I did not have the emotional strength for it and, at fourteen weeks, was into my second trimester. I was running out of time, and scared, so I stuck with Abby.

She brought up the money again in the car.

"Remember," she said, interpreting my silence, "what you have borrowed from me is also covering your flights, your hotel, me and Polly. Charrings is a bargain, compared to what you'd have to pay in the more well-known places. You can repay the money in the time we agreed, instead of having to put it up-front."

I nodded listlessly. I was aware of the benefits of doing this Abby's way, even with the interest she loaded onto the repayment price. The most important thing was that I was not by myself on the journey. So I jumped quickly from surprise to utter terror when Abby bid me goodbye outside a housing estate in a sprawling suburb.

I looked around, not understanding. Where was the clinic? More pressingly, why was Abby leaving me?

She noticed my fingers grasped tightly around the door handle of the car, and my shaking leg.

"Trish," she put a hand on my knee but it would not stop twitching, "this is it. Charrings is in there – in Number 10."

I followed her pointing finger to an ordinary house in the middle of the row. Two storeys, semi-detached, with a small, unkempt front garden.

"It's . . . a house?" I stuttered stupidly.

"Of course," Abby replied with a mixture of amusement and annoyance. "This is a low-key clinic. It's for women – like you, I might add – who don't want anyone to know what they're doing." Her tone changed abruptly. "You think it's wrong, don't you? Abortion."

I said nothing. She was right. My mother was head of Pro-Life Ireland. The act was illegal at home. I was raised to be against it. I certainly understood the arguments. Without it, a little baby would be born in nine months. But I had to escape the situation I was in, not just for me but for any future children I might have when I was ready – financially prepared, married and able to give them a real life. The abstract arguments of right and wrong evaporated as I stared at the house. Abortion was my only way out. I had to agree with it. I needed it.

Abby sneered. "Even if you could afford it, would you really

147

march up to a world-renowned abortion clinic in central London, with protesters constantly hanging around outside?"

My legs went weak at the thought. Abby correctly interpreted my silence.

"Exactly. You may not want to admit it, but you judge women who do this. You don't want to be associated with them. It's a quiet service you want, so you can go back to your life and pretend this never happened. Avoid the ridicule you know others would fling at you because you would do the same thing to them if fortunes were reversed."

I opened my mouth to object, but Abby suddenly yielded. "The clinic is all set up in there. Go in, give them your name. I'll be here in an hour to collect you."

"That soon? It'll be done in an hour?"

She nodded. "It's a short procedure. Shouldn't take more than fifteen minutes. Wait for me. Don't go wandering off."

"But – you're not coming with me?"

She looked at her watch. "Polly and I have to collect our five o'clock. Good luck, Trish. You'll be fine."

I continued trembling as I emerged from the car. I imagined Abby referring to me in that numerical way. *Sorry I'm late – my one o'clock had a freak-out and I had to calm her down.*

I glanced up and down the street but it was deserted. No kids playing soccer on the road, no mothers with prams. No elderly neighbours leaning on walls, chatting about everything and nothing, the way they do at home.

I watched Abby's car speed away before walking up the driveway. Weeds poked up through the cracked pavement. I walked tentatively to the door, thinking about Abby's line that it was all a show – a pretence to spare judgemental hypocrites like me the torture of exposure. There was no bell. I shivered.

Even as I lifted the rusting knocker, I knew this was not a place where I should be handing over my body for surgery.

Chapter eighteen

TRISH

The woman who answered the door did not smile. She beckoned me in, blowing a bubble of chewing gum. Some of it stuck to her lip as she sucked it back into her mouth.

The reception was a skinny table in the hallway. It blocked access to the rest of the house so I was forced to stop in front of it. The woman pulled in her stomach and shuffled sideways between the end of the table and wall, to get to her chair on the other side. She was a girl, really. I doubted if she was eighteen. She shouldn't be working in place like this, I thought crossly, then immediately chastised myself. This was what Abby meant when she accused me of being judgemental.

I gave the girl my name. She directed me past the stairs behind her and through a door off the hall into a makeshift waiting room. I was alone, which calmed me a little. I rummaged in my bag, checking I had all the necessary items Abby had suggested. A couple of changes of underwear. Sanitary towels. As I was fourteen weeks, it was to be a surgical procedure. There might be excess bleeding.

I remembered when Josh's wife became pregnant with their first child. He raced into work one day and, although I indicated to him that I was in the middle of a call with an important client, he lingered around my desk until I hung up. He ordered me into his office and for a moment I thought I was in trouble. When he announced it to me, I squealed with delight and hugged him fiercely. But his next words, those were the ones I remembered while sitting in the waiting room of the Charrings house. "We've been dying to tell everyone for ages, but we had to wait until we were twelve weeks. That's when it becomes real."

I was two weeks over that magical mark and yet I felt nothing. No kicking or squirming, or any connection to what was inside me. No joy. Nothing but fear.

A man wearing a white coat appeared in the room. "Patricia Olden?"

I was out of my seat swiftly, relieved it was finally happening. I needed it to be done before I could dwell on it any more.

"You can call me Trish," I said, shaking his hand.

He smiled blandly. I followed him back into the hall and past the table where the receptionist was slouched over a magazine. The stairs groaned under my feet as we made our way up. I took in my surroundings with increasing foreboding. The walls were streaked and the carpets threadbare.

He led me into a small bedroom. It was decorated like a doctor's surgery with an office table and chair in the corner. A slim hospital bed lined the far wall. A plastic curtain hung from a rail around the bed. It was off-white and grubby at the bottom where it trailed on the floor.

"Are you allergic to any medication, Patricia?" he asked.

He did not look at me, but sat at his computer and scrolled down through a document on screen. He was tall, and though thin he was muscular. With a tanned complexion and long eyelashes, he was oddly striking. He could have been attractive, had the intensity emanating from him felt kind, rather than hard.

"No," I whispered, my breathing coming ragged now. I did not feel safe, and the enormity of what I was about to do was overpowering me.

150

"I know," said the doctor, who had yet to introduce himself. "I have all your information here, but that's one we always ask a second time, just in case." He winked, as if revealing himself to be a true professional. "Now, if I can ask you to remove your bottoms and hop up on the bed there."

I looked at the bed, then back to the doctor. "We're doing it now?"

"No time like the present."

I stayed seated, recalling the website of the prominent abortion clinic. It had described scans. A full consultation. Care and planning and a nurse to hold my hand.

I wasn't prepared but found myself shuffling over to the bed and pulling the curtain around me. I stripped off my trousers – a baggy tracksuit, at Abby's recommendation – and my underwear. Tears pricked my eyes. Every waking and dreaming thought I had experienced in the past week had been of this moment.

The curtain whipped aside. I clambered up on the bed. When I looked at the doctor he had a surgical mask covering his face. I wondered whether it was necessary. I swallowed. I had so many questions about what was about to happen to me but I did not have the wherewithal to ask. All my courage was taken up just existing in this strange reality.

"A sedative will be the best option for you," the doctor said. "No need to knock you out completely at fourteen weeks."

His accent was tricky to place. I thought it was English, but I couldn't be certain. I simply lay there. When he touched my arm, his fingers were cold.

I jumped as a needle pierced my skin.

The doctor laughed. "Come on, now. You're all right. It will kick in momentarily."

Within minutes, I began to experience a strange sort of slackening in my muscles. My mind spun too.

Then it started.

I floated in and out of consciousness. The pain tore at me. As I moaned, Abby lifted a cloth from my head and replaced it with a cold one. I tried to push her away with all of my ineffectual strength.

The sedative had worn off hours ago but I felt as if something foreign was still running through my veins. Without needing Abby to tell me, I knew it was a fever. What had he done to me, that man? I had read there might be cramping during a surgical abortion, but he had entered me with force, brutally. I was remembering other descriptions of the procedure from the professional clinic's website – medication to soften and dilate the cervix, painkillers. I had tried to scream but the sedative had affected my tongue. I had no control of it. He had reached under his white coat, and whipped his leather belt from his trouser buckles.

"Bite on this, then, if you can't handle it," he said harshly as he shoved it between my teeth.

I crunched down as he ducked between my legs, his cold hands holding me firmly in place.

Finally, it was done, and he was by my side again.

"Some people have a lower threshold of pain," he said as he put his hands under my arms and pulled me into an upright position, the belt slipping from my mouth. I flopped over and he lowered me back down on the bed.

"Fine, stay there for a few minutes until you feel better." He tossed a blanket on my legs and disappeared behind the curtain.

Sometime later – I have no idea how long – Abby entered the room. She covered my forehead with her hand. It felt beautifully cool. The next few hours are a blur. I remember her exchanging words with the doctor. Not harsh words, but urgent. She assisted me down the stairs – I recall stumbling a number of times and her cursing as she struggled to keep us steady. There was a car. I assumed Polly was in the front but the driver did not speak. Then I was in bed, sleeping. For how long, I don't know.

I woke, thirsty, in the dark. I sat up to see Abby dozing in a chair under the window. I tried to sit up but the effort was weakening and I collapsed onto the pillow. I had felt this way once before – when I had glandular fever at the age of sixteen. But this time there was sharp pain in my stomach. Had something gone wrong? Bile rose in my throat – what if he had not removed it properly? I cried out and Abby leapt from the seat.

"Trish, are you okay?"

I wanted to scream that no, I was far from okay. I was scared and hurt and very, very ill. That doctor – he never told me his name – had savaged me, I could feel it. Did I have blood poisoning from a dirty instrument? Excessive bleeding from the roughness of his extraction? Something was wrong with me.

I grabbed Abby's arm. "Hospital," I croaked.

She shook her head. "You don't need a hospital, Trish. You're just experiencing some after-pains."

I shook my head, and spoke in what I hoped was a firmer pitch. "I need a doctor."

Abby brushed a stray hair from my face. "Trish, I've done this a thousand times. You need to rest. Here, drink up."

The glass of water sparkled through the dark room as she tipped it into my mouth. The relief was immense and for a moment my trust in her was renewed. But as I lay my head down, a slicing sensation, more twisting than the worst period pain, drew in my breath sharply. A tear ran down my cheek.

"Abby, please," I begged. "I need help."

"You need sleep," she insisted, lifting my head to tip more water into my mouth. As I tried to resist, she held up two large pills. "For the pain. You'll be better in the morning, I promise."

I wept as I swallowed them and let her lower my head onto the pillow. Then, mercifully, I slept.

Over the next two days my body burned as I tossed in the sheets. Abby was always there but never willing to get me medical help beyond generic painkillers.

On Friday morning, Abby messaged my boss from my phone to tell him I had decided to stay in London for the weekend after all. She read out his reply which was not only understanding but congratulatory. Finally, I was taking time for myself, enjoying my life, spreading my wings. I buried my head in my pillow and tried with all my effort to fall asleep, away from this torment. It did not take long.

After about two days of blurriness, I finally emerged into the shining clarity of full consciousness. I could hear Abby in the bathroom. I sat up and took a sip of my water. My head swam, but it was different to the past few days. I knew it was only from a lack of food, and hours spent lying in bed. I no longer had a racing fever. That had broken, and I felt somehow free, as if the torture of the last few days had finally ended.

Abby's tired face twitched into a smile when she came out of the bathroom to see me sitting upright in bed.

"Trish!" she gushed, rushing over to sit beside me. She touched the back of her hand to my forehead. "You look much better."

"What day is it?" I asked.

"It's Saturday morning," she announced like it was an achievement. "Honestly, you've been sleeping on and off for two days."

"Why didn't you get me a doctor, Abby?"

"Trish," she did not break eye contact, "you got an infection. One that I knew you would fight off with a few days of rest. A doctor would have said exactly the same thing."

"Why did I get an infection?"

She shrugged. "It happens. Not often, but I have seen it. Nausea and cramping are common – don't worry if you experience those for another few days. But would you really have had me get a doctor? Brought you to hospital? I thought you wanted this kept confidential?"

"I do. But who would have found out?"

"Don't be so naïve," Abby said crossly. She began packing bits of clothing and toiletries into a bag. "Abortion is a constant hot topic. It never goes away. You don't know who would see you in the hospital, what nosy pro-lifer is hanging around waiting to expose you." She stopped her shuffling suddenly and spun around to face me. "I did you a favour, Trish," she spat. "I've spent days in this room with you."

My default emotion of guilt was quashed by an anger I could not contain. "I didn't ask you to do that, Abby. You're not a doctor. Don't Charrings Clinic have an aftercare service?"

"Now you listen to me, you stuck-up bitch!" Abby was suddenly by my side, leaning over me. "I have done more for you than I needed to do. I took care of you while you were sick. I protected you because I knew you wanted this to be private. I have paid for your extra nights here and booked you onto a flight tomorrow evening at no extra cost. It's fine for you, sitting in bed like Lady Muck. I'm the one making this happen for you, and don't you forget it." She wagged a finger in my face.

I nodded, frightened by the fury in her eyes.

She sat back, her demeanour settling. "Why don't you have a shower? It will freshen you up. I'll go get you some food. You'll need to get your strength up for the journey home tomorrow."

After she left, I flopped down on the bed.

With the lucidity of aftermath, with the procedure finished and my fever dissipated, I finally saw what I should always have known. Abby was not one of the good guys. She was not defending women's rights or giving desperate girls a way out. Her game was extortion. The amount of money I had to repay her over the next few months must be triple her costs.

She took me to a dirty house in the middle of nowhere. I was so scared, I let a man who had not identified himself thrust a hand into me and wrench the foetus out of me with such force I had passed out, even with sedation. Abby was right – in the cold light of unmedicated reflection, I was glad she had not brought me into the open, calling to doctors and nurses that I had an abortion. You can't go anywhere these days – who knows who would have seen me? But she did not do that for me. It was to protect the clinic.

I lifted my phone and connected to the internet. I searched for 'Charrings Clinic' but there were no results. It was as if it didn't exist. I closed my eyes. Why hadn't I done a search for it at home in Dublin? Deep down, had I been afraid of what I might find?

There was cramping still, but it was a duller sort of discomfort, not the outright pain of the previous two days. I clambered out of bed, determined to leave this place tonight. But the exhaustion of the fever coupled with lack of sustenance was immense. I would need more rest before I boarded a plane.

I managed to shower and put on a clean set of clothes. When I came out of the bathroom Abby was back, changing the sheets for me. I thanked her for the food she had brought but when she sat into her chair in the corner, I insisted she leave.

"You need sleep too, Abby. I'll be fine now, don't worry about me."

She did not argue and I was glad when she was gone.

I tried to eat. I managed a few pieces of dry bread but it churned in my stomach. There was another pain too, a stabbing one, lower, in my womb. I placed a hand there, but it didn't feel empty compared to a few days ago. The baby within me had never seemed real, and still didn't now. Perhaps I was devoid of any emotional or human connection. No wonder Alan left me. There was something seriously wrong with me. I barely had the energy to weep.

I sat in Abby's chair in front of the brick-wall view. It was over. The relief that flooded through me mingled with another sensation. I felt violated.

I bent in the seat. I had no right to feel that way. The abortion had been my choice. No one forced me to use Abby – I chose her rather than revealing the truth to my mother, or my friends. I made the decision not to ask for help or to borrow money to travel to a legitimate abortion clinic. I did not consider any option, other than termination.

I rose from my chair, unable to sit with these thoughts any longer. Despite this being of my own making, I felt damaged. My body had been invaded, treated with disregard. I had been kept here by Abby, unable to move with the sickness flowing through me.

I considered going to a doctor before leaving England. But my flight was tomorrow and Abby would be back for me in the morning. There was no way I could visit my local GP when I got home – he treated my entire family. It was too much of a risk.

The worst was over, I convinced myself. I didn't need a doctor.

I climbed into bed and stared at the ceiling. A strange calmness descended upon me. This experience had changed me but I wasn't going to let it destroy me. I was going to repay Abby everything I owed her as soon as possible, and then cut her from my life.

With such empowering thoughts, I slipped toward slumber. My hand caressed my twisting gut. The physical pain would dissipate eventually, I knew. But my insides would never be at peace, because that was where I would keep this secret. Locked away deep inside, where no one would ever find it.

Chapter nineteen

STEPHEN

I don't sleep.

I have considered asking Lisa about spending part of our remaining savings on a more comfortable couch, but she would simply smirk. Besides, what would I say to my friends when they ask why we got a new one? They know we are short of money. *Lisa won't let me sleep in the bed so I need a longer couch.*

But I have a feeling that even if I had the most luxurious mattress in the world, I wouldn't be able to sleep tonight. The look on Lisa's face when she intentionally pushed me down the stairs is imprinted on my mind like a luminous neon sign.

I reach into my trouser pocket and take out the business card. It is slightly crumpled following my fall down the stairs. I run my finger gently over the words.

I have had this business card for years. While I was still working in TJ Simons, there was an active *Women in Business* network. The male accountants were encouraged to attend the lectures and discussion groups they organised, though we sat through them with a mixture of indifference and underlying condescension. One afternoon, a woman from the charity *Heal the Hurt* came to discuss domestic violence.

At that time, I hadn't even met Lisa. My experience of violence in the home took the form of a father-son relationship, but that wasn't what the *Heal the Hurt* woman wanted to discuss. Her talk was a warning to other women – how to see the signs before it's too late, how easy it is to get sucked in and not realise that you are being abused long before the hitting begins.

"Emotional, spiritual, financial abuse," she listed on her fingers like a teacher. "Not only are these real, they are often precursors to physical violence. Be vigilant, and speak out as soon as you can. The longer you leave it, the harder it is to acknowledge."

I remember some of the women on my team sniggering on the stairs as we returned to our offices after the talk – "Next time Barry asks me do the dishes . . ." one grinned.

"Or when Oisín tells me to hurry up getting ready . . ." another added.

I butted into their conversation. "Sounds like you should ditch those losers before they get violent." We all laughed at how dramatic the talk had been. I wonder now if there had been anyone else descending those stairs with us, searching for the strength to speak out to a friend about abuse at home, but who clammed up on hearing our mockery.

I stare at the business card. The woman had handed them out after her talk. Having politely slid it into the back of my wallet, I promptly forgot about it. A few weeks ago, I was ten cent short at the supermarket and began digging around in my wallet for any bits of loose change. I pulled out my blood donor card, an old coffee shop loyalty card with only two of the potential ten coffee cups stamped, and the *Heal the Hurt* card.

Terrified Lisa would find it, I marched over to the nearest bin and was about to throw it away when I paused. For some reason, though I had no intention of calling them, I couldn't quite bring myself to toss it.

Back in the car, I tucked it away inside the car safety booklet gathering dust in the side pocket of the driver's door.

Tonight, when I finally heard Lisa's snores upstairs, I sneaked outside as quietly as I could and retrieved the card. I held my breath as I returned to the house, but her snoring continued to flow lightly through the air.

The card is basic. It has a white background and blue logo on one side identifying the charity, with a generic helpline number and email address printed in bold on the other side.

I glance up, half-expecting to see Lisa's silhouette in the doorframe. Nothing. Her snoring has stopped, but that happens as she tosses and turns in the night. I lick my dry lips. Have I reached a turning point? Pushing me down the stairs is a new low for Lisa. Perhaps it will be enough to give me the courage to act.

I think about Gerry, as I often do when my situation takes a turn for the worst. Trish and Ciara believe he took the easy way out, but I see the heroic nature of his actions. He couldn't control the illness devouring him, but he could still have a say about when he would go. My own bravery does not compare to his. I have no bravery.

What would I say if I called these people? Would they be surprised to hear a male voice on the end of the line?

The woman who gave us the talk in TJ Simons had focused on women being abused by their male partners, as that was what they overwhelmingly saw. However, she did make the point that the opposite happens. "There are examples of abuse across the spectrum – in all types of relationships. Never be afraid to contact us."

But I am afraid. If I make the call, they may offer me some comforting words, or give me instructions as if I haven't already thought of them – *just leave, walk out the door, stand up for yourself.* But what good would that do? If Lisa finds out, I dare not imagine how she would react. It's not worth the risk.

Even if I could somehow man up and face the fear, I still don't think I could make the call. I am embarrassed.

My legs carry me without forethought to the kitchen. I reach into the drawer under the sink and pick out a box of matches.

Striking the side of the box, it illuminates with not only a flash, but a small whoosh.

I stare at it.

The card wavers in my hand. I cannot take any chances. Lisa is too volatile right now. I need to see this out, wait until she calms down. Maybe then I will consider leaving, or telling a friend, or phoning a charity anonymously. Until that happens, I cannot let her find this card.

I move it a fraction and the flame catches it. Shaking the match out, I watch the card burn until there is nothing but cinders in the sink. I blow away the ash and drop the remainder of the match in the bin.

Then, without feeling guilty or ashamed – without feeling anything – I walk back into the living room and curl my knees into my chest. I squeeze as best I can onto the couch.

Lisa is asleep, I tell myself. Nothing more will happen tonight, and everything else is tomorrow's problem. With hours of peace ahead of me, I finally feel my eyes start to droop close. I ignore the twinging in my neck, and concentrate on drifting off to a safe place all on my own.

Chapter twenty

CIARA

It is the morning after the Charrings Clinic story breaks before I feel truly back to normal. I take it easy for the day, a bit of Pilates in my room my most vigorous activity. Without training to occupy me, my mind feels as restless as my body.

I watch the baby drift off in Orla's left arm as her right hand continues to wipe up the kitchen counter.

"I'm sorry," I say, when she finally places the baby in my arms to make dinner. "I hadn't intended staying more than a night or two."

"Don't be stupid," she murmurs absent-mindedly as she carries armfuls of vegetables from the fridge to the kitchen counter.

I coo into Donal's soft skin. He has lost that immediate new-born baby smell, but he is still intoxicating. That is because he is my darling nephew, I think crossly, not because I crave one of these little creatures for myself.

I balance him carefully as I message Nikki, apologising for my long absence and describing my illness self-pityingly. I hope she will be softened into explaining about the mysterious Ann, but she merely responds that she is glad I am feeling better. I ask if I can call over at the weekend. She responds positively, and mentions that there had been a stream of congratulatory visitors during the week. I am not surprised – I have been inundated with messages from well-wishers. Now that I am better, I go through each individually, explaining my late reply by reference to the fever and thanking them profusely for their backing.

When I have replied to the last one, I scroll down to the number I saved under the pseudonym "**Homewrecker**". Despite her lies, I feel guilty about sneaking around behind Nikki's back. Time has tempered the initial shock of seeing those messages. But while there might be an innocent explanation, I have yet to hear it. If Nikki isn't going to give me a straight answer, I'll have to find it out myself.

The problem is, I have yet to come up with a way of starting a dialogue when I ring Ann. I contemplate coming right out and identifying myself as Nikki's partner. But what are the chances she'll do anything other than hang up and block my number?

I know nothing about her, other than her first name. I have no pretext under which to contact her. I need to clear my head. I get to my feet, baby Donal dozing undisturbed in my arms.

"I'm in the way here, Orla," I say as she scoots around me to throw carrot peelings in the bin behind me, while yelling into the other room at Liam and Kate to stop their messing. "Why don't I take this little guy out for a quick stroll around the block? I could use the fresh air."

"Good idea. I don't suppose you want to take the other two terrors with you?"

I hesitate a second too long and she laughs.

"Don't worry about it. Even if you were in the full of your health, all three of them at once is tough going."

I lay the baby in his pram, and tuck in the blankets around him. As soon as I step out the door and breathe the cool, late-September air into my lungs, I realise how ill I have been. My legs are unsteady beneath me and my head light. The air helps and by the time I reach the end of the road, I am feeling stronger. I watch Donal's stomach rise and fall with his rhythmic sleeping breaths. Babies sleep so soundly, so peacefully. It almost seems a punishment that such angels have to grow up into the pressured world of adulthood.

I think about Trish's little nephew and how different Orla's life would be if Donal had been born with Edward's Syndrome. It should put my own troubles into perspective. But even empathy for a sick baby cannot rid my mind of Nikki, her arm draped around a beautiful woman named Ann, both of them snickering together at my ignorance.

By the time we reach the park, I have finalised my plan. It is a long shot, but it is all I have. I sit on a park bench, looking around to make sure that no one is near, and double-check the brakes on Donal's buggy. I pull his blankets around him. I take out my phone and stare at the name "**Homewrecker**" for a few moments. I press the call button and hold it to my ear.

After one ring, a female voice answers with a friendly lilt.

"Hello?"

I swallow. "Hi, is that Ann . . . O'Sullivan?" I use the first surname I can think of, that of the poor girl from the news last night.

"No, this is Ann Preston."

It is amazing the personal information people will give away to total strangers if prompted. Now I have a surname. I curl my fist into a ball and punch the air victoriously, trying not to let my grin colour my response.

"Oh, I'm sorry. I must have dialled the wrong number."

I have decided that the only way to ease my conscience about going behind Nikki's back in this way is to give her the benefit of the doubt. Despite the lies and sneaking around, there could be some explanation I have not considered. Nikki's main groups of friends are the crowd from her teaching diploma, and the teachers at her school. I take a chance with this Ann Preston.

"Oh – I may have got the surname wrong. The Ann I am trying to reach, she's a teacher. That's not you?" I add an innocent inflection.

"No, I'm sorry. I'm not a teacher. You definitely have the wrong number."

I delay with a fake cough, trying unsuccessfully to think of another angle. I don't want to arouse her suspicions so I apologise once more and hang up. Reaching into the buggy, I lift out the baby. He wriggles but does not wake. I rock him tenderly, for my own comfort as much as his.

Suddenly, my phone rings. I jerk at the sound and grab it up eagerly. A name flashes on the screen. It's Nikki.

My jaw tenses. What are the chances she would ring at this moment, right after I had rung Ann? Does she somehow know? Is she there with Ann? Had she heard my voice through the phone?

A man jogs by me with his dog. "You know, the traditional thing to do is answer it!" he calls back with a good-natured chuckle.

I look up at him, confused, then down at the phone I am holding at arm's length like a grenade. I am tempted to shout a smart remark but can think of none before the man runs out of sight.

I let the call ring out, and sit staring at it for another minute. No voicemail. The cool air whips around me with renewed vigour so I bundle the baby into his buggy.

Orla meets me at the door, worrying a kitchen towel in her hands. "What took you so long?" she snaps. "It's freezing out there."

"He's fine. I wrapped him up so tight he probably thinks it's summer." I point down at the many layers smothering him.

"I wasn't talking about him, he's grand." Orla pushes the pram inside without as much as a glance at her baby. "I mean you, Ciara. You haven't been out of the house in three days and you disappear for an hour? Thomas, get into doctor mode and say something, would you?"

Thomas emerges from the kitchen with Liam crawling up his back and Kate squirming delightedly under his arm. "A bit of fresh air is the best thing for her, love," he says, grinning at me.

Orla mutters mutinously, and shoos me up the stairs to change for dinner. As soon as I am alone in my room, I fire up my laptop and open the internet.

I type '**Ann Preston**' into the search box and watch impatiently as the results start appearing. A famous doctor from the eighteen hundreds. Loads of Facebook pages and LinkedIn profiles. An elderly artist. I try different spellings of her name, but nothing of use is revealed.

Frustrated, I slam the lid down. I am at a dead end. Unless, of course, I talk to Nikki.

I can understand her frustration. If she came to me and accused me of having an affair I'd be equally angry and unwilling to engage with her until she admitted I would never do that. But then I remember the messages on her phone, the lies. Anger rises inside me again.

Before I realise I am doing it, I am dialling the Homewrecker again.

"Hello?" the same person answers.

"Ann, my name is Ciara. You know my partner Nikki."

There is a pause. "Who?"

"Nikki Garrison," I say with authority.

"Oh, Nikki, yes, of course." Her voice suddenly changes, dropping low. "Ciara. I've heard a lot about you."

"I bet," I say snarkily. "Is Nikki with you now?"

"No," she answers, suddenly sounding worried. "Why, have I missed an appointment? I didn't think I was due to meet her until next week?"

I hear papers shuffling in the background. My heart leaps. This doesn't sound like a torrid love affair. Less than a second later, my stomach drops weightily. Have I wrongly accused Nikki? But no, I had good reason. I need to find out more.

"Maybe I made a mistake, Ann – when are you next supposed to meet her?"

"Not until Monday, I believe." Another pause. "Is everything all right?"

"Yes, I just – I didn't know Nikki was meeting you until recently. I thought we . . . could you tell me why you are meeting her?"

"Wait a second . . ." Ann's tone changes again, this time to a suspicious drawl. "Did you ring me earlier today, looking for a different Ann?"

I try to think of an explanation, but she does not give me the chance.

"What the hell is going on?"

"I'm sorry," I say quickly, "I just want to know why you and Nikki are meeting."

"Talk to Nikki," she says gruffly, "and don't ring me again." A dial tone bleeps in my ear just as Orla calls me downstairs.

I try to get into the spirit of the kids' high-jinks at dinner but I continue to be preoccupied by my conversation with Ann. Orla notices my quiet demeanour and insists I overdid it on my walk earlier. She orders me to bed early. Although I can feel my muscles screaming for more exercise, I obey.

I crawl into bed and take out my phone. My heart pounds as I see a missed call. It is Adrian. Orla rang him yesterday but refused to let him speak to me. The message is gruff. He asks after my health begrudgingly and demands that I contact him as soon as possible. I message him, promising that I'll be in touch once I'm better. No one is more conscious than I am of the need to keep to a training schedule, but Orla is right about one thing, I am exhausted after the fever. My fight with Nikki is taking up all my mental energy. I need to sort that out first, or I won't be able to concentrate on my training properly.

I stare at the phone, furious that my preparations for my dream are being usurped by the Homewrecker. I could call her once more, and demand an explanation. Or I could do the sane thing and talk to Nikki, apologise for jumping to conclusions and calmly ask her to explain the messages. As I am wrestling with the decision, Orla knocks on the door.

"Hot cup of honey and lemon tea?" she asks, easing inside with two steaming mugs in her hands. I take one willingly and sniff in the freeing scent. Orla sits on the edge of the bed, cradling her own drink.

"Ciara, I want to talk to you about Nikki," she says.

Something about the tightness of her declaration catches my attention and I look up. Her face is pained with worry lines. I say nothing.

"She hasn't called back, even after I messaged to tell her you were unwell."

"She did get in touch with me after that, but I didn't want to see her. Not until she's prepared to tell me about that woman Ann." When Orla doesn't answer, I keep going. "Look, maybe it's not an affair, but something's going on. There have been too many lies, Orla. Too many nights when she's sneaked off without telling me where she's going."

"Well, that's what I wanted to talk to you about," Orla says, her breathing shallow. "I don't know who Ann is or how often they've been meeting. But I can tell you that she hasn't been with Ann every time she's disappeared on you."

I place my mug on the nightstand and sit upright. "What are you talking about?"

Orla sighs. "Remember I told you that no one is ever truly ready for parenthood? Well, it only gets harder when there's three of them. Kate needs extra care with her bad lungs, the baby needs full-time attention and we have to be careful not to overlook Liam. Thomas works so much – I'm alone with the kids for most of the day."

"Are you saying you're struggling, Orla? Because I can help out more. But what has this got to do with Nikki?"

"One day, about six months ago, I was in the supermarket. The baby wouldn't stop crying, Liam had run off down the sweets aisle and Kate was throwing a tantrum. I was this close," she holds up her finger and thumb with a minute gap between them, "to losing it altogether when Nikki appeared around the corner hand in hand with Liam."

I blink at my sister. Neither she nor Nikki ever mentioned this to me.

"Nikki took one look at my worn-out face, then bent down and asked Liam and Kate if they wanted to drive home with their Aunty Nikki. Of course they thought that would be a great adventure, and before I knew it I was left with only one child for an hour. Absolute bliss. Nikki met me at home with the kids a while later. I was at the end of my tether, Ciara." She sounds suddenly more urgent,

169

apologetic. "It's not that I chose to open up to her instead of you. She happened to be there at the time, and it came pouring out of me. I couldn't stop it. How tired I've been, how I haven't been able to give each kid proper one-on-one time because there's always another one hanging off me. I guess . . . sometimes I don't feel like a very good mother."

To my horror, she dissolves into tears. I lean forward instinctively and wrap my arms around her. She shakes as she tries to cry quietly so as not to disturb the rest of the house.

"Orla!" I half-laugh despite her upset. It should be obvious to her that she's a fantastic parent – how can I possibly express how amazing she is? I force her hands from her face. "Orla, you are the *best* sister anyone could ask for, and a wonderful mother. The kids adore you. They're little darlings . . . well, when they're not screaming at each other."

She laughs wetly.

"Come on, now, Orla. Don't cry. It's natural to need help. Three kids is a lot. I'll help more."

"Well," she sniffs, "that's exactly what Nikki said. She was going to tell you, but I knew you were too busy training. I think that was the week you were building up to an important race. European qualifiers or something."

"You're my sister." I pull back from her. "You are way more important. You should have told me. Nikki should have told me."

"She wanted to, like I said. But I insisted she leave you alone, at least until that race was done. Then the Olympic qualification times were announced and you were even busier. So Nikki took to popping in. Sometimes for a short visit, to take one of the kids off my hands. Other times she stayed for hours. She was adult company when Thomas was working. It helped, Ciara. It made me remember that I have an identity beyond being Thomas's wife, and a mother."

I bite my lip. "I'm glad you had help."

She must hear my hesitation. "We never spoke about your relationship. Nikki knows I'll always be on your side. She offered to bring you here with her some evenings but . . . to be honest, I asked her not to do that."

"Why, Orla?"

"I don't know. I guess I was ashamed. The state I was in when Nikki came upon me in that supermarket. If a social worker had rounded the corner they probably would have taken the kids from me on the spot – I was a wreck. I didn't want you to see me like that."

I understand. Even though your family are the ones who'll love you no matter what, they are the ones you can't bear to disappoint.

Orla wipes her eyes. "I'm sorry if Nikki being here made things difficult between you. I shouldn't have asked her to keep anything from you."

"It's all right, Orla." I rub her shoulder. "You needed help. I'm just glad Nikki could give it to you. Anyway, that's not the real problem. There's still the question of Ann."

"Well, I definitely don't know anything about that. Nikki never mentioned anyone called Ann to me. But if Nikki is so intent on having children now, as you say, why would she jeopardise that?"

I shrug, but cannot help voicing my other concern. "I bet being around your kids didn't help with her broodiness."

"Give me a break! They have some sets of lungs on them – if anything they would have put her off!"

We laugh together and I send her off to bed with assurances that I don't blame her for anything.

I lie back on my pillow with a renewed determination to smooth things over with Nikki. I thought Thomas and Orla had the model life but, it goes to show, there are pressures and problems even in seemingly perfect households.

I send Nikki a message. **Sorry I missed your call earlier – was with the baby**. It's only a white lie. **Will be home this weekend. Looking forward to seeing you. Love you**.

After a few minutes, she sends me a message with a single kiss. I smile. Perhaps we can work through this after all.

Chapter twenty-one

TRISH

After the news about Mary O'Sullivan's death finally exposed Charrings Clinic, my job proved to be a blessing once more.

As I jumped the gap from the bus to the kerb outside Dublin airport and clacked hurriedly into the terminal, dragging my case behind me, I felt like I was running away. But it was a legitimate escape, I told myself, because my job demanded I leave the country. I kept my head down as I checked in my crew luggage. I knew I was being silly to fear Abby finding me in this crowded airport, but I felt her presence everywhere.

Lisa's call the previous week finally made sense, but that resolution brought me no relief.

Charrings was the hot topic of the week. The crew were discussing it intently when I boarded the plane, and it kept cropping up throughout the flight.

"My little sister's best friend in school had a cousin who did the same course as Mary O'Sullivan, you know," had been one of the many pathetic attempts to associate with the tragedy.

I kept busy, loading and unloading refreshments repeatedly to avoid getting dragged into the conversation. Thankfully our shared last name was not enough for anyone to connect me to my mother, though a few mentioned the news appearances by the pro-life front, mostly with derision.

One of the younger crew piped up after a while. "Well, at least that awful place will be shut down now."

It was at that point I excused myself. I pulled the sliding door behind me and sat on the toilet seat, my head in my hands, my knees touching the door in the cramped space.

"Get a grip, Trish," I whispered. No one had any reason to link me to Charrings. There was nothing to gain from confessing my connection at this stage. I shook myself as much as the small space would allow, and plastered a smile on my face before squeezing out into the main section of the plane.

The flight was a haze of screaming children and irritated passengers. I was exhausted by the time we landed.

As soon as we arrived in our hotel, I connected to Wi-Fi and scoured the news sites for any updates. There was nothing. That night, I slept fitfully, and spent most of the next day rereading articles on Charrings Clinic.

Desperate for distraction, I joined a few of the more energetic crew members for drinks in the hotel bar. We stayed up until the late hours, and they cursed me early the next morning when I knocked on their doors, seeking company for a sightseeing walk. A couple of them joined me, albeit sleepily, and that night we hit the town.

Our Saturday flight home was through the night, so I managed to get a few hours in the hotel gym before leaving for the airport. I was tired by the time we boarded, but also slightly more at ease. The days away numbed the immediate shock of the Charrings announcement.

Not for the first time, I said a silent prayer of thanks for my job. I imagined how my week would have been if I was still working in Orwell Travel. Fear of Abby lurking around Dublin city would have made me twitchy. Josh would not have failed to notice, and I probably would have ended up calling in sick. Of course, sitting at home would only have magnified the terror.

It was the aftermath of my trip to Charrings that ultimately propelled me into the job with Aer Clara.

I had arrived in work early on the Monday after my trip to London. At a few minutes to nine o'clock, knowing Josh would be on his way, I took up my place by the door, swinging my arms by my sides. I had to convince him my London holiday had been a success. I had spent the morning scribbling a list of the sights I could have seen – Buckingham Palace, Leicester Square, Big Ben.

Josh bounced in the door as usual, and furrowed his brow immediately. "Trish, sweetheart, you look awful. What's wrong?"

To this day, I don't know how I managed to hold in the tears. I had directed all my efforts at appearing normal, yet at a single glance Josh could tell I was suffering. He had no choice but to accept my repeated assurances that I was hungover from a crazy weekend with my friend in London. His narrowed eyes made me realise the transparency of my trauma. If he noticed, others would too.

So I hid. Ciara and Stephen made some efforts to reach me, but put my aloofness down to the combination of my break-up with Alan, and Gerry's death. I avoided my mother as much as possible, keeping to my room. When she demanded my presence downstairs I made up excuses and spent hours sitting in the park, staring at the swans floating gracefully yet without purpose on the pond.

During the next few months, as my depression festered, Josh fussed about me. He lingered around my desk asking if I was feeling all right and kept offering me more holidays. Although he meant well, his constant mothering was suffocating and ultimately spurred me on to quit my job.

There were also practical considerations. My mother took me in after the break-up on the agreement I pay her rent. I did not begrudge her that but it put a strain on my finances, especially with my repayments to Abby. I needed more money than Josh was able to offer.

But the real trigger was Gerry's six-month anniversary. It was then that his family spoke for the first time about his pancreatic cancer. We had learned from the priest on the day of his funeral that when he leapt from that cliff he had only months to live. His parents were too distraught to share any more detail. Six months later, as his father opened up at the remembrance Mass, I heard Ciara weep quietly beside me. I held her hand as Stephen gripped my knee.

Gerry's father was stooped like an old man at the pulpit, his face wet with tears. "Gerry did not warn us what he was planning to do. He did not leave a hint of where he was going that day. It was to spare us all months of painful goodbyes." He had sighed then. "Even though I understand, I wish he hadn't done it. Every extra day, hour, minute with him would have been a gift. If anyone out there ever thinks leaving your family will spare them, please know that is not true."

It was as if he was speaking directly to me, and I felt the full meaning of his plea. All Ciara and Stephen talked about for the rest of the day was how they wished Gerry had confided in them. I knew I wasn't going to end my life as he did, but I couldn't let myself get much worse. I had to pull myself out of my cocoon of distress.

I needed a break. A new start.

I handed in my notice to Josh the day after the anniversary Mass. Josh went through the stages of grief in a flash, from denial to acceptance. He proclaimed that he'd miss me, that he'd never find another assistant who would muck in like I did. But he was happy for me, he said with a knowing smile. I was a beautiful young woman who should be out exploring the world, not stuck behind a desk licking envelopes her whole life. He asked me what my new job would be, and could do nothing but blink rapidly when I admitted I had not got that far.

"You will work here until you get something," he said sternly.

I didn't bother to remind him that he was not my father, mostly because it had been short-sighted of me to quit with nothing else lined up. So I kept working in Orwell Travel and spent my evenings on job websites, searching for something interesting that paid more than peanuts. Without further education, my options were limited to the type of role for which Josh had employed me.

Two weeks after I handed in my notice, Josh rang me at home. He was giddy with excitement.

"We have a really important client coming in tomorrow." His words tripped over his tongue, slurring with anticipation. "I'm going to need you to help me with him. Wear your best suit – look as professional as you can, will you?"

Josh ran an informal office. If he wanted me dolled up, it must be for something big – expanding the business or getting in a partner. He was too upbeat for it to be anything negative or a downsize. My loyalty to Josh was absolute, especially since he had been so decent about my decision to leave.

The next morning I put on my best navy skirt and jacket and applied a modest amount of make-up. I was at my desk early, but Josh did not show until eleven o'clock. I recognised his companion immediately. Two years previously, there had been air-traffic-control strikes in the south of Portugal and many of our customers were stranded. As Josh rushed around putting out fires, I took a call from Mr Farrell, the head of one of Ireland's premier international airlines, Aer Clara.

I stayed in touch with him throughout the crisis, assuring him all his passengers were being kept up to date with the options available to them. We were one of three travel agents who had groups of more than one hundred tourists stranded, and he was apparently impressed with our business over all the others. He remembered me immediately, though I was to learn later that Josh had been talking me up all morning.

He shook my hand enthusiastically and, when I brought them coffee in Josh's office, he asked me to sit. Josh was beaming, his neck flushed red.

"Ms Olden," Mr Farrell began, "I hear from Josh that you're leaving Orwell Travels in search of something different?"

I stiffened. Surely Josh had not called in this man to persuade me to stay? I opened my mouth to answer politely, but he continued and at his next question I was silenced.

"How would you like a job with Aer Clara?"

Both he and Josh sniggered at what must have been my stunned face. It took me another minute to fully appreciate the situation, and realise that Josh had dressed me for an interview.

Mr Farrell sat back, his greying hair somehow enhancing the striking aspect of his muscular figure. "I met Josh a year ago at an industry event. I remember the assistance companies like his gave to us during the Portuguese strikes."

Josh cut in, unable to resist. "A few months ago I invited Mr Farrell to speak at the annual conference of the Travel Agent's Forum. When you said you wanted to leave Orwell to try something new, I thought of him."

"I had mentioned to Josh that we are expanding this year. There will soon be a trawl for everything from pilots to engineers. And . . ." he paused, "cabin crew."

I had only ever once been on a plane – to London – and it was not an experience I wished to repeat.

"Now, employment has to be on a merit basis," he said, "so I cannot offer you a job. You will have to go through the same process as everyone else. But I can give Josh a few tips to help you with your CV. You certainly have the customer-service temperament and experience required, and you proved yourself able to handle a crisis. I see no reason why you would not be accepted if you pass the training."

I gubbed like an idiot, contradicting his faith in me. I don't think I recovered from the shock for several days. Surprise soon soared to hope. It was a chance to put my harrowing past behind me.

Josh was determined this should happen for me, and coached me extensively for the interviews. I'm convinced Mr Farrell put in a good word for me. Suddenly, there was something positive in my life to talk about.

I rang Ciara, the first time I had done so since Gerry died. Unable to contain my excitement, the prospect of working as an air hostess spilled from my lips. Ciara squealed in delight.

I smiled at the obvious joy of my friend on my behalf.

"Think of all the free flights you can get me," Ciara laughed, without a mention of my recent absence from her life.

I grinned with genuine humour for the first time since Alan left. Since Gerry died.

Stephen had been equally enthusiastic, and we agreed to travel to the midlands to cheer Ciara on at a race in Athlone the following weekend. It was a short race, one she was doing mainly for practice so she was delighted when we showed up. Afterwards, the three of us spent hours in the pub, chatting about everything and nothing. I felt a warmth in my bones that I had forgotten could exist.

Less than two months later, I discovered I had the job. It was conditional on passing their training course, which I did within another few months. Ciara and Stephen both came to my wings ceremony. I cried with a fervour they attributed to happiness, but for me it was pure relief. I had a future.

On my last day in Orwell Travel, Josh presented me with an envelope. Inside was a cheque for two extra months' salary. My hands shook as I tried to press it back on him. He insisted, and whispered in my ear that his networking with the Aer Clara hobnobs was paying off. He was planning on launching new package holidays to some of their more exotic destinations. "Things are looking up, kid. I can afford it and you've earned it. Take it, and don't go saving it in the bank. Splash out. Spend it on something nice."

I took his money with thanks, knowing exactly where it was going. Repaying Abby was more difficult than I had anticipated. The interest was significant, and once, when I was one day late with a payment due to a banking error, she charged me an extra fifty euro. I did not argue. I did not want to see her, or even talk to her on the phone. The mere thought of her brought back vividly the leering face of the doctor with no name, the slicing of my innards.

The debt swallowed Josh's money into its black hole. I feared I might be paying it off forever. The first few months of my job with

Aer Clara were sullied with the constant stress of being indebted to Abby and tied to my Charrings' experience. Then, an uncle of my father's passed away down the country, leaving a significant sum to me and Beth. Had my sister known it would be so difficult to conceive, she might have saved her half. I took my share of the money with useless guilt. I had never met this great-uncle. He died in a nursing home. I only hoped he had been treated well, and had not been lonely in his final years. The solicitor who passed me the cheque assured me that he had been well known in his local community, and died peacefully.

I transferred to Abby everything she was owed. She was stunned and callously charged me an 'early repayment' fee. I paid it without objecting, knowing any connection with her was now severed. With a lightness I had not felt in over a year, I boarded a flight to New York. Perhaps my relief shone through my face, because something made the handsome passenger in seat 15C smile at me constantly. He put his business card into my hand at the end of the flight and asked to take me for a drink. Shocked but filled with a strange confidence, I smiled back.

"Thank you, I'd like that . . ." I glanced down at his card, ". . . Brian."

Now, as we touch down on Irish soil from the trip to LA, the temporary escape my job offered me is over. I try to convince myself that the Charrings Clinic story will have been overtaken by more recent news at this stage, but still I feel my stomach clench as I step off the plane.

One of the cabin crew catches up with me as I power-walk through the terminal, desperate to get home.

"Trish, do you have your car?"

"No," I sigh, once again bemoaning my decision to leave it at home.

"Would you like a lift? I'm dropping Karen home, and you're on the way."

I hesitate. I'm exhausted after the flight, and tense about being back in the same country as Abby. The last thing I want to do is make idle chit-chat on the journey home. But I look out the window at the rain and, at the thought of dragging my bag across town on the bus in this weather, the fight goes out of me.

"Thanks, Sophie," I smile at her. "That would be great."

"Great, we're going to have a quick tea to warm up in the café over here and then we'll get going."

I curse inwardly. I just want to get home. But I see Karen waving us over and Sophie is already strolling toward her. I sigh. A quick breakfast would probably be the best thing – I'm not sure I have much in the way of food waiting for me at home.

I order a large croissant to go with my coffee, and join the girls at a table in the middle of the floor. They are both staring up at the television in the corner. I glance up as I lift my mug to take a sip, expecting one of the morning shows, or perhaps a soap omnibus. I stop the motion just as the mug reaches my lips.

On the screen is what looks like a press conference. A tag line runs along the bottom of the screen – **Latest in Charrings Clinic story – Minister for Justice to make announcement.**

Chapter twenty-two

TRISH

I freeze, staring at the screen.

"Are they still talking about that?" Sophie mumbles through a mouthful of scone.

"Looks like there's something new happening," frowns Karen.

"Or 'happened', past tense," says Sophie, pointing up at the new text rolling on the bottom of the screen. "Looks like this is a repeat from Friday."

I lower my mug to the table, all sense of hunger vanished. The noise from the television ramps up as a woman in her forties steps up to a podium. Cameras flash and journalists shout questions at her. She holds up a hand for silence.

"Isn't she a politician?" asks Karen.

I try not to roll my eyes. It's the Minister for Justice, Elaine Masterson, again. She's one of the most vocal politicians in the country. She never fails to comment on social issues, such as the lack of support for victims in the justice system, lenient sentencing in criminal cases and, most frequently, women's rights. She has been in trouble more than once for airing her personal views over those of the party, and commenting controversially on issues outside her ministerial portfolio of justice. But I don't think she is the loose cannon many make her out to be. Rather, she won't stay silent on an issue if she thinks her influence could help. Mum hates her because she's actively pro-choice.

Minister Masterson looks down at the crowd, preparing to speak. She is a tall woman with severe features – a sharp nose and chin that juts out alarmingly. She is wearing one of the power suits for which she is well known.

"*Thank you all for coming,*" she says into the microphone. "*I have a short statement and then I'll take some questions.*"

I look around. There are five other people in the café and, despite this press conference being a repeat from two days ago, all of them are gazing raptly at the screen. Even the woman at the cash register is leaning forward on the counter, staring up at it. I swallow and refocus my attention on the Minister.

"*As details have emerged about Charrings Clinic and the tragic death of Mary O'Sullivan, the UK authorities have made a number of discoveries. While there is much we do not know at this stage – I can tell you the following. Charrings Clinic did not advertise. The women who went there did so partly because it was cheap, and also because it was 'off the radar'. In other words, their abortions would not be discovered.*"

Sophie takes a bite of her scone. "Tell us something we don't know."

Minister Masterson continues. "*We are certain there was at least one contact on the ground in Ireland who arranged Charrings Clinic appointments for desperate women. Women like Mary O'Sullivan who believed she could not afford to have a baby, and was too embarrassed and frightened to come clean with her loved ones. It seems these women were promised financial assistance, but were ultimately threatened with exposure of their secret abortions if they did not pay back horrendous interest.*"

I squirm in my seat. I am not entirely sure where the Minister is heading with this. Finally, she gets to the point.

"*The UK authorities are conducting their own investigation into Mary*

O'Sullivan's death, and Charrings Clinic specifically. But we have a responsibility in Ireland too, to protect women from those who would take advantage of their vulnerable state. We believe girls like Mary O'Sullivan are being targeted. Such people are no better than loan sharks. The Gardaí have set up an investigative team to seek out anyone involved in what I would describe as extortion. If you have any information, please come forward and speak to the Gardaí. You will be treated with the utmost sensitivity and confidentiality. I am taking a personal interest in this, in the name of justice for Mary O'Sullivan, and to prevent another Charrings Clinic popping up elsewhere. Thank you."

She looks down as if to take questions from journalists but Sophie and Karen have already begun dissecting her speech.

"How will they know where to begin looking for the people involved?"

"I bet that doctor they arrested gave up some juicy information in exchange for leniency, the bastard," says Sophie, scrunching up her face in disgust. "The minster is not going to let this go, I can tell you. She'll want results. There's an election next year – this would keep her name in the papers."

"Don't be so cynical. It sounds like she really does want to crack down on anyone involved in Mary O'Sullivan's death. Poor girl. Do you reckon anyone will come forward?"

"I don't know, I mean there must be more women. Trish, what do you think?"

I look up at my name. Sophie and Karen are staring expectantly at me. I shrug. "I suppose so." They resume their conversation, and I try to nod along.

I am now desperate to get home but it seems like an age before the girls are finally ready to leave. I try to keep an upbeat manner in the car but an increasingly heavy tiredness pervades me.

Sophie drops me off at the end of my road with a cheery wave.

As I make the short walk home, soft Sunday-morning rain dampening my hair, I allow myself to consider the possibility of speaking to the investigation team. The Minister promised confidentiality, but this will ultimately be a Garda investigation so

she won't have any say in the way it's run. It's too much of a risk –
these things have a way of leaking. It's not just about me anymore
– if the public get wind that Beth Barkley's sister had an abortion,
she and Mum will be tainted. I could probably live with that, if it
wasn't for Conall. I can't risk the donations stopping.

Besides, what good will my coming forward do now? Charrings
Clinic is shut, the doctor with no name has been arrested. Of
course, there's still Abby – the facilitator of Charrings Clinic. The
investigation seems directed at her. But she'd never forgive me if I
was involved. And Conall would be the one to suffer.

I bundle into the cold house, never so delighted to be home.

I draw a bath as I unpack from the journey. I laze in it until the
water has chilled and my toes have shrivelled to prunes. After I dry
my hair, I doze for a few hours. Hunger eventually rouses me. I am
poking around in my relatively empty cupboards when my phone
rings.

My mind immediately leaps to Abby. I lean against the door, my
heart pounding. Furious with myself, I stamp my foot. I will not let
Abby paralyse me this way. I grab the phone out of my bag and with
a surprise that almost dispels the fear encasing me, I see Brian's
name flash across the screen.

I raise it to my ear. "Hello?"

"Trish, it's me."

"Hi, Brian."

There is a loaded gap as I swallow and he takes a loud breath.
He apologises for ringing out of the blue, and asks a few standard
questions – how is my job going, is Conall doing well? I answer
but do not return the politeness. Stephen admitted to me after their
last golf game that Brian is dating other women. He had been
reluctant to tell me, but felt I should know in case I bumped into
them in town, or heard about it from some busybody aiming to
wound. I was glad it came from Stephen, but was not ready to hear
details.

As if reading my mind, Brian finally jumps to the point. "The
reason I'm ringing, Trish – have you seen Stephen today?"

"Stephen? No, I only got in the door from LA this morning. I haven't spoken to him since Tuesday."

Brian's response is tinged with frustration. "Well, I'm in the golf club. We're supposed to be teeing off in ten minutes but there's no sign of him. He's not answering his mobile and he hasn't sent a message to say he's running late."

"That's not like him." I frown.

"It's not our usual slot so I probably should have rung to confirm," he says levelly, but I can hear his annoyance.

"Why don't you try Lisa?" I say, my tongue sticking on her name, as her warning call gushes back with the power of flowing water.

"She's not picking up either. I might give Ciara a buzz."

"Good idea," I say vaguely, though a hysterical plot is forming in my mind. I am not clear on Lisa's involvement with Abby, but if she was dispatched to warn me there must be some connection. What if Lisa has threatened to expose Abby to the Minister's investigation? What if Abby has done something to Lisa? And hurt Stephen too?

Even as my brain invents these theories, the rational part of me knows they are ludicrous. But I see a flash of Abby's empty eyes and hear her cruel words as I begged her for a doctor in that hotel room.

"Brian," I say suddenly, "if Ciara doesn't know where he is, let me know, will you?"

The last thing I want to do is go to their house. The need to avoid Lisa is almost as strong as my aversion to Abby right now. Brian promises to message me either way, and we hang up with stilted goodbyes.

I slump down onto the kitchen chair. Despite my earlier nap, I am still exhausted after hectic days in LA followed by working through the night. But I need to stay up or I won't sleep tonight. My phone rings again. Hoping it is Brian calling to confirm Stephen's safety, I pick it up. My sister's number is displayed on the screen.

"Hi Beth," I yawn. "Is everything all right?"

Her reply sounds stuffy, like she has a head cold. "No, Trish. Nothing is all right."

Chapter twenty-three

CIARA

It is Sunday before I find the courage to return home. It has been more than a week since I have seen Nikki and my heart quite literally aches for her. If I can suffer severe pain when I pull a leg muscle while running, then it is no surprise that an injury to the toughest and most tender muscle of all would hurt this much.

I am jittery with a sort of excitement, as if I am on my way home from a trip abroad. I want to rush over and throw myself into her arms. But the memory of our conversation from yesterday afternoon stifles my fervour.

"Nikki, it's me," I had said when she answered. "I was going to come home later but Orla and Thomas are going out for dinner tonight so I thought I'd baby-sit as a thank-you for this week. Is that okay? I do really want to see you. I'll be home tomorrow."

"Whatever you want, Ciara."

I breathed out a relieved sigh. "Thanks. Would you come over here instead?"

"Actually, I've been invited to dinner tonight. If you're not

189

coming home, I'll go to that."

I tensed. My conversation with Ann yesterday had thrown up many new scenarios. It sounded like they had more of a professional relationship than anything – was she a doctor? Could Nikki be ill? Or was this something to do with the baby Nikki wanted so badly? But their language had been so secretive, they sounded intimate to me. I could not stand the thought of Nikki meeting her again without explaining it all to me. I swallowed deeply, knowing how much worse I would make it if I was wrong. Yet I was unable to stop myself. Competitiveness is vital for my career but it pervades the rest of my life too, like a sickness.

"Dinner with who? Is it Ann?"

"Oh, for the love of God!"

"I'm sorry," I said immediately, enraged by my own stupidity.

"It's Brian, okay?" she snapped. "It's been hard for him – he didn't just lose Trish, he lost all of us. He wants to meet for dinner. Unlike you, I think about people other than myself once in a while."

The accuracy of her accusation stung me and I held my retort in my throat. After a few seconds, her voice wavered faintly.

"Come home tomorrow. But, Ciara, I need to know that you trust me. After all our years together, if you don't believe I'm committed to you then it says a lot about your own loyalty."

I did not engage in further back and forth. She had a point. I promised to come home the next day and hung up, unsure whether to be satisfied with the call or not.

Now, as I am packing, my mobile rings. I make to answer it when I see Brian's name flash up. I imagine him and Nikki talking about me over dinner last night, and do not answer.

Orla watches me pack the few possessions I had brought into my small rucksack. I thank her for all the clothes and toiletries she lent me during the week.

"Not to mention taking care of me and feeding me up like a cow before slaughter."

She points a teasing finger at me. "I don't want to hear any

190

excuses about your training slipping. You're fit and healthy so get back into the routine as soon as you can."

I promise I will. We lapse into silence as I think about Adrian's most recent phone call. Losing a week's training so soon after my new PB could be disastrous, but he claims to be reworking my schedule so I will be ready for the trial in November.

Orla changes the subject as I start worrying about the intensity of Adrian's plans. "Do you think you'll work it out? With Nikki, I mean? I didn't think a week would go by without one of you caving."

"It's difficult, Orla." I look at my sister thoughtfully. "Here's the dilemma. I want to trust Nikki. But there is evidence that she's been lying to me. Any objective person would say I'm being taken for a fool. Isn't it natural that I ask her about it?"

Orla shifts in her seat. "Two years ago, shortly after Kate was born, Thomas got his new consultancy position and was working all the hours in the day. I needed him at home, but it seemed to me that whenever he had a choice, he opted for work. We arranged a special night for our anniversary. That day I cooked a romantic meal, managed to get the kids to bed early, and waited. He never showed."

My mouth falls open.

"I rang the hospital to find out when he'd be home, and the nurse on duty told me he was out to dinner with his boss. His female boss," she added, tilting her head at me. "Objective evidence, right? Sufficient to warrant me marching down to the restaurant and demanding an explanation?"

"Definitely." I nod fiercely. "You were dead right. What did he say?"

"Oh Ciara," she says with a hint of something like sympathy, "I didn't disturb him, I didn't question him. Yes, it would be logical to worry he was having an affair. But I'm not an objective outsider. I know Thomas. He loves me, he dotes on the kids. It's not in his personality to cheat."

I cock one eyebrow at her. "People cheat all the time, Orla. It's naïve to think otherwise."

191

"Well, yes," she agrees. "Some people cheat. But Ciara, some people *don't* cheat. And I knew Thomas well enough to be sure which category he fell into. So I waited until he came home."

A small smile spreads across her face.

"He apologised for being late. Without knowing that I had rung the hospital, he told me straight away that he had been out with his boss. He needed time with her away from work to explain that he couldn't keep it up. The hours were killing him, especially with Kate being such a sickly baby. He had asked for unpaid leave for a month to be with us at home, and extra staff on his team when he returned. His boss agreed."

My head drops with the shame of ever having suspected my devoted brother-in-law.

"I'm not saying that Nikki is innocent," Orla says. "Maybe she is cheating on you."

I look up so fast I crick my neck.

"But the evidence won't tell you. She won't tell you. You already know, Ciara. Deep down, you know whether or not she's cheating on you. So? Is she?"

I shake my head. "Of course not."

"Great!" Orla waves an arm theatrically toward the door. "Then get home to her and sort out this nonsense."

I am strangely emotional leaving my family at the door. Liam and Kate cling to a leg each, grinning mischievously as I try to shake them off. Thomas kisses my cheek and holds out the baby for me to snuggle.

"Are you sure you don't want a lift, Ciara?" he asks again.

I shake my head. I need some space to think before I see Nikki. I hug my sister tightly. Our talk opened my eyes to how hurt Nikki must have been when I assumed she was cheating. I am still determined to get answers. I know I can trust her, but it must be reciprocal. She has to trust me enough to give me the real explanation about Ann. When she does, everything will be well.

With my own faith renewed, I feel confident when I push open my hall door. I call out to Nikki as I enter. She emerges from the kitchen, walks across the hall and stops a few paces in front of me. I hesitate as I lean in to kiss her. Just before my lips touch hers, she steps back. I falter on the spot.

She folds her arms, her eyes glistening. "You rang Ann?"

I curse my own idiocy and hold up a hand. "Yes, and I'm sorry. You wouldn't give me answers. I thought she would."

Nikki presses her lips together and shifts her weight to her other foot. Her arms remain crossed tightly across her chest. "And did she?"

"No, and I'm glad." I move toward her. "I don't want answers from her. I want them from you. And I'm not scared."

She frowns.

"I don't know why you've been meeting this woman or why you lied about it. But I know that there must be a good reason. You're not cheating on me. You would never do that."

I inch nearer. She does not retreat.

Heartened, I continue, my mouth dry. "Do you remember our first date? You took me to your cousin's new seafood restaurant in town."

Despite her anger, Nikki's face loosens a fraction. Another person might not have noticed, but I saw the lines around her eyes relax.

"You had pre-ordered," I continue, "and I didn't tell you I'd never had shellfish before because I didn't want you thinking I was uncultured. You were so sophisticated and pretty. I was never out of my leggings and runners."

"You were from Donegal – right on the coast," Nikki replies as though this is the first time we are having this conversation. The smallest hint of a smile shapes her mouth. "I assumed you were used to fish."

"Cod and salmon, yes," I exclaim. "Not mussels or oysters."

"I was trying to be romantic. How was I to know you were allergic to shellfish when you didn't know yourself? I had to meet your sister for the first time in a hospital. My cousin was freaking out that you'd sue the restaurant."

We stare tenderly at each other. I cannot believe I ever doubted her.

"The staff were rushing around like mad yokes, Nikki. But I was perfectly calm. I knew even then you were the one for me. You might have poisoned me, but you'd never hurt me."

"That doesn't make any sense," Nikki laughs.

"Neither does this," I say emphatically. "Just like then, I know you'd never hurt me. But you have spread a venom. You lied. I trust you, Nikki. Now you have to stand up for us."

She lowers her eyes. I reach out and take her hand.

"It's okay, Nikki," I whisper. "I'm here, whatever it is."

When she looks up, I see tears shimmering in her eyes. I lead her through the kitchen and out to the garden. I sit on the back step, considering Nikki as she stands before me.

"So," I say as nonchalantly as I can. "Who is Ann? What's the big mystery?"

Nikki takes a deep breath.

I hear it shuddering inside her throat.

"She's my counsellor."

I blink stupidly. "You're seeing a counsellor?"

Nikki sits heavily, like an old woman, on the plastic chair beside her. "Ciara, I want us to have a baby. Haven't we been discussing this for the past year?"

"Constantly," I say before I can stop myself.

"Ann specialises in helping couples who can't have children naturally, like us. People who are considering adopting, or who are actively doing it, or who are thinking about other options like sperm donation – or surrogacy in some cases."

I swallow. "But she's a counsellor, Nikki."

"So?"

"So, you're not talking to sperm banks or adoption agencies. People go to counsellors because they're depressed."

She shrugs. "I need someone to talk to about it. Someone who knows about the processes and what I'm going through."

I stare at her. Is Nikki so obsessed with having a child that she needs professional help to cope? My stomach lurches as I remember what happened the last time a friend slipped that low – I imagine

Nikki diving gracefully off a cliff, and bite down on the inside of my lip. I taste blood.

Nikki moves to sit on the swing, the motion soothing her as I know it always does. "Ann has been meeting me every couple of weeks. Sometimes, if it doesn't suit, we have a call. It's an informal thing – there's no doctor's office, or clipboard or medication. It's more akin to a sponsor. We have dinner. We chat. She supports me."

I kneel before her, not caring that my knees are damp on the cold grass. I rest my hands on her legs, and the swing pushes back with our weight.

"Nikki, I'll support you. But don't be sad. Please don't be sad. Not like Gerry was."

I bury my face in her lap, the tears falling with more force than they ever have before. The pressure of the past few weeks – from the stress of the race to finding those messages from Ann – it pours from me. My shoulders shake as Nikki soothes me. Eventually, I shudder to calm.

"Ann had an idea," Nikki says, stroking my cheeks. "I kept wanting to thrash it out with you, but there was never a right time."

"What does she suggest?" I sniff.

Nikki's legs twitch under my arms. "Single people can adopt, you know. And, of course, use sperm donations. She said that, maybe, if you weren't ready – if you weren't ever going to be ready – I should consider whether to do it as a single mother."

I stare up at her. She is a stranger, the woman who comforted me so familiarly seconds ago. How is it possible she is planning a family without me? Would she really leave me behind – or simply leave me?

"You'd have a baby without me?" I whisper.

She leans forward, her eyes soft and inviting. "I want to have a baby *with* you, Ciara. But you're putting it off. You'll debate it with me, we'll go over the pros and cons. But at the end of the day, you're not ready. What if you never are?"

"B-but," I stammer, my heart racing, "I love you."

Nikki kisses my forehead. "I love you too."

My heart contracts painfully. Could this be it? Are we breaking up?

"Nikki," I say thickly, my mouth like a desert, "you are the most important thing to me in the world. I think we are a proper family, right now. Just the two of us. I don't need anyone else."

"Well, I do," she answers straight away, refusing to be guilted into giving up on her dream. "That doesn't mean I need you any less, Ciara, and you know it. We have to move forward. I can't wait another ten years, only to realise you'll never be ready to have a child."

I want to argue. My reasons are rational and ready. But all I can see is her, my steady pacemaker, abandoning the plan and sprinting ahead. Leaving me behind in the most important race of my life.

"You won't wait for me."

She does not falter. She strokes my face, resigned. "I would wait. Just not forever. And I think that's what you're asking of me. I've been honest with you, now it's your turn. Will you ever be willing to have a baby with me?"

The truth is I don't know. But how can I tell her that? Even committing to doing it in one year, or two, or five seems dishonest. I lay my head in her lap and close my eyes, letting her stroke my head. I could stay here forever, if only she would too.

Chapter twenty-four

STEPHEN

Trish warned me about Lisa from the start. Not about her violent nature, Trish could not have known about that. Rather, she remembered how my girlfriend used to act as a teenager, when she was best friends with Trish's sister Beth. They had one of those sneering, bitchy friendships where each was happiest if the other was miserable.

They do not see each other often any more. According to Trish, Lisa found it difficult when Beth got married. Beth wallowed it in smugly and the friendship ultimately spoiled.

The night I met Lisa, when she was having drinks with Beth on Dawson Street, was a rarity and apparently one of the last times they met. Beth had thrown herself headfirst into the 'new wives' club in her area, and she was becoming consumed with the idea of children.

Lisa was uninterested in such domesticity. From the earliest days of our relationship, we planned on travelling and living the high life. I was earning well – I surprised her with romantic weekends to Paris and jewellery that I had Trish and Ciara help me pick out. I noticed Lisa's condescending attitude early on, but it always seemed to be in jest. Plenty of women are domineering. It's supposed to be a positive trait these days to be attracted to strong, powerful women. It is only now I can recognise that Lisa is not those things. She is just controlling.

I have tried to decipher a pattern in our relationship.

We soured to poison about a month after I lost my job in TJ Simons. At first, Lisa had been bracing, encouraging me to send out CVs and actively chase my contacts. When, a few weeks in, it became clear there was no immediate prospect of employment, she started to withdraw from me. The fabric of home ripped further apart with every exasperated question.

"Have you heard anything yet?" "Who did you talk to today?" "What is your plan now?"

I stayed out later, which probably wasn't the best way to handle the situation. Then, one evening, I stumbled home from the pub late to find Lisa sitting on the stairs in her pyjamas. I'd had a few drinks but I sobered in a second when she started shouting.

She had never spoken to me that way before. I backed up against the door in shock as she pointed her finger up at me and unleashed a verbal tirade, her eyes wild.

"*You're useless, Stephen!*" she shrieked. "*You can't get a job. You're spending your nights in the pub with a bunch of unemployed nobodies. No wonder TJ Simons let you go. You're good for nothing!*"

Flecks of spit flew from her mouth onto my face, but I didn't move. All I heard was my father, uttering those same sentiments. I guess there are only so many times you can be told you're worthless before it becomes ingrained in your reflection.

The shouting continued after that first night. At first, I hoped it was a once-off. I blamed myself, as she did, for her frustrations. What sort of man spends his nights in the pub when his girlfriend is sitting lonely and worried for him at home?

Lisa did not hit me until two months ago. It was just a slap. The type women are always inflicting on their loser boyfriends in Lisa's endless romantic-comedy films. I was used to her nagging rants by then. They weren't having any effect. She needed to get my attention. The slap was a warning.

It worked. I apologised. I stopped drinking at night. I made more of an effort to come home straight after work, cook her dinner, tidy the house exactly as she demanded. The slaps kept coming. I burnt the potatoes. I didn't sweep under the table. I hadn't had any interviews in weeks. There was always a reason. They became increasingly sharp and severe. Despite her height and skinny frame, she knew how to use her hand. A carefully placed chop on the shoulder. Endless smacks to my torso.

One night, she threw her glass at me. I ducked and it shattered against the wall.

"What are you doing?" I cried instinctively.

She came right up to me. "This is your fault. You made me do this," she hissed. "Clean it up."

I wanted to argue, I truly did. I felt the words form in my mouth but they dissolved at her blazing stare. I had learned many years ago where arguing got me. Obeying meant an easy life.

The punches came soon after that. They barely hurt – but every one shattered another part of me. I curved over as I took the blows, punctuated by her screams of anger.

I knew I was pathetic, inadequate, an idiot – all the things Lisa shouted at me. She never treated me this way when I was a real man, with a job that provided for us, with a life and friends and the sense of self I had gradually built up in the years after escaping my father's clutches.

I still hoped we could find a way to some sort of normality but I scarcely remembered a time when I had felt affection for her.

When Lisa first told me, after pushing me down the stairs, that she didn't want me leaving the house except for work, I assumed she was being dramatic. But every night this week, she has been standing at the door, waiting for me. I have spent the evenings sitting at our kitchen table, reading recipes by various up-and-coming French chefs. Lisa buys new cookbooks every few months, and leaves them out for me to read. She never cooks, or bakes or does anything in the kitchen. That's my job. Just one of the little ways she controlled me from the beginning. I can see it now, but it is too late.

Three days ago, on Thursday evening, as I scanned one of the newest cookbooks, a sigh slipped from my mouth without me realising.

"Bored?" she asked.

"No," I said quickly. "Lisa, I haven't gone jogging in ages. Maybe I'll go for a run."

She simply laughed. "That's not how it works anymore, Stephen. If you feel the need to exercise, let's work out to my fitness DVD."

"I don't think so . . ."

"Come on!" she smiled brightly, taking my hand and pulling me off my chair. "You'll like it." It was more a demand than hopeful statement.

I felt stupid doing jumping jacks alongside her in the living room. I couldn't reach my toes without bending my legs, and my back cricked constantly. It has been bothering me since I 'fell' down the stairs.

She seemed happy by the end of the workout, and I smiled tightly. The key was keeping her happy – then maybe she would lift this ridiculous rule and let me out of the house.

On Friday evening, I remembered my pre-arranged golf game with Brian. I cooked one of Lisa's favourite dishes, roasted haddock, and that seemed to put her in a good mood. Afterwards, I was sitting fretting, wondering how best to broach the subject, when I was distracted by the news. The Minister for Justice was talking about Charrings Clinic.

I chanced a sideways glance at Lisa. It was my mention of Mary O'Sullivan on Tuesday night that set her off. She was staring with wide eyes at the television. We listened in silence about the Garda investigation and to the minister's request that other women come forward. When the news segment was over, neither of us said a word.

Suddenly, Lisa's voice cut through the air. "*What?*" she asked loudly from her seat.

I froze, uncertain what she wanted me to say.

"You're rocking like you're on the verge of saying something. So spit it out."

"I have a golf game organised with Brian this Sunday," I said quietly. It was better than asking her about Mary O'Sullivan again.

She sighed and stood. "Here," she said, handing me my phone, which she had confiscated every evening since the night she pushed me down the stairs – the night it all changed. "Ring him."

I took it and swallowed deeply before lifting my hand to dial the number. I was millimetres from pressing the call button, when Lisa's small hand covered mine.

"Tell him you can't make the game."

My breathing came faster. "But I promised him."

She swiped the phone from my hand. "Then you can't call him at all."

Yesterday was Saturday so we were stuck together in the house all day. It was one of the worst days of my life. Lisa dominated with renewed vigour. In the morning, after I spent another night curled awkwardly on the couch, she handed me a list of jobs to do around the house. They didn't seem so bad, but Lisa was on hand to pick and nag at my incompetence. She insisted on holding the ladder while I cleared the gutters in the back garden. As I clambered down she wobbled it. I barely managed to hold on. Her high-pitched laugh cut harder than my hands as they blistered clinging to the ladder. She made me cook lunch, but only let me have a small plate, even though I was starving.

The whole time I knew all I had to do was walk out of the house. If she threw herself on top of me, she couldn't stop me. I was too strong. Just not strong enough to try.

Last night, she invited me into bed with her. I hardly dared believe it was not a trick. I inched in slowly, expecting a rebuttal. When she started caressing my arms and stroking my leg with hers, I pulled away. I had learned not to challenge her, but it seemed impossible that she wanted to make love to me.

"Do it," she whispered harshly.

I shut my eyes and kissed her neck, straining to recapture the pleasure it used to give us both to lie together. As soon as we were done, she ordered me out of the bed again. I spent another night on the couch, staring at the ceiling, willing an end to this torment.

I woke this morning feeling bad about bailing on Brian. We hadn't been in contact to confirm but I knew he would be at the club today, waiting for me.

So, after lunch, when Lisa goes to the bathroom, I grab the opportunity and swipe my phone out of the pocket of the cardigan she has inadvertently left hanging on a kitchen chair.

I call Brian, and scrunch my fist in frustration when it rings through to voicemail. "Brian, it's Stephen. I'm sorry for the late notice but I won't be able to make it." I stop. I want to shout out for help. Knowing I can't, I turn my head, searching for an excuse, when I see the ladder propped against the wall outside. "Lisa has me doing some work around the house. DIY stuff, you know."

It comes from behind. A sharp thump. I collapse forward, falling on top of the phone. I scramble upright. Lisa curses, and kicks the phone from under me. I shout out instinctively as she stamps repeatedly on it with the thick heel of her shoe until it is shattered and scattered across the floor.

"Learned your lesson, then?" She plants a kiss on the top of my head.

I watch her walk away with a storm brewing in my stomach. I could launch at her and put an end to this once and for all. Or run out the front door.

But as I watch her walk from me I hear her voice and my father's mingle together as one. I'm not cut out for bravery. For anything. I crawl to my usual seat at the kitchen table. I lower my head and stare at the recipe book without reading.

It is not over. I will pay for this with more than a broken phone. Tears well in my eyes. I blink them away.

"Stephen," Lisa calls sweetly from the living room, and I sense danger, more danger than I have felt before. "Can you come in here, please?"

Chapter twenty-five

TRISH

The receptionist is cruelly slow. I drum my fingers on the countertop as she scans the computer. "Third floor," she says in a monotone after a full three minutes.

I don't bother to thank her, or wait for the lift. I take the stairs two at a time.

The third floor is eerily quiet. I creep along, searching for Beth. I am reminded of Conall's birth, just over half a year ago. My mother rang me in hysterics to say Conall had survived and to get to the hospital as soon as possible. My chest had contracted with shock. I had assumed he wouldn't live. I hadn't expected to meet him until he was laid in a coffin.

As I raced through the hospital on that occasion, I worried holding a new-born might make me regret the decision I made all those years ago to let Abby take me to Charrings Clinic. I am embarrassed now to admit that I stalled, though I knew I probably had limited time to meet my nephew. The smell of disinfectant was so putrid I almost retched.

On the day of Conall's birth, I found Larry and my mother in the corridor, conversing in undertones. Larry was wearing a shirt with the sleeves rolled up, his hair tousled and deep crevices under his eyes. He hugged me with an unusual display of affection. I returned his embrace, unsure how else to greet him. The usual "Congratulations" on the birth was clearly inappropriate. The baby remained on the brink of death.

They had ushered me in to Beth before the nurse in charge of restricting visitor numbers could spot me. In the dull light of the room, I saw my sister lying on her side, her eyes red-rimmed and protuberant. She was staring at something beside her bed. I made to go to her, until my eye caught the incubator.

My legs carried me to him instinctively. Suddenly, he was there, in front of me. This tiny, oddly-shaped baby with wires binding his arms and chest, and taped to his cheek. My eyes began to water and I gulped out a sob. I never felt so mighty an emotion before or since. The need to gather him in to me, to rip off those tubes and caress his baby skin was so overwhelming I didn't realise I was falling. Mum and Larry caught me as I crumpled to the floor.

I picked myself up, embarrassed. I should have been supporting Larry, not the other way around. But Beth seemed to understand. She reached out an arm, though it was such an effort she hardly managed it. I grasped her hand in mine and rubbed it. Our eyes locked. It was the first real sisterly moment we ever shared.

"We've named him Conall," she said croakily. "It means 'strong'."

Charrings could not have been further from my mind then. Nothing but Conall occupied my thoughts.

Now, in a different hospital, I hope my fears will melt into hope as they did on first meeting my nephew. A nurse emerges from a side room, querying my presence crossly. When I mention Beth and Larry Barkley, her expression transforms into one of sympathy. I preferred the anger.

I follow her to a room at the end of the corridor. The cartoons and colours shining from the walls, though clearly appropriate for a children's hospital, are off-putting. They clash with the silence of the ward which is dark despite it being the middle of the day.

The room I enter is small. Maybe that's why the monitors seem to loom so large around the baby. Larry is dozing in the armchair under the window. The *Toy Story* curtains are pulled shut. Beth is sitting forward, leaning over a cot. She looks up as I come in, tributaries of tears streaking her cheeks.

"He's beautiful," she sighs, gazing back down at her son. "I mean, I know if he wasn't mine, I wouldn't think so. But he is, isn't it?"

"He is, Beth." I mean it. It's not that I cannot see the disproportionately sized head and jaw, the birdlike flimsiness of his body. But it seems so minor – two millions soldiers in perfect formation, just one with a finger out of place. Staring down on him as a whole, my heart swells. There are no more chairs in the tiny room, so I stand opposite Beth on the other side of cot. The baby lies still but for the rise and fall of his chest. Tubes and wires are stuck to his arms and legs. His little mouth twitches, as though preparing to yawn.

"I want to hold him," my sister cries out. Her hand drifts over him. "I can't find a place to touch him that won't dislodge one of these damned tubes."

A scream of torture could not have radiated more pain. I wish I had words for her, but any attempt at bolstering would be callous.

"How can I help, Beth?" I ask. Conall has been rushed to hospital many times before, but this is the first time she called me. It must be serious.

"They thought he could really go this time." Her voice sounds hollow. "He's rallied though, my little fighter."

"Where's Mum?" I ask, glancing around.

Larry remains comatose in the corner, his head resting on the wall behind him with his mouth hanging open. There is no sign that anyone else has been here, which is odd. Mum is usually first on the scene.

"She doesn't know we're here."

I furrow my brow, trying to fathom the situation. "Do you want me to ring her?" I ask, although I have no wish to see my mother.

I have managed to avoid her since the Charrings story broke.

Beth does not answer my question. Instead, she looks up at me. "Did you see Mum on the news last night?"

"No," I say immediately, wanting to steer the conversation away from this dangerous course. I don't meet her eye, fixing my attention on the baby. I can feel her eyes drilling into me.

"She's been on the television and radio every day since that announcement came through on Tuesday."

I glance up at the accusatory tone. Beth has been as passionate a pro-life advocate as my mother, if not as openly militant with those who verbalise the opposite view. She cannot be surprised that Mum is on the media trail. I would have expected her to be pleased. The more publicity Mum gets, the better for Conall. It seems to be the pro-lifers who have the money and are willing to donate. Beth's eyes are hard.

"What's wrong?" I ask.

She shakes her head, looking down again at the baby.

There is something odd about my sister's demeanour. I must figure out what's going on.

"Beth? Come on, you can tell me."

She stands, knocking the chair against the wall behind her. Larry shuffles but remains asleep.

"Larry has been awake for nearly twenty-four hours," Beth explains. "He stayed up with Conall last night, and we decided to call the ambulance this morning." She stops for a second before continuing. "I don't want to be around Mum right now."

"Why not, Beth?"

"You should have seen her on the news. Berating that young girl, Mary Whatever-her-name-was."

I swallow. "But you're pro-life."

"Of course I am," she snaps. "I always have been. I just feel sorry for that girl, Mary . . ."

"O'Sullivan," I say.

"Right, Mary O'Sullivan. I don't agree with her decision to have an abortion, but, God love her, what she went through must have

206

been horrendous. Mum is not showing her any compassion." She pauses. "Mum's hurting the cause."

The manner in which she throws in 'the cause' as an afterthought confuses me. While Mum would have launched straight into a fiery debate on the morality of Mary O'Sullivan's actions, Beth seems to be empathising with her. In the darkness of Conall's room, without Mum around to fire Beth up, I feel safe and reckless enough to chance the question I had never dared to ask.

"Is this about Conall?"

Beth sits, resting her arms on the cot and sobbing wretchedly.

I walk around to rub her shoulders. Kissing her head, I whisper platitudes in her ear. "He'll be fine, Beth. You said so yourself – he's a fighter."

She sits up. "Look at him, Trish. He's suffering. He is hurting every single day. Why should he have to be a fighter? It's not fair."

"What are you saying?"

"I'm not an idiot, all right?" Beth brushes her fingers past Conall's head. "I know what Edward's Syndrome means. In those moments, when I see him writhing in agony, I wonder if I should have done it." She laughs harshly. "I mean, we'd put down a dog if it was in pain, wouldn't we? But we let a sweet angel like Conall endure it because we're too selfish to let him go."

"Beth," I whisper.

She wipes her eyes. "I don't mean that, obviously. Life is the most precious thing. I haven't changed, I'm still pro-life. But since Conall was born, I have a different perspective. I understand why some women choose abortion. I don't agree with it, but I understand it. Mum doesn't see that, and she's been so vile about Mary O'Sullivan all week – I don't want to see her."

"Well, I'm glad you called me," I say, my confession never so close to my lips as in this moment.

I know I can never tell her the truth, but I want to, so badly. I am bursting to confide in someone, anyone. But the only reactions I will elicit are gasps of horror. It's a doomed desire – the hope of acceptance.

She fixes on Conall. "He wasn't supposed to have survived an hour out of my womb and in spite of everything he's going strong. I'm so grateful I kept him."

"Conall! Conall!" Larry leaps from the seat in a panic, searching hysterically around the room.

Beth is by his side in a second. "It's all right, sweetheart. You were dreaming. Conall's fine, see?"

Larry blinks furiously and lets Beth lead him unsteadily to the cot. He starts on seeing me. "Trish, what are you doing here?"

"I came to see if I can do anything," I say. "I'll leave you now. Beth, ring me any time."

I don't offer to call Mum, because I know it's not what Beth wants. I have no desire to talk to her either. She won't be happy when she realises her grandson is in the hospital and nobody told her. I linger at the door for a few seconds as I leave, watching my sister and her husband hold hands as they look down at their baby.

Though I hate leaving them here, I am suddenly impatient to get home, away from Beth, away from all of this, which seems to follow me wherever I go.

Chapter twenty-six

CIARA

We are standing apart in the garden, staring deeply as if it's the last time we will ever see each other. The gaze is a desperate search for a reason to stay.

Eventually, we take a break. The openness of the garden has not been enough this time to free the stifling intensity of our fight. The side issues, the emotions, the distractions are all fading away. We are finally getting to the nub of the problem and it scares us both because there is no obvious solution.

I leave Nikki in the kitchen to have a shower upstairs. I take my time, the everyday sounds of her frying a lunch downstairs soothing to my ears. After a while, I hear the doorbell ring. I listen at the door of our bedroom to Nikki greeting someone, and that person coming in. I frown. We are in the middle of an important discussion – why couldn't she just tell whoever it is to go away?

I walk noisily down the stairs and into the kitchen. Nikki is tipping the last of the sausages from the pan onto a plate.

"Ciara," she says but I don't look at her. I am staring instead at the woman sitting at the table, drinking tea. She rises slowly.

She is a short woman, not much over five feet I'd guess, with thick glasses. In her sixties at least, she wraps her woollen cardigan around her as she stands. Nikki sounds breathless.

"Ciara, this is Ann."

"Hello, Ciara," the woman smiles, stepping forward with an outstretched hand. "I believe we spoke on the phone."

I open my mouth, and close it again. There are too many emotions to process – I can't tell if I'm angry with this woman for showing up, mortified meeting her face to face after my deceptive phone call or furious at Nikki for inviting her in the first place.

I stare at her proffered hand. The manners drilled into me as a child force me to take it.

"I wanted you to meet her," Nikki says breathlessly. "She's been such a help to me. We're not getting anywhere discussing it. I thought maybe Ann could help."

"Help?" I say incredulously. "This is between us."

Nikki places the plate of sausages on the table beside the bread and butter, and the pot of tea.

"Help yourself, Ann," she says, ignoring me. "Ciara's on a strict race diet so the sausages are all yours." She turns to me. "I'm going upstairs. I want you to talk to Ann."

"Why?" I can barely get the word out. "I want to talk to *you*, Nikki."

She pecks my cheek as she passes me. "Just do this for me. Please."

I grab her arm but she slips from my grasp and takes the stairs two at a time. I stare after her until I hear Ann clattering with her cutlery behind me. I sit wordlessly and watch her make a sandwich. She takes a large bite and sits back. She says nothing. She simply stares at me.

"So," I say eventually. "What's the big plan? You convince me that becoming a parent is the best thing I could do with my life?"

Ann sits forward. "I'm not here to convince you of anything. I've counselled many couples over the years to try to help them make the right decision for them. There are many options open to couples who cannot conceive naturally."

I nod.

Ann continues. "But there is one option no one wants to discuss."

I raise an eyebrow, waiting for her to elaborate.

"Not having a child. Sometimes couples are so intent on finding a way, they don't consider the possibility they might be just as happy without children. That is one of the options Nikki and I have spoken about at length."

I stare at her, not knowing whether to believe her or not.

"I'm not in the business of telling my clients what's best for them. People have to make their own choices. Here is what I do know – when you make a decision as a couple, whether it be to buy a house, or get married, or have a baby, both of you have to be okay with it. That doesn't mean you need to be over the moon. Compromises have to be made, sometimes outside forces intervene. But you both have to be willing to go down the road you've taken. If you cannot agree on a journey, then maybe you need to go your separate ways."

Fury boils inside me. "Is that what you've been telling Nikki? To break up with me? To have a baby on her own?"

"Of course not," Ann snaps.

I am startled enough by her reaction to stay silent while she continues.

"I don't tell anyone what to do. I ask the questions – you have to find the answer. So, I have a question for you. Why did you call me? What were you hoping I'd say?"

I look down. "I thought Nikki might have been having an affair."

Ann throws her head back and laughs, a chortling, guttural laugh. "I'm not sure my husband of forty-two years would be too impressed," she grins.

I give her a small smile.

"It nearly would have been easier, wouldn't it? If she was having an affair?"

I open my mouth indignantly but Ann does not give me time to answer. "That way you wouldn't have to make a decision about having children. Plus she'd be the bad guy, so no one could blame you."

The accuracy of her statement stings.

"I – I don't want to break up with Nikki," I stammer.

"I know," she says gently. "Neither of you is the bad guy here. Not her for reaching out to a counsellor. Not you, for having doubts about being a parent."

"I promised her," I say, out of nowhere. "I did promise her we would start the process this year."

"Do you really think keeping your word is the best reason to have a child? There's nothing wrong with the way you're feeling, Ciara. And there is nothing wrong with the way Nikki is feeling either. I don't have a quick fix. You two are doing the right thing by talking about it."

"Why did Nikki ask you to come here today?"

Ann gives a sad smile. "She didn't. I asked her to call me when you came home and had time to talk. I'd like to have a session with you. Some day that suits you, just for an hour. Free of charge."

That was the last answer I was expecting. "Why?"

She leans to the side to rummage in her pocket. She pulls out a wallet and opens it. A picture of a red-faced boy smiles out at me. "That's my son, Ronan," she smiles. "He's a lot older now. Has a little boy of his own, and a baby girl."

"Cute picture," I smile.

"He's adopted. Took us ten years to get a baby, but he was worth the wait. It was a horrible ten years though. My husband and I, we watched all our friends have their first babies – then second and third babies. It was heart-breaking."

"I'm sorry," I say.

"I took to the drink quite heavily. In the end, at my husband's insistence, I went for counselling. I felt like such a failure going into that room for the first time – like I was admitting failure. I didn't say a word during the first session. I just cried and cried. Strangely enough, even that made me feel better. It sounds trite but, over the course of a few months, talking about the stresses and anxieties lifted a weight from my shoulders."

She sits back and takes another bite of her sandwich, as if this is the most normal conversation she has ever had.

"In the end, we got Ronan, but I never forgot how much counselling helped. That's why I decided to train myself. But, Ciara," she leans forward again, "what has surprised me most over the years is that people come to me for counselling when they want a baby, but end up talking about other things. It's amazing how much unburdening helps."

I stare at a small scratch on the table.

"Look, you and Nikki obviously communicate well. But you are also clearly going through a challenging time. Maybe I can be of some assistance. I like Nikki. I want to help you both."

She stands.

"I'll go now. If you decide you want to meet me, apparently you have my number." She grins slyly, and I raise my eyes to meet hers, half-ashamed, half-amused.

At that moment, I hear Nikki jog down the stairs and into the kitchen. She holds up her phone. "Sorry to interrupt, but can I borrow Ciara for a minute? There's a call we need to take."

"No problem, I was leaving anyway," says Ann, all business. She grabs her coat from the back of her chair and picks up the remainder of her sandwich. "I'll take this to go if that's all right," she says over her shoulder as she walks past us to the door. She stops before walking through and looks back. "Talk to you soon, girls."

Nikki and I stand there until we hear the front door close. When we turn to each other, her face reflects something like uncertainty. I think mine must too.

"Who is it?" I ask, indicating the phone.

She puts it to her ear, keeping her eyes on me. "Brian? I'm putting you on speakerphone."

I glance at her questioningly before looking down at the phone as she holds it between us. I greet Brian briefly, remembering his call that I ignored earlier, wondering what he could have to say to us both.

"Hi, Ciara. Listen, I was just saying to Nikki – sorry to jump past the pleasantries, but have you heard from Stephen?"

My eyes dart to Nikki, who shrugs. "Stephen? No, I haven't talked to him in ages actually. Why, what's wrong?"

"I don't know," Brian says, sounding out of breath. "I was supposed to meet him for golf earlier. He didn't show up. He and Lisa aren't answering their phones, and Trish doesn't know where he is either. A few minutes ago, I picked up a garbled voice message."

"Where are you now, Brian?" Nikki asks.

"I'm at home. I must have missed his call while I was driving. Stephen was supposed to meet me a couple of hours ago. After a while, I just gave up and drove home. In all the time we've been playing, Stephen has never bailed on a game."

"What did his message say?" I ask, looking down at the phone instead of at Nikki.

I hear Brian sigh wearily. "He said sorry for the short notice but he'd have to cancel because he needed to do some work on the house with Lisa. Then I heard some kind of commotion."

Nikki's eyes narrow but I ignore her. The last time Stephen's name was spoken between us she was all but accusing him of beating up his girlfriend. I won't give credence to that by acknowledging her suspicions now.

"I heard this sort of banging in the background and raised voices," Brian continues, "and then it cut off. I'm a bit uneasy. I think maybe I should call over to him."

"We'll go to Stephen and Lisa's place now," Nikki interrupts. "He's just cancelled on you – it would be less weird if Ciara and I happened to drop by."

Brian agrees to this plan, relief dripping from his thanks.

Nikki hangs up.

"Do you really think there is a need to go traipsing over to Stephen's?" I ask, somewhat impatiently. "So he missed a golf game, big deal. Look, I'll give him a ring."

Nikki watches me with a blank face as I take out my mobile. The call goes straight to voicemail.

"I don't want to give us something else to fight about, Ciara, but I told you what I saw the day I had coffee with Lisa. And it's not just the missed game – that call to Brian sounds strange. Something's not right."

I tut. "You're catastrophising."

I am inclined to dismiss Brian's concerns. Stephen probably forgot about the game and, most likely, he is now doing exactly as he said – some DIY jobs for his demanding girlfriend. But Nikki is already marching outside so I follow her, seething. I haven't seen Stephen in three weeks, not since we drank beer and ate chocolate in Trish's house in an effort to console her after the *Current Times* interview. Normally, I'd be delighted with an impromptu visit. But Nikki and I are in the middle of a potentially life-changing discussion. That she can drop it all to run to the aid of another is one of the reasons I love her, yet it fans the angry flames kindling around my heart.

We sit into our car with a mingled atmosphere of anger and concern cascading around us.

"Did you ever ask Stephen about the bruises I saw on Lisa's wrist?" Nikki asks, reversing out of the driveway.

"Of course not!"

"Funny thing," she says, somehow implying the opposite, "that you would jump to the worst conclusion possible after you went snooping around my phone and found those messages from Ann. Yet at the mere suggestion that Stephen might be less than perfect, you leap to his defence."

I bite down on my tongue, not wanting to have another argument. But I cannot hold it in any longer.

"You let Ann come to the house without telling me? Really?"

"She wanted to meet you," Nikki says defensively. "You did call her out of the blue trying to get information on me. How could you go behind my back like that?"

"I told you I was sorry. And you were the one who left me

215

wondering who the hell she was. It's not strange that I jumped to conclusions."

Nikki sighs. "Look, we both made mistakes."

I pause. "Ann said neither of us is the bad guy."

She gives me a sideways smile. "I'd like to think she's right."

We travel the rest of the journey in silence, though it is very loud inside my head.

Nikki cuts the engine on the road outside Stephen's house. She turns to me.

"Look, Ciara —" she begins.

I cut her off. "Let's deal with one disaster at a time."

"I was just going to say I'm sorry I jumped to conclusions about Stephen." She smiles hesitantly. "We'll probably find him up a ladder painting, with Lisa directing him from her armchair."

Together, we get out of the car. Their driveway is long, with tall bushes blocking our view from the road. As we walk to the door, I notice weeds poking up from the ground and wet leaves clumped by the drainpipe. They have really let the place go. The outside of the house could do with a coat of paint. Clearly, work does need to be done on the house. Stephen was telling Brian the truth. There's nothing wrong. I don't know why I experience such a strong sense of relief – I never doubted him in the first place.

I lift my hand to ring the doorbell when I hear a yell. It is a high-pitched woman's scream. Nikki and I jerk our heads simultaneously to the living-room window. They had expensive triple-glazed windows installed before Stephen lost his job last year and the sound is muffled. We wouldn't have heard it except that we are right by the house.

"Sounds like they're having a domestic," I whisper, embarrassed to have caught them fighting. "Maybe we should go."

"Go?" Nikki asks, as if it's the craziest suggestion she has ever heard.

"We wouldn't want people nosing about in the middle of our arguments, would we?" I grab her arm as she makes to move to the window.

Nikki shrugs me off. "We let off steam in the garden. We're hardly secretive about it."

"Come on!" I start to creep away as I hear more yelling. I cannot make out what Lisa is saying, but she is clearly enraged.

Nikki has already picked her way over to the window and is staring inside.

"Nikki?"

She ignores me, maintaining her gaze, transfixed by what she's seeing inside. Unable to take the suspense, I stamp across to her and squint in through the glare shining on the window.

Stephen is squatting on the floor, curled into a ball, his hands shielding his head. At first, I cannot grasp the scene before me. Then I see her. Lisa comes toward him, a wineglass in her hand. With another shout – this time I hear it clearly – she brings the glass down upon him. It shatters on his hands, glass splintering outwards, washing over him like a shower.

The smash releases us from our dream-like denial. Together, as one, Nikki and I scream, pounding our fists against the glass.

Chapter twenty-seven

STEPHEN

Panic engulfs me. With a physical lurch of nausea, I spring to my feet. I have an insane urge to leap in front of Lisa – to protect her from Nikki and Ciara banging on the window.

Lisa and I lock eyes like co-conspirators. My legs waver with contradictory impulses. I want to flee from the beatings, the shouting, the terror of the past few days. Minutes ago, all I wanted was a chance to escape the hold Lisa has on me. Now that saviours are here for me, I'm paralysed.

Lisa teeters, as if trying to decide whether to scream at them to get away or attempt damage control by coming up with an excuse. Ciara disappears from the window. Within seconds, there is banging on the door.

Nikki is rooted to the spot. I look at her reluctantly. In her eyes I see everything I had feared about discovery – pity for the pitiful man. Her head jerks away from the window suddenly at the sound of breaking glass. Lisa and I both jump at the noise. Through the door leading to the hall a small rock rolls into sight.

After a few seconds, Ciara steps into view. Her scarf is wrapped around her hand. My mouth falls open as I realise what she has done.

"Did you just smash our door?" Lisa asks in outrage.

Blood stains the cream scarf. She must have cut herself reaching in the broken glass panel of our door to unlock it from the inside.

In an unusual role reversal, it is Ciara who stares at us with tears welling in her eyes while Nikki barges past her, striding across the room until she is nose to nose with Lisa.

"*Sit down*," she says with a menace I have never heard in her voice.

I want to intervene but my throat is empty. My whole body is hollow.

Lisa opens her mouth as if to argue when Nikki pulls her phone out of her pocket and holds it up. At her jerky movement Lisa flinches, as if expecting a blow. When none comes, she flushes red and sits on the seat behind her without looking at any of us.

"We're going into the kitchen," Nikki says, staring down at Lisa. "Don't leave the house, or I'll call the Gardaí and I swear to God, Lisa, I'll have you charged with assault by the end of the day."

Without waiting for an answer, she strides over to Ciara who is swaying on her feet by the living-room door.

"Let me see, sweetheart," Nikki reaches out and lifts Ciara's hand. A red circle is oozing through the scarf.

Without thinking, I follow them into the kitchen. Ciara's face is a grey-white. She does not object as Nikki sits her on a chair and starts to unwrap the scarf. The cuts are deeper than I would have expected, and I recoil at one particularly ugly gash above the knuckle on her index finger.

Nikki grabs a tea-towel and holds it under the tap. For a moment I tense. Is the kitchen clean enough for visitors? The irrelevance of such a concern is almost funny, but humour seems beyond me. I hover behind Nikki as she sits and dabs Ciara's hand. When the towel touches the raw gashes, Ciara flinches away, crying out. Nikki asks me to fetch a glass of water and something sweet, to give Ciara a sugar boost.

I rummage through the cupboards. When I turn around, Nikki has her phone to her ear.

"What are you doing?" I drop the box of Roses and rush over to her. She does not back away.

"Orla?" she says into the phone, continuing to stare at me in what could be a reassuring or threatening way. "Ciara has cut her hand."

There is a pause as we examine Ciara, whose eyes are slightly unfocussed.

"I don't know if it needs stitches, Orla. Can you come here and take a look?"

Nikki gives the address and hangs up, slipping the phone into her pocket. I pick up the sweets and hand them to her. She takes a toffee from the packet, removes the crinkling paper and pops it into Ciara's mouth.

She unwraps another sweet. "No point us sitting for hours in the emergency room only to be told she doesn't need stitches after all. Orla is a nurse, she'll know what to do."

I nod and watch as Nikki tilts Ciara's chin upwards to feed her a second sweet. I turn from the tender scene like the intruder I am. I pour a glass of water. Ciara takes it from me with a weak smile and sucks in small sips. It seems to help, and within a few minutes a pinch of colour is restored to her face.

Satisfied, Nikki sits. "Do you have a first aid kit, Stephen?"

I find a box of plasters and slings in the cupboard under the sink. Nikki cuts a strip from the long bandage and begins to cover the wounds. Ciara moans while Nikki murmurs words of comfort.

I wring my hands as I watch them. Ciara is not prone to self-sympathy or dramatics. Her ligament injury – the one that stopped her competing in the Olympics four years ago – must have been incredibly painful but all she cared about was the race. Her whimpering as the bandage brushes her exposed cuts tightens my chest.

Nikki looks up at me and points to the first aid kit. "Do you need anything?"

221

I shake my head immediately. The wineglass had broken on my hands but had bruised rather than cut me. I had brushed away the stray splinters without injury. My ego was irreparably damaged, but nothing from the first aid kit was going to help that.

We sit for a few more moments, until Ciara looks up. "I'm fine," she says weakly. Nikki cuts the excess bandage away and stands slowly, moving behind Ciara. She faces me, placing her hands on Ciara's shoulders.

Together, they contemplate me, Nikki with compassion etched into her face and Ciara with the wide eyes of a confused child.

A terrific shame burns at my heart. None of us know what to say.

Eventually, Ciara rises, with effort. She reaches her arms around me and buries her face in my chest, the tears falling once more.

"I'm sorry," she manages. "I didn't know."

"Stephen," Nikki says, watching me curl my useless arms around her girlfriend. "How long has this been going on?"

I want to deny everything but I cannot find the words. My back is stinging from Lisa's latest blows. A horrible pounding beats in my eyes and I dare not blink. Thankfully, Lisa's voice floats in from the living room.

"Nikki?" she calls.

Nikki's mouth tightens and Ciara untangles herself from me. Before I can stop them, they have marched into the living room. I follow.

Lisa is standing in the centre of the room, her jaw set.

"I hope there hasn't been a misunderstanding," she begins.

I taste a flare of anger from the pit of my stomach. That defiance, which bubbles to the surface sporadically, but which Lisa's put-downs have always quashed, is fed by the presence of my friends by my side. Although the revelation of our secret is horrifying, it is also liberating. I remain silent.

"There's no misunderstanding," Ciara says. "We saw exactly how you treat Stephen, and you're completely deluded if you think you can explain it away."

"Stephen," Lisa gestures to me, her body shaking, "Stephen, tell them it's not what it looks like."

I don't know what to say. I feel as if I'm swimming underwater. When I say nothing, Lisa appeals to Nikki.

"You saw the bruises on my wrist," she says imploringly.

I finally find my voice. "I was just trying to stop her." I press into the words, needing to convince my friends that, though I'm not perfect, I would never do to Lisa what they saw her do to me through the window.

Lisa growls at me. Nikki steps closer, as if to shield me. The motion appears to anger Lisa further.

"*Why couldn't you mind your own business?*" she screams, so suddenly Nikki jumps.

"Stephen is our business," Ciara says coldly. She turns to me. "Brian was worried about you," she says unsteadily. "He said it wasn't normal for you to cancel golf. He thought something was up when he heard a commotion during your voice message. So did Nikki. But I wasn't going to come here, Stephen – I assumed you were fine. I'm sorry."

She makes to hug me again. I don't know if I can cope with any more consoling affection.

"Where is Brian?" I ask, to distract her but also because I had thought that if anyone would arrive at the house today it would be him. I had been dreaming about it like a pathetic princess. When Lisa's rage reached fever level during the past two days, I was scared I would never escape the house without a rescuer.

"He's gone home," Nikki answers, not taking her eyes off Lisa.

After a few more seconds of silence, Lisa shrieks again, clearly unable to handle the tension. "*What do you want?*" She flails her arms once more.

"Screw this," Nikki says viciously. "I'm ringing the Gardaí."

Lisa's eyes dart to mine, willing me to stop it. Expecting that I would defend her, defend us. But my friends are my armour against her power, and it makes me strong enough to at least do nothing. I cast my eyes to the floor.

"Stop." Lisa's voice is commanding and spoken with a calmness born from confidence. "Don't call anyone."

"Sorry, sister," Nikki shakes her head. "You've been abusing your partner for who knows how long. That's assault. You're not getting away with it."

Lisa rounds on me instead. "Are you going to let them do this? What will people think of you – unable to defend yourself against little me? No one will believe you and those that do, well, they'll despise you for your weakness."

"I swear to God, I'll be doing some assaulting myself if you don't shut up," Ciara snarls. "Nikki, make the call."

"Wait, Nikki," Lisa says, sounding strangely serene. "I didn't want to have to do this, but you're leaving me no choice. If you tell anyone what's been going on in this house, I'll let out a little secret of my own."

"What secret?" asks Ciara. "I think we've discovered the worst of your skeletons."

With a full view of the room, I see what a mess we have made of it. Glass is scattered across the floor, the coffee table lies on its side and the seat cushions are upended. Yet it is her face I notice most of all. It has that smugness she gets when standing above me, preparing to strike.

"This secret isn't mine alone," she sneers. "It belongs to Trish, too."

"Trish?" Nikki says in astonishment. "What does Trish have to do with any of this?"

"Oh nothing," Lisa replies smoothly. "Except that I happen to know a little something about her. Come on, Stephen," she says, strutting across the room toward me. In their confusion, my friends do not stop her. "You've been poking around this issue for days. Surely even you could have figured it out by now."

"Back off him, Lisa," Nikki warns, her voice dropping deep.

Lisa leans in to me and whispers into my ear so only I can hear. "You know why she and Brian broke up, don't you?"

Ciara marches over and shoves Lisa from me. In the scuffle, she must have knocked her hand because she cries out, clinging to it. Nikki rushes to her. I stare past them to Lisa, who is nodding elatedly.

My mind feels like mush, but I trudge my way through the facts Lisa is so convinced will bring me to the right conclusion.

Brian and Trish, I learned recently, broke up because she didn't want kids. What has that got to do with anything? Trish mightn't be blabbing it to everyone but it's hardly enough for Nikki and Ciara to let Lisa get away with what they saw.

Out of nowhere, it crystallises. There have been recent, odd connections between Trish and Lisa – a woman named Abby I never heard of until this week, and a young twenty-two-year-old who died in a clinic in England. Trish had been near hysterical when her death was announced, and a mention of Mary O'Sullivan pushed Lisa over the brink of sanity, and me down the stairs.

Yet neither of them had ever mentioned a Mary O'Sullivan before. Could it be that it was not the person, but the place that terrified them both?

Without thinking, I blurt it out. "Are you trying to tell me you had an abortion?"

"What?" cry Ciara and Nikki together.

Their heads twist between me and Lisa. It must seem such a random, irrelevant comment. I couldn't stop the question bursting from me. The thought that Lisa had somehow been a victim of that clinic mixes with revulsion that it was my child she went there to destroy.

"No, I didn't have an abortion," Lisa says, and for a moment I am lightheaded with relief.

I sink into the couch behind me. She allows me a second of peace, before shattering it all.

"But I did get pregnant, and I did go to Charrings Clinic."

"Charrings Clinic?" the girls exclaim, again in unison.

Lisa is in control once more. "Do you want me to tell the story or not?"

"I think not," Nikki says indignantly. "I'm sorry you have a

225

history with that place, Lisa. From what they're saying on the news, it must have been awful for you." Her slightly quelled tone tightens once more. "But I'm calling the Gardaí."

"Give me five minutes," Lisa says, "and you will understand. Or else go ahead, ring them. But you'll spend every waking moment of the rest of your life regretting it, and wishing you had spared me five minutes."

"I want to hear this," I say authoritatively. "Please, Nikki, Ciara," I look meaningfully at them, "let her say what she has to, and then we'll leave."

Nikki shifts on the spot. After a moment she throws her eyes upward in defeat and steers Ciara onto the couch, fixing the cushions before lowering her down. She sits beside her and points to her watch. "Five minutes, Lisa," she says.

For a second, Lisa freezes, as if uncertain where to start. Then she crosses her arms and begins.

Lisa discovered she was pregnant, apparently, the week after I was let go from TJ Simons. She claims she was overwhelmed – afraid to tell me because I was already under so much stress. She knew that, without my job, we could not afford to raise a child.

I observe her carefully, trying to read her expressionless face. Perhaps she has beaten all the trust out of me, but I cannot believe her. I was unemployed, but not destitute. We weren't homeless, and I had options. Moving abroad. Tightening our belts for a few years – the economy would pick up, I would get something.

But that's not Lisa. She doesn't want to be poor and she wouldn't put her life on hold for anyone, not even a baby. For Lisa, success is a stage filled with sparkling things, not midnight feeds and college funds. There is nothing wrong with that. Lisa doesn't have to want a child. Except I thrust one into her, and she panicked.

"I wish you'd told me," I say.

Her eyes water. "I was waiting. I thought if you got another job, maybe we could make it work."

I shake my head sadly. "No, you didn't. You were never going to have that baby. It's okay," I rush on before she can interrupt, "I know

226

kids aren't your thing. But this wasn't just about you. We didn't have a one-night stand. We were living together, for crying out loud. I deserved to know."

"It's my body," Lisa spits irately.

I hold up a hand, finding it surreal that I can challenge her. "I'm not saying I would have forced you to have it," I say. "But I had a right to know, Lisa."

"It would only have upset you," Lisa whispers.

I feel Ciara and Nikki tense beside me. I cannot blame them for doubting her altruistic motives after what they witnessed.

But I know Lisa in a way they do not. She is a complex person, scarred from an unloving home. She brought the viciousness of her own father to our relationship, but she is not wholly at fault. After all, I came with my own baggage – so put-down that I was unable to confront her.

The way she treated me, it created a hatred inside of me. Now that the truth is out, I am finally free to see her clearly, and I see the good as well as the bad. Lisa has redeeming qualities, though she may have lost them recently. I believe her when she says she considered my feelings. But it is all too late now.

Ciara cuts across our regretful gaze. "Lisa, get to the point."

"I made my decision to go to England, to get rid of it." She looks down. "But I was scared. I didn't want to do it alone. So I contacted an old friend, one I had cast aside years ago because she had an abortion herself."

"Wait a minute," Ciara frowns, "is this the friend Deirdre Olden had expelled from your school?"

"Yes," Lisa nods. "Abby. She agreed to go with me to England. I had the abortion clinic all picked out, and the appointment made, but she said she had a special connection with a different clinic. More discreet, and cheaper. They specialised in keeping things under the radar. It sounded like exactly what I needed, and I wouldn't be alone. Plus she would lend me the money."

My mind spins. How could Lisa have trusted her?

Pre-empting my question, Lisa looks at me. "Abby knew what it was like to go through that, with everyone against her. I thought she'd understand. But she was just using me. She was using all those girls." She speaks quietly. "The clinic was cheap, but she was not. I had to borrow from my boss to pay her back. He thought it was for bills, because you'd lost your job, Stephen. I still owe him a fortune."

"We'll pay him," I say fiercely. "Don't worry."

"Don't worry?" Nikki cuts across. "You've got to be kidding, Stephen. She lied to you. She – she's been abusing you, for God's sake!"

"Hang on," Ciara holds up a hand. "Why are you telling us this, Lisa? If you think it'll make us feel so sorry for you that we'll forget what you did to our friend you're mistaken."

Lisa gives an oddly calculating smile. "No, I know you're not going to let this go. Which is why I'm telling you. I'm not the only one Abby brought to Charrings Clinic."

"Lisa, no!" I try to stop her but it's too late.

"Your friend, Trish. She had an abortion."

Ciara simply laughs. "No, she didn't."

"Yes, she did. Years ago, before she ever became an air hostess. Abby told me all about it. It was shortly after she and her long-term boyfriend had broken up."

Ciara's eyebrows flicker. "No. She would have told us."

"Would she?" I shake my head.

Ciara jerks around to look at me.

"Ciara, you know Trish is so private, even with us. She probably wanted to get it done and forget about it."

"Why are you saying all this, Lisa?" Nikki's eyes are blazing. I can tell she already knows the answer.

"Because Trish Olden would rather die than have her family find out her secret. Can you imagine the reaction of her nut-job of a mother? And with her sister on a moral crusade to raise funds to keep her baby alive? How do you think it would play to the media for the youngest Olden daughter to have had an abortion? To be associated with the worst back-alley clinic since the 50s?"

Our laboured breathing is all that fills the silence.

228

"So," Lisa says loudly, causing the girls to jump, "you stay out of our business, and we'll stay out of Trish's. No one needs to know about her connection with Charrings."

"We're not leaving Stephen here with you!" Ciara says with equal vigour.

"I know that," Lisa snipes. "But if anyone asks, we broke up because we wanted different things in life, or whatever. There is no need to involve the Gardaí. Agreed?"

I agree so readily Ciara and Nikki stare at me in shock.

"I'm fine," I touch Ciara's arm, trying to convince her, "and we can't let Trish take the fall for this."

Ciara growls. "You are a Class A bitch, Lisa."

The doorbell rings. "That must be Orla," Nikki says.

"Wait a minute." They all turn to me. My eyes are fastened on Lisa. "Earlier you said you never had an abortion. Why did you say that?"

Lisa gives a sort of shrug. "Because it's true. It's not an easy decision, you know, to terminate a pregnancy. I was stressed and worried and indecisive."

"Are you saying you had second thoughts?"

"Yes," she whispers. "I could sort of distract myself from the reality of it, while I was making plans with Abby and trying to hide it all from you. When I got over there, I started to doubt whether I was able go through with it. I was scared. I didn't know what to do. I told Abby and at first she was sympathetic but when I continued talking about pulling out, she got mad. She said I'd made a commitment and she'd spent a lot of money helping me, and people needed to be paid and I had to go through with it."

I glance at Ciara and Nikki, who are staring at her with open mouths. I know what they are thinking. Opinionated, abusive Lisa – she should have had no trouble kicking this Abby to the kerb.

The doorbell rings again but we all ignore it.

"You don't know what it was like." Lisa sits heavily. "I was nauseous. I was so tired as I tried to figure it all out. It wasn't until I was outside the clinic that I made up my mind."

"What do you mean?" Nikki asks, apparently unable to contain herself. "Made up your mind to do what?"

"It doesn't matter," she says blankly. "It doesn't matter whether I decided to have an abortion or keep the baby. Because standing in front of that building, having made my decision, I felt a warm wetness trickle down my leg. When I looked down, I saw red."

Nikki gasps, and Ciara's hand flies to her mouth.

For a stupid second, I don't make the connection. Then I blurt it out. "You lost the baby?"

She nods as a choking sob escapes her lips. I have the strongest urge to go to her. I hold off, almost swaying on the spot with indecision, as she must have been while delaying outside that clinic.

The doorbell rings, this time followed by a knocking. Nikki bustles distractedly into the hall to open the door. Ciara follows her. I stare down at Lisa, drying her eyes on her sleeve. My heart pulls as my throat tightens.

I back away from her to join my friends in the hall.

Chapter twenty-eight

TRISH

A slashing sensation cuts through my head. I dry-swallow two paracetamol. My brain is too full – I need help to switch it off. I click on the heating and pour myself a generous measure of red wine.

Brian messaged earlier to say Stephen left a garbled voicemail – something about doing jobs around the house for Lisa – and that Ciara was planning on popping in to him anyway. Glad that at least one drama has been averted, I settle in for a night on my own. I plan on drawing a bubble bath – my second of the day – then sitting in my robe with a box of chocolates and watching a cheesy film on television.

But the parting image of Beth and Larry holding hands beside Conall's cot fills me with guilt. I am considering driving back to the hospital when the doorbell rings. I ignore it. Who would be calling on a Sunday evening?

It rings again. I sigh resignedly and slouch out to the hall.

I pull open the door with such little expectation that, when I see

231

her standing there, it takes me a minute to grasp it is really her before me.

"Hello, Trish. It's been a long time."

I slam the door shut instinctively.

Abby's foot kicks out, stopping the door before it closes. She barges inside.

"Thanks," she says pleasantly, as though I had graciously welcomed her in with a sweep of my arm. She scans the hall. "So, this is your house. Not too shabby, Trish. I heard you snagged yourself a fancy new job."

She runs her finger along the wall as she strolls into the kitchen. "Dusty. Could do with a repaint."

I gaze out the front door she has left open and contemplate running through it. But where would I go? No one will want to help me once they find out why I'm seeking to escape her and, besides, she would find me. I close the door slowly and follow her into the kitchen like a new breed of Stockholm prisoner.

She spins around, her lips stretched wide. "Drinking alone, I see. So sad."

I watch her as she walks calmly around my kitchen, inspecting it. She looks older than I would have expected after a mere seven years. She hides it well, with her stylish outfit and blow-dried hair. But the bags under her eyes are long and grey, and she has lost weight in her cheeks.

I am revolted by the fear that envelops me. When I look at her, I see not only her face, but his. The doctor with no name. I clench my groin muscles at the memory of his cold hands on me.

The terror I have been holding in for this past week is released. Tears cascade down my cheeks and I don't stop her when she comes to me, tilting her head in sympathy. She wipes away the tears. I cannot bring myself to object as she wraps her arms around me. She is the one person who knows what happened to me over there, even if she is the cause of my pain.

After a few minutes, I pull away from her.

"Better now?" she asks in a motherly way.

I nod and walk around her into the living room. I sit in the armchair and take long, deep breaths, listening to her clattering around the kitchen. She comes in a few minutes later with two glasses of wine. She passes one to me. I take it.

"What happened in here?" she asks, gesturing to the paint-splattered wall with her glass as she eases onto the couch under the window. I don't answer. It is a lot better since Stephen helped me scrape the bigger blobs away, but it is still a mess.

Abby takes a noisy sip. "It's a stressful time, isn't it?"

I nod. She must be wondering if I have become completely mute.

"Listen, Trish," she speaks in a tone that implies utter reasonableness on her part, "there's no need for you to worry. Everything will go on as it did before. It's been – how many years since you travelled to England with me?"

"Seven."

She smiles. "You see? It's nobody's business and you have managed to keep it that way. No reason that should change now."

A flash of annoyance pierces my temples. "You changed it," I say, a daring nerve coming from nowhere. "You told Lisa."

She bows her head and takes another sip of her drink. I copy her, needing the help.

"Yes, I did."

That tiniest fleck of an admission, though it falls far short of an apology or basic explanation, is enough to embolden me. It has been many years since I followed Abby meekly to Charrings. I am older, more experienced. I know myself better. The uncontrollable bout of tears that took over when Abby first crossed my threshold has exorcised the worst of my terrors. I can, at least in the security of my own home, confront her.

"Why did you do that to me, Abby? To all those girls? Mary O'Sullivan – just a college kid?"

"She was over eighteen," says Abby quietly.

Further bolstered by the apologetic quality of her statement, I cross my arms. "Is that your cut-off point?"

233

Abby sets her glass down on the coffee table with such force that the red wine sloshes over the sides onto her hands. She doesn't acknowledge the spill.

"Yes," she says without a hint of remorse. "Eighteen is my cut-off point."

I shake my head sadly. "You might not be exploiting children, Abby, but you're doing it to vulnerable, scared young women who need a friend."

"No one was ever my friend." She wipes the redness on her grey trousers. "I was only sixteen. Your mother led the marches against my mere presence in your school after I travelled to England."

I say nothing. An ingrained loyalty will not let me apologise on my mother's behalf, especially when I know she is not sorry.

"My own family kicked me out after that. I had to fend for myself. Sleep around, sell drugs. I used to rob houses in the area just to have enough to eat."

I cannot help asking. "Did my sister not help you? She was your friend."

Abby leans back, the plump cushions absorbing her. "I thought that too but she bailed on me. Beth was brainwashed by your mother, and as for Lisa – well, she knew which side her bread was buttered on. Siding with the baby-killing drug addict wasn't going to help her escape her own family, was it?"

I stand, folding my arms across my body. The blotched walls shimmer before me. I take a deep breath.

"Why did you talk to Lisa about me? She could tell her boyfriend, who is one of my best friends. She could tell my family. You can't have missed the media attention around Beth, surely?"

"Of course not," says Abby with a strangely satisfied cadence. "I watched you, simpering nervously on Margaret Elderfield's couch."

My stomach drops. The thought of Abby with her eyes on me is sickening.

"You promised you wouldn't betray me, Abby." I am surprised at the depth of my indignation, considering she put me through worse. "You were responsible for my experience in Charrings, but I trusted you with my secret. Now you've outed me to someone in my closest circle of friends. Why?"

Obviously Abby senses that my agitation is swelling to aggression. She holds up a hand. "Trish, I'm in trouble. You're not stupid – you must be able to take an educated guess at the number of women I've helped. Most of them experienced no negative after-effects."

"But some did," I cut in.

"Yes, like you, some did. Mary O'Sullivan was the worst. No one ever died until her, Trish. I'm convinced she must have had other problems that caused the internal bleeding."

I stand, my arm trembling as I shake a finger in her direction. "Don't you dare blame her! That man gave me a leather belt to bite away the pain. It was only a matter of time before he murdered someone. I'm surprised it took seven years. You're avoiding my question. Why did you tell Lisa about me?"

Abby's face has gone pale. "Mary O'Sullivan had her operation on a Friday. There were complications from the start. I took care of her all through the night, but by Saturday morning it was clear she was spiralling. Even though it meant putting Charrings on the line, I had to get her help."

I cock my head in disgust at the tinge of self-sacrifice in her voice.

"I knew it would be worse if she died. I've never had to bring anyone to hospital in the ten years that I've been taking women to Charrings. I know you think it's the worst place in the world, but you survived, didn't you?"

My stomach flutters at the memory of begging Abby for a doctor. "Why didn't they arrest you at the hospital?" I ask.

She rolls her eyes. "Do you think I'd waltz in with her? I might as well have handcuffed myself there and then. Polly and I dropped her off around the corner. All she had to do was walk in. I assumed she'd live and confess everything. I needed time to work it out. I honestly didn't think they'd fail to save her."

"It wasn't their failure, Abby," I say harshly. "It was yours."

"Out of all the women I helped," Abby says loudly, over me, "there are about twenty who really hold a grudge. I needed to warn them straight away not to react when Mary O'Sullivan woke up and the news leaked. I hold their confidence, so they need to keep mine. Lisa was one of the first I called."

"When did she go to you?" I ask, thinking of Stephen.

Abby's response is quiet. "Less than six months ago."

"But that doesn't make any sense." I shake my head. Lisa would have been able to afford one of the proper clinics. That was after Stephen lost his job but he got a redundancy payment. They would have had savings. "She wouldn't have needed a loan from you."

Abby takes another sip of wine. "She had her reasons. Can you not remember when you were in her shoes? She needed a friend to help her through it."

I shake my head, unable to believe that Lisa would not pay for the best.

Abby shrugs again, indifference oozing from her. "Something about her having a joint bank account with her boyfriend. He would have wanted to know why she needed such a large sum. And I suppose she felt she could trust me. I have experience with this, as Lisa knew only too well."

My legs shudder under me. "Then why did you ring her first? Why is she one of the twenty who hold a grudge? What did you do to her?"

"Don't be so melodramatic," Abby snaps. "She didn't get the abortion."

"What do you mean?"

"She lost the baby before she could go through with the termination."

I gasp.

Abby stands and continues, completely unaffected by what she has just revealed. "The point is, Lisa still owed me money and she wasn't happy when I insisted on payment." She pauses, as though reassessing. "That's putting it mildly. We had blazing rows. I was on the cusp of telling her boyfriend about our arrangement. Eventually,

236

she paid me, but she said I'd live to regret the way I treated her. As if she hadn't been the one who came to me for help!"

I watch her without saying a word. She is worrying her hands in a way that could be threatening.

She looks up suddenly, as if wanting to get this over with as fast as possible. "I rang Lisa to make sure she'd stay quiet. She laughed at me. She said she had been hoping someday she'd have the opportunity to get back at me. She said I would be undone by Mary O'Sullivan – that she wasn't scared of me anymore. She was testing me, Trish. That's why I had to tell her about you."

"What do you mean?"

"If you feel so bad for poor Mary O'Sullivan, why haven't you come forward yet?"

I say nothing.

Abby smirks. "Because it's not about you any more. Beth is relying on the generosity of pro-lifers to fund her baby's healthcare. Don't think I'm oblivious to the ticker-tape running along the bottom of the screen whenever your mother and sister show up on television. *Donate to Conall. Help keep Conall alive.* Beth's credibility will be shot if your association with Charrings is ever revealed." Her face contorts with a sneering smile. "Not that it would bother me, given how Beth abandoned me, and how instrumental your mother was in my downfall. It would give me great pleasure to watch their worlds crumble."

I bite down on my anger and impatience. "What's this got to do with Lisa?"

"Most women I bring to Charrings keep it a secret because they are embarrassed, or ashamed. They worry about what their parents or friends would think. But you have something more important to think about than your own reputation. Yes, your family would disown you, your mother would probably publically shame you. But worst of all, your sister's campaign for her sick baby would be compromised." Abby leans forward. "If I was willing to tell *your* story, Lisa would not doubt that I'd expose anyone else without a second thought. Including her."

My ears hum loudly. "But you only told Lisa, right? You didn't tell anyone else, Abby?"

She smiles. "Of course. Your secret is safe with me – and with Lisa. Once she saw that I was willing to reveal you, she knew I wouldn't hesitate to tell her boyfriend. She called my bluff and she lost. Do you know, I think she was under the ridiculous impression that, because we had been friends long ago, I would never actually out her. Even though she's the one who abandoned me when I needed her most!"

Abruptly, Abby starts walking to the front door.

"This visit is a formality. I know you won't reveal me to the investigation, because I would destroy your sister in return. Now I can be sure that Lisa won't either. Her boyfriend would learn not only of her own trip to Charrings but that, by telling the world about me, she caused me to reveal *your* secret. You're one of his best friends. Do you think he would ever look at her the same way again? She won't risk it."

She smirks at my fallen face. I watch her open the door and slam it behind her without another word.

As quickly as she charged back into my life, she is gone.

Chapter twenty-nine

STEPHEN

Nikki's face is ashen as she leads Ciara's sister into the living room.

"Stephen, Lisa, this is Orla," she says with forced civility.

Orla nods to us briefly before striding across the room and taking Ciara's face between her hands. The baby dangling from her chest squeals happily as he is pressed between the sisters. Ciara strokes his stomach with her good hand, holding up the other for her sister to see.

Orla surveys the upended room. "What on earth is going on here?"

Nikki speaks first. "There was an emergency. We had to break the window to get in and Ciara went a bit overboard."

Orla looks at each one of us in turn, waiting for someone to tell her the truth. Finally she steps away from Ciara and lifts the baby from her sling. She holds him out to me and Lisa. "Will one of you take the baby while I examine my sister?"

"Stephen," says Nikki urgently. "Stephen will take him."

She nods at me meaningfully. Lisa does not react as I take the squirming bundle. Orla eyes me sceptically but clearly trusts Nikki's judgement enough to leave her baby with me. She leads Ciara into the kitchen, passing Nikki her car keys.

"Get my nurse's aid kit from the boot. I'll need the antiseptic wipes."

I remain in the living room, bouncing the cooing baby, staring down at Lisa. I try to imagine us with our own baby. A crib in the corner and a stream of visitors bringing presents. It is as unreal as an alien world. Possible, but not in my lifetime, not in my reality.

The door slams as Nikki makes her way through the hall with the aid kit. She stops at the door of the living room and peers in at us. For a second, I think she is about to ask if I am all right but she seems to think better of it and carries on. There is consoling murmuring from the kitchen and I strain to hear if the girls are telling Orla about what they saw. It is a dangerous game. The more people who know about how Lisa and I have been living, the more likely it is to become public knowledge. I have no doubt Lisa will expose Trish out of spite if I try to press charges.

After a few minutes of silence, Lisa stands and twirls away from me. The baby gurgles. I pat his back. In many ways, she is a victim. Emotionally neglected as a girl, her father demeaned her at every opportunity. She was not beaten to the extent I was, but there were drunken punches out of nowhere, stinging slaps when she tried to rebel.

How difficult it must have been for her to have stayed quiet, when her father berated her. Her explosions of emotions in recent months were born of years of repression. Funny really, that she had to lose control in order to control me. But perhaps it is not surprising that she resorted to the default of her childhood when crushed by the enormity of a lonely miscarriage.

Nikki and Ciara would say I am being too easy on her. That she was always a selfish person, who was attracted to my money and status. She is an adult – responsible for her actions.

"You won't really tell anyone about Trish, will you?"

She doesn't hesitate. "That depends on whether Ciara and Nikki can keep their mouths shut."

I swallow.

Nikki calls my name from the kitchen. Relieved, I walk in to them.

Orla glances up as I enter. "She's going to need stitches. I'll take her to the emergency department – hopefully it won't take long."

"Stephen, go home with Nikki," Ciara says. "Orla will drop me off there later."

"What about Lisa?" I ask.

Nikki and Ciara exchange a look. Orla eyes me cautiously as she packs away the last of her aid kit.

"Best to give her the night to pack up," says Nikki. "Tell her to be gone by the morning."

Orla reaches out her arms to take the baby. I pass him over and he starts to whimper.

"You're good with him," she smiles. My eyes water, and her countenance melts into one of compassion. "I'm sorry you and your girlfriend are breaking up."

Ciara rises noisily to distract Orla from my impending meltdown. Without a glance toward Lisa in the living room, the sisters head out the door. I take the stairs two at a time. In our bedroom, I throw a few essentials into a bag. My movements are robotic and my mind clear. I purposely keep my gaze from falling on the photo of us on the nightstand – a relaxed, smiling picture of happier times.

When I arrive downstairs, Nikki is waiting for me in the hall.

"Stephen," she puts a hand on my arm, "are you okay with this? Coming home with me and Ciara for a few days? When we tell Trish what's been going on, she'll probably insist we go to the Gardaí anyway."

I shake my head, gleaning strength from protecting Trish instead of being the victim myself. "Trish can't know about this. I'll stay with you guys for a few days until Lisa's gone, then I'll get on with my life."

"Stephen –" She stops, her face pained. She tries again. "When I

241

saw Lisa's bruises, I suspected you were hurting her. I'm so sorry."

Her voice breaks. I stroke her arm and do my best with inelegant words to reassure her. I could not blame Nikki for anything, not after she saved me.

I think of Orla's baby and the way he sat contentedly in my arms, although I was a stranger to him. As an only child, I am not used to kids. I had approached my career with such single-mindedness, I never considered having children. Like Lisa, my goals were material.

I imagine Lisa on the kerb of that clinic in England, my baby bleeding out of her. What if her decision had been to keep it? That could have changed everything. If, rather than hurting me, she had come to me for protection. My motivation for finding a new job would have rocketed. Everything would be different.

Of course, if she had decided to go through with the termination, who knows what that hatchet-man might have done to her on the operating table. She could have been another Mary O'Sullivan.

Morbid speculation will do no good. The reality is I lost my job. She miscarried. Together, we were unable to cope. What followed was months of brutal beatings, degrading orders and the physical dismantling of what was once a loving relationship. Maybe I will be a father one day. But it won't be with Lisa.

Nikki's hand is on my arm. "I'll wait outside," she promises. "Say goodbye, and let's go."

I part from her as she goes straight out the hall door. I turn into the living room. Lisa is sitting with her head in her hands. I walk over to her and squat down in front of her. It is not without apprehension.

"I'm going to stay with Nikki and Ciara tonight," I say. "I want you to be gone by the time I'm home tomorrow evening."

She nods.

"Where will you go?" I ask with genuine curiosity. Lisa has few friends beyond superficial acquaintances with her work colleagues.

Her mouth slants to the side in the condescending way to which I am so accustomed. "Do you care?"

I say nothing. The truth is, I don't care anymore. The rescue I so badly needed has released me emotionally too.

"No one will report you," I say. "But if I hear a whiff of a story connecting Trish to Charrings . . ."

I don't have to finish. She reaches out and strokes my cheek. I shut my eyes, trying to remember when that was a gesture that comforted me. Now, her palm is cold on my skin. My back cricks as I stand. I feel her tense, knowing it was her beating that is causing the pain.

Our eyes meet one final time. I don't know what I hoped to see there, but they are empty. Without hesitation, I walk out of her life.

Chapter thirty

CIARA

Orla is not stupid. She knows something is up. But, bless her, she doesn't push. She doesn't even ask me whether I patched things up with Nikki.

I sit in the back of the car beside Donal in his baby-seat, entertaining him with my good hand. There is something calming about interacting with a baby. They offer their entire attention and ask for nothing but eye contact in return.

He is full of chat, babbling indistinct noises, which I answer with enthusiasm. I can sense Orla's eyes on me in the mirror. It does not take long to reach the hospital. Orla has a word with the receptionist as I lower myself onto one of the plastic orange chairs in the waiting room.

"The receptionist says there's not a long queue today. You're lucky," she says, sitting beside me.

"Orla, I'm sorry about all this."

She glances sideways at me as she jiggles an orange finger-puppet at her gurgling baby. "Do you want to tell me what this is all about?"

My eyes water. "I can't. It's not my story to tell."

"It doesn't take a genius to guess. You smashed a window to get into that house – you must have been trying to help someone. One of your friends was being hurt."

I nod. "Stephen's a good guy," I say, telling her the facts without having to say the words. "It's Lisa we'll never speak to again."

My sister gives a low whistle. "Just goes to show, you never know what's going on behind closed doors." After a few minutes of silence, she changes the subject. "How's Nikki?"

I shrug.

She pats my knee. "Well, let's get your hand sorted first. One thing at a time."

I smile gratefully.

Orla takes me for dinner once the stitches are in. At first, I tell her I'd prefer to go home, anxious to see Stephen.

"You've had an injury. Your body needs building up. I'm taking you for some carb-loading," she insists as she pulls into the car park of a pizza restaurant.

"Adrian won't be happy," I warn her.

"He'll get over it," she says dismissively.

I admit to feeling more energised after a decent feed.

I give my sister an extra-long hug as she drops me off at home. "You're a terrific sister, you know that?" I murmur into her shoulder. She squeezes me tightly, and then ushers me out of the car. She waves as she drives off into the night.

I glance at my watch, twisting my key as quietly as the lock will allow. It is nearly ten o'clock.

The house is quiet. I hear shuffling upstairs and take a deep breath, knowing my discussion with Nikki is not over.

But before I can face her or Stephen, there is one thing I must do. I tip-toe into the living room. I don't bother clicking on the light. The dark feels warmer. Fumbling with my phone, I use my good hand to dial the number and hold it to my ear.

"Hello?" Trish sounds muffled, with a strange gushing noise in the background.

"Hi, Trish, it's me," I say softly. "Can you hear me?"

Her response is loud in my ear. "Yes, I can hear you. What's up, Ciara?"

"I just wanted to give you a ring. I haven't talked to you in ages. Are you at home?"

"No, I'm out. I can't stay on long. Is everything okay?"

I almost laugh. Everything is so far from okay, I feel like I've fallen through a rabbit hole. My life with Nikki is teetering on the edge of a precipice. Only for her, I would have ignored Brian's warning earlier and left Stephen in the clutches of a boyfriend-beating psychopath. And now I am talking to Trish, her with a secret I cannot tell her I know. The maze of mysteries with which we are all grappling is silencing us, strangling our friendships.

"Trish," I try to steady my voice, as my watering eyes liquefy everything else, "I want to see you. Can you call over tomorrow?"

She answers but the gushing noise muffles her voice. I suddenly recognise the sound. It is wind.

"Where are you, anyway?"

"Just out. Look, I'm not sure tomorrow will work. What's wrong, Ciara?"

I don't want to tell her over the phone. I'm not sure I want to tell her at all. But I cannot pretend it didn't happen. "Nikki and I called to Stephen earlier. I don't know how to tell you this. Lisa has been abusing Stephen."

"What?" she says loudly and confusedly.

I can picture her pressing the phone to her ear, sure she has misheard me.

"Domestic violence, Trish. She's been beating him. We saw it with our own eyes."

Trish listens in silence as I give her a rundown of our day. When I finish, I am almost in tears. Trish starts to say she will call over, but I interrupt.

"Stephen is upstairs, I think he's asleep. There's no point coming now. I promise you he's fine, Trish. We'll ring you tomorrow."

"Okay," she says reluctantly. "I can't believe it. I wish I'd never introduced Stephen to that bitch."

I rub my eyes, knowing I should admit to Trish that I learned about her connection with Charrings Clinic. I don't have the energy for it now. "Trish, I want you to know that you're a good friend. And I'm here for you."

For a few seconds, all I can hear is the wind.

"What do you mean?" she asks.

I curse myself. Of course, with Charrings now a national conversation, she will be waiting for – almost expecting – exposure.

"I just mean – Gerry never told us when he needed help. I want you to know if you ever need me, you know you can tell me anything."

Trish's voice changes – sounding almost harsh. "Why are you talking about Gerry?"

A heavy silence hangs between us.

"I cut my hand," I say wildly, hoping to distract her. "I had to get stitches."

"Oh. What happened?"

"Lisa wouldn't let us in. I had to smash the glass panel in the door." I bend over, squeezing my eyes shut. "Trish, I'd better go. I'm sorry I haven't spoken to you since the race. Things have been – busy. I'll get Stephen to ring you tomorrow. Let's catch up next week, okay?"

"Bye, Ciara. Take care of yourself."

She is gone before I can bid her goodnight.

There is a chance she is more annoyed than I realised – I did barrel out of the running club after the race without thanking the people in my life who made an effort to be there for me. I am finally realising the extent of my selfishness. My friends have been in pain. My partner has been craving the most basic of needs – a family – and I switched off on her. Even my sister was struggling. Yet all I cared about was my own goal.

"Ciara?"

I jump. Stephen's broad shadow slopes into the living room and hovers above me. I take in his imposing figure. He probably doesn't see it, but the fact that he could never use his physicality to hurt Lisa is a strength beyond anything. I pat the seat and he sits beside me in the dark. It's easier to talk this way, hiding from the true feelings shining in each other's eyes.

He coughs. "I wanted to say thanks. For today." He gingerly picks up my bandaged hand. "How is it?"

I pull away. "No lasting damage. Four stitches on my index finger, and another three on the palm of my hand. Dissolvable, so I don't need to have them removed. I'll be back to normal in no time."

We sit for a few minutes until he breaks the silence.

"Nikki said you were staying with your sister for a few days."

If it was anyone else, I would tell them to mind their own business.

"She needed some help with the kids," I say cautiously. Then I sigh. "Nikki and I were taking some time apart."

"I know. She told me. She said you guys had a fight."

My fists clench. "Did she tell you what about?"

"No. I think we've established that ours is a group of secrets." I can hear the smile in his voice.

The horrible accuracy of that sentence winds me. I lay my head against him, his warm skin comforting through his T-shirt.

"I don't want that," I say, barely recognising my own voice. "You'd think – after Gerry – we'd be better at sharing."

"So share then." He shrugs and my head slips from his shoulder.

It is the last thing I want to do, but I know he is right. If I ask for his confidences, I have to be willing to engage. I take a deep breath.

"Nikki wants kids." I pause, my throat closing.

"And you?" Stephen asks softly.

"I don't know."

There is so much more I could tell him – postponing my promise to become a parent; my first instinct when I saw those messages being suspicion; Nikki finding herself so unhappy that speaking to a counsellor was preferable to me. But ultimately they all boil down to the same issue – Nikki and I are grasping hands tightly yet pulling in separate directions. Our shoulder-sockets burn as we try to hold on. It will not be long before one of us relents.

Stephen shifts beside me on the seat. "That was why Trish and Brian broke up."

I shake my head. "Well, now we know there was more to it than that. Who knows what tortures Trish went through in that hell-hole of a clinic? It's not surprising – her aversion to pregnancy."

Although I can only make out a blur of motion in the dark, I hear Stephen rubbing his stubbly chin. "Brian might have handled that. I think the real reason they broke up is because she never told him the truth. She kept things in. Have you and Nikki been doing that?"

I think about Nikki unburdening to Ann. I nod. "But we're trying to make it right, to be completely honest with each other. As you, me and Trish should be, too. By the way, don't be surprised if you get a call from Trish. I just spoke to her."

Stephen whips his head around. "You didn't tell her about Lisa, did you?"

I pucker my brow. "Well, I didn't tell her about Lisa's threat, about Charrings. I told her . . . you know, how Lisa was treating you."

"Ah Ciara, why did you do that? I told you not to say it to her."

"No, you didn't," I say defensively. He had said no such thing, and all I had done was try to be honest with my friend.

"Oh," Stephen scowls. "Sorry, it was Nikki I told, not you. But damn, Trish, now she's going to want me to go to the Gardaí. How am I supposed to explain to her that I'm not doing that without telling her about Lisa's threat?"

"Sorry, Stephen," I say meekly. "I didn't think. I wanted to talk to Trish, and I figured she'd find out anyway."

Stephen pats my leg, his anger disintegrating. "Don't worry, we'll figure it out." He yawns. "I'm going back to bed. Nikki made up the spare room for me. Oh, and she gave me your old phone."

I turn to stare at him through the dark. "Why? What happened to your one?"

He pauses briefly. His voice is strangled when he answers. "Lisa broke it." He coughs as I put a hand on his knee. "Nikki's waiting for you. I think you should go upstairs and speak to her."

"Stephen." I move my hand to his arm as he makes to stand. "I'm sorry about Lisa."

He gives me a scratchy kiss on my cheek. As he leaves the room, he puffs out a resigned sort of sigh. Whatever problems I have with Nikki, at least we haven't resorted to power games like Lisa. We can talk as equals. I watch Stephen's shadow trudge up the stairs, and sit for another few minutes gathering courage.

When I eventually stand, I feel nervous. The tension spreads as I walk upstairs, my legs tingling as they carry me upwards. Nikki is sitting on the bed in her pyjamas. She lifts her head when I come in. Without a word, she walks to me and examines my hand.

"Seven stitches," I whisper, sounding smothered.

She nods, then pulls at my sleeve to help remove my top without hurting my hand. Then she pulls me to her, nuzzling into my neck.

I try to push her away without any real conviction. "We have to talk, Nikki."

"I know," she murmurs into my neck. "But not tonight."

She is right, of course. We have been through enough today. We are both exhausted. And more than anything else, we need each other. Indulging in my deepest want, my truest desire, I lean into her and let my mind rest.

Chapter thirty-one

TRISH

I strain my eyes in the dark to see the hand on my watch as it ticks over to midnight. I know I should go home. The temperature has plummeted in the past hour.

Midnight. The start of a new day. Of a new week. It is technically Monday morning now – all round the country workers are bedding down for a solid's night sleep before routine recommences. I pull my coat around me, shivering.

Gazing outward from the top of the world is calming. There are mountains all around, some with dizzying vertical drops, others rippling down, sliding to flatness below. I stand at the edge of the highest cliff, with a dazzling view beyond. The city sparkles up at me, mirroring the dots shimmering in the sky. Up here, in the dense darkness, the stars shine brighter than can be seen from below.

Still, they are mere specks, probably burned out already in a distant galaxy. Not enough to light the abyss, only steps away. How easy it would be now to end it all. No more mother, no more sister. Not even my friends. But they will disappear from my life anyway.

Tomorrow, once they find out the truth, they will be gone as quickly as gravity would pull me over the cliff.

I cannot make out the drop with only those useless, dead stars to guide me. I could close my eyes and run until the ground disappears and I fly, landing with a crack I will not hear on the rocky ground below.

I imagine Gerry watching the sky that morning as darkness faded away, basking in the beauty of the world he was about to leave.

Ciara's call has changed everything.

She rang while I was walking toward The Kite. I had parked the car half a mile down the road, not wanting attention drawn to it when the pub closed for the night and the car park emptied.

It was difficult to hear her as the wind picked up on the exposed road. She sounded upset. For an awful moment, I panicked that she had somehow discovered my secret. The reality was much worse. Stephen. Lisa. Abuse. I shake my head against the image. I picture Ciara breaking the window to rescue our friend. I should have been there. I should have asked Ciara whether an injured hand will affect her Olympic chances.

The Kite was closing for the night when I arrived. I loitered on the corner watching the last of the customers leave, curling into their bulky jackets, their breath puffing out as they jogged to their cars. By eleven o'clock, the owner was locking the front door. He bundled up in protective biking gear and threw his leg over his motorbike with the ease of a professional before scooting off down the road.

I crunched my way across the gravel, straining to hear anyone else, but the place was deserted. I cupped my hands around my eyes and squinted in the grimy windows. Chairs were stacked upside down on the wooden tables. A dish cloth lay abandoned on the bar.

Tracing Gerry's last steps was strangely soothing. He is the one I need to channel now. Seven years ago, he left his car here, in the grounds of The Kite. The bar would not have been open that early in the morning, but he might have hung around, like I did tonight, enjoying the solitude. Remembering the good times. The four of us used to come here regularly. When Ciara was abstaining from alcohol as part of her training, we had a ready-made driver. Stephen, Gerry and I would tease her with our cool pints of cider on summer evenings and mulled wine during the winter. She would raise her chin defiantly, gulping her virgin drinks with slurps of fake enjoyment.

I took the most direct route to the spot from where Gerry jumped, though it involved winding through brambles and over rugged terrain. I am used to the trek – I do it every year during my private moments of reflection on his anniversary, before Ciara and Stephen arrive at The Kite. It was harder to navigate in the dark. The stars were pinheads, too tiny to offer real guidance and the slice of moon was too meagre to show the way. I stumbled more than once.

When I was almost there, I tripped on a mossy clump of grass. I crashed down, gasping, thinking I had reached the edge. But it was merely a dip in the ground. My knees smarted from the knock. I should have worn warmer clothes. Pulling my hood over my head as far as it would reach, I breathed in the icy air, and continued to the edge.

I realise I have been standing here for almost an hour.

"Gerry!" I call out. No one answers. "*Gerry!*" I scream his name this time, out over the gaping expanse.

The wind cuts upwards, blasting against me. I shuffle sideways and squat down, a large rock sheltering me. I settle into a sitting position alongside the mossy boulder. From this angle, I can make out the overhang, and the sheer drop to the rocky crevice below.

"Was it easy, Gerry?" I say, quietly this time. My words are whipped from my lips and carried outwards on the wind. "Once you had made up your mind, was it easy to jump?"

Silence. Guilt. I am getting off lightly, confessing to Gerry – he cannot question my motives or have his say. Still, I have never admitted it to anyone, not even to a dead man. My knees quiver, though only the ghost of my friend will hear.

"I had an abortion," I blurt out. That familiar phrase, repeated for years in my head, booms loud in the open world. I grip my stomach, the words pouring from me. "I didn't have any money, or the strength to organise it. So I went to Abby, a woman I'd known as a girl. I'd heard rumours she could help people like me. But instead, she took me to Charrings Clinic, a back-alley butcher shop."

My voice shakes now as I allow myself to cry. I wrap my arms around my body, wishing they were Gerry's. I close my eyes and relive the one time I did allow him to comfort me in that way.

"You remember it, Gerry," I say, my voice velvet. "Don't you?"

Alan left during the summer. On a steamy July day, when we would otherwise have been strolling along the seafront with ice creams, he walked out of our flat for the last time. Hauling the final box into his arms, he stared around at the empty room.

"I'll miss this place," he said despondently. "A lot of happy memories."

I broke down then, as he repeated what he had said the day we decided to split up weeks before. He would miss me. We were moving on, but he would always cherish what we had. Such meaningless clichés, yet every word reflected my own sentiments.

He left on a Saturday, and boarded a flight to his new life the very next day. I spent that Sunday in the flat, weeping for Alan and avoiding the future. I awoke the next morning to the sound of the bin lorry outside.

It was too much then. Sunday had been a sleepy, quiet day, like the world was mourning with me. But now, everyone was getting on with their days as normal. A new week. A new life.

Gerry's place was a ten-minute walk from mine. I jogged there in less than five. I caught him as he was leaving. Dressed in mid-summer casuals, he was pulling the front door behind him, his bicycle helmet tucked under his arm.

"Trish!" He recovered from the surprise with a warm smile that disintegrated when he saw my blotched face. "What's wrong?"

When I couldn't answer, he opened his door and ushered me inside. He flung his bag on the kitchen table and dropped his helmet on a chair. He clicked on the kettle and began preparing coffee for me.

A dog-eared script had slid out of the top of the shoulder bag, and I picked it up.

"What's this?" I sniffed, flicking through it.

"Just a screenplay I've been writing."

I was momentarily distracted from my own misery. "You're writing now? I thought you wanted to direct?"

He shrugged, clanking the mugs together as he lifted them down from the cupboard. "Directing takes time. I got impatient, I suppose."

For many years afterwards, I recalled that conversation. He must have known then that he had only months to live. Did that explain his sudden venture into an area of film the timing of which he could control? When he died, the manuscript was not found. His family insisted they had searched every inch of his flat. His colleagues at Make It Films – where Gerry had been so thrilled to have found basic work as a runner, exposing him to directors and allowing him access to film sets – also denied any knowledge of the work.

That morning, I had stared at it, impressed, but had not read it, not even the title. Gerry had turned the attention back to me.

I sobbed once more at Alan's departure, my impending move home to my controlling mother, the general lack of direction in my life.

"I'll direct you," Gerry had smiled, touching my arm.

I gave a watery grin, and bent forward to rest my head on his shoulder. I don't have a clear memory of how it happened, except for the naturalness of it all. It was as though we had kissed many times before. His warm skin brushing mine felt familiar. There was no hesitation. Quite the opposite – I selfishly took his love without objection.

It was only looking back, after he jumped from the cliff, that I recognised my own wretchedness mirrored in him. The frantic way he pulled me down, how his fingernails dug into my skin, holding me to him.

"I didn't come here for this," I gasped as he fumbled with the buttons on my shirt.

"I know," he said, meeting my eye, "but I want it anyway."

"Me too," I whispered.

We regarded each other shyly, in total understanding.

It only happened once. We met a few times over the next two months, always with Ciara or Stephen in tow. Neither of us mentioned it. We conversed cheerily, and managed to avoid being alone together. At least, that's what I thought he was doing when he always left the pub early. Now I consider the possibility he was exhausted from the illness. Ciara had commented once on his recent weight loss, but he had made a flippant remark about cutting sugar from his diet before changing the subject.

"I'm sorry," I say aloud into the darkness. "I didn't realise that you needed me just as much as I did you." I falter, the real confession clinging to my lips. "I'm sorry I didn't have your baby."

I knew from the start it wasn't Alan's. We had always used protection, and besides, we had officially broken up two weeks before Alan moved out. We had not touched each other since then.

For weeks after I called to Gerry that morning, I did not notice I was late. Adjusting to life without Alan was all-consuming. I had lost a boyfriend and with him the future I had expected. My mother was my housemate now, and I was struggling financially with the rent she insisted I pay. It was not her fault – she thought I had been diligently contributing to Alan's mortgage. That had of course been my intention, but it was often too much for my meagre salary and Alan had covered my share on an embarrassingly regular basis. Now, with my mother standing by the door every Friday, palm open for her rent, I was regressing.

Then Gerry jumped.

The truth about his pancreatic cancer came out at his funeral. I remember sitting beside my friends as the priest gently revealed it on behalf of Gerry's family. Ciara had squeaked in disbelief, while Stephen's mouth dropped open. I held a shaking hand over my eyes, thinking how kind Gerry had been the morning I cried about my break-up with Alan. How pathetic must that whining have sounded to a man on a countdown? He had not asked for my consolation in return. Conceivably he was being brave, but I felt so inadequate recalling that lack of trust. A weight of shame curved my shoulders and dragged down my spirits to a much worse place than they had been.

In the weeks following, I failed to notice my second missed period, and put bouts of nausea down to stress. It seems incredible to me now, but it took me twelve full weeks to properly snap out of my daze, and realise that something more serious was happening to my body.

At first, I didn't consider pregnancy. In my defence, it had been months since I had taken solace in Gerry's arms – it seemed too long ago for it to be a real possibility. When I finally asked the pharmacist for some over-the-counter suggestions to combat tiredness and a constantly swirling stomach, she had grinned at me.

"What don't you try this?" She winked as she passed me a pregnancy test.

I took it with a blank stare.

The elderly woman beside me at the counter nudged me. "Congratulations," she whispered, as though the box in my hand was a result.

Jolting to alertness, I flung a random note on the counter – to this day I have no idea if I over or underpaid – and raced out the door. The journey home was a short one, but it was torturous. I knew, as soon as the pharmacist had passed me the test, that I was pregnant. The mystery was how it had taken me so long to figure it out.

I dropped my bag and shook off my jacket as soon as I stepped inside. I called out for my mother but thank God she was out of the house. Striding into the kitchen, I downed three full helpings of water, then locked myself in the bathroom and waited.

It didn't take long for my bladder to empty, but the two-minute wait for the result crawled by. I sat on the bed with my head in my hands, grabbing it up every ten seconds or so, but it took its full time. Finally the two little lines lit up.

In that moment, I knew I couldn't have a baby. There were so many reasons why I should go through with it. The morals of my mother's pro-life declarations were not lost of me. I was carrying my best friend's baby – what better way to keep him alive than to bear the only offspring he would ever have? There were reasons not to go through with it too – financially I was far from ready to be a mother. Emotionally, I was a wreck.

But even in those first few seconds, as I sat staring at the positive pregnancy test, I knew all the arguments in the world were redundant. I just couldn't do it. It was too much, far too huge for reality. Gerry was dead. I was all alone. I was not able to take this on and that was the end of it.

"So that's it, Gerry," I finish through chattering teeth. "I think all the time about how you could have changed things if you hadn't come up here seven years ago. If you had known about the pregnancy before the cancer took you. Would you have helped me? Convinced me to have the baby? Paid for my abortion – sparing me the need for Abby?" I sigh heavily. "But maybe not. Maybe I wouldn't have told you. I might have gone to Abby anyway. I'm sick of wondering. Of the guilt defining me. All I have is what really happened – the way life has turned out. And I don't like it any more than you did."

My numb fingers grapple for my phone in my pocket. Amazingly, there is some signal on this rock in the middle of nowhere. I dial the number of the real victim of this whole affair.

"'Lo?" he groans.

"Brian, it's me."

"Trish? What–what time is it?"

I hear a crash and a curse, and almost smile as I picture him fumbling around for his clock before knocking it and the contents of his bedside table to the floor.

"I'm sorry to ring so late, Brian. But I need to tell you something. There's something I have to do, and you deserve to know the reason why."

He is awake now. His response is alert and his voice thick with worry. I will not let him talk me out of it. It is too late.

After a long and distressing call, during which he cried as much as I did, I walk slowly to the edge of the cliff. The air is pure out here, and I breathe it in deeply. I try to conjure up a clear image of Gerry, but instead an unexpected face flares before me.

It is a face I have never seen outside of photographs – at least not that I can remember. My father. The man Beth always described as a tender counterpoint to Mum's authoritarian ways. I feel more connected to him than I ever have now that I have finally admitted aloud why I went to England seven years ago.

During that awful interview with Margaret Elderfield, Mum claimed my father suggested abortion to save her from having to raise two children alone. That might have been the excuse, the reason he gave. But I think I am more like him that anyone realises. I think the pressure of having another child when he was deteriorating must have been overwhelming. How stressful for him to have to consider increasing his family at that time. Denial would have seemed the sole option. Like me, he just couldn't do it.

But, of course, it wasn't his decision. It wasn't his body. My mother was determined not to compromise her morals, no matter how much harder it made her life. I do love her for that, because it wasn't my mere existence that complicated her life. I have never achieved anything for her. Never paid her back for her years of raising me – if anything, I continued to be a burden right through into adulthood. From returning home after my break-up with Alan, to my natural shyness that makes me worthless in any campaign for her grandson, I have been a disappointment.

I wish I could tell her I'm sorry. I suppose I could ring her, as I did Brian. But any apology will sound hollow once she realises what I am about to do.

With the finality of my plan causing me to tremble, I do something I haven't done in a long time. I bend my knees – they crick as I drop – and clasp my frozen hands together. If there is a God, he must surely have given me up for a lost cause after

261

everything I have done. I lied to my family and friends for years. I let Charrings persist with its work knowing how dangerous it was, and Mary O'Sullivan died because of it. Perhaps worst of all, I stole God's power over life and death and chose not to carry Gerry's unborn offspring.

Maybe, in this moment of confession, of regret, of repentance, God will be merciful and offer me what I am asking. It is a small favour, really.

Some courage, that's all I need. Not a lot. Just enough so I can finally do what I must to end my suffering.

Chapter thirty-two

STEPHEN

I wake up to the slam of the front door and burst into consciousness. I must be in Ciara's house – she is the only person I know who is utterly incapable of shutting a door quietly.

The warmth of familiarity washes from me as the memories flush through me like a fever. I remember why I am in Ciara's home. Lisa and I are over. I try to place the emotion running through me. I am not pining for a lost love, or fearful of her reproach. All I can conjure up is relief. I burrow under the duvet, grateful for the safety of this house.

Eventually, I peel back the covers and ring work. Coughing as authentically as I can, I fake a cold. The secretary who takes the message doesn't sound too convinced, but then she never seemed to like me. Perhaps I let my disdain for the work seep out. I have no one to blame but myself.

Nikki has left a towel on the edge of my bed. I stand under the steaming water until my flesh reddens. With messy, towel-dried hair and in my bare feet, I pad downstairs. There's a note on the table.

Gone to Pilates with Nikki. Home before nine. Ciara.

I glance up at the clock, ticking loudly above the cooker. It is almost nine already. For a second, I panic at the expectation of company. Then I remember. Lisa is not here to complain when I walk around without socks on or berate me for not dressing properly for breakfast.

The tears come from nowhere. It is not often I cry. Even during the worst of Lisa's abuse, when my skin stung and my ego shrivelled to nothing more than the darkest self-loathing, crying was not my reaction. Now, in a house where I am under the protection of my friends, I can finally release. My deep wailing is distressing to my ears and I gulp in air in an effort to stop.

Thankfully, by the time Ciara's key turns in the lock, I have recovered and splashed cold water on my eyes to soothe the swell. If she notices, she does not comment. She kicks off her shoes and sits down at the table.

"Morning," I say cheerily.

"Hi, yourself," she smiles. She looks a model athlete with her hair pulled tightly back from her face and her black Lycra gear shining in the fluorescent glow of the kitchen. Her luminous yellow socks shine up from her feet. "How did you sleep?"

I nod as I shovel the last of my cereal into my mouth. "Great, thanks." I pick up the bowl and stand with my back to Ciara, rinsing it under the sink. Before I realise it she has moved and her arms wrap around my body. She rests her head on my shoulder-blade, sighing into me. This is the nearest we will get to light-of-day candidness, so I pat her hand in thanks.

Feeling the bandage under my fingers, I turn around to inspect it.

"Oh, it's fine," she tuts impatiently before I can ask her about it. "Showering this morning was a pain though, and I was pretty hopeless in Pilates."

"You shouldn't have bothered going. You should be resting it."

She drops her eyes. "Nikki and I go every Monday. I didn't want to miss it."

She speaks with a low lilt that stirs my curiosity about their relationship. I don't press her further. It's not because I don't care, but I think she wouldn't know what to say.

I squeeze her left hand. "Promise me you'll talk to me if things get bad."

She shrugs. "Things are already bad. But I don't want to talk about it now."

"You don't want to let it continue without talking to someone, Ciara." I swallow deeply. "I'm living proof of that."

"You're going to be fine," she says. "You're stronger than you think. You don't give yourself enough credit."

I laugh at the preposterousness of her faith in me but she shakes her head.

"I mean it, Stephen. We all know Lisa had a crappy childhood, but so did you. You didn't turn out like she did. You're a better person. A decent man. And you're not alone. You have me and Trish." Her head snaps up suddenly. "God, Trish. Stephen, had you any idea?"

I shake my head. I tell her briefly about Trish's reaction when we watched the news break about Charrings Clinic. "She said she knew that girl, the one who died. But now I think that must have been a cover to explain why she was so upset."

Neither of us says a word. Ciara walks into the living room and sits wearily onto the couch. I follow her, my mind still on Trish.

"I'm sorry about Lisa losing the baby," Ciara says.

I squirm on the seat. "It makes it easier to say sorry when it's a miscarriage, doesn't it? It's harder to talk about when it's an abortion."

Ciara runs her hand across her head. "I know. You'd think with all the campaigning about abortion, on both sides, we'd at least be able to talk about it. I read the latest stats on my phone while I was waiting in the hospital last night. Do you know that twelve women a day travel to England for abortions?"

I prod my head forward in disbelief. "Twelve women a day?"

"That's only the women who give their address as Ireland and

265

not counting those who go to countries other than England. Oh, and it doesn't include the ones who buy abortion pills on the internet."

"I had no idea it was that many." That's quite the sizeable market for someone like Abby to exploit, I think angrily. "Lisa and Trish both seemed genuinely afraid of Abby."

Ciara, who has been sitting with her arms folded in full-on debate-mode, creases her brow. "Do you think they'll report her?"

I shake my head. "Not a chance. They'd be too terrified she would find out it was them. Maybe we should talk to Trish. If we tell her we know, and that we're okay with it . . ."

"Are you? Okay with it?"

I think for a moment before answering. "It's different when it's Trish, isn't it? To be honest, if it was someone I didn't know, I'd be thinking about the father. Did he not get any say? But this is about Trish – not abortion."

I just want my friend to know we accept her, whether we agree with her decision or not. Ciara told me I'm strong, when I assumed the world would label me as weak. I have to pay that generosity forward.

Ciara clicks through to Trish's number. "No answer," she frowns after a moment. "Do you think she's ignoring me because I was so weird last night?"

I give her my best reassuring smile. "That doesn't sound like Trish. But look, let me try her." It rings until I hear Trish's pre-recorded message followed by a long beep. I click off the phone without saying anything.

"She's probably still in bed, or out of signal somewhere," I say, as Ciara bites her lip. "What are you worried about? Did she say something to you last night?"

Ciara shakes her head. "No, she didn't. But it was hard to hear her. She was definitely outside – I heard wind whistling around her."

"What time did you call her?"

"It was after ten anyway." Ciara scratches her head. "Maybe she's flying today," she says uncertainly, more to herself than to me.

I shake my head. "No – I saw her last Tuesday when the news about Charrings came out. She kicked me out because she was flying the next morning, and I specifically remember her saying she had Sunday and Monday off this week."

Ciara stands. "Come on, let's call over to her house."

"Why?" I ask, not moving from the couch.

Ciara is already in the hallway. She comes back into the living room and sits on the arm of the chair with her shoes in her hands. She thrusts her feet into them hurriedly. "Trish was distracted last night, Stephen, not like her usual self. The past week must have been horrendous for her. We should see her."

A metallic taste swirls in my mouth. "We'll have to tell her we know."

"Yes," Ciara says. "We don't have to tell her about Lisa blackmailing us. We'll just say you're considering your options about reporting Lisa and leave it at that."

I don't see any particular need to be rushing over to Trish right now, and I'm not looking forward to another emotional conversation. But Ciara is already out the door. Reluctantly, I run upstairs to put on my shoes and jacket before following her outside.

I grin as I see her sliding into the driver's seat. I walk over to her car and put my hands on my hips. "Nice try."

She rolls down the window. "What?" she says stubbornly. "I can drive."

"Like you could do Pilates this morning? Can you wriggle your fingers?"

She holds up her arm. The white bandage twitches pathetically. I tilt my head, the argument won. She screws up her face like a petulant child but gets out of the car without further argument.

We say little on the journey to Trish's house. When we arrive, the curtains are drawn. I say again that she's probably in bed, but that doesn't stop Ciara banging on the door. I point out that Trish's car isn't in the driveway.

"Well, she's got to be somewhere," Ciara says, looking around uselessly. "It shouldn't be that hard to find her."

"Let's just leave her a voice message and she can call us when she's home."

Ciara holds up a hand. "Stephen, I know you think I'm being dramatic but our friend is going through something huge at the moment. I just want to make sure she's okay."

I take a deep breath, remembering the last time I saw Trish. She had been far from okay, and she all but kicked me out of her house after her hushed phone call with Lisa. I take Ciara's old phone from my pocket. Ciara stares at me quizzically. I hold up a hand, pre-empting her question.

The phone rings five times before Lisa finally answers.

"Lisa, it's me," I say loudly, determined to keep some semblance of control. "I need to ask you something, and I want you to be honest."

"All right," Lisa says warily.

"Have you talked to Trish since I left your house yesterday?"

"No," she says without hesitation.

I believe her.

"What about Abby? Did she contact you last night?"

Lisa pauses. "How did you know that?"

"I don't have time, Lisa. Answer the question."

"Yes, Stephen, she came to the house yesterday evening. She had just been to see Trish."

I repeat Lisa's words for Ciara. Her eyebrows fly upwards. To my surprise, she walks back toward the car, punching at her phone.

I turn my attention to my ex-girlfriend again. "Lisa, listen, this is very important. What did she say to Trish?"

She must perceive the urgency because she does not challenge my reason for asking. "I don't know what she said exactly. Abby told me that Trish won't be talking, and that I am to make sure I keep my own mouth shut too."

I pause for a moment to question why on earth Lisa would submit to this woman's wishes now that I know the truth. But I don't have time for such trivia. I hang up without an explanation.

I watch Ciara talking on the phone until she beckons me over to the car. She cups her hand over the mouthpiece, and hisses at me to take down a number.

"Go ahead, Mrs Olden," she says, and repeats a phone number back to me. She thanks Trish's mother and hangs up.

"I didn't want to make her suspicious so I said my mobile had somehow wiped all my phone numbers and that I wanted to get in touch with Trish about dinner. But she's not there – Mrs Olden hasn't seen her all week."

"Maybe we should try her sister."

"Way ahead of you." Ciara nods at the phone in my hand. "Go ahead, ring her."

The call goes straight to voicemail. I lower the phone. "Maybe she's with Trish. Both their phones are ringing out – they could easily be somewhere together."

Ciara thinks about that for a moment. "Yes, maybe. You could be right. But what are the chances Beth is in a place where she can't answer her phone – like in hospital with the baby – and Trish is somewhere else, maybe out of signal?"

"You're catastrophising, Ciara," I say gently.

She looks at me sharply. "That's exactly what I said to Nikki before we called to you yesterday. I wouldn't have gone if Nikki hadn't convinced me. I'm not making that mistake again."

I tense at the mention of yesterday. Although Trish's suffering gives me no pleasure, thinking about her allows me avoid the fact that less than twenty-four hours ago I was trapped in a corner while Lisa struck me, blow after blow. Sensing myself slip into that low place in my mind, I force myself to focus on Trish.

"Well, where else could she be then?"

"I don't know!" Ciara barks. "But Lisa told you Abby called over to her last night. She must have threatened her. Why wouldn't she come to us?"

We lock eyes. I know she is thinking the same thing I am – the last friend we had who chose not to confide a secret in us ended up jumping from a cliff.

"The wind," Ciara whispers. "Last night when I called her it was windy. Like she was somewhere exposed . . . like a mountain."

I try to inject authority into my voice. "Come on, Ciara. She could have been anywhere windy last night. By the sea, walking through an open park . . ."

She interrupts as though she hasn't heard me. "On the day Trish was filming that *Current Times* interview, I was running up by The Kite and I rang to wish her good luck. She could barely hear me – the wind was so loud around me. I don't like this, Stephen. I have a bad feeling. Please, let's just take a drive up to The Kite. What if she . . ." her voice catches.

I shake my head automatically. "Trish would never do what Gerry did."

"Wouldn't she, Stephen?" Her voice is pitched high. She paces alongside the car. "She must have been living in constant fear since the news about the clinic came out. That woman Abby is back on the scene. Trish has no one to talk to about it. She didn't tell us, so who else is she going to go to? Her pro-life fanatic of a mother? Beth, mother of the miracle baby? She's all alone, Stephen, and you know Trish – she has such a gentle personality. What if it all became too much for her?"

My lips are dry by the end of her speech. I doubt Trish has done anything drastic, but if she was considering it, following in Gerry's footsteps would be the most obvious choice.

I crack my knuckles distractedly. I saw Trish's reaction when she thought Abby was merely phoning her – I imagine how horrified she must have been when the woman showed up at her door.

"I know she's probably fine," Ciara says, though her voice implies otherwise. "But I won't relax until we check. What else will we be doing anyway? I'm not due to meet Adrian until this afternoon and you're obviously not going into work." She points at my jeans.

I know better than to argue with Ciara when she has her mind set on a plan. I open the car door.

"Come on then," I say. "Let's go."

Chapter thirty-three

CIARA

Though it's my car, Stephen is driving. He has been through so much in the past few days, he shouldn't be exerting himself. I stare down at my hand. It's throbbing slightly. I meant to take painkillers when I got home from Pilates. I am anxious for it to heal. Not just so my training can resume or because I am an impatient person by nature and detest being deprived of normal activities like driving or Pilates, but because Stephen has been eyeing my injury with a mixture of guilt and shame.

I cast a sideways glance at him. He doesn't notice. He is concentrating on the road.

He might not realise it, but he is a proud person – in the best possible way. Stephen's pride is what makes him strive to be a good man. It is what prompted him to pay for his father's nursing home, whereas someone else would have taken pleasure in depriving the man after so many years of mistreatment. I fear it's what stopped him disclosing to me, or Trish, the way Lisa was treating him. Having to be rescued by his friends must have been humiliating for

271

him. His imposing physicality makes him a natural protector. My hurt hand must remind him of the role reversal, and I long to strip off the bandage.

"Nearly there," says Stephen suddenly. He nods to a faded sign with an arrow pointing the way to The Kite. "That's the biggest car park around here. Let's start there."

From outside, the pub has the appearance of a typical country cottage, with old-fashioned curtains and whitewashed walls. Inside, it sprawls into nooks and crannies. Irish poetry covers the walls along with paintings of rebel heroes. Upbeat trad music hums from corner speakers and the barmen are the friendliest you'll ever meet.

Not surprisingly, the car park is empty first thing on Monday morning. A couple of old men stroll in the door of the pub as we cut the engine.

"Morning!" calls an older man with a leathery face, as he wipes down the wooden tables outside.

I wave as we approach him.

"Hello there," says Stephen. "I take it you work here?"

"I don't wear this apron for the ladies," he grins widely. "They tried to make me retire last year but I was having none of it. Been a barman here for thirty years! The regulars kicked up a right fuss and they let me stay on."

I smile back at him. "Say, you haven't seen a woman about our age this morning, or last night? A bit taller than me, skinnier, with brown hair. Probably on her own. She's a friend of ours."

The barman scratches the back of his head. "Well, I wasn't working last night but there's been no one here this morning except my two regulars and your good selves."

"Do you mind if we park here for a while?" Stephen asks – clearly conscious, as I am, that we are using the facilities yet turning away from the pub. "We're going for a walk, but we'll pop in for a coffee on our way back."

"No problem." He indicates the empty car park. "You're not taking the spot from anyone else."

Stephen thanks him and steers me away. "Come on, let's go to Gerry's cliff."

It takes us longer than expected to find the exact place. We've been there before, but after the first few years Stephen and I took to hanging around The Kite instead. I had found it unsettling, making a sort of pilgrimage to the exact spot from which he must have jumped. But Trish found some comfort in it so we let her go alone. Perhaps that had been a bad idea.

The terrain is rocky and bunches of brambles scratch my jacket noisily. Finally, we reach the place.

Seeing the drop before me, I don't want to go any further. "I've changed my mind, Stephen. Let's go."

"Trish isn't Gerry," he says with conviction. "She didn't jump. I'll prove it to you."

"No, Stephen!" I cry out piercingly. I don't know why this sudden fear is closing in around me. I want to go home.

He holds up a hand to calm me, and takes short, shuffling steps toward the cliff. As he reaches the edge, he bends down onto his knees to steady himself against the sudden wind that can whip up without warning from the crevices. He pokes his head over the side, scanning the rocks below.

My hands clench into fists by my side.

He turns and smiles, relief shining from his eyes. "I told you. There's nothing down there. Definitely not Trish."

My breathing calms and I cover my eyes with a shaking hand. "We shouldn't have come here," I whisper. Stephen picks his way over to my side. I lower my hand as he curses, staggering over a clump of grass on the way, falling onto his knees. I sigh loudly. "How can we tell Trish we thought she'd do something like this?"

"We won't tell her," Stephen says, wiping his trousers as he starts to stand up.

"More secrets." I stamp away.

Stephen calls after me but I ignore him, until his voice suddenly darkens. My name cuts through the air, laced with panic.

I swing around to see him staring at the ground. I watch as he bends and thrusts his hand into a patch of brambles. He winces as the thorns cut him. He pulls his arm out. Dangling from his fingers are a set of keys.

He holds up one of bright blue metal in the shape of an airplane. "It's an Aer Clara keychain."

I stumble to him and grab the bunch from his hand. As well as the chain and a cluster of smaller keys, there is a car key. I meet Stephen's eyes, knowing our thoughts have aligned. If Trish dropped these, there is no way she left the mountains in her car. Stephen shouts as I race past him to the edge and lean over. I crane my neck, certain he missed something. All I can see below is jagged rock. I stretch still further until suddenly I am reefed back.

Stephen clings to me as I gasp for air.

"For God's sake, Ciara. You could fall yourself."

"She was here, Stephen," I cry, struggling against his grip. "She was here!"

My mind is swirling with images of Trish on this mountainside alone, fearful of even her best friends finding out what she did seven years ago. Every moment with us since then has been a lie – but she kept silent for a reason. My lips purse as I think what Deirdre Olden's reaction would be if she ever found out.

We are thirty years old. Our parents' views should not interfere with our decisions – yet they do. The power they hold over us – perhaps even they do not realise the full extent of their influence. Deirdre Olden is not a source of support for her daughter. She is the worst kind of campaigner, and they exist on both sides of the debate.

I saw them for myself, about three years ago. I happened to be in town shopping when a pro-choice march heading north on O'Connell Street met a pro-life demonstration coming the other way. I bounced on my tip-toes as a line of Gardaí blocked our exit from the side streets.

"What's going on?" I asked the man in front of me.

"Clash of the know-it-alls," he said despairingly, shoving past me. "I'll find another route."

Curious, I pushed my way to the front of the crowd.

"Sorry, love," said the Garda who was blocking my way by linking arms with his colleagues on either side. "We'll let you through in five minutes, once these have passed."

"No problem," I smiled. I had a perfect view past his head to the centre of the street.

Flustered Gardaí were attempting to siphon the pro-life brigade down the west of the street, while shunting the pro-choicers along the opposite path. Both groups roared at each other, each waving placards denouncing the evils of their opponents.

"Baby murderers!"

"Controlling fascists!"

It was then I spotted Trish's mother, leading the pro-lifers. Her placard read, *"Cherish all human life equally."* I couldn't disagree with the sentiment. I craned my neck as the march continued down toward the river. Pushing through the impatient crowd, I walked hurriedly through the side streets parallel to O'Connell Street until I reached the water. The pro-life march chanted by the bridge for about ten minutes, until finally they started to disperse. I wandered amongst the thinning crowd. Finally I saw her shaking hands with a group of women.

"Mrs Olden," I called, unsure why I was seeking her out. She looked at me blankly. "I'm Ciara Kavanagh. Trish's friend."

She smiled pleasantly. "Of course – Ciara. Sorry, out of context. How are you, dear? I didn't see you. Were you taking part in the march?"

"No," I laughed, "I'm afraid not."

"Oh?" she said, seeming mildly offended. "Not an issue that interests you, then?"

"Well, it's hardly a predicament I'm likely to be in, is it?"

She stared at me in perfect confusion, until it clicked. She flushed red in embarrassment. "It's a problem that affects everyone."

I frowned, noticing some of the demonstrators watching our exchange with interest. "Is it?"

"Well, of course, dear," Mrs Olden smiled. "I won't be getting pregnant at my age, but that doesn't mean I don't take the welfare of all our citizens seriously."

I knew I shouldn't get into an argument with her, but I couldn't help it. "What about women whose babies are destined to die painful deaths within hours of being born? Girls who have been raped? Do you care about them, Mrs Olden?"

She puffed out her chest, reminding me strongly of a bird protecting its nest. "Yes, I care about all of them. I wouldn't want them doing something they regret. Don't think for a second they wouldn't regret murdering their own babies."

"You know, Mrs Olden, you're perfectly entitled to your opinion. But you should know that bald language like that can be hurtful to some women who believe they have no choice."

"They always have a choice," she snapped. "In this day and age, there is plenty of help available for mothers."

I was itching to fight back with persuasive arguments about a woman's right to bodily autonomy but I knew Trish would be mortified to think of her mother and friend battling it out in the streets. "I don't want to argue with you, Mrs Olden. I just thought I'd come over and say hello. We should still be able to have a friendly conversation, even if we disagree about abortion, am I right?" I purposefully kept my voice light. All she had to do was agree, and we could have been on our way.

She was hesitating when suddenly a young woman in her twenties leapt in front of us.

"*Stay away from my body!*" she screamed. "*I'll do what I want, and bitches like you won't control me!*" She spat at Mrs Olden's feet and raced across the nearest bridge.

I watched her with my mouth hanging open.

"You see, Miss Kavanagh," Mrs Olden leaned close, causing me to jump, "these are the sort of people who will kill innocent babies without a thought. This issue is about life. The value of human life. If you cannot agree with such a basic moral value, I don't see much point in speaking with you at all. Good day."

I had phoned Trish immediately after that confrontation with her mother to apologise. Trish was dismayed to learn we had quarrelled, but assured me she did not blame me. She did not appear surprised by the behaviour of the young spitter and, while she seemed to recognise her mother's behaviour as aggressive, I hung up none the wiser as to Trish's own personal beliefs.

I recall the depth of Mrs Olden's mindset as I stand beside Stephen at the clifftop. If she truly believes all pro-choice advocates are taking a dark path, how could Trish ever tell her mother about her experience in Charrings? More importantly, how hopeless would Trish feel if she believed the truth was about to be exposed? Would she be desperate enough to come to this spot?

"Where is she?" I push away from Stephen, whirling around.

For the second time in as many days, my heart tightens in fear for a best friend. This time, there is no window to smash, no attacker to confront. There is just Trish, lost on the mountains, and I have no idea where to find her.

Chapter thirty-four

STEPHEN

"She was here, Stephen. Where the hell is her car, if not at The Kite? It has to be somewhere."

"I know," I say irritably, running a hand through my hair. "There are other places to park around here other than The Kite. Let's go."

We plough through the overgrown area until we arrive at the road. The Kite is ahead of us, but there are narrow roads veering off on either side.

"Should we split up?"

I shake my head fervently. "No, we stick together."

I don't know why I am so relieved when she doesn't object. There is nothing to be afraid of out here. The sun is slicing through the clouds. The morning has matured into a crisp autumnal day. Yet I feel a strong urge against solitude.

Without a reason, I take the road to the left. Ciara follows me. She seems content to let me lead, though it was only yesterday that she and Nikki discovered how pathetic I really am, as I crouched beneath Lisa's iron arm.

Trish's disappearance coupled with Ciara's subsequent panic has propelled me back to the first emergency I faced in TJ Simons when the head of our team was away. My junior colleagues had looked to me for instructions. I had gathered them around and stood with my legs steadily apart, my arms by my side. I spoke calmly and quietly. They listened, followed my instructions and then congratulated me when it was all over, though they had done the actual work. All I did was provide an assured atmosphere.

I learned a valuable lesson about leadership during that crisis. Anybody can do the work that solves a problem but a leader is needed to create the environment for them to do that.

Now, Ciara needs support. Without Lisa around, I remember how to provide it. Even with her runner's legs, Ciara has to power-walk to keep up with my hurried and naturally long stride.

We pass fields and a few country bungalows, but no more than two cars are parked along the sides of the road. We loop around toward The Kite again then pass behind it and through a public walkway to get to the main road on the other side. Cars zoom along and we keep near to the hedgerows to avoid getting hit. Burnt golden and brown leaves crunch under our feet, sliding into mush nearer the grass.

"Stephen!" Ciara calls out as I weave to avoid a particularly muddy patch.

I jerk around and follow her hand, pointing down a side road. It is in fact more of a laneway, seemingly leading nowhere. There, at the very end, parked so tight into the trees I missed it, is Trish's car. I grab Ciara's arm and together we sprint across the road and down the lane.

I squint into the front of the car. It is empty. Ciara cups her hand against the back window.

"There's no one here," she groans.

My eyes are drawn to the boot. Zombie-like, I walk into the trees and rummage around on the ground. I ignore Ciara's calls until my hand finds a large enough rock. I emerge from the trees and walk around to the driver's seat. Ciara stares as I lift my arm and fling the rock through the window. I turn my face away as the glass shatters.

Beside me, Ciara screams. "What the hell do you think you're doing?"

"I wouldn't be much of a gentleman if I asked you to do it again, would I?" I say, without a hint of comedy. Brushing the broken glass away, I reach in and unlock the door from the inside. I open it, bend down and pull the lever to pop the boot open.

Ciara gapes as I lift the boot door, holding my breath. I let out a relieved sigh. "Empty."

"What did you think . . . that Trish was in there?" she stammers with incredulity. "You've been watching too many films, Stephen. Why did you smash the window? For God's sake, *we've got the keys!*"

A hotness flushes up my neck. I had completely forgotten about the keys. But I do not apologise – it was a legitimate moment of panic. It is not just fiction films I have seen. Real life *Crime Watch* specials have a habit of ending with women being found dead, stuffed in the boots of their own cars. Ciara is staring at me, incensed. She must be deliberating the lasting damage Lisa has done to my psyche.

"Right," she says faintly, letting the incident go for now. "Trish's car is here, her car keys were at Gerry's spot and there's no sign of her at the bottom of the cliff or in the surrounding area. She's not in The Kite and we don't know of anyone who has seen her since last week."

The summary makes my stomach swirl. "Except for Abby."

"What?"

"Except for Abby," I repeat loudly. "Lisa said Abby called to Trish yesterday. We need to ring the Gardaí." My mouth is suddenly dry. "If she took shelter somewhere, or tried to walk home in last night's weather, she could be in danger of exposure."

I pull my phone from my pocket. Shaking it furiously, I growl. "I have no signal."

Ciara glances at hers, cursing loudly. Glaring around, she points to the trees. "We're too shaded here. We'd probably be better off near

281

Gerry's spot – at least it's an open space."

"Let's head to The Kite," I suggest calmly, though my insides are churning. "We can call from there."

Ciara nods. We decide to leave Trish's car in the laneway, in case its position turns out to be important. We jog back toward the pub. It does not take us long. As we make our way over to the entrance, Ciara's phone rings. My heart leaps that at least we have signal, but almost instantly constricts at Ciara's face as she watches the name flash up on the screen.

She snaps her neck up. "It's Brian. Oh God, what will I say? Should I tell him about Trish?"

My chest pumps rapidly. "See what he wants first."

She answers with a shaky hello. I bend down with my ear to hers, so I can hear him.

"Ciara, it's Brian. Are you near a television?"

The randomness of his question confuses me.

"A television?" Ciara repeats, staring up at me. "Brian, now isn't a good time –"

"It's about Trish," he interrupts.

"What about Trish?" She cannot hide the urgency.

"Switch on the television to RTÉ – there's a breaking news conference."

"Breaking news?" She looks at me and I feel my legs go weak. There is only one reason I can think of for breaking news – someone has been found dead.

Brian is speaking again. "Can you give Stephen a ring too? He'll want to see this. Oh," he adds as an afterthought, "did you manage to speak to him yesterday after I left the golf club?"

I move away from Ciara, not wanting to get drawn into a conversation with Brian right now.

"We saw him," she says breathily. "He's here with me now."

After rushed goodbyes, she hangs up. She gapes open-mouthed at me for a second, then rushes into The Kite. I scan the pub and see a small television perched in the corner. The man from earlier is cleaning glasses behind the bar.

"Hello again," he greets us cheerfully.

"Can we switch on the TV?" Ciara asks without preamble.

He scrunches up his face in an apologetic way. "Sorry, the regulars don't like it on."

"This is an emergency!" she cries with a harsh edge to her voice.

The barman cocks an eyebrow, apparently unimpressed with Ciara's tone. I place a quietening hand on her shoulder and lean onto the bar.

"I'm sorry, but this really is an emergency. There's breaking news, and we think it has to do with a friend of ours who's missing. *Please.*"

He eyes us for a moment. Our genuine anxiety must shine from us.

"Sorry, lads," he calls to the two old men in the corner.

They mutter grumpily but do not kick up a fuss as the television fuzzes into life.

Ciara grabs my hand. "Stephen," she says, her voice fading away.

"I know," I whisper. "Don't worry, it's going to be okay."

I don't believe my own promise but I say it aloud anyway, for Ciara. I grasp her hand back. Together, we stare at the screen, waiting with pounding hearts for news of our friend.

Chapter thirty-five

TRISH

The noise is a whip to my eardrums. It is unceasing. So much has happened over the past twelve hours.

After I spoke to Brian, admitting to him the truth about Charrings, the pain in my chest eased considerably. He had not hung up, or berated me, though he was clearly shocked.

"Brian, say something," I had pleaded.

"Why didn't you tell me this years ago, Trish?" he asked, his voice dripping with regret.

"When I met you, I was still new to my job. I was finally moving on after what I had done, and what I had been through in Charrings. I didn't want to relive it. When you proposed to me, I was so excited about being your wife I didn't want to spoil it."

I spoke for another five minutes, trying to explain, crying as I did so. I heard him weep on the other end of the phone. I stared out across the mountains at the city glistening in the distance. It would have been so easy to be envious of all the couples down there, happily falling asleep together before another ordinary week. But they must have problems too – if not as amazing as my story, at least as relevant for them.

I knew my confession to Beth would be even more complicated. I would have to meet her. I trudged back to my car, planning on driving to her house. I was so preoccupied figuring out how best to wake her this late at night without disturbing the baby, I didn't realise I had lost my keys until I reached the car. Rummaging frantically in my pockets, I swore loudly and kicked the tyre. I tried to retrace my steps but it was too dark to properly scan the roadside. By the time I made it to The Kite, I gave up.

I sat on one of the wooden benches outside the deserted pub. The clouds were still threatening rain but so far they had held off. The whipping wind, however, was gaining momentum. I huddled into the shelter of the building and dialled Beth's number.

"Trish?" she whispered as a greeting.

"Hi, Beth. Sorry to wake you."

"You didn't, I've just got Conall down to sleep. Hang on a second."

A door clicked in the background and the volume of her voice normalised. "I'm here," she said. "Trish, it's after midnight, what's wrong? Are you okay? Is Mum all right?"

I rushed to assure her there was nothing wrong with Mum, and asked after Conall. She promised impatiently that he was fine, firing questions back at me.

I took a deep breath. "Beth, I need to tell you something."

That silenced her. I tensed at the pause. I chickened out, at least until I could see her.

"I'm at The Kite pub and I've lost my car keys."

"The Kite? Up in the Dublin Mountains? What the hell are you doing up there after midnight? Are you on your own?"

I interrupted before she could continue her Mum-like barrage of questions. "It's a long story, Beth. The bottom line is I've no way of getting home short of walking."

"Do you want me to send Larry up?"

I shook my head. "I want you, Beth. Can you come? Please. You know I wouldn't ask if it wasn't important."

She agreed, thankfully without probing further. After I hung up, I sat back against the whitewashed wall of the pub. There was nothing more I could do until Beth arrived. I allowed myself to relax, merely existing in the dense darkness. From this seat, the city lights were blocked by the mountains. Only the twinkling of distant stars lit the world.

I knew this was the last moment of peace I would experience. The final few hours before my family learned the truth and disowned me forever.

Beth arrived at The Kite in record time. She was always a fast driver, although she keeps to the speed limit when she has Conall in the car.

She swung into the car park. I rose as she cut the engine, my heart racing. Beth and I might not have been friends as kids, or as young adults, but since Conall's birth I had become stitched into her life. It saddened me that I must now lose that little bit of sisterly intimacy.

"Are you all right?" she called as she slammed the car door and buttoned up her full-length coat. The wind howled as she battled her way over to me. She stood in front of me with wide, trusting eyes. Unable to take the tension any longer, I blurted it out.

"Beth, I had an abortion."

For a second, she did not move. Then, slowly, she took a step back. Tears pooled in my eyes. I wanted to reach out and grab her, to tell her I was still the same person. That I loved her. She eyed my stomach, as though maybe I had done it wrong and there was a little cousin for Conall inside me.

"Why?" she gasped, the stormy wind forgotten. "When?"

The second question was easier. The words flowed, now that I was no longer hiding anything. "Seven years ago. After I broke up with Alan, I had a one-night stand with my friend Gerry."

"Gerry . . . who died?"

I couldn't help appreciating that she remembered, having never met him.

287

"Yes," I smiled sadly. "He died before I realised I was pregnant."

"Hang on," Beth said, looking around.

I couldn't wait for her to piece it all together. "Yes. He threw himself off a cliff near here."

Beth tilted her head. "Trish, what are you doing up on this mountain? Tell me."

I chomped in a deep breath. Already, we had come to the point. "I came to talk to Gerry. I know it sounds crazy, but it's true. I've made a decision. I need to come clean about what happened. To you. To Mum. To everyone."

"To everyone?"

I crane my neck up toward the sky, as if gravity might suck the tears back into my head. "When I found out I was pregnant, I didn't want to tell anyone. I *couldn't* tell anyone. So I went to the one person I knew who had an abortion – Abby."

"Abby? Abby Walsh? From school – who Mum . . ."

"Yes, that Abby. She took me to England. To a place called Charrings Clinic."

This was too much for Beth. She gripped her hair with her hands and turned from me. She started toward the car and for a moment I thought she was going to leave me. But she paced around in a circle, ending up in front of me again.

When she finally looked at me, her face was gleaming white through the blackness of the night. "That place," she choked. "A young woman died there."

"I know. I didn't have a good experience either. The abortion was a success, but it came at a price. Beth, just tell me, do you hate me?"

"Hate you?" she asked with such confusion I almost cried. "Why would I hate you?"

"Beth, I had an abortion. What do you think Mum will say?"

Then, to my surprise, she threw herself onto me, hugging me fiercely. "You're so brave," she whispered, weeping onto my shoulder.

"Brave?" I pushed her from me, astounded.

"I considered it," she blurted out, wiping her eyes.

I blinked, not understanding. She rushed on, the truth bleeding from her.

"I was so convinced, always, that abortion was wrong. Mum and I worked for the pro-life cause for years. It was the basis of my relationship with Larry – we met at an anti-abortion rally, for crying out loud. When we got the diagnosis of Edward's Syndrome, Mum and Larry didn't waver. It wasn't even a discussion. I couldn't tell them what I was thinking – that I was scared to keep carrying a doomed baby. That ending it might be the kinder option, if he was to suffer."

She broke off, crying into her hands.

"But – Beth," I stammered, "you never said anything. You were always so certain you would keep him."

"I just wanted to talk about it, to consider it as an option. But Mum would have disowned me. As for Larry, do you think our marriage would have lasted through me aborting his child against his wishes?"

I finally realised what she had been trying to tell me in the hospital.

"Beth," I said, "you can't blame yourself for any suffering he goes through. His pain is managed with medication, and he is looked after so well. He's the most beautiful person I've ever seen. You made the right decision."

She threw her hands upwards. "I didn't make any decision. I let other people make my decision for me. I'm not saying I would definitely have had an abortion – and yes, you're right, I'm so glad now that I didn't, seeing him live beyond expectations. But I'm not brave. I'm a coward."

"Beth, come on. You were just sticking by what you thought was right. You have always been pro-life."

"Of course I have!" she shouted into the beating wind. "Didn't I abandon Abby completely when she became pregnant? Haven't I marched with Mum through the streets and attended rallies all over the country, long before Conall. But it all changes when you're in the situation yourself." She regarded me thoughtfully. "You must know what I mean."

I nodded so hard my neck cricked. Never, in seven years, had I felt that anyone truly understood my plight. "I do, Beth. You know me, I was never a fanatic like you and Mum —"

"Thanks," she gave a half grin, brushing the tears from her face.

I blurted out a tension-relieving laugh. "You know what I mean. I never demonstrated, or spoke out in any way. To be honest, I never thought about it much. I suppose I believed Mum's underlying argument that we have no right to intervene in the life of an unborn child. But when it happened to me — God, Beth, I couldn't go through with it."

I see her biting her lip. I have to be completely honest.

"There was no mitigating circumstance — no Edward's Syndrome, I wasn't raped. Nothing that might make even a pro-lifer sympathetic." I bow my head. "You think it's wrong, don't you?"

"Yes," she said without hesitation. Then her voice softened. "I wish you hadn't done it. But I'm not Mum. I'm not Larry. I used to be, until I had my own doubts. I know how awful it is to worry about being demonised for even considering abortion. You're my sister, and nothing will change that."

Beth came to me again, and this time our embrace was tender. Shielding each other from the worst of the wind, I drew strength from her acceptance and channelled it back to her, wrapping her in to me.

After a while, she drew back.

"So, what are you going to do now?"

I took a deep breath, knowing I could still lose her over this. "Abby didn't take me to Charrings Clinic out of the goodness of her heart. It was pure extortion. She needs to be outed."

"I agree," she said fiercely. "Abby put your life in danger. I won't stand by when someone who used to be my friend hurt you in that way."

"Beth," I said, my courage growing, "a few hours ago, I was floundering. I couldn't decide whether I should say anything. I came here to talk to Gerry, but it was dangerous. I was so low, who knows what I might have done."

"Trish!"

"I wasn't planning on doing what he did. Honestly. But I was so scared, so alone. I could have snapped. But then I got a phone call from Ciara. She told me something awful. Your old friend Lisa – I'm sorry to tell you this, Beth, but she's been abusing Stephen."

For a second, Beth stared at me. "What do you mean?"

"Just what I said. Beating him up."

"But," she sort of laughed, "Lisa's tiny."

"We tend to hear more about battered women than men – but it does happen. Emotional abuse can escalate. He couldn't stop her. We don't know how long it's being going on but Ciara and Nikki happened to call to his house and saw it."

Beth ran a hand down her face. I was suddenly proud. Out of her school-friend trio, Abby targeted vulnerable women for profit and Lisa became an abuser. But Beth, she's the most caring, dedicated mother I've ever met. I wanted to tell her this, but there was too much to get through.

"Ciara and Nikki intervened and they stood up to Lisa together. Stephen found the strength to leave her, and is staying with Ciara tonight. It was only when speaking to her on the phone that I realised it takes seemingly impossible courage to stand up for yourself. But sometimes all you need is a little help from a friend."

"Did you tell her what you just told me?" asked Beth.

I shook my head. "No. I came to you. I need your help, Beth, and it's not going to be easy. There are too many girls like me – controlled by Abby and living in fear of exposure that they chose Charrings as their escape. I have to bring Abby down, for them. It's not abortion I'm championing, it's those girls. Their lives must be consumed with keeping it quiet." I bit my lip, the awful truth bubbling up. "Maybe if I had spoken out sooner, Mary O'Sullivan would be alive today."

Beth rubbed my arm. "You can't blame yourself for that."

"Abby has always threatened to reveal me if I unmask her. If this comes out, you know the pro-lifers will turn on me, and probably Mum too. Which is bad news for Conall."

My sister blinked. "You're right. It will affect the donations." She paused, looking far into the darkness with a furrowed brow. After a few seconds, she focused on me again. "Trish, honestly, if I asked you to keep your secret, would you? For me, and Conall?"

I had been so sure this was the right plan. I expected her to judge and yell, and somehow that would have been easier to counter. But her reasoned plea made me stop. I didn't want to make another mistake. The answer came easier than I expected: the most important person – the one who mattered more than me, or Mum, or Beth, or – God forgive me – Mary O'Sullivan, was Conall. If he needed me to carry this burden, I would do it for him.

"Yes, Beth," I said quietly. "If you think that's what Conall needs, I'll say nothing."

She leaned in to hug me again. "Do it," she said, pulling back and wiping a tear from her cheek. "Conall has an aunt who is willing to put him before her own needs, and the needs of hundreds, maybe thousands, of woman around the country. What more does he need?"

I stared at her, not quite believing.

"We'll handle Mum and Larry. This is something you have to do, and I'm going to be there with you. Now, let's get out of this cold."

Chapter thirty-six

TRISH

I clutch my head in my hands, trying to stifle the noise. It only rises, the voices calling out sharply, the stamping of feet and hustling growing louder. The moment of admission is inching nearer. I watch Brian being escorted away from me into the main hall. My conversation with him moments ago had calmed me.

I had been sitting with Beth, waiting for it all to begin, when I heard my name. I rose from my seat.

Brian was walking toward me as fast as the two Gardaí accompanying him would allow. He stopped in front of me, his body rocking slightly as if unsure whether or not to hug me. He glanced at Beth in surprise. She nodded at him and glided away.

"Trish," he took my hand, "I don't know what to say."

"I'm sorry."

His eyes softened. "I wish you'd told me earlier."

I studied my feet as they scuffed the floor. "I know. I should have explained. But it wouldn't have changed anything. You want children, Brian, and you deserve that."

He stroked my hand with his fingers. "Maybe when this is all out in the open, you'll feel differently about children."

I opened my mouth to respond when Garda Connolly appeared at my side, an expression of urgency on her face. "Mr O'Connor, can I escort you to your seat? We'll be starting any minute."

I leaned in and kissed Brian's cheek.

"Ring Ciara and Stephen, will you?" I asked. "They're my best friends. They deserve to see this."

He nodded. I watched his back as Garda Connolly led him into the fray.

Brian was the first person I told about my plan to make this announcement. After I phoned him from the cliff last night to confess about Charrings, I confided what I was planning to do. I expected some resistance. After all, he had just learned the truth. It was a lot to process. Yet he was as supportive as if we were still engaged to be married.

"I think you should definitely do it, Trish," he had said emphatically and without hesitation. "This has cast a long enough shadow over your life. Your family will learn to live with it. Conall will be fine – as fine as the poor child can be in any case."

"Do you mean that, Brian?" It was not a matter of placating him. My nerves were wavering, and no one's opinion meant more to me than his. We had once been a unit, a real team. I destroyed that by not sharing one of the most important and awful experiences of my life – one that defined me, in a way. Yet, Brian still knew me. He was able to read my heart, and I wanted his blessing for this.

"I do, Trish," he said. "You don't have to go public, you know. You can insist on anonymity. But I think it would be good for you. Get it all out in the open. It will give you control of it."

I nodded, even though he couldn't see me alone on that rocky mountainside.

I linger in the wings with Beth. Bowing forward, I see the room more full than even the noise level indicates. The few rows of seats the small media room accommodates are full. I watch while Garda Connolly impatiently scoots one of the juniors from his seat to let

Brian sit down. Journalists stand with their camera crews along the walls. Latecomers shove their way in the doors at the back.

Suddenly, there is a lack of air. My breathing picks up speed. Garda Connolly returns and pats my shoulder, giving me a reassuring smile. Though she has a young face and cannot be more than a few years older than me, she has the protective air of a parent. Perhaps it is the uniform, or the way her long hair is tied professionally into a bun that makes her appear older than she is. Her smile tilts naturally sideways. It puts me at ease.

"Just stick to what's written in front of you," she says gently. "If you need a break, I'll take some questions."

I nod. My body feels hollow.

A man dressed in black beckons us onto the raised stage at the front of the room. Garda Connolly leads the way. I shuffle after her like a bold schoolgirl. Beth follows me. I can sense her shaking behind me. Garda Connolly walks straight to the podium in the centre of the stage and calls for silence. The audience falls dumb immediately, but the scraping of chairs and vying for space persists rowdily.

"Thank you all for coming this morning. As indicated, we have had a significant breakthrough in our investigation. Minister for Justice Elaine Masterson is at this moment being briefed by Gardaí on the next steps. I would like to introduce Patricia Olden, who made her statement to the investigation unit on the condition that she be allowed to tell her story in public."

I glance up from my feet to see all eyes flick from Garda Connolly to me. I hastily revert my gaze to the floor. Cameras flash. I blink furiously.

"Ms Olden will be reading a short statement. I may take some questions as we go along, but please do not direct any to Ms Olden, as she has been instructed not to answer. You will all be aware of the sensitivity around any potential legal actions arising from our investigation. I will give you whatever information I can. Please be patient."

Abruptly, she turns to me and indicates the free spot at the podium. I wobble up to it. A dense hush descends on the room. My paper crinkles as I pull it from my pocket and smooth it out on the podium. Skimming my eyes over the floor of expectant journalists, I see Margaret Elderfield halfway along the wall. I take a deep breath.

I have avoided public speaking my entire life. The thought of addressing more than a handful of people at a time has always terrified me to the point of near collapse. Even now, my legs are shuddering beneath me and my notes vibrate dangerously in my hands. But I know I can do this. I have to do this.

"Good morning." I hear my voice, solid and clear, so unlike my insides right now. "My name is Trish Olden. I stand here today because I have made a statement to the Gardaí who are officially investigating the circumstances in which young women have been lured across the water to Charrings Clinic."

Having the exact words to read makes it easier, but still my knees quiver violently. I feel a small pressure on my arm. I know it is Beth, steadying me.

"I cannot say as much as I would like in case criminal charges are brought. But I wanted to make this statement publically, to let the person responsible know it's over."

I suck in the air, trying to ignore the blinding cameras.

"Seven years ago, I had an abortion at Charrings Clinic. I could have made this statement privately to the Gardaí but I want the world to know that Charrings Clinic is as bad as it has been portrayed. No woman goes there unless she is desperate. So to all the women who have survived Charrings, and who have kept it quiet all these years, I want to say I understand and I am here for you."

Somehow I am holding back the tears, but the effort is choking my throat. I can speak no more.

Beth leans across me to Garda Connolly. "Can you take some questions while she composes herself?" she asks quietly. "She's not finished yet, are you, Trish?"

I shake my head and stand back to let Garda Connolly step into my place in front of the podium. Immediately, there is an explosion of noise. Journalists shout up at her, waving their arms as if they are on a Wall Street trading floor.

I close my eyes, needing to escape this madness. With Garda Connolly in control and Beth linking my arm, I let my mind slip once more to last night.

Beth and I did not drive home from The Kite immediately. We spent at least the next half an hour sitting in her car with the heat blasting, reviewing the plan. I rang our local Garda station where the sleepy young man on reception told me he could take a statement if I came in but, for the official Charrings investigation team, I'd have to wait until morning.

"It is nearly one in the morning," I conceded to Beth when she cursed his attitude.

"Screw that." Clicking onto the internet, she shushed me as she tapped rapidly. She made me take down a number from the website she was searching. When I read it back to her, she dialled with the same smug face Mum gets when planning her pro-life rally speeches.

Beth switched to speakerphone as a man answered groggily.

"Mr Masterson, may I talk to your wife?"

"Who is this?"

"I am a member of the public with a vital message for the Minister."

"For God's sake!" he shouted. Beth jumped. "It's after one a.m. My wife is a politician but she is also a human being. You can't just ring up in the middle of the night and . . ."

"Tell her I have information about Charrings Clinic."

"Lady, I couldn't care if you're the president. If you think my wife gives a rat's ass about Charrings Clinic at one o'clock in the morning . . ."

There was a scuffle in the background and a woman came on the phone. Beth and I smiled knowingly at each other. It transpired the irritable man's wife cared very much about Charrings Clinic at one o'clock in the morning and, after a short, rather blunt conversation,

297

an interview was set up for less than an hour's time.

It was almost two o'clock when Beth and I arrived at the station. Minister Masterson was there to meet us. I almost walked past her, not recognising her out of her usual power suits. She had thrown on a baggy pair of trousers and a hoodie, but when she stepped forward to greet me, her attire did not diminish her.

Though the investigation team were as anxious as I was to get on with the interview, to my surprise it was the Minister who insisted both Beth and I sleep for at least three hours. She admitted it was not pure kindness – she didn't want sleep deprivation to be used as an excuse for anything controversial I might say in my statement.

So, in narrow single beds in the Gardaí's private staff area, I collapsed into a dreamless sleep. Beth shook me awake some hours later. She had filled Larry in on everything. He was not happy, but she was determined. Thrusting a plastic mug of lukewarm coffee into my hand, she left to contact the national newspapers.

The Gardaí were not impressed when they realised I was calling a press conference but, once they realised there was nothing they could do to stop me, they decided it would be better to maintain some sort of control of the situation. Minister Masterson chose not to attend the conference, but to hold a separate press meeting later that day. She didn't want to be overshadowed, she told me frankly. If she held her own meeting, there would be no distractions from her comments. I was surprised how forthcoming she was about her priorities. It was refreshing. I thought maybe I'd vote for her in the next election.

I was as honest and detailed as possible in the interview. Beth had insisted that she stay in the room with me. When I described the doctor with no name, and how I still wake up to the touch of his cold hands on my legs, I broke down. They were glad Beth was there to comfort me then.

Just one of the three interviewers was a woman. Garda Connolly had clearly been assigned as my baby-sitter and I was glad of it. She was the only person who did not try to talk me out of going public.

She accepted my decision immediately and prepped me for the press conference with a sympathetic demeanour.

Garda Connolly walked us through the station to the door of the media room. As I prepared to walk through it, Beth grabbed my arm.

"I didn't call Mum," she said urgently. "Should we do that first?"

I shook my head rapidly. My plan might be altruistic, but this was the one selfish part. My mother will not accept this. She will see it through the only prism her eyes allow – that of her pro-life cause. The decision I made will be a personal attack on her and her morals, which for her are intrinsically coupled. I could not handle telling her before I made my statement.

Beth seemed to understand, and began ushering me to follow Garda Connolly into the waiting area beside the media room. I felt a sharp tug on my arm and my body jerked backwards.

"What's the matter?" I hissed, rubbing my arm.

Beth was staring at me. "I remember our father," she swallowed thickly, "better than Mum knows. I remember him bounding into the house the morning you were born. He pulled me out of bed and made me dance around the room with him. Whatever thoughts he may have had at the beginning – he wanted you." She sighed at my vacant expression. "You might not have any memories of him but you had a father. Mum will be angry. Don't let her use him to make you feel worse when all he did was have the same thoughts I once did."

I took her hand and squeezed it. "Thank you," I managed to say, before taking a seat alone, my head in my hands in a doomed attempt to block out the noise building in the media room.

I open my eyes, but I am no longer sitting in the safety of the wings. I am on the stage, watching Garda Connolly attempt to quiet the crowd. She is almost shouting to be heard over their demands. Her face reddens as she calls for calm, for one question at a time. Then she simply waits, her arms folded, and with the raised eyebrow of a sanctimonious teacher. Finally, they calm down to a mutinous murmur.

She points at a grey-haired man in the front row. "Tom," she says, offering him the first question.

The man named Tom directs himself toward me as he speaks. "Have you arrested the person Ms Olden referred to as 'responsible'? Can you tell us about this person?"

A shiver runs through my body but I manage to control myself. I stare straight ahead into the crowd.

"We are questioning a woman in her thirties,' Garda Connolly says. 'I won't say any more about her at this stage. No arrests have been made. Next question."

The room roars again. I stare down at Tom. I had asked about whether Abby would be arrested in my interview, though of course I got a similarly evasive answer.

Beth had been more concerned about me. "Is my sister going to be in any kind of trouble?" she asked before we had even sat down at the table.

"Absolutely not," the Garda leading the interview had insisted. He motioned for me to sit, keeping eye contact. "It is illegal to have an abortion in this country, but there is nothing stopping you travelling to England. You did nothing wrong. It is this woman —" he looked at his notes, "Abby Walsh — that we are interested in pursuing."

I cleared my throat nervously. "But I'm the one who had the abortion. She just arranged it."

"It's not the abortion we're interested in," he insisted. "Even if you had it here, can you imagine us actually arresting a woman for having an abortion? The whole country would go spare."

"We'd never get out of here for the demonstrations," shuddered Garda Connolly.

The main interviewer leaned forward. "Look, Trish, the media are calling this the Minister's investigation, but that's just political posturing. We're the ones running it, and if it turns out this woman extorted money from you, we will recommend to the DPP that she be charged. So let's get all the facts."

I gave all the details I could remember, no matter how painful. It was like pushing through the worst turbulence. I felt lightheaded by the end.

Garda Connolly is scanning the audience. She points to a young woman a few rows behind Tom. "Laura, what is your question?"

"I see Beth Barkley up there beside her sister. Her funding campaign for her baby has been driven by, and targeted at, the pro-life community. I think everyone who contributed to her family will want to know why she is aligning with her sister."

I can't help my eyes drifting to Margaret Elderfield who is trying unsuccessfully to push her way through the throng to the front. She must be bursting to alert the room to her part in all of this. After all, the one part I played in Beth and Larry's campaign was on her show.

"Mrs Barkley will not be giving a statement today. She has asked me to convey two messages to the public. First, she and her husband are enormously grateful for the contributions that have helped keep her son alive. Second, there is nothing more important to Mrs Barkley than family, and she is standing by her sister one hundred per cent. She will not be making any comment so please do not address any questions to her directly."

With every eye in the audience on her, Beth slowly and purposefully places her arm around my shoulder.

The next few minutes pass in a blur. Suddenly needing to get this over with, I touch Garda Connolly's shoulder.

"I'm ready," I whisper and she steps back graciously.

"Remember, keep to the script," she whispers in my ear.

A hush falls over the room. Everyone is staring at me – all these strangers. I think about Ciara and Stephen, and lift my head to the cameras.

"I want to apologise," I say, "to my mother, Deirdre Olden. She has championed a creed that all life is precious. She has chosen to dedicate herself to protecting life, even – maybe especially – the tiniest, most vulnerable human lives. I think those who do not share her viewpoint can at least admire her for that."

It won't be enough for Mum to forgive me, but all I can do is offer her the tolerance she is sure to deny me.

"I hadn't planned on getting pregnant," I glance down at my notes, "and the person I turned to for help took advantage of my youth, my vulnerability and my lack of knowledge. That person charged me more money than I would have paid to a reputable clinic, but allowed me repay in instalments, making it the only viable option for me. That person offered me something more important – companionship and apparent understanding. I scooped up that crumb of care eagerly, not tasting the bitterness until it was too late."

I take a deep breath. The eloquence of those words are Beth's, written a couple of hours ago. My preference would have been to shout raucously from the podium – "Abby Walsh! It was Abby Walsh – she did this to me!"

Being denied the chance to name her publically came as a huge blow. I have already leapt over the line by giving her up to the investigation team. She will know it was me as soon as they interview her. I wanted to take that final step by speaking her name aloud.

The Gardaí called to her house before my press conference to bring her in for questioning. But deep down, I do not believe she will ever suffer jail. It will be difficult to secure a conviction on any charge. How will accusations of exploitation be proven?

She will never hurt another woman again, and that is enough for me. Still, the Gardaí are right. Just in case, I do not want to prejudice any charges they bring against her. So I use Beth's speech, until I reach the section about her. That I wrote myself.

I squint into the constant flashing of cameras. Aside from their clicks, a captivated silence pervades the room.

"I am almost done," I say, my only slide from the script. It is for my own reassurance. "My sister Beth chose to have her baby, and he is now seven months old. Many generous contributions have been made from members of the public, all of which have helped enormously with Conall's medical care. I speak directly to those benefactors now. Please do not let my statement today change anything. Beth is on this stage because I am her sister, and she is a compassionate and loyal person. But that doesn't change Conall's needs – please do not withdraw your support from him. None of this is his fault."

I can see Brian at the back, staring up at me. My phone vibrates in my pocket. I know it is my mother. I ignore it. I imagine Ciara and Stephen sitting together, watching my secret unfold. Most importantly, I feel a presence floating around me. I hope it is Gerry, forgiving me.

"I am not here today to advocate pro-life or pro-choice. I am merely saying to others like me – I am here for you. If you have been to Charrings Clinic, and survived, please contact me. We can help each other. Finally," my lips almost touch the microphone, "I want to extend my sympathies to the family and friends of Mary O'Sullivan. Charrings Clinic was just one small part of her life, and I hope you do not let it define your memories of her. Thank you."

That is it. I have said all I am allowed to say. All I have the energy to say right now.

Leaving the podium, Garda Connolly beckons me to follow her. Beth's hand is on the small of my back, steadying me. The room explodes into a thunderous boom of questions. I can hear Margaret Elderfield above them all, calling to me as though we are life-long friends.

I have learned who my real friends are, and I hope they will remain so.

With my admission, I am calling time on this part of my life. But it is only the end of one chapter. There are many more to come.

Turning from the flashing lights, I walk out of the room and into my new life.

CIARA'S EPILOGUE

I was in utter awe of Trish's bravery. I did not suspect there was more to the story.

We did not manage to get near her until the day after the announcement. The press were all over her, and the Gardaí were loath to let her out of their sight until they were certain she knew exactly how to handle media questions in a way that would not jeopardise any eventual trial.

The next day, she invited me, Nikki and Stephen to her house. We arrived together, shoving each other out of the way as she opened the door in our rush to embrace her. She and Stephen had a long hug in the hallway. Eventually they separated, Trish drying her eyes with the back of her hand.

We talked about Lisa. Trish's face became more pinched with every description of what we had seen. So far, Stephen had not elaborated on Lisa's treatment, and we hadn't asked. A small part of me didn't want to know, but just thinking that made me feel guilty.

The conversation moved on to Trish's press conference. She

seemed relieved that it was over, and assured us she didn't regret her decision. She felt she needed to apologise for not telling us in person.

"You must have got a shock," she said quietly. "Finding out about my past."

I looked at the ground. Stephen's voice was pained as he recounted how we had learned about her connection with Charrings the previous day. Her lips pressed tightly together as she listened to Lisa's ultimatum.

"Well, my story is out now," she said, bitterness lacing her words. "So there's nothing stopping you reporting her to the Gardaí, Stephen."

He squirmed in his seat. "I'll think about it," he said evasively. "So, Trish, has Alan contacted you about all this?"

She shook her head. "He has no reason to – he's not the father."

We listened in utter disbelief as she admitted that the baby's father had been Gerry, not Alan as we'd all assumed. Gerry had died before she made her decision. She knew she was giving up his chance at procreating. She was denying Gerry's parents their sole chance at grandparenthood.

Nikki and I have always been firmly pro-choice, but I suppose it is natural that we would identify with the marginalised women, rather than the faceless fathers. Somehow, my friendship with Gerry tainted the decision I would always have said was hers. The need to stand up for him is only strengthened by his inability to speak for himself.

"I know it's hard to accept," Trish said, facing our horrified expressions bravely, "but since I'm being completely honest, I didn't even think about Gerry, his legacy, his parents. I couldn't think about anything. Panic. Fear. That was all there was inside me."

"Do you think you made the right decision?" Nikki asked, with genuine curiosity.

Trish's lip trembled. "I don't know. I made the wrong decision trusting Abby, that's for sure. Charrings Clinic was the biggest mistake of my life, and I'll have to live with the consequences forever. But at that time, in the moment, it honestly wasn't an active decision. It was all I was capable of doing."

Later that night, Nikki and I fell asleep holding hands. The depth of the loneliness in which my friend must have been drowning was unfathomable. Gentle, kind Trish, who always put others first. To have been so consumed with fear – it frightened me. I didn't want to end up that way.

Nikki and I had agreed not to discuss our future while Stephen was with us. The wait exaggerated the drama in my head – was this our last few days together? Every time Nikki urged Stephen not to leave too soon, was it because she was avoiding our inevitable conversation? I was doing the same.

Stephen stayed in our house for nearly a week, even though Lisa did as she was told and moved out of their house within twenty-four hours.

Then, today, he announces he is going home. Both Nikki and I are at pains to convince him there is no rush. But Stephen simply smiles. "You two don't need me here."

The problem is, of course, we do need him. He is our buffer – our excuse for delaying.

We see him off at the door. When he is out of sight, I lower my waving hand and Nikki takes it. Together we walk inside. In the living room she drops my hand and we hover, inches apart, waiting.

"So," Nikki says eventually, twisting her fingers together. "Alone at last. Will I pour us a glass of wine?"

I shake my head and motion for her to sit. I stay standing.

"This is difficult," I breathe. "We have let our problems fester for so long, we are not going to be able to solve everything here and now."

She nods slowly, clearly uncertain whether I am advocating that we work on our issues over time, or give up altogether. I stare down at my beautiful girl.

"Nikki," I say, "it's a matter of priorities. Trish stood up for herself this week, and Stephen finally put himself first. I need to do the same and fight for what I really want."

"Gold," Nikki says, unable to stop disappointment coating the word.

"*You.*"

She gives a little laugh. "You have me."

"Not any more. You come with a baby now."

"What are you saying?"

"I'm saying this isn't as straightforward as Stephen's problem – Lisa was clearly in the wrong. Or in Trish's case, her decision was already made – she just needed a spark of courage to speak out about it. But for us, we are going to have to compromise."

Slowly, I pull a folded envelope from my back pocket and hand it to her. She stares at it for a moment, and frowns curiously as she opens it.

"What's this?" She scans the form, trying to decipher it.

"It's our appointment time for next week with a doctor who specialises in sperm donation."

She looks up, her face completely blank. I reach over and place my hand on hers. It's shaking.

"I rang Ann during the week and she put me in touch with this doctor – apparently she comes highly recommended. We were lucky to get an appointment so soon. Of course, that is just one option. Adoption would take longer, so if we decide to go down that route we should start the process soon."

She tilts her head, taking me in. "Just like that, you'll have a baby?"

"I've been stalling, putting it off, because I didn't know if it's what I wanted. But the hell Trish and Stephen have been going through has made me look at things differently. I assumed a desire for motherhood would come naturally, but life doesn't happen that way. It's messy. People get abortions, and live with abusers, and yet life continues." I blink back tears. "I'm not losing you, Nikki. I'm afraid of growing up, of having a family. And – I'll admit it – I'm afraid of being an old married woman at home, past my racing prime. But there's something that scares me more, and that's living without you. So let's do it. Let's have a baby. There won't be a more

308

loved kid in the world."

We find a dusty bottle of champagne in the corner of the cupboard, and toast to our future together. I allow myself one small sip, and then another. Adrian will never know. For once, I am not at all apprehensive.

"Wait a second." Nikki stops midway through pouring her second glass. "You said we'd both have to compromise."

"I was wondering when you'd remember that." I punch her arm playfully.

She watches me thoughtfully.

"Nikki," I sigh, "I still want that Gold. Give me the support I need to give it my all in Rio. We can start the process, but I don't want a child before then."

"Done," says Nikki, so quickly I cock an eyebrow.

I had expected her to ask how she can trust me to stick by my pledge.

She mirrors my sceptical look. "Come on, Ciara. I wouldn't want you to give up on your dream. I want our child to point to the Gold medal we hang above the mantelpiece and ask what absolute legend won that."

We laugh until we are doubled over. No one in the world makes me laugh like her. I take her hand, grabbing up the bottle of champagne in the other.

"Come on, love. Let's go outside. The neighbours must be sick of our fighting. Let's give them some good news."

Together, we squeeze out the door, clinking our glasses to our future together, whatever – and whoever – it might bring us.

STEPHEN'S EPILOGUE

It's Nikki birthday the week after I leave their house, and the party is epic. It rocks like the old days – us bunch of eejits on the town, toasting to every stupid joke that comes into our heads and dancing until the early hours.

Brian shows up halfway through the night with a bunch of flowers. Ciara and Nikki scream excitedly and drag him straight to the bar, even as he tries to object that he cannot stay as he is already late for another friend's birthday party. They are having none of it and detain him a full half hour, forcing him onto the dance floor and trapping him inside a circle with a group of Nikki's teacher friends.

He cranes his neck, looking to me for rescuing, but I merely tip my glass in his direction and laugh.

I was not able to tell Brian about Lisa in person. Somehow, it is more mortifying to admit my weakness to another man. So I asked Ciara to explain to him the real reason I had abandoned him on the golf course.

Three days after I arrived back at my house after staying with Ciara and Nikki, Brian knocked on my front door armed with beer. For a second, we stared at each other.

"Any chance you're watching the match?" he asked tightly.

At that exact second, a roar went up from the television, as the teams ran onto the pitch. We grinned and I waved him in. The game provided enough distraction so that the serious topic about which neither of us wanted to talk had to be squeezed in between tries.

I did my best to convince Brian that I was fine, and not regretting my decision to break up with Lisa. As soon as possible, I switched the conversation to Trish.

"Did you know about any of it?"

Brian shook his head. "Not until she rang me the night before the press conference to give me a heads-up."

"How is she now?"

He shrugged, banging his fist on the table suddenly and yelling at the red-faced player who missed an easy conversion.

I waited for a few minutes, but could not let the opportunity pass. "Brian, are you and her getting back together, now the truth is out?"

He shook his head. "I thought so, at first. Watching her admit everything to the entire country, I convinced myself that was what was holding her back from having kids. Now everything was in the open, I thought she'd reconsider."

"But she won't?" I felt my eyebrows rise.

"No. She's quite insistent. I guess the whole experience has put her off pregnancy."

"Would she consider adopting?"

He shifted slightly. "She seems dead against that too. I don't really know why. Ciara gave me the number of an adoption counsellor if Trish really felt carrying a child would be too painful. But Trish won't hear of it. I think in her mind she doesn't deserve to be a mother after Charrings."

"I'm sorry, mate." It's all I could say, really.

We resumed our angry critique of the match.

After the game, we shook hands firmly and I promised to reschedule our golf slot in the coming weeks.

I don't get much of a chance to speak to him at Nikki's party. When he finally escapes the dance floor, we barely manage a few minutes of chat before he has to leave.

"I really do have another party," he says, glancing down at his watch.

"I'm sure you're desperately sorry to leave this lot," I grin, nodding at the group of women who had imprisoned him on the dancefloor, still screeching and flailing raucously to the music.

He claps my shoulder and looks around. "I was hoping to catch Trish," he says.

At that moment, she appears from behind a group gathered on the other side of the bar. He makes his way over to her. I watch them talk without touching. His conversation with her is brief and ends with a stilted wave. I turn my head away, embarrassed.

I am unable to understand her decision to write off having children, if considering it would mean she and Brian could try again. I thought Ciara's obvious radiance at having made the opposite decision would inspire her. But I am not in a position to be giving relationship advice, and she has been through too much in the past few weeks for me to be pontificating. If I have learned anything from the way in which Ciara and Nikki saved me from Lisa, it's that the essence of friendship is unconditional acceptance.

So instead of questioning Trish when Brian leaves, I put my arm around her and steer her to the bar for another drink. The shot is sticky. The next morning, I can still taste it on my tongue.

I wipe the sleep from my eyes and sit up, the room spinning around me. It is no surprise my head is thumping. I stumble downstairs and knock back two aspirin. I get a strange kick from leaving the glass on the counter unwashed. Not having to conform to Lisa's every whim is freeing.

But despite flashes of smugness that I don't have to cook Lisa's dinner or tidy up every speck of dirt as I go, the break-up has mostly left me deflated.

Ciara called over the day after I left their house to tell me she had made an appointment for me with a personal trainer.

She sniggered at my horrified reaction. "It'll only take an hour."

"I'm already seeing a psychologist, at Nikki's insistence," I added, a tad grumpily, although the first session had been less painful than I had anticipated.

Ciara waved away my complaint. "I'm talking about keeping you occupied on a day-to-day basis. You need a focus so you don't spend your evenings pining after Lisa. Exercise is good for you – it gives you more energy, and releases endorphins . . ."

I gave in to avoid a lecture and, similar to my experience with the psychologist, I actually found my meeting with the trainer satisfying. He listened to my sporting history and came up with a two-month plan to increase my general fitness. I'm to have another session with him in eight weeks to update it. Ciara was not wrong – the runs, though tiring, have been exhilarating.

But this morning, with a banging headache, I am tempted to abandon the running schedule and enjoy the quiet of the house. As if to tease me, the doorbell rings.

I pull my robe around me as I answer it. I am greeted by a dishevelled Trish and bleary-eyed Ciara.

I grin. "You two look as hot as I feel."

"I'm fine, just tired," says Ciara defensively as I invite them into the living room. "I wasn't drinking – I'm on a strict diet with the trial race next month."

"You can hardly say the same, can you?" I say to Trish as she lowers herself gingerly onto the couch, her hair knotting further around her fingers as she tries to untangle it.

"Stephen, do you have any painkillers?" she asks groggily.

I laugh and take the packet out of my robe pocket. "Miles ahead of you, Trish." I toss them to her and point to a bottle of water on the coffee table. "So, what are you girls doing here at this ungodly hour the morning after the world's greatest birthday party?"

Trish slouches back into the couch, pointing a limp finger at Ciara. "This one showed up at my door and insisted on dragging me here."

Ciara grins. "I'm starting a new tradition," she says brightly. "On

Sunday mornings, the three of us are going to do brunch."

"Brunch?" I can't hide my aversion.

Ciara pats her bag. "It won't seem so girly when you're wolfing down what I have in here. Sausages, rashers, black pudding, eggs . . ."

Trish moans longingly.

I jump up. "Give them here. I'll cook them."

She grins and tosses me the bag. I always had an active palate. Perhaps cooking for my friends, who unlike my father and Lisa are not forcing the chore on me, will be a pleasure.

I listen through the kitchen door to the girls chatting as I pre-heat the grill and unpack Ciara's bag of cholesterol. They are discussing swapping brunch for evening catch-ups on the weekends Trish is scheduled to fly.

The idea of a new tradition, even if it is on a Sunday morning, fills me with a fresh warmth. Suddenly, I am eager to tell my friends my plan, though it is not yet fully formed.

Tomorrow I plan on handing in my notice to Zedmans.

I spoke to an old colleague last week who now works in the bank. He somehow managed to wangle me a student loan. I am going back to college. I found a course that staggers the start of its year to accommodate mature students with work commitments. I can begin in January – a yearlong Masters in Finance. It has an international element, which means at least one semester will involve travel to both Luxembourg and New York. Even with the loan, it won't be easy. But I can do it. Trish's public confession awakened courage in me. Ciara and Nikki's willingness to choose the hard compromises to secure happiness with each other further fuelled my decision. The only way not to drown in regret and loss is to move forward. I will study next year, meet new people, travel. Maybe I'll meet another woman, one who will want children with me in the future. If not, at least I will always have my friends.

"Smells like heaven in there," Trish calls, as the sausages spit fat under the grill.

"Just wait!" I shout over the noise of the extractor fan. "It's going to be like nothing you've ever tasted before."

TRISH'S EPILOGUE

The funeral is a web of pain. Grief oozes like a breeze from the very pores of those left behind. I keep my head down, trying to avoid the stares. As if it is somehow my fault. Ciara and Stephen sit on either side of me, holding a hand each.

It has been over three months since my press conference. The flashing of cameras as I stood on that podium still wake me at night.

It is not just my dreams that are invaded by the monsters from my past. The police in England have contacted me about testifying against the doctor with no name. I have said I will think about it. That's all I can bring myself to do for now. Abby has been questioned, and warned to stay away from me, or she will be arrested for harassment.

I have been offered protection if I feel threatened. I have had no need to accept. Abby has so far not come near me. She has lost her hold over me. Her threats are useless since I admitted the truth. That is at least one of the positive outcomes of my confession.

The most immediate effect has been the evaporation of fear.

While exposure has led to new stresses, I feel a constant form of relief. My shoulders have dropped, my muscles loosened. I think this is the beginning of peace.

Of course, not everyone accepts me. My mother's reaction was beyond anything even I anticipated. After the interview, Beth and I asked Garda Connolly for an escort to her house. Journalists were already outside when we arrived. They called questions as Beth put her arm around me and steered me past them.

I felt a nugget of hope swell in my chest when my mother opened the front door and stood aside to let us in.

Beth slammed the door behind us. "Vultures!" she spat, peering out the window.

I faced my mother. The stinging crack across my cheek caught me unawares. I staggered back into Beth.

"*Mother!*" Beth cried.

"Don't call them vultures, Beth," she said calmly. "You need them, now more than ever, to be on your side. For Conall."

"I came to say I'm sorry, Mum," I said before Beth could respond on my behalf. "I know you're disappointed . . ."

"Disappointed? *Disappointed?*" Mum shrieked. "You *murdered* my grandchild!"

"Mum," Beth cut in. "Get a grip."

"No, Beth!" Mum wagged a finger at her as though she was five years old. "I understand why you had to appear beside her on television. You need to come across as the loving sister if you have any chance of keeping the public on your side. But you can't tell me you agree with what she did?"

"It doesn't matter what I think, or what you think. It was Trish's decision. We don't know what it was like for her."

"I do." Mum stamped her foot. "If you'll remember, her own *father* wanted her dead before she was born. I was on the brink of losing my husband to cancer, about to be thrust into the role of sole breadwinner for the daughter I already had. I had no family, no help. Yet I made the brave decision. But you, Patricia Olden, you chose to be weak and pathetic. You always were. You're a failure."

318

"I am not a failure," I said loudly. "I did what I thought was right at the time."

"*You knew full well it wasn't right!*" Mum screamed. "You were raised to know how wrong abortion is, and you did it anyway. I've never been so ashamed."

My heart tightened. All I wanted was to throw myself into her arms and have her tell me everything was all right. I stared at my mother's bulging eyes, and knew that would never happen.

I left without another word and have waited every day for her to call. The phone has not stopped ringing. It has not once been her. My mother was not the only person I had to meet in the days after the press conference, but I knew her reaction would be the worst. To have survived that confrontation, awful as it was, geared me up to face the rest of the world.

Both the pro-choice and pro-life sides of the abortion debate had serious issues with the investigation, so I was nobody's friend. While both groups cautiously welcomed any measure that would tackle the exploitation of young women and harmful abortion clinics, neither felt it went far enough. My experience was claimed simultaneously as proof that abortion is never a good option and that criminalising the practice in Ireland serves to endanger women. Just like Mary O'Sullivan, I became reduced to a weapon with which both sides could attack each other.

I ignored the many calls from journalists over the next week – chief amongst them, Margaret Elderfield. That she thought I would choose her as my mouthpiece is laughable.

Instead, I set out to meet the people who were important to me. Beth's husband Larry was almost as militant against me as Mum but Beth promised she'd talk to him. The next time I saw him, he had mellowed enough to let me hold his son, though a coldness blanked his expression. I could not blame him. I have learned that some of the ongoing donations to Conall's medical fund were cancelled within an hour of my interview.

"That's more of a reflection on those people than on us," Beth had insisted, with a knowledgeable air. "They saw me stand by my sister and, because they didn't agree with her actions, they took much needed help away from a little baby. Try to figure the logic there."

My conversation with Ciara and Stephen was nearly as difficult as facing Mum. There was no need to tell anyone about Gerry – indeed I have been surprised at the lack of interest in the father – but they deserved to know. As four lonely friends in summer camp, we became a family. No more secrets.

I was nervous. It is easy to side with a friend, but what about when one friend wrongs another?

They gazed at me as though they had never seen me before, and for a second I thought the decision I took to bring Gerry's baby to Charrings would be too much for them to forgive. But though they regarded me with uneasy eyes, they did not run.

Now, their hands grip mine. I need them to keep breathing through this funeral. The loss is so extreme it seems to take up every fibre of my being, even the space for air.

Brian is here too, sitting a few rows behind me. He had raised his hand in sombre greeting as we filed into the church. We have not seen each other in months, since he finally accepted it is over between us. He thought my secret had been the problem, and that once I admitting my Charrings Clinic connection to the world, we could move forward. It took him some time to realise that will not happen. He thought I would change my mind about children. But I have not. And will not. For a reason I have not told him.

It is the one part of this whole situation I have kept to myself. It is the one secret remaining, and I know I will never tell another living soul. Not my mother or sister. Not Ciara or Stephen. Not even Brian, though a part of me thinks it might help him understand. I was firm and, even without that understanding, he has finally accepted it. We are over.

The priest starts to talk. His voice is low and rumbling. He stares down at the family in the front row with sympathetic eyes. He has done this before, many times. Though perhaps not for such a little person.

I am not in the front row. Mum would not allow it, and I didn't want to upset Beth any more by arguing about it. My sister sits, hunched forward, with Larry and Mum on either side. The coffin is so tiny I cannot bring myself to look at it for long. Larry carried it down the aisle with ease. I don't want to think about Conall in that white box, cold and alone. I close my eyes. If only that would make it disappear.

It was a matter of time. We knew that from the beginning. To have reached nine months is a miracle. But he defied the odds so often and for so long we may have begun to hope for a longer life for him. The priest repeats the word 'miracle' often during the funeral Mass. But it is not the miraculous nature of Conall's life that I will remember. It is the everyday things. The peach-like fuzziness of his cheek. The soft sigh he would exhale as he fell asleep in my arms. His eyes, so wide in his oddly-shaped head, staring into my own as though seeing right into my soul, and loving me despite it.

I gulp out a loud cry. Ciara and Stephen squeeze my fingers tighter. Beth and Mum swivel around. Even Mum's expression softens with sympathy at the agony etched into my face. Beth gives a comforting twitch of her lips, before once again facing the coffin. She has barely taken her eyes off it since they placed Conall inside last night and shut the lid.

The funeral is a gentle affair – Larry's nieces read poems they penned for their little cousin. A capella hymns mesh with the collective weeping that floats through the air. I hope the fullness of our affection can somehow be a buoy for Beth, but she merely stares at the coffin as though she has X-ray vision.

After the burial, we make our way back to Beth and Larry's house. Neighbours frantically scurry about with trays of sandwiches and endless supplies of tea. Feeding is all they can do. I try to help Larry's sister in the kitchen but, after many exasperated laments, she barks at me to get out of the way. It is too cramped, apparently. I am about to argue that surely there must be something I can do, when I remember that Larry first met Beth at a pro-life rally, through his sister. She is of my mother's mind. I return to the living room.

My sister is alone in the corner. I sit on the floor at her feet and rest my head against her knees. "Beth," I breathe, allowing a tear slide down my cheek. She rests her hand on my head and runs her fingers slowly, rhythmically, through my hair. I allow my eyelids to droop heavily.

After some time, my friends take me from my sister's side. They push tea into my hand and shield me from unwanted well-wishers. Eventually, I notice that the afternoon sunlight has started to dim. I don't have much time.

I lean around Stephen to see Beth being fed some pills by my mother. "She'll be asleep soon," I say. "I'm going to go."

"We'll take you home," offers Ciara.

"I'm not going home. I need to –" I stop. "Never mind."

They press me until I admit I need some time alone, with Gerry. They exchange startled looks.

"I'm not going to do anything stupid, guys," I say somewhat irritably. "Talking to him really helps me. So don't make a big deal of it, okay?"

"We're coming with you," Stephen says. "We'll leave you alone to talk to Gerry," he adds, "but you're not driving up there alone. Remember your last expedition up that mountain? Let us drive you, Trish. We'll wait for you at The Kite."

It is not what I want, but it is easier to agree.

Within an hour, they are settling into one of the benches outside The Kite, where they will have a clear view of me returning.

"Don't be long," Ciara shivers.

"Be careful, it's going to get dark soon," calls Stephen as I trek away from them.

I find the spot easily.

"Gerry," I say into the dusty sky of late-afternoon dusk, "it's over. Brian has finally accepted that we're not getting back together."

Silence.

"I couldn't tell him the truth. He thinks I won't be having children because I don't want any. Of course that's not true. God, Gerry, poor little Conall. He didn't deserve to die. He was such a

322

sweet baby – even when he was in pain he would barely whimper. I miss him more than I miss you."

I wrap my arms around my body. It's amazing how, a few weeks ago, I thought Abby coming back into my life was the worst thing that could happen to me. Now, I would lock myself in Charrings Clinic with her and the doctor with no name for all eternity if it meant the chance to smell Conall's head one last time.

But that cannot happen. All I can do is grieve, and move on.

What Brian does not realise is that, after Charrings, I did try to move on. With him. When he began peppering our wedding discussions with hints of the family life we would enjoy afterwards, it prompted me to wonder if there was a way to give him what he wanted. What I wanted, too. I had suspected for some time that my experience in Charrings might have had a more lasting effect. There was no physical explanation – I just felt it, deep inside. The emptiness.

So I went to a doctor. I had the tests. The results were conclusive.

"Gerry, I lied to Brian. I told him I didn't want a baby. But if I could give him a baby, I would. The truth is, I can't."

There could have been one cause, or many. The infection festered long after I left England, though the symptoms were not sufficiently severe for me to seek medical help. It died eventually, along with my hopes of ever carrying a child to term. There are other ways to have children, as Ciara and Nikki know, but how could I ever hold a baby in my arms and call him mine, call her mine? A barren life is my punishment, and I must accept it.

That is the real secret I keep. The reason I broke up with Brian. Why I doted on Conall – the nearest person I would ever have to a descendent.

"Trish?"

I whip around. Ciara and Stephen are trudging toward me. I wipe my eyes hastily.

"What are you doing here?" I ask accusingly.

Stephen points at Ciara. She gives him a shove.

"I'm sorry, Trish. We were worried. We lost Gerry here once, and we don't want to lose you too."

323

"I told you I'm not about to jump!"

"We know that." Ciara holds up her hands as if surrendering. "But you're using this place, the memory of Gerry as a comfort. Listen, you don't have to confide every detail in us. But you don't need to use a ghost as your crutch either. Come with us. Let's have a drink in The Kite – "

"Come on, Trish," Stephen says. "We'll be back here next year on Gerry's anniversary. Until then, let's stick together."

I look at them both, my two best friends. The future, whatever it brings, holds these two. That will be enough for me.

Turning my back on the cliff edge, I gesture forward with my arm for them to lead the way.

THE END

If you enjoyed this book from
Poolbeg why not visit our website

www.poolbeg.com

and get another book delivered straight
to your home or to a friend's home.

All books despatched within 24 hours.

POOLBEG

Why not join our mailing list at
www.poolbeg.com and get some
fantastic offers, competitions,
author interviews and much more?

@PoolbegBooks   facebook.com/poolbeg

ALSO AVAILABLE

LEVI'S GIFT

JENNIFER BURKE

Inside those walls was a man, as young as I was, learning how to become a man of God. He owns my heart to this day.

Levi's Gift tells the story of Lena and her daughter Mattie who has just given birth to a stillborn son. Following Mattie's spiral into depression, Lena takes her from their home in America to Italy in an attempt to rescue her and rekindle in her the sense of family and identity she lost after the death of her child.

But this requires Lena to reveal what she experienced as a young woman in Italy – the love she has secretly treasured all her life.

She hopes that by encountering the past together, they can find hope for the future.

poolbeg.com

ISBN 978-1-78199-9431